# SKYFALL

'Operation Prometheus is a joint Soviet-American project that combines the specific knowledge and talents of both countries in a way that will benefit the whole world.' . . . The mighty 2,000-tonne Prometheus is the largest piece of space hardware ever launched. The nerve-racking predicament of its crew of six—incarcerated together with their fears, emotions and frictions—shrinks to nothing beside the horrifying destruction which threatens hundreds of thousands of people on earth if no way can be found to move the satellite from its decaying orbit. The lethal radio-active fuel, Uranium 235, which the vessel is carrying gives the crisis an acute international urgency, and the politicians play out their power games in the light of this desperate knowledge. . . . This masterly and suspenseful novel vividly portrays the kind of global disaster that could one day become a dreadful reality.

# SKYFALL

★

## HARRY HARRISON

**THE
COMPANION BOOK CLUB**
LONDON AND SYDNEY

This edition, published in 1977 by
The Hamlyn Publishing Group Ltd,
is issued by arrangement with
Faber and Faber Ltd

*Made and printed in Great Britain
for the Companion Book Club
by Odhams (Watford) Ltd*
60087219X
9·77/319

This book is for
HILARY RUBINSTEIN
and
CHARLES MONTEITH
without whose
enthusiasm and encouragement
it would never have
been written

Particular thanks to Gerald M. Webb, F.B.I.S.,
for unstinting technical guidance

## 1

*Baikonur—USSR*

'CHRIST . . . it's *big*,' Harding said in a hoarse whisper. 'I didn't think anything could be *that* big.'

Big was too small a word. A gleaming skyscraper in the flat plain; a windowless tower of metal that dwarfed the buildings round it. Not a building; a spacecraft. 20,000 tons that would soon roar flame from its engines, shudder and rise, at first slowly then faster and faster, and soar arrow-like into space. The largest spacecraft men had ever built or dreamed of.

Large as their four-engined jet was, it was dwarfed to insignificance. It was a fly buzzing round a steeple. Here were the six gleaming boosters, each of them identical, each larger than the largest American spacecraft ever built. In flight the outer five would drop away once their fuel had been expended, leaving the central core booster to hurtle on with the payload. But payload was too trivial a word for this *Prometheus*; Prometheus the mortal who stole fire from the gods and brought it back to Earth, now Prometheus the machine that would circle the Earth 22,300 miles up, would reach out silver arms and seize the sun's energy and hurtle it down to Earth. The answer to mankind's energy problem, the ultimate solution that would supply unlimited power. For ever.

This was the plan. The enormity of it was driven home to Patrick Winter now by the sheer size of Prometheus. When his aircraft had completed its circle he straightened the wheel and eased it forward, dropping towards the waiting runway. But his mind wasn't completely on his task and he was a good enough pilot to know it.

'Bring her in, will you, Colonel?' he asked.

Harding nodded and took control. He knew what the other man was thinking. Like an after-image the memory of that burnished metal tower hung before him too. He brushed it away and concentrated; the multiple wheels touched down and he reversed thrust on the engines, braked and slowed. Only when they were rumbling along the taxiway towards the buildings did he speak.

'And you're going to fly that son-of-a-bitch?'

It was halfway between a statement and a question, perhaps a suspicion that something as big as that couldn't ever lift off the ground. Patrick heard the tone and understood; he grinned slightly as he unbuckled and stood.

'Yes, I'm going to fly that son-of-a-bitch.'

He went back to the main cabin and I. L. J. Flax signalled him to come over. Flax sat on the couch, lolling back, the telephone handset almost lost in his big hand. Flax normally didn't enjoy flying because he was too cramped. Over six feet tall, he must have been over six feet around the middle as well; with his legs wide apart he filled the couch. He had a tendency to sweat and his shaven, bald skull was dotted with droplets.

'Yes, all right,' he said in his clear, ever-so-slightly accented English. 'Keep the line to them open. I'll call again as soon as formalities are over.' He could have been talking to anywhere in the world. Air Force One had the communications capacity of an aircraft carrier. Flax hung up the phone and pushed it away, scowling unseeingly at the window.

'Still under observation but the medics seem to agree that it's appendicitis,' he said. 'They'll operate in a couple of hours. Wonderful. You'd think a doctor would take better care of himself. Why the hell should a *doctor* get appendicitis?' He shook his head in unbelief, his loose jowls flapping.

'Maybe you don't believe it, Flax, but doctors have appendixes too.' Patrick stood in front of the full-length mirror and knotted his tie. At thirty-seven he didn't look too bad. An Apollo next to Flax—but then anyone was. His gut was still flat and he exercised enough to stay in shape. Handsome enough so that girls didn't run away screaming, although his jaw was on the large size and his hairline had a tendency to

8

creep a little higher every year. He pulled the knot tight and reached for his jacket. 'And Kennelly does have a back-up. We've all worked with Feinberg and he'll do the job all right.'

'Ten will get you twenty he never shows,' Ely Bron said.

Ely was sitting by the window, his long nose in a book—its usual position—and hadn't appeared to be listening. But he had the maddening ability of being able to read and talk at the same time. He could win an argument and re-member every word of the chapter he had read while doing it. He turned a page.

'What's the bet?' Patrick asked. 'Feinberg's our only back-up medic. He has to show.'

'Really? Then let's see your ten spot.'

'It's a bet,' Flax said. 'Do you know something we don't, Ely?'

'Know, guess, ear to the wall. It's the same thing.'

'I'll take another ten if you're throwing your money away,' Patrick said. He buttoned his uniform jacket and brushed some invisible dust from his major's oakleaves. It was prob-ably ten bucks thrown away since Dr Ely Bron had a way of usually being right about things and of winning bets. And he would let you know too. Patrick tried hard to like his nuclear physicist colleague but was aware that he did not always succeed.

'Let's go,' Flax said, heaving his bulk to his feet as they slowed and stopped. 'Band, guard of honour, politicians, usual crap.'

'Is it good afternoon or good evening?' Patrick asked, look-ing at his watch.

'*Dobry Vyecher* is good at any time,' Flax said. 'Or *Zdract-vooyeti*.'

Through the open door came the first notes of the Star Spangled Banner, slightly off key and with the beat wrong, sounding more like a Russian folk song than the siege of Fort McHenry. The ranked batteries of cameras clicked when they appeared at the head of the stairs, and the recep-tion party stepped forward. There were some mercifully brief speeches of welcome, in Russian, followed by equally

9

brief statements of pleasure at being able to come—then it was inside for the vodka and caviar. And the press. Patrick was relieved that Flax fielded most of the questions, switching from Russian to Polish to German to English without hesitation. Ely Bron seemed to do just as well in French and German, no doubt learned in his spare time at MIT when he wasn't getting another master's or doctorate. Patrick had worked hard on his technical Russian and knew he could work a space flight in it—but he wasn't up to conducting any interviews. It would have to be English or nothing. A short man in a very wrinkled suit pushed through the crowd towards him. His glasses were stained and he had a tendency to spray fine droplets when he talked.

'Pilkington, *World Star*, London,' he said in faint cockney and pushed a microphone towards Patrick. 'Major Winter, as Commander of this venture I imagine you must have very definite ideas about it. Firstly the danger. . . .'

'I don't think venture is quite the right word.' Patrick smiled when he spoke; he had met Pilkington's type before on both sides of the Atlantic. There were reporters who wanted facts, hard news. And there were others who wrote primarily for people who moved their lips when they read. He had read *World Star* occasionally and thought it made ideal catbox lining, but remembered his training. 'Always be nice to the press.'

'Operation Prometheus is a joint Soviet-American project that combines the specific knowledge and talents of both countries in a way that will benefit the whole world.'

'You mean the Russians are better at something than the Americans?' The microphone hovered close and Patrick, still holding his sincere smile, thought how much better it would be pushed down Pilkington's throat.

'What we're doing is beyond political or national rivalries. The Prometheus operation will supply pollution-free energy at a time when traditional sources of power are running out. Eventually it will supply this energy to every nation on the face of the earth. . . .'

'But now only the Russians and the Americans are going to get any?'

'Right now just the Soviets and the Americans are building and financing the project which has cost twenty-two billion dollars to launch. Once in place it can be expanded far more cheaply. In any case any increase in total world energy supplies will benefit everybody.'

Pilkington wiped his lips with the back of his hand and twitched, then took a new tack. 'The danger, that's the thing the whole world's worried about. This death ray you'll be shooting out, it could wipe out whole cities, couldn't it?'

'That's not quite true, Mr Pilkington, I'm afraid you must have been reading your own paper.' A quick thrust instantly half-regretted. 'Colonel Kuznekov developed the technique and it has been tested as thoroughly as anyone knows how. Electricity is generated from sunlight in space by simple thermal means, a turbine-driven generator, then broadcast as a beam of high-energy short waves. These are received on Earth and converted back into electricity.'

'But couldn't this death ray get out of control and wipe the countryside right out?'

'The *radio* waves are the same as the radio waves that are all round us now. They're just stronger; more concentrated. Admittedly if you stood in the right spot they could cook you.' His voice left no doubt as to who it was that needed cooking. 'But this is a very remote possibility. The receiving antennae are located in extremely remote buildings, and there are a great number of automatic controls to stop the broadcasting if any emergency should arise.' Patrick looked across the room, over the reporter's head, and saw Nadya standing against the far wall. 'You'll have to excuse me, I'm needed over there. Be sure and tell your readers that Britain's power grid is ideally set up to distribute electricity of this kind. Eventually it will supply all the UK's power needs—incidentally getting rid of all the pollution you get through the burning of irreplaceable coal and oil. Thank you.'

He ducked round the microphone and pushed his way through the crowd, reaching out to take two of the tiny glasses of icy vodka from a tray. She turned as he came up. The remembered face with the transparent, ice-blue eyes

11

with the little tilt at their corners, the hair golden as Ukrainian wheat. She was in uniform, a wide leather belt tight about the long jacket, a row of little medals on ribbons pinned over the swell of her breast.

'Nadya. . . .'

'Welcome to the Soviet Union, Major Winter.' She took one of the glasses and raised it, unsmiling.

'Thank you, Major Kalinina.' He drank it down with a single motion and his eyes never left hers. Her fixed expression did not change. 'Nadya, after this thing is over I would like to talk to you. . . .'

'There will be many opportunities for conversation, Major, during our official duties.'

'Damn it, Nadya, you know what I mean. I want to explain. . . .'

'I do know what you mean, Major, and no explanations are needed. If you will excuse me.'

Her voice, like her expression, never altered, but when she turned around her skirt swirled out and dropped back to her polished leather boots, swirling faster perhaps than she had intended. Patrick watched her receding back and smiled. She was still a woman. Maybe she hated him but by God she wasn't indifferent to him.

What had it been, just four months since she had left Houston? After those long, long weeks of training on the Prometheus Flight Deck simulator. At first he had felt like all the other Americans in the programme, felt angrier if anything because he would have to fly with her as his co-pilot. Sure, everyone knew that the Russians had women in their space programme, Valentina Tereshkova had been the first and others had come after her. But Prometheus was too big a project for anything but the best—and the Soviets had sent a woman. A political publicity ploy, nothing else. Good old USSR, home of female and racial equality, shining example to capitalistic USA where male fascists cracked the whip over women and the darker races. Maybe that had been the idea behind their choosing Nadya, there was no way to tell, but she had done her job and had done it so well that no one had ever found anything to bitch about. She was too good at what she did. From the very first moment they had met in Houston, she had had Patrick on the defensive. . . .

'*Ya orchen rad votretitsa s vamy,*' Patrick had said.

'How do you do, Major Winter. You have a very good accent and I am sure when we speak Russian during operations that there will be no problem. But wouldn't it be better if we spoke English now?'

*Sure, because your English is perfect and I probably sound like an illiterate coal miner from the Caucasus.* But he couldn't be sure of this because she quickly added that she had never been in an English-speaking country before and she hoped he and everyone would permit her to talk with native speakers to perfect her knowledge of the language. Feeling like a very native speaker, he had agreed.

The training had been rough but she had hacked it without getting a hair out of place. Like Patrick, she had first trained to fly fighters, then gone on to be a test pilot. Unlike him she had gone back to school for a degree in orbital navigation. She had flown a number of missions on Soyuz and then on Salyut. At times he felt lucky that he had one more space mission than she had—plus the fact that the last stage of Prometheus was an American design. Or he would have been working as co-pilot for her. She had even been made a major a month before he had. It was enough to give a normally superior male intense feelings of inferiority.

Not only that but she was goddamn good-looking. The blonde hair, blue eyes and tilty-nose bit was okay, though she rarely smiled and wore a baggy jump suit for training. But Sundays were always free, a NASA rule in Houston, and on her second one she had accepted an invite for a hamburger barbecue around the pool at Doc Kennelly's. Doc was a stocky, smiling Irishman with a doting wife and seven noisy kids who was, behind the jokes and the Irish whiskey, the best space medic in the business. Nadya may have tried to dodge the invitation but she never had a real chance to say no. She showed up at the party in a Russian cotton dress of such massive ugliness that she appeared more feminine and attractive by comparison. May Kennelly had taken one horrified look and whisked her into the house and behind closed doors. Some form of feminine argument, backed up by the stewpot climate of a Houston August, had got Nadya into a wispy blue bikini that brought on a whistling round of masculine applause. She accepted it with a small bow then did a smooth dive into the pool. The afternoon had been all a breeze after that. Once out of uniform Nadya seemed to be a more accessible person, ready to talk about trivial things, ready to smile. When Doc shouted *Come and get it*, Patrick grabbed two paper plates and loaded them up. Nadya was drying her hair with a thick towel and looking very good indeed in the bikini.

'Hungry?' he asked.

'Ravenous. Like a Siberian wolf.'

'Then you're in luck. Doc's burgers have no relation to those rubber shoe heels we get in the commissary. Ground sirloin, Bermuda onions, Canadian cheddar—along with May's secret formula bean salad, cole slaw, garlic pickles, french fries, that's the way, douse them with ketchup, and all the rest. Dig in.'

She did, with an appetite as good as his, washed down with cans of Jax beer from the ice-filled washtub. 'This is very good,' she said.

'You better believe it, real American home cooking for a Sunday afternoon. If you were back in Russia what would you be eating now?'

'That would depend where you were. The Soviet Union is very large you must remember, with many different peoples. At my home, in Leningrad, there would be herring and brown bread, perhaps cucumber in sour cream, very good in summer, and *kvass* to drink.'

'*Kvass?*'

'You do not have it here. It is a drink made from old bread. . . .'

'Doesn't sound so great.'

'Oh, no, it is. Like a beer. Very good in hot weather.'

It was easy talk, not really important, but still fun. Nadya lay back on the grass, her arms behind her head, and even

14

if he had wanted to Patrick could not have ignored the rise and fall of her breasts.

'Have you a family back home?'

'Yes, one brother and one sister. Both married and I am an aunt three times now. When I go home there is always plenty of family to see.'

'And you never married?'

'No. One day perhaps, but I've been too busy up until now. But *you* shouldn't talk. In all the publicity releases from NASA I read that you are the only unmarried astronaut. What is your reason?'

'No reason, really. I guess I like being a bachelor and don't want to be tied down. I suppose I just enjoy playing the field.'

'This expression, I do not understand it.'

'Slang. You know, like playing around, only not so much the same thing. Going out with girls and enjoying a healthy sex life without worrying about hearing the wedding bells chime.'

Nadya sat up abruptly and pulled the towel around her shoulders, her unrevealing working expression back on her face. 'In the Soviet Union we do not talk about this sort of thing.'

'Really. Well we certainly do here. You get some of these wives alone and you'll hear some utterly fascinating things. Relax, Nadya, it's just reality, you know. I'm a healthy male of thirty-seven. You wouldn't really believe I was a virgin, would you? And you are, what did the release say, thirty years old, and damn good-looking too so you . . .'

'You must excuse me.' She rose swiftly to her feet. 'I must thank Dr and Mrs Kennelly for their hospitality.'

They never talked this way again. Not that Nadya was distant or even unfriendly, just that the relationship always stayed a professional one. If they did have a chance for small talk, between training sessions in the simulator trainer when the computer was having problems, it was the kind of talk two pilots who barely knew each other might have during a flight. Trivial but never personal. This situation continued right through their months of training, right to the very end. They worked well together and both did their job in a highly professional manner. Period. After work they never saw one another unless it was at some official function, like the going-away party. This stage of the training was ended. In the morning the Soviet team would be jetting back to Baikonur—Star City—the big Soviet rocket complex. The next time they would all meet would be at Baikonur, for the launch.

It was hot and the air conditioner was overloaded, they were all in uniform and drank a lot of toasts. Patrick realized that it took three good blinks before he could focus his eyes well enough to read his watch. After two in the morning. Time to go. He had brought the car and he still wasn't so wiped out that he couldn't drive it home easily through the wide, empty streets. But no more drink. Stepping over a broken glass, he found the front door. On the steps two Russians were holding up the unconscious form of a third. Patrick walked around them digging out his keys. Someone was standing quietly under a tree near the cars and as he came close he realized it was Nadya.

'Good night,' he said. 'See you in Baikonur.' He walked on, then stopped. 'Having trouble?'

'No. It is nothing. I just don't want to drive with those three.'

'I don't blame you. If they don't pass out before they get to the car they'll add to the highway mortality figures by morning. I'll drive you home.'

'Thank you. But a cab has been called.'

'Many are called but few arrive. This time on a Saturday night you stand the chance of a snowball in August. Get in, you're only a block away from me.'

Knowing he had drunk a lot, Patrick drove with slow concentration. Staying under 35 and obeying the stop signs instead of easing through slowly in the traditional Hollywood Stop.

Despite this, and the empty roads, they almost added to the mortality figures themselves.

The car roared around the bend towards them, high beams blinding, on the wrong side of the road.

Patrick responded with a test pilot's trained reflexes. The other car might swerve back, so if he tried to pass it on the left there could be a head-on smash. Small houses on the right, set back from the road, lawns and shrubs in front, no trees.

He twisted the wheel hard, smashed into the kerb and up over and on to the sidewalk, the grass. Hitting the brake and fighting the slewing surging machine. The other car was gone by in an instant, never stopping. Then Patrick had the twisting ton of metal under control and back into the street, stopping.

'You dirty son-of-a-bitch,' he said, watching the tail lights vanish around a turn in the distance.

'Is everything all right?'

'It is now—but that screwball bastard was out to kill us.'

The street was silent. No lights had come on in the dark houses, no one was interested. Maybe screaming brakes were the norm around here. The careening black marks of their tyres sliced through the lawn and flowerbeds. 'I'll get you home. Call the police and report this thing. My insurance will buy this guy some new rose bushes.'

All of the drink had worn off, quite suddenly. He parked in her driveway and Nadya unlocked the front door of her apartment. By the time he was off the phone he wondered why he had bothered. No one hurt, no cars smashed, the Houston police were massively uninterested in even recording the details. He gave them all the information in any case and slammed the receiver back down. Nadya was standing behind him with a very large Scotch on the rocks; he realized suddenly he was completely sober and very much in need of a drink now that the burst of adrenalin was wearing off.

'Blessings on your head,' he said taking the glass and drinking deep. He put it on the table and placed his hands lightly about her waist. 'You know that was pretty hairy for a moment.'

'It did look dangerous.'

'Deadly. Those nut cases were out to kill us. Set back the joint American-Soviet space programme ten years it would.'

Suddenly it did not seem funny at all. 'I was frightened. For you, not me. I didn't want anything to happen . . . to you. . . .'

Words ran out and, without conscious thought, he pulled her tight to him and kissed her with a passion that was not artificial, that surprised him with its intensity. Kissed her and she returned the kiss, her lips and tongue hot in his, nor did she pull away when his hands went down her body, moving with their own will.

Her underwear was very non-proletarian, dark lace, very delicate. The rug was soft under them and everything was just right. Until he realized, suddenly, that he was all alone. She was there, yes, naked and lovely beyond belief, but she apparently felt nothing. Her body did not move and her hands lay at her sides. What they had felt together, what they *must* have felt together, was gone. He ran his fingers over her breast and down the firm roundness of her stomach and she lay quiet.

'Nadya,' he said, then did not know what more to add. Her eyes were open but she was not looking at him. 'I'm too old for rape.' He sat up, regretting the words the instant he spoke them.

Whatever regrets he had were too late. The bedroom door slammed behind her and the bits of lace and the crumpled dress were the only reminders of what had been just short instants before. He talked to her through the door, tried to apologize, explain, but she never answered. Nor was he very clear in what he said because he was not sure himself just what had happened. In the end he dressed, poured another large drink, left it untouched on the bar and stamped out into the hot night. At the last moment he had even caught the door as it slammed shut behind him, fury instantly becoming concern, closing it quietly and wondering just how he did feel about her. About everything.

He never had made his mind up completely. Some things seemed clear, he thought he had the right answers, but seeing her there in the stuffy room in Baikonur changed everything one more time. Four months. Nothing had changed. The same exit, the same closed door.

18

He envied her her certainty of decision. Exactly how he felt was not clear at all.

'*Tovarich*,' a deep voice said and he turned with relief and took the proffered glass of vodka from the Soviet officer.

'*Mir, mir* in our bloody time and for ever,' he said, and drained the glass.


'*Reilly, do you realize that it's only nine in the morning and it's already so hot you could fry an egg on this oscilloscope. This place is worse than the Cape.*'

'*I feel so sorry for you, Duffy. If you don't like it why did you sign up?*'

'*For the same reason you did. When they folded the C5-A project NASA was the only place hiring. What does this bunch of screwball letters mean?*'

'*The alphabet is called Cyrillic, Duffy, don't flaunt your ignorance. Zemlya 445L. Connection of that number. Yevgeni . . .*' *He turned to the stolid technician who stood on the platform beside them and rattled off a quick question in Russian. Yevgeni grunted and flipped through the thick manual he held and found the correct diagram. Reilly squinted against the intense sunlight, then read the translation aloud.* '*Secondary starter circuit first stage servo disconnect.*'

*Duffy removed the stainless steel screws from the support collar and examined the multi-connectors where the looms passed through a bulkhead into a high-pressure helium tank. He carefully pulled back the clips and with a rocking motion pulled out the uppermost fifty-way plug and sprayed cleaner on the gold-plated pins. Satisfied, he reconnected it and nodded to Yevgeni who made an entry in the thick manual.*

'*Thirteen down and maybe four million to go,*' *Duffy said.* '*Ask your buddy where the next one is in this system. You know, I been wondering, how come a good mick named Reilly speaks this lingo?*'

'*My adviser in college said it was the language of the space age, that and English.*'

'Looks like he was right. I took two years of Spanish and I didn't even learn enough to argue a buck off the price when I got laid in Tijuana.'

The Russian technician worked the controls and the inspection platform rose slowly between the towering cylinders of the booster rockets. The ground was three hundred feet below them and the figures of the other men on the ground appeared tiny as ants. Above their heads the stainless steel wall rose another hundred and fifty feet. Great braces joined the boosters to each other and to the core body. There were hydraulic lines, fuel exchange pipes, power cables, oxygen drains, computer monitoring readouts, telemetry hardlines, hundreds of connections for services of every kind joined the units of the immense vehicle together.

They were all needed. They must all be able to function perfectly. The failure of a single component among the thousands and thousands could jeopardize everything.

If Prometheus exploded, it would be the largest non-atomic bomb ever made by man.

## 2

GREGOR SALNIKOV heard the car when it was still far away, a hum no louder than the bees busy in the flowers beyond the open window. There were other houses farther down this road, and no shortage of cars among the officials here at Baikonur. A shortage of paving though, whenever a car passed a cloud of white dust rolled along after it. Apart from the dust he was unaware of the cars that went by; they had nothing to do with him. He carefully spread peach preserve on the thick slice of bread, then poured the heavy glass full of tea. The car stopped in the road outside—then the engine was turned off. Here? A car door slammed and he stood up to look out. It was a big, black Czechoslovakian Tatra, more of a tank than a car. An old one too, with the triple tail fins, and there was only one like it in all Star City. He went down the passageway and his hand was on the knob just as the knocker sounded.

'Come in, Colonel,' he said.

'Vladimir, if you please, Gregor. I think we know each other well enough by now. And what would the Americans think if it was "Colonel Kuznekov" and "Engineer Salnikov" all through the flight.'

'I'm sorry, Vladimir, come in please. Bad manners, the heat . . .'

'I always told the men in my outfit don't complain, don't explain. Though you are not in my company I give you the same advice for free.'

They were a study in contrast, in age and in every other way. Colonel Kuznekov was a rock of a man in his middle fifties, stocky and hard, his grizzled hair as tough as wire. Gregor Salnikov was a head taller and twenty years younger, blond, easy-going, still with the accent of his native Georgia. He led the way to the kitchen and while the Colonel dropped into a chair he put fresh tea in the pot and filled it with boiling water from the samovar.

'I thought I would bring my car and take you to the meeting,' Kuznekov said. 'Very important, very high level, the world watching.'

Gregor looked up at the clock. 'But there's more than an hour yet, plenty of time.'

'Good. We can enjoy some tea first.' Kuznekov dropped a slice of lemon into his glass and mashed it with his spoon. Instead of adding sugar he held a lump between his teeth and drank the tea through it in the old-fashioned manner. He did a lot of things like this and some people were foolish enough to take him for a rustic. 'You have a very pleasant house here, Gregor,' he said.

'Yes,' Gregor said, looking around, his face falling as he did so. He had never learned to hide his emotions. Kuznekov nodded, understanding.

'Excuse me if I speak out of turn, but I think we are good enough friends for you to hear me out. You wear a black band on your sleeve—but you also wear one around your heart. I know it hurts you to talk of this, but some things must be discussed. How long is it now, two months since the plane crash? Those old Ilyushins, some of them should have been retired ten years ago. Your wife and small daughter. . . . But you have to go on, eh?'

Gregor sat heavily, his hands clasped before him, head lowered. 'There are times when I don't feel like going on.'

'Yet those are the times when we must. You look at me. An old family man, grandpa twelve times over. But it wasn't always that way. I was nine years old when the Germans came to our village.' His voice did not change much, but was suddenly harder, emotionless, his face the same. 'Black uniforms, lightning bolts on their collars. Our people were in the way so they just wiped them out. Like beetles. I was lucky. I was out with the cows and they didn't see me. They shot the cows though.' He shook himself and took a long noisy sip of tea before he continued.

'So what was I to do? No one else there and all the Nazis between me and the rest of the country. I went to the forest and thought about it and met Pyotr there who was in the same fix. Only he had done something about it. He had a nice new German rifle and a wallet of ammunition and was cleaning blood from his axe.' He finished the tea with a happy sigh and put the glass down. 'In the partisans we fought behind the enemy lines for the rest of the war. I killed my first man before I was ten years old. I tell you this simply to show you that life must go on. *Your* life must go on. I know how you feel but if you continue like this you'll be dropped from the Prometheus programme. And whoever replaces you won't be able to do your work as well as you can.'

'I know this. I've been trying. But it's hard.'

'Nothing in this world is easy, my friend. But you owe it to yourself and to the rest of us to try.'

'Yes, I will, of course. Thank you.'

'Don't waste time thanking me. Just get into my eighteen-year-old racing car and break some records for the two-kilometre dash.'

# 3

'MR PRESIDENT, these are the ladies and gentlemen of the Council for Good Government of Topeka, Kansas.'

There were murmurs of greeting and some hesitant bows from the women in the delegation. President Bandin nodded his great head in solemn welcome, managing to convey a strong resemblance to Pope John bestowing a benediction. He did not stand, but met them eye to eye, for his chair was on a raised platform behind the great desk. His bandy legs did not match the noble breadth of his forehead, but none of his visitors were aware of this for the ceremonious hush of the Oval Room impressed and subdued even the most cantankerous. This was the heart of America and here, under the Great Seal of the Presidency, was the head of state.

'It is my pleasure to meet with you fine people from the great midwest, and I cannot tell you how much I back your efforts for good government. Though I understand that good government is not the reason that brings you so far to see me.'

President Bandin waited expectantly, the massive head tilted receptively to hear their pleas. Charley Dragoni, the presidential aide, touched the leader of the delegation on the arm, and nodded towards the President. The man took a step forward, coughing to cover his embarrassment, then spoke.

'Mr President, I, that is we, want to . . . thank you for seeing us today. It's a great honour, believe me. What we come about is not so much government, I mean good government, like the name of our organization says, you know . . .'

'Get on with it, Frank,' the elderly woman beside him hissed behind her hand. The spokesman stammered and his words rushed on.

'You see it's the grain prices at the exchange. We been taking a beating with futures and some people are making a fortune sellin' to the Russians while some of us got to take bank loans for fertilizer and seed crop. 'Tain't fair to the independent producer. . . .'

'You sir, ladies and gentlemen, I do know your problem.'
The spokesman's voice was cut off instantly as President
Bandin spoke. 'I know it well and to be honest it's something
that concerns me both night and day. Right here, on my
desk at the present moment,' he tapped a thick folder that
lay under his right hand, 'is the latest study on this important topic and the draft of my plan to alleviate the situation.
If there are profiteers they will be punished and they will
profit no more. You people who work the soil with your own
hands must prosper, not greedy speculators. You are the
heartland of this great country and your crops the blood
that feeds us all. Your voices will be heard. Thank you.'

With these words as a clue, and the final impressive nod,
Charley Dragoni pushed on the nearest arms and began
moving them towards the door. An old man, nearest to the
desk, was shaking with controlled passion and he called out
hoarsely,

'Mr President, I gotta be frank, I didn't vote for you last
election. But being here, meeting you like this, it's something, Mr President, and you got my vote and everyone in
my family.'

'Thank you, sir, I appreciate your sincerity and know it is
a free choice in a free society.' The President thought for a
second, then pulled out his tie-pin with the presidential seal
upon it. 'Your honesty humbles me. Please, take this as a
reminder of this visit. It's the last one I have.'

Dragoni passed the pin to the man and his emotional
thanks were audible as they all left the room and Dragoni
closed the door behind the last blue rinse.

'Is that it for today, Dragoni? I hope to Christ it is.'
Brandin settled back heavily in his chair and loosened his
collar while his assistant consulted a card.

'Yes, sir, the last until four this afternoon when you're
meeting with the delegation of Puerto Rican Congress-
men.'

'More trouble from the spics? They're getting to be worse
than the nigs these days.' He took off his jacket and the
waiting Dragoni was there to take it and hang it in the
closet.

'And don't waste your time in there,' Bandin called after him. This message was quite clear to Dragoni who rattled quickly in the concealed bar and emerged with a large bourbon and branch. Bandin drank heavily and smacked his lips with pleasure, then dug a presidential-seal pin out of the top drawer of the desk and pushed it carefully into his tie. After this he opened the heavy folder under his right hand and took out the betting form and handed it to Dragoni.

'This one with the red line under it, fourth race at Santa Anita. A thousand to win. What about the Prometheus doctor?'

'Finalized, sir. There was some initial problem with Doctor Kennelly but he sees reason now. It's a national emergency and he's a government employee.'

'I'll say it's a national emergency when that bastard Polyarni came up with a girl cosmonaut. After those nice talks at the tractor exhibition; hands across the sea, co-operation, all that crap. And this broad waiting in the closet ready to be pushed on at the last minute. But wait until he has to face his comintern buddies when he finds out what *we've* got in *our* closet. Oh, baby, how I wish I could see his face then! I'd give a hundred grand to any CIA spook who could bug the Kremlin room when he tells them.'

'Are you serious about that, sir?'

'You have no sense of humour, Dragoni, none at all. Fill up the glass again.'

# 4

ALL PEOPLE CARE ABOUT is their own tiny corner of the universe, I. L. J. Flax thought to himself.

'You gentlemen do realize that in just forty-five minutes I must be at the first press conference here for Prometheus? Satellite relays for television, the world press, the works.'

He spoke in English to Vandelft who headed the American engineering team, then turned and said the same thing in Russian to Glushko, his opposite number on the Soviet side. What little they spoke of the other's language had long vanished in the heat of the moment. One from Siberia, the other from Oshkosh—it was amazing how much they resembled each other. Gold-rimmed glasses, thinning hair, tobacco-stained fingers, shirt pockets stuffed with pens and pencils, the inevitable calculator slung like a gun in a holster on each hip.

'I know that, Flax,' Vandelft said, his fingers tapping nervously on his clipboard. 'But this won't take fifteen minutes, ten, you've just got to do something. What the hell is the point of a news conference if all the final testing's held up? We're never going to launch on time if that happens.'

'There is no trouble,' Glushko said, his eyes murderous and cold as he avoided looking at his opposite number. 'It is the Americans who have stopped the work. We're ready to proceed at once.'

'All right, I'll come, for the sake of unity, peace, *mir*. Remember this is a joint project so I'd appreciate it if you would both at least act as though you wished to act jointly.' He repeated this in Russian as he lumbered out of the door and into the full heat of the day, the beads of sweat turning to rivulets as the sun smote him. Vandelft was at the tiller of one of the golf carts the NASA personnel used for getting about the sprawling base, and Flax squeezed in beside him. The Soviets scorned this effete form of transportation and Glushko was already on his bicycle leading the way.

You just never get used to the size, Flax thought. And in a couple of days I'm going to be sitting in Mission Control and coaxing this bird into orbit. It's a long way from Pszczyna.

Flax rarely thought of his native town, for America had been his home since he had been eleven. But Poland was the land of his birth, German Poland really and his family had still been considered Germans though they had lived there for generations. His father was headmaster of the local school, an educated man by any standards, and had raised his son the same way. German was spoken at home and Russian and Polish in the streets and in school, so young Flax was native in all three languages, an ability his father had not permitted him to lose when they had emigrated to the United States when threats of war were in the air. Bookish and always overweight, he had few friends, and no girl friends. The refusal of the Army to draft him because he was so fat only added to his humiliation and drove him further into his studies. He was studying engineering at Columbia University then and he smelled opportunity when the first course in electronics was offered, a field so new that they didn't even have a textbook and had to work from mimeographed notes done the same day of each class. He had gone into radar research, then, when working for the same army that had refused him entry a few years earlier, he felt that justice was coming his way at last. When NASA was organized he was there at the inception, his technical knowledge and linguistic ability keeping him on top when the German rocket scientists were whisked away ahead of the advancing Russians. After this he had never looked back; some people thought that Flax was Mission Control and he never told them differently. Now with the joint Soviet-American project he was at the peak of his career. But it did get tiring.

The fast elevator shot up inside the servicing tower and they emerged into the air-conditioned comfort of the Prometheus Assembly Building. PAB was a building without a base, a five-storey structure perched high in the air on top of the servicing tower that enclosed the entire upper structure of the spacecraft. Not only were the immense boosters and core body too big to be put together in a normal Vehicle Assembly Building, but they would have been too massive to move once joined. Therefore they had been assembled and joined in the open with temporary shelters covering the sensitive stages. They had been designed with this in mind and would not suffer from exposure.

But Prometheus itself could not be treated in this cavalier manner. It had been built at the Kennedy Space Flight Centre under the usual sterile and controlled conditions, air conditioned at all times to protect the circuitry from corrosion and the computer from temperature failure. After disassembly the various parts had been flown to the Soviet Union by a specially modified fleet of C5-As. Therefore the need for PAB, perched above the rockets, a building with the correct environment where the components could be re-assembled.

Technicians moved aside when the three men crossed the floor to the entry hatch. Flax led the way, puffing as he pulled himself through the opening, and looked round the now familiar Flight Cabin.

As in any other Flight Cabin the controls and instruments dominated everything. Yuri Gagarin went into space as a passenger facing a panel with twelve different instruments. Things had changed a bit since his time. Systems of all kinds proliferated and with each new system came controls, with the controls meters and readouts, until every available inch of space on all sides of the two pilots' couches was thick with them. Just learning the position and function of the instrumentation required thousands of hours of study, then hundreds of hours in the Flight Cabin Simulator putting this knowledge into practice.

'Just look at that,' Vandelft said, angrily. 'Look how the Russkies have fucked everything up!'

'Fook up!' Glushko shouted. In his months working with the Americans he had at least picked up that much English.

'Gentlemen, please,' Flax said, patting the air with both hands, trying to hush them. 'I see the problem, the matter under discussion. Now if you both kindly shut up we'll see what we can do about it.'

He had to find an answer that would satisfy both parties —and it would not be an easy one. Under every switch, dial or readout a clearly lettered plate was fixed describing its function. Labels such as PDI ABORT or RCS did not make much sense to a layman but they were vital to the pilots. Next to each of these abbreviations was the same information spelled out in Cyrillic. But something new had been added.

On all sides, under and around the original labels, there were bits of paper that had been pasted on. Some of it was yellow paper, others ruled sheets from notebooks, and all of it covered in crabbed Russian handwriting.

'The whole thing looks like a notice board in a supermarket,' Vandelft said. 'Are we selling spare tyres and baby-sitters or are we flying a goddamn spaceship?'

'These are necessary because of the inadequate information and labelling in English,' Glushko shouted, his voice drowning out the other engineer's. 'My technicians must check the circuitry and for that the labelling must be in Russian. Besides—*see*—you do the same thing! So why should not we?'

He pointed triumphantly to some neatly lettered bits of card that Patrick Winter had attached to some of the most important readouts he would use in take-off. Specific information about limits that should not be exceeded, figures to be watched.

'I don't think this is quite the same thing,' Flax said, raising his hand as the Russian engineer started to protest. 'However we can compromise. Your labels stay up as long as your technicians are working here. Then they come down —*all* of them. What benefits them on the ground has nothing to do with the need of the Soviet pilot in flight. Glushko! Hear me out before you stamp off in a huff. The paper labels come down, but your pilot may attach any special labels she might need, just as our pilot has done. They can discuss it and we'll all abide by their decisions. Okay?'

They would accept the compromise, they had to. He looked at his watch. Good Christ! He was late already.


They had started without him. The auditorium was half filled with newsmen and photographers, bright under the big lights for the television cameras. The platform seemed even more crowded than the audience as all officials of the partner nations who could, got into the act. Top NASA brass was matched by their opposite numbers in SCSE, the Soviet State Commission for Space Exploration. The astronauts and cosmonauts seemed lost in the crowd. There was an empty seat next to them they had saved for him. Flax hated making a late and obvious entry, particularly since everyone would find him more interesting than the Soviet official now nattering away. It couldn't be helped. He took a deep breath just as someone touched him on the arm. An MP captain stood there, flanked by two sergeants. All three wore sidearms.

'Top Secret communication, sir, from the code room. Could I please see your ID.'

'For God's sake, Captain, you've known me for over a year. . . .' The protest faded away in the light of the officer's impassivity and Flax fumbled out the card. The captain studied it carefully, as though he had never seen it before, and nodded.

'Sergeant, note this number, then the time and date.'

Flax moved from one foot to the other as the sergeant took out a pad and slowly wrote down the particulars. Only when this was done did the officer unlock an attaché case chained to his wrist and take out a sealed buff envelope that was stamped TOP SECRET in angry red letters. Flax stuffed it into his pocket and turned away, but he wasn't through yet.

'Please sign the register, sir. Here . . . and here . . . and initial in this box . . . and here on the second sheet.'

Finally free, Flax walked swiftly down the aisle, uncomfortably conscious of heads turning curiously to follow him. Only the minister droned on, unaware. Flax stood at the foot of the steps and waited until the red light blinked off on the camera doing a panoramic shot of the entire stage and the light came on on the close-up camera covering the politician. As fast as reasonably possible he climbed the stairs and rolled across the stage to his seat. Ely Bron, in a well-tailored and obviously expensive charcoal-grey suit, leaned forward and whispered in his ear.

'I hope she was worth the delay, Flax. Can I have her name when you get tired of her?'

'Shut up, Ely. You're a real pain in the butt,' he hissed back.

The Russian sat down, to a mild flutter of applause, and was replaced by a NASA official who said approximately the same things the other had, only in English. Flax mopped sweat from his head as subtly as he could, and waited for his breathing to calm down. Then he remembered the communication in his jacket pocket.

SECRET was stamped over almost every paper he touched, but top secret with all the signing and guards and such was much more rare. Whatever it was would surely be a bit more interesting than the speeches. He slipped the envelope out of his pocket and, in the concealment of his crossed legs and massive hands, managed to work it open and take out the message inside. He waited until the close-up camera was on the speaker, then swiftly read it.

Then read it again, sweat bursting from every pore.

After that he just sat numbly until Ely tapped him on the arm.

'Flax, wake up, you're on. Give 'em hell, boy.'

Flax walked slowly to the podium and adjusted the microphone in front of his lips. Cameras clicked and the blank eyes of the television cameras stared directly at him. The whole world was watching. He coughed a bit into his hand then began to speak.

'As the man in charge of Mission Control it is my job to act as liaison between the crew of Prometheus and the machines and men on the ground, link the two into a single functioning unit. My job here today is to introduce the astronauts and cosmonauts who will be on this first flight. However, before I do, I would like to read to you from a communication I have just received from the Space Centre in Houston. As you can see there are only five people beside me on the platform where there should be six. Doctor Kennelly, the space physician who was to go in Prometheus, has been suddenly taken ill. It's not serious, not serious, that is, in that he is in no danger. He was operated on yesterday for appendicitis with certain complications and the prognosis is for complete recovery. However, he will not be in any condition for this flight. Therefore another NASA doctor has been appointed in his place. As you all know we have standbys for everyone on this mission, since the health of any single individual cannot be allowed to affect the entire operation. I will now read to you from the communication I have just received.'

Flax took out the sheet and the cameras clicked even faster.

'It begins with a description of Dr Kennelly's condition, then adds, "Considering the present incumbent inoperative procedures have been optioned for qualified trained back-up replacement now en route Houston Baikonur ETA 1500 hours your time. Replacement physician is Doctor C. Samuel attached Houston Space Medicine Research Centre. Doctor Samuel is 32 years old and a graduate of Johns Hopkins University in Baltimore, Maryland. After graduation she interned at Johns Hopkins Hospital . . ." '

A rising murmur from the press cut him off as those who understood English caught the meaning of what Flax was saying. The simultaneous translation droned on and short moments later the Russian speakers jerked to attention and the murmur grew. Flax stood silent and immobile and waited for silence.

'Ely, did you hear that,' Patrick said angrily.

'Politics, my friend, politics.'

'You're damned right! A woman cosmonaut one up to Moscow, so as soon as Doc Kennelly got sick they must have started scratching around in every NASA lab to find a woman to slot into the programme in his place. She can't have been trained so quickly. Seems they're going to sell Prometheus down the river just to play politics one more time. . . .'

'If I may continue,' Flax said. 'After graduation Doctor Samuel interned at Johns Hopkins Hospital. All of her biographical material is in this message and will be available to the press after this meeting. Doctor Samuel is a midwesterner, that is she grew up in Detroit although she was born in Mississippi. Before going to Johns Hopkins for pre-medical training she obtained a BA in education at Tuskegee Institute.'

Only the Americans were completely aware now, the rest of the international audience listening and taking notes. Ely sat so quietly his silence was a message. Patrick's jaw was tensed so hard the muscles stood out in ridges. Nadya, sitting next to him, heard him curse under his breath. Now she was angry too.

'Why do you speak like that?' she whispered. 'Don't you think a woman is fit to come on this flight? Are women inferior?'

'Politics. They're playing politics.'

'So what if it is politics? If she is qualified it is a very good thing.'

'But don't you realize just how dirty a game they're playing? The Soviets have a woman on this flight, so they must have a woman too. Only they've gone one better. This will really buy the votes and put a finger in the old Russki eye.'

'Why are you so vicious?'

'Why? Didn't you understand? Didn't you hear the name of her school, Tuskegee?'

'I did, yes, but I do not know this centre of education.'

'Well I do. It's *black*. An all-black school. Now if you don't think replacing a pot-bellied Irish-American with a black woman isn't playing politics, then I'd like to know just what in hell is?'

# 5

*Cottenham New Town, England*

'YOU TURN ON the telly dear, while I clean up the tea things,' Irene said, stacking the dishes while she spoke.

'Right,' Henry Lewis said, pushing himself away from the table. He walked slowly into the front parlour and switched on the set. It was an old one and took a long time to warm up. His favourite chair was already in front of the screen and there was a packet of Woodbines on the table next to it. He lit one and opened the week's *TV Mirror*.

'I thought so,' he called out. 'Repeat of that Leeds United game. The one we missed when we were at your mother's.'

The screen flickered and came to life as he reached out a finger and punched ITV. A man with a neck like a bulldog was talking a foreign language while another voice translated into English. Irritated, Henry pushed BBC-1 only to find the same man speaking there. ITV was still the same so, in a last forlorn hope, he did what he rarely did and pushed BBC-2 and got just what he deserved. Three men sitting on wooden chairs blowing horns.

He kicked off his slippers disgustedly and pulled on his boots. Taking his cap and jacket he called to his wife, 'Christ knows what they're up to. Going for a stroll.'

'See you at closing time.'

It was a perfect summer evening and he really didn't mind being out of the house. At the end of the terrace he turned down New Town Road past the tall council flats of the estate. He didn't like them. More like barracks than proper flats. He came abreast of The King's Arms but went on. All plastic and fizzy keg beer with a juke box; he had been in there once and never gone back. Not a decent place at all. It was ten minutes farther to the old village, but worth the effort.

This was a bywater, surrounded on all sides by the new town. The main road to the plant from the motorway had sliced away half the village, while the housing estates loomed on all sides. But the remaining bit of village was built in a steep valley and perhaps it would have cost more to fill it in than leave it. There were some cottages, a shop or two, and a half-timbered building with a peeling signboard swinging in front of it. The Horse and Groom, Free House.

Henry thumbed down the iron latch and pushed open the heavy wooden door.

'Evening, Henry,' the landlord said, wiping down the bar.

'Evening George.'

Henry leaned both elbows on the dark wood and watched quietly while George pulled a pint of mild and pushed it over to him. He took a deep draw and sighed happily. George nodded in agreement.

'That's a good barrel, that one is,' he said.

'All right. Not the way it used to be.'

'What is?'

'You can say that again. Even the bloody weather's gone to hell.'

'They say it's those rockets.'

'Rockets! That's what they had on telly this evening instead of the football. Yanks and Russians and more rockets. Nothing to do with us, thank Christ. As if things weren't bad enough. At least we aren't wasting money on capers like that.'

'Can't afford to, that's why. Those bloody politicians would if they could.'

'You're right, George. Wet politicians and watery beer.' He drained the glass and dropped it back to the bar. 'Give us another one.'

# 6

'FLAX, I AM GOING to blow the whistle on the whole thing, so help me I will.'

'Patrick, think first! Put it into gear. You weren't born yesterday. You know you have to compromise in politics and politics is what keeps NASA going. You don't need me to tell you that.'

They stood inside the heavy glass door looking out at the setting sun, a red ball of fire on the horizon. It was air conditioned inside the building but still warm outside in the Russian evening. The two MPs beyond the door, one Soviet the other American, had dark patches under their arms and looked wrinkled and hot. The road beyond them was empty.

'You told me she was on the way,' Patrick said.

'The plane landed, the car was waiting. But you know the kind of delays the Russians get into at the airport here.'

'Ely knew something was happening. Remember that bet? He knew or guessed. But who'd have thought they'd pull *this*? Not they, this is too big a con even for the NASA brass. I can smell Bandin right behind this whole mess.'

'No mess, Pat. She's a qualified doctor. . . .'

'The world's full of doctors, but very few fit for space crew. You know what they used to call him when he was first in the Senate? Rubber Bandin. He could stretch in every direction and always snap back. The last of the old wheeler-dealers. You don't hear it much any more. The PR boys sold him to the American public like a bunch of bananas. But he's still plain old Rubber Bandin. Anything for a vote or a buck.'

'He's not a bad president. . . .'

'And not a very good one either. Maybe not as crooked as Tricky Dicky, but he's craftier. Look at this bit. He may louse up the entire Prometheus Project—but by God he's really latched on to the women's vote and the black vote. But I'm not going to buy it.'

'Patrick, relax. Think clearly.' Flax had him by the arm, his fingers hot and damp through the thin fabric. 'You've been in the space project what, nine years? It's your career and this flight is the topper, the big one, and you're the pilot. If you say anything you'll get chopped. The people who own the newspapers are on Bandin's side and they own the people who write for the papers. No one will ever know what you're talking about—and you'll be down the chute and out of a job. They'll make it look like sour grapes and crucify you. And Prometheus will still take off on schedule with another pilot. Is your backup as good a pilot as you? If not—*you'll* be jeopardizing the project. Just by opening your mouth.'

'It's dirty, Flax. You make it look black and white but it's politics and it's dirty.'

'Patrick, you know better. It's all politics. Remember the old science fiction stories about rockets to the moon? Some rich industrialist builds one in the back yard, or a mad professor puts one together out of wash boilers and off they go. None of those writers got it right. None of them ever wrote about middle-aged Army and Navy pilots landing on the moon. None of them ever thought of the fact that the space race would be just that. A race. National glory and wave the flag. If we don't get there first the Soviets will. Hurry, hurry and pour the money in, take chances and hope you luck out.'

'There's a car coming. And you're trying to tell me it's still that way?'

'You had better believe it. The Soviets have the big boosters. We've the rest of the hardware and the technology. Neither of them alone could get this project off the ground for another ten years—if then. Putting the co-operation package together has been the biggest piece of creative politics in the history of mankind. Don't louse it up at this late date. All right, Bandin's making political hay out of it. So what? If it works it works for us all and that's the name of the game, buddy boy.'

A black Lincoln Continental, American flag snapping on its hood, pulled to a stop outside. A full Colonel and one of the embassy aides climbed out, then turned to help the other passenger.

Patrick watched, trying to hold down his doubts and his anger, still not sure what to do. A girl climbed out and walked towards the entrance.

She was here. Smallish, just up to the shoulders of the two men who flanked her. Dark skin, not very black but dark enough. Hair cut short and neatly curled. Pretty. Nice features, almost an Egyptian nose. Good figure too in the cream summer suit. Sound hips, practical legs, good walk. Christ, what was he doing? Judging a beauty parade or looking at the space medic who could make or break the flight?

Then they were inside and introductions all around. Her hand was cool, her grip firm. It didn't last long and then they were alone with Flax.

'I'm sorry to put you right to work, doctor, but the interview was scheduled. . . .'

'Coretta, if you please Dr Flax.'

'The same in return, Coretta. Flax is what everyone calls me. As you can guess we need good PR. *Newsweek* has seen things pretty much our way and they have a reporter out here now to do the lead for their special issue. Name of Redditch, one of their top people. He's talked to most of the others here and should have left but he waited for you. If you're not too tired.'

'Not in the slightest. It was a lovely flight, and I'm still excited. I'd love to talk to him.'

'Great. In here. Patrick, you know the way.'

It could have been no accident that the large window of the PR lounge faced the launching pad where Prometheus stood. The giant spacecraft was framed neatly and stood out against the rose clouds of dusk. Coretta stopped involuntarily and clasped her hands together.

'Ohh, my goodness! That is something, really something!'

'May I quote you on that?' he asked, a thin stoop-shouldered man by the bar with a drink in his hand. He had big ears and a potato nose and radiated a sort of shambling good will. But his eyes were attentive and he missed nothing.

'Dr Samuel, this is Mr Redditch of *Newsweek* magazine,' Flax said. 'Would you like something to drink before we begin?'

'A bourbon on the rocks, not too strong.'

'I'll get it,' Patrick said, turning to the well-stocked bar. The best booze was always brought out for the press. He poured himself a large Chivas Regal with soda and a Jack Daniels Green Label for the girl. They were sitting round the coffee table now and the reporter had a tape recorder in the centre of it. Flax shook his head *no* when Patrick lifted a drink in his direction, eyebrows raised. Patrick put the drinks on the coffee table and joined them.

'I hope you people realize that I'm no science reporter,' Redditch said. 'Our technical boys have been producing figures and charts and we'll have plenty of that. But I'm doing the lead. I'll do the personal pieces, readers like personalities, and all the general non-technical stuff. All right?'

'Most fair, we're happy to help,' Flax said.

'Fine. If I could start with you, Coretta, since you're the newcomer and the only one I haven't talked to before. Can you tell me something about yourself?'

'I can't add a thing to that press release you must have seen. Just school, then research, then more research with NASA.'

'I'm sure your life has been much more interesting than that. Certainly a woman succeeding in a man's field is something people will be interested in. And a black woman as well. You've come a long way against what must have been difficult odds.'

'I don't see it that way,' she said calmly. 'America's a civilized country and given the skills a woman can do as well as a man. And skin colour doesn't enter into it.'

'*Really*?' Redditch said, his eyebrows lifting. 'That'll be good news in the ghettos.' He made a note on his pad. 'Can I be frank, Coretta? I've been a newsman for a number of years and I know the facts. And I can't stand bullshit.'

Her face was calm but her voice was icy. 'I'm giving you the facts and they're not bullshit.'

Redditch threw his hands up in mock surrender. 'Okay! No fights. You call them as you see them and I'll write it down.' He flipped through a wad of NASA releases. 'Now, in this copy about you, it doesn't seem to mention anything about either your marriage or your divorce.'

'You've been doing your homework,' she said calmly, then sipped at her drink. 'The marriage lasted less than a year. An old school friend. It was a mistake on both our parts. There were no children. We're divorced but still see each other once in a while. Would you like names and dates?'

'No thank you, I have all that. Just your personal point of view. Another question if you don't mind. Do you think there was anything political in the fact that you, a newcomer to the space programme, were chosen to go on this flight?'

This was the cruncher, the big one, the question that Redditch had been setting up. The early stuff was just teasing. Patrick sat unmoving and saw the sudden reddening of Flax's neck. Neither of them said anything. Redditch

39

made an adjustment on the recorder while Coretta sipped her drink, then put it down.

'I don't think so,' she said in a calm, unhurried voice. 'I'm no newcomer to NASA, in fact I have been connected with space research for five years. I have always wanted to practise my speciality in its proper setting, in space. I'm sure my age helped me. Some of my colleagues are senior to me but they may not have the physical resiliency for a long space flight. I was just lucky that my number came up now, for a flight as important as this one. I am very happy to be a member of the crew.'

Well done, Patrick thought, then went to pour himself another drink. Cool delivery, no fluster—and every word smacking of the NASA speech writers. She had learned her lines very well. Redditch was going to have a hard time flustering this baby.

Redditch never did. He asked the same question from a couple of angles then appeared to lose interest. Was Coretta's smile a bit wider as he turned his back? Flax was at the bar and pouring himself a large glass of ice water, then a second. Redditch flipped the cassette over and turned to Patrick.

'Now the sixty-four thousand dollar question. I know you have been asked it about three hundred times already but I hope you won't mind if I ask again now. What is Prometheus for? Over to you.'

'Before I say what the project is for, or designed to do, can I fill in with a bit of history?'

'Say it any way you like, I have all day. But keep it non-technical. I'm the guy who failed first-grade arithmetic in the eighth grade. Take it from there.'

'Right. First, think of the energy shortage. No politics now, greedy Arabs, profiteering oil companies, all that stuff. Just the physical reality that, at the present rate of consumption, we're going to burn up all the Earth's oil in a couple more years. So we've got to do something drastic about it. Prometheus is that drastic thing. Oil is really two things. Not only the stuff we burn in our cars and planes, but a basic raw material for most industries, chemicals, fertilizer, the lot. So every drop we burn is a drop wasted for this other vital need. Therefore if we get our energy needs from something other than petroleum we have *all* the oil for its other uses. Okay so far?'

'Perfect. Clear as a bell. More.'

'Right. Alternative sources of energy. Primarily all our energy comes from the sun.'

'I don't get that. Coal? Oil? Wind? What do they have to do with the sun?'

'Everything. Coal and oil contain solar energy stored away by plants millions of years ago. The sun heats our atmosphere and it moves and we get winds. The wind blows and makes ocean waves, so even wave power is indirect solar power. The time has come to utilize the non-polluting, eternally available energy of the sun directly. The Prometheus Project.'

'Slow down. It's going to take billions of dollars to even begin this project. Wouldn't that money be better spent on earth, say tapping the solar energy in the desert?'

'Negative. The atmosphere interferes, the sun doesn't shine at night so the supply isn't continuous, construction is expensive, a number of things make it difficult. It should be done, yes, but it can never equal the size and sheer efficiency of Prometheus. Eventually Prometheus will supply *all* the world's power needs, supply free power for ever. That's what we plan.'

'How?'

'Look outside the window. The largest spaceship ever to be launched. The first of fifty. This is a big and overpopulated world we live on and it needs a lot of power. Fifty shiploads for this project, then who knows how many after that.'

'That sounds expensive.'

'It is,' Patrick said. 'But once launched the project will be self-sustaining. The electricity will be sold at a rate of two and a half cents a kilowatt hour—which will be enough to finance more launchings and generators. Once the payload is in orbit the generation of electricity is simplicity itself. The biggest part of our payload is the same kind of plastic

41

you wrap around left-overs when you put them in the refrigerator. Since there's no gravity in orbit, no friction from the atmosphere either, this very thin plastic can be spread out to cover square miles of space. It's coated with aluminium so it acts like a big mirror to reflect sunlight to a focus where it will heat a fluid that will, in turn, drive a turbine that will generate electricity. Simple.'

'Very simple. But you haven't told me how the electricity gets back to earth. Isn't this where the death ray bit comes in?'

Patrick smiled. 'The old rumours are the hardest to kill. Any kind of radiation can be called a death ray—but only if it's strong enough and concentrated enough. A light bulb will warm your hand, but stand in front of a military searchlight and you'll be fried. If you've a small boat you can get a radar set that will help you find your way. Yet if you could manage to get at the focus of a big search radar you would find yourself cooked, coagulated like a hard-boiled egg. Degree and concentration. Once the electricity has been generated in space it will be converted to radio waves, low density microwaves, and beamed back to earth. The double directional aerial will beam to a receiver in Siberia and another in the State of Washington. The amount Russia receives will supply most of her Siberian needs. What we get will supply the five Western States. Free power from space.'

'Sounds okay but I hate to leave the death ray so quickly. It seems to me that the amount of power to do all that, even in the form of radio waves, might be a *little* strong when it hits the earth?'

'Absolutely correct. Firstly, the radio beam is locked on to the receiver and is self correcting. Secondly, if despite this the beam should waver too far it will be automatically shut off. The theory suggests that the beam of radio waves will not be strong enough to cause damage on Earth, but as a further protection the receiver will be situated in the mountains, miles from the nearest habitation.'

Redditch reached out and snapped off the tape recorder. 'That makes sense—and it seems to wrap it up. Thank you for your time. I'm going to run, there's a plane I can just make.'

There were polite good-byes and the door closed behind the reporter.

'Now I can have that drink,' Flax said, heaving himself up to the bar. 'I was afraid to even look at booze with that son-of-a-bitch of a reporter here. You want a refill, Coretta?'

'Yes please,' She sat, poised and at ease, her hands folded neatly in her lap. Patrick poured another drink for himself and wondered how she could remain so calm.

'You're just out of Houston,' he said. 'Hear anything more about Doc Kennelly?'

'Just what you probably know. The operation was successful and prognosis fine.'

'Quite a coincidence, wasn't it?'

'What was a coincidence?'

'His getting sick at this time. And whatever happened to his backup, Feinberg? Wasn't a Jew ethnic enough for Prometheus. . . .'

'Patrick,' Flax broke in. 'Why don't you just shut up and let Coretta get some rest, she must have had a long day.'

'No, let him talk, Flax. Let us get this one out in the open. I have no idea of what happened to Dr Feinberg. No one bothered to tell me. I was just started on a hush-hush space orientation programme about seven weeks ago. Centrifuge, free fall in the plane, all the rest. Just two days ago I was told I was going on Prometheus. That's all I know.'

Patrick laughed without humour. 'That's all we know too—Seven weeks! That bastard Bandin has been planning this all along. I wonder if Doc really had a hot appendix. They could have faked that too——'

'That's enough!' Flax said, heaving his bulk forward between them. 'Get to your quarters, Patrick. You've had a lot to drink, go sleep it off.'

'No,' Coretta said. 'Will you please move aside, Flax. This thing has been started and we're going to finish it. Right here and now.' She stood in front of Patrick, looking up at him, fists clenched and emotion showing for the first time. She was angry. 'It's pretty obvious what you're thinking.

43

That bastard Bandin, as you call him, has been playing politics. The Commies got a woman into the space programme which gave him a shot in the political eye. Now if he could see them with another woman, then raise them with a *black* woman, he would be having a shot in the political arm instead. Was it *possible*? Could Kennelly get sick enough to drop out of the programme? His backup could have been replaced earlier for other reasons, no problems there. If this were done—who could be pulled in quickly enough to take Kennelly's place? Why look, there's nice little Dr Coretta Samuel way in the back of the NASA lab, not only proving that NASA is an equal opportunity employer, but she's really good at analysing calcium samples. She should be. She's been doing it for five years. Why not give her a chance at a place on the Prometheus team? That's what you are thinking, isn't it—or something very much like that?'

She leaned close to Patrick in her anger, so close he could feel her breath warm on his face. He did not speak, but only nodded slowly in response. Coretta leaned back and sighed, then turned away.

'Well do you know something, Mr Pilot—that's what I have been thinking too.' Then she wheeled about and stabbed her finger at him. 'I think the way it was done stinks and the stink is of politics so strong I can smell Washington right from here. But you want to know something else—I don't care! However I got into Prometheus doesn't matter a damn. I'm *here*! Mr Redditch knew I was lying about the place of the black man in America. Not to mention the black woman. But I'm not making race propaganda out of Prometheus. Others are doing that. All I've to do is go along for the ride. And I can do it. I can hack the job. I'm going into space and I'm going to do the work I've been trained to do then come back to the roars of the crowd. I've worked hard and come a long way to get where I am now. There was a great man in the history of our country, name of Martin Luther King. They killed him for what he was doing and his wife carried on his work. God knows how many thousands of little black girls were named

44

after her—I'm just one. Now I'm going to take that name into space and do my job. It will be a woman who'll have done it and a black woman who does it and they'll *never* be able to take that away from us.'

She slammed her glass down so hard on to the table that it jumped and fell over and ice and bourbon spilled across the shining surface. Before anyone could say anything she had turned and was out of the door and gone.

*'Reilly, this whole damn thing is a plumber's nightmare. Not made any easier by the fact that I can't read a word of it.'*

*'I will teach you, Duffy, ten bucks a lesson. Well worth it. In a little while you will speak Russian like a native and will also be earning like me, an extra fifty a week for being bilingual.'*

*'Not me. I barely speak English. Now tell me, what are all these squiggles at this junction?'*

*'Standby bilateral fuel transfer pump tank 23 feed line 19 to feed line 104 tank 16B pressurization point switch normally off 734LU.'*

*'Thanks, I feel a lot better for knowing.'*

*The master schematic for the section was spread out on the deck; it measured two metres by two and was in six colours.*

*Duffy muttered to himself as he checked the circuitry. He blinked once, lost his place on the diagram, then sat up to rub his back.*

*'So we check the circuits,' he said, pointing to the open panels and dangling electrical leads. 'So great. We have continuity between the flight cabin controls and the computer and the relays and sub-unit motors and servos. But so what? We gotta take tovarich and his buddies on trust. All the Russki plumbing's sealed away and pressurized with nitrogen and we can't even get to look at it.'*

*'They checked and double checked. You've seen the records.'*

*'Yes—but how do we know?'*

45

*Reilly shrugged and picked his teeth with the positive probe from the digital voltmeter, watching the numbers flicker on the readout. 'I guess we don't. Take it on faith, baby. Give them credit where credit's due—these big bastards really fly. Raw power and up and up they go. Multiple motors and fuel supplies so if one motor or pump kicks out the others keep on functioning. They really lift.'*

*'They really blow up too, or is that just a rumour?'*

*'One of them did, we're pretty sure of that. A satellite photo in 1968 showed one of the first of these big babies on the launching pad. Picture taken next day showed that it was gone—and so was the launch tower and all the buildings for a mile round. It must have blown right on the pad. But that was an early model.'*

*'So you say.'*

*'It's on the record. They've done all their launches for a couple of years now with these boosters, and all of them have worked and worked well. They've had their troubles with their shuttles and they have had a lot more payload trouble. But these big babies can really dig in their toes and lift.'*

*'Time for a coffee break yet?'*

*'No. We do this one next.'*

# 7

'AND NOW our little holiday begins, hey?' Colonel Kuznekov said, smiling around at the five others. Behind his back the heavy door hissed shut and the bolts rattled into place.

'It's quarantine,' Ely Bron said. 'I don't think we can look at it as a holiday.'

'But we can, Dr Bron,' Kuznekov insisted. 'Ninety-six hours of peace while the final countdown begins. Right now the technicians are, how do you say it, in a bloody sweat making sure everything goes right? While us—what do we have to do? We are locked in this magnificent block of flats where nasty bugs and bacteria cannot get at us. We're sealed in with cooks to make our food and maids to look after our clothes and bedding. We all have work to do, the pilots most of all, I see them studying those big books all the time. But we don't work as they do. So we've time to meet each other without politicians and publicity and newsmen and a thousand other things to distract. To talk with us they must use the phone and we can always be busy when it rings.'

The phone rang. They were all silent for a moment—then burst out laughing. 'Who shall I say is busy?' Patrick asked, as he reached out to take up the phone.

When he did so the lights came on. This was more than a simple telephone, really a closed-circuit television set-up. The chair in front of the phone was bolted into place and a TV pickup focused on it. Across the desk was a screen with the image of the caller.

It was I. L. J. Flax.

'What's up?' Patrick asked. 'We're not even locked in yet and you're on the phone already.'

'Sorry. Reporter wants to interview Coretta. Should have been here a day ago but had trouble with plane connections.'

'Who is it?' Coretta called out.

'Girl by the name of Smith. Says you promised an exclusive interview for *Black Woman* magazine.'

Everyone was aware of the conversation; no one was looking at Coretta. She hesitated a moment, then answered.

'Tell her to wait a bit, I'll be in touch with her. There's no time now.'

'Pull out the cord when you hang up, will you, Patrick,' Ely said.

'I'd like to. But let's do like Coretta. Don't take calls. Call *them* if we want to talk. Colonel Kuznekov is right. We all have things to do before lift off. But let's get to know one another. We're a team and we're going to have to learn some more about each other to function as a team. Nayda and I are the pilots and we know how to work

47

together. At this moment I'm in command and I'll stay there until we're in final orbit and the engine is shut down. At that point the Colonel takes over and issues the orders.'

'Not quite, Patrick. The generator is my responsibility, and I am in charge of assembly. I'll need strong people who can space walk; for this I'll issue orders. But for everything else, maintenance of our space station, communications, the rest, to the Commander. You must still be in charge.'

'Makes sense, Pat,' Ely said, turning the page of his book as he spoke. 'You're captain of the ship and you stay that way. With Nadya your first mate. The fission engine is mine, but I just fire it up for the single burn into orbit, then shut it down. After that I play rigger to Colonel Kuznekov's solar generator.'

'We all have our roles, like an ant hill in space,' Kuznekov said. 'Patrick and Nadya get us into orbit, then keep all the machines operating that keep us alive in that hostile environment. I'll supervise the assembly of the generating plant and once that's done, electricity's turned over to Gregor here.'

Gregor nodded. 'While the generator is being assembled I will be erecting the broadcast antennae on Prometheus. The output will be low to begin with but will serve to operate the pilot programme. Conversion from the turbo-generators to 3.3 GHz then beamed to the receiving stations on Earth. I do not envisage any problems. The equipment has been tested and functions as designed.'

'Well, bully,' Coretta said. 'That leaves me as odd girl out, with nothing to do except help you people carry around the equipment. But I must remind you that the only machine on this trip *not* designed to function in space is the human body. We will be in orbit, in free fall, for at least a month before the relief flight of the space shuttle. So my job is to see that we all stay functional for that period, possibly longer. It must cost a million dollars each to put an American or a Russian body into orbit, so the longer we can stay on the job functioning well, the better it will be. See me with all your complaints, aspirin and sympathy at all hours.'

Coretta hit the right tone. Somehow they had each summed up their work for the others, once started they had to go on. But she had topped the conversation and made them laugh.

Patrick sensed this as the correct moment to stop the business and get social. They had to learn to live together before they could work together.

'The drinking light is lit,' he said. 'I know there are no teetotallers among the Americans, or among the piloting staff. How about you, Colonel?'

'I drink only vodka, brandy, beer, *kvass* and wine, though during the war I learned to like German schnapps and Scotch whisky.'

'You won't be hard to please. That leaves you, Gregor.'

The blond engineer looked around. 'Please, I am no problem, a small glass of wine perhaps. Though I am willing to try anything.'

'Boozers all,' Patrick said. 'As CO of this outfit it is my pleasure to throw out the first bottle. It's going to be a native product of ours, a sour mash bourbon, and you'll like it. If you don't like it we'll try something else.'

Patrick poured the drinks and passed them out. Nadya nodded thanks, without looking up, already deep in conversation with Gregor. Perhaps she found him attractive; maybe he was, in a depressing Russian way. A sad-looking engineer, a widower of only two months, must bring out the maternal instincts in any girl. Perhaps even more than that. She might be holding his hand next to cheer him up. Or more. Well, fine, it would make for a happy ship, wouldn't it? It didn't matter to him. She was pilot and he was commander and that was all there was to it. Yet as he reached for the bottle to pour more drinks he saw her image clearly before him, as she had been that once, nude and smooth as silk beneath his fingers, her lips still wet where they had pressed against his. This memory was so strong that he had to pause for a second and resist the impulse to blink or shake his head. With a steady hand he poured a drink. That was all in the past, a moment out of time, something unimportant. It had looked good for a bit, then something had gone wrong. He had no idea what it was nor did he care to find out. There were other women in the world, right on this flight in fact. Femlib with a vengeance. And he could understand Coretta a lot better than he could Nadya. Maybe there was something after all to the east is east, west is west bit. It was technology and a common need that had lifted the Prometheus Project off the ground, not the crying need for each country to vote in the other's elections. Ely and the Colonel had the right idea; keep it technical and there were no problems. Patrick brought them their glasses.

'Listen, Patrick,' Ely said. 'Did you know that our friend the Colonel here was the man who developed, with Patsayev, the superconductor cable that we're laying now in Alaska?'

'I didn't know it but I would believe it. Probably because I know very little about superconductors.'

'The greatest thing in physics since the discovery of the monopole. Shows how stupid the CIA boys can be. A fifteen-page report on the Colonel, all about what year he joined the Communist party and the name of his dog, but nothing about his real work. Don't stand there looking like a shocked virgin, Patrick. Do you think the Colonel doesn't know that we've had inch-thick security reports about everybody on the crew?'

'Or is there doubt on your part that we have had the same about you?' the Colonel said. Taking a long swig from his glass, he nodded approvingly. 'Not vodka; but a certain charm of its own.'

'Yes, it has,' Patrick said, then relaxed and smiled at himself. 'I'm sure the security people are earning their money on both sides of the fence. And I guess it doesn't really matter a damn. Prometheus is a joint project that both countries have been booted into because we both need new energy sources now the old ones are running out. In the US we've had our big blackouts in Seattle and 'Frisco, then the fires. You've had those crop failures and the famine in Siberia, or maybe that didn't hit the papers here?'

'Our press is reluctant to spread bad news,' the Colonel said dryly. 'But the enthusiastic broadcasts of the Voice of America and the BBC keep us informed of all disasters.'

Coretta sat alone, looking into her drink, and Patrick thought it would be a good time to repair some wobbly fences.

'About our first meeting,' he said.

'What about it?' She did not intend to make it easy.

'I think you misunderstood——'

'I don't think I did, Major Winter.'

'It's going to be a long flight. My name is Patrick.'

'If I call you that, you'll be calling me Coretta, and I'm not quite ready for that yet.'

'This is not a fight that anyone can win, Dr Samuel. All we can do is all lose. If we should keep fighting, the flight will be in jeopardy and one of us will have to be replaced. What would that accomplish? Can't we just start even— like we'd never met before, as if I'd just come in the door? Then I could sidle up and say that you remind me of a girl I used to date in high school, almost my first date as I remember. Don't narrow your eyes like that, I mean it. I know I'm the right colour and everything else to be a racial bigot, but appearances can be fooling. I remember her name was Jane and she was a Negro, that was before the word black came along, and I thought she had a real great build and I asked her to the drive-in, me borrowing my father's car. I thought it worked real peachy-dandy, particularly the wrassling in the back seat, but when I took her home she said she didn't think she would be seeing me again. Now this was a blow to the old male ego and I asked her why, didn't she like me? I remember she gave me this nice pat on the cheek and said, sure she liked me, I was a real good necker and she liked that. But the conversation was just too boring. I remember she went on in school and had her degrees years before anyone else, and now she's teaching sociology at Columbia. Of course I didn't feel too humiliated because at that time smooching was more important than books, but I have never forgotten it.'

'Patrick Winter! Is that story true?'

'So help me. And I'll show you her picture in my high school year book with a big red lipstick kiss right over her signature.'

'And she was a black girl?'

'Well—not exactly. I changed that part to capture your attention. She was really a *chicana*, Mexican-American. All her family were migrant workers. But I thought a minority is a minority to make the point. Fins?'

She was tense for a moment longer, then relaxed and smiled. "You know, you're not so bad for an ofay.'

'You're not so bad yourself for a femlibber who has spent her life keeping the male fascist pigs at bay. Drink to peace—and the success of Prometheus.'

'Why not.' She clicked her glass against his and they drank. 'But why not success? Is there any doubt of it?'

'There is always doubt about any flight. The more things that are involved, the more that can go wrong. On the first Apollo to the Moon the LM touched down with two and a half per cent fuel left. The Soviets, us, we've both had our problems with the space programme. Now we have six of the largest boosters ever made strapped together in one lump. They have to take off together and put Prometheus into low orbit, this payload also happening to be the largest one ever as well. Then when we are in this low orbit, which is what is called a decaying orbit, meaning we will drop back to Earth pretty soon if we don't get out of it, we have to fire up Ely's fission engine to take us out to our final orbit. Now this engine, while the theory and smaller models have been ground tested——'

'Let me guess. This engine has never been flown in space before?'

'Bang on. And you ask me if there is any doubt about this flight. But, before I depress you too much, let me say that a lot of people have been working a number of years to bring the doubt factor as close to zero as possible. By the odds you are a lot safer in Prometheus than trying to change a tyre on a California freeway. Your life expectancy there is twenty-five seconds if you try to change it on the outside, next to the lane.'

'You've cheered me up. As long as I stay away from California, I am safe.'

A tall man in a chef's hat appeared at the open door. 'Dinner is served,' he said in thickly accented English.

'What are we having?' Ely called out, but the cook's linguistic knowledge was exhausted and he fled.

'A specially selected menu,' Nadya said. 'I talked to the cook and he is very proud of it. Borscht, then herring, followed by beef stroganoff and noodles. Caviar and vodka too, of course.'

'Russian soul food,' Coretta said. 'If I get the chance, I am going to show your chef some real American cooking like collard greens and ribs. Let's go, I'm starving.'

# 8

*Cottenham New Town*

FOR SIR RICHARD LONSDALE, breakfast was always the best part of the day, and breakfast on a morning like this perfection itself. The table had been set by the open french windows; a robin was hopping about the rose stems and blackbirds were busy on the lawn beyond. The air scarcely moved. His *Times* was by his plate, the two boiled eggs in their cups, the toast still warm on the rack. He poured himself a cup of coffee. He was alone. He loathed speaking to anyone at this time of day. Emily would appear just before he was ready to leave, no earlier. Before opening the paper he sipped more coffee, keeping the moment of peace extended before letting the world interpose again.

Richard Lonsdale was managing director of Pharmaceutical Chemicals Ltd., a job for which he received a substantial salary garnished with a number of agreeable perks. The papers he had taken home were all safely packed into his briefcase, along with a cassette of letters for his secretary to type. New problems would arrive soon enough. He delicately sawed the top from the first egg, shook on salt and pepper, and spooned out a bit. Just right. He looked at the headlines in *The Times* and the day had begun.

The business news was always depressing so he never looked at that until he was in the car. As usual, little good seemed to be happening in the Near East, Spain again, Korea. GRAVE DANGER PREDICTED FOR PROMETHEUS PROJECT. That was more like it, a bit of the old scientific Cassandra to keep the blood flowing. What one bunch of scientists invented the next bunch predicted would despoil the world, destroy the environment and give everyone cancer in one loathsome form or another. Unfortunately they were usually right. He finished his breakfast and read the article with some attention. He was just folding the paper when his wife, in her floor-length dressing gown, swept in.

'Good morning, darling,' Emily said, giving him an offhand peck on the forehead. 'Don't forget to be in time for dinner tonight because that man from abroad's bringing people around afterwards. You arranged it last week, remember? I'll have some coffee if there's any left. What a most appalling thing! Look at that headline. I know they exaggerate a bit, but this does sound absolutely ghastly. Earthquakes!'

'In Russia, my dear, *if* the rocket should blow up and *if* there's a ground fault where the man says there is.'

'But what about all the other things, the death ray and all that?'

'My dear, I assure you that what happens to Prometheus can have no effect in any way upon us at the present time. Now, I must be going.'

The Rolls was waiting outside when he emerged promptly at 8.15. The chauffeur was removing an invisible fleck of dust from the black bonnet and he turned with a smile to hold the door open.

'Lovely day, sir. Vintage day, that's what my old mum used to call it.'

'Your mum was right, Andrew. We haven't had a summer like this since seventy-five.'

Gravel crunched softly under the wheels as the car rolled

sedately down the drive. The fact that it was a company car and Andrew a company employee did not diminish the pleasure. With the window open and the Third Programme playing a Bach trio, the morning was a good one indeed. So good that Sir Richard never opened his paper to the business pages. They would wait and this day wouldn't. From his home to the plant was about ten miles, an easy fifteen-minute drive, mostly through country lanes. If they had taken the motorway it would have been less than a mile more and would be much faster. They never did. It would be rush and modern times, high speed and telephones all day; the longer the rural peace lasted the better. Stone walls flowed by, then green meadows with grazing Guernseys, a field with sheep. The lambs were big now and losing their early charm. A thickly wooded copse was replaced by farm buildings, then the cobbled high street of the village of Dry Etherton. The shops were just opening and Harry Moor stood in the open door of The Dun Cow lazily working his teeth with a matchstick. He raised his hand as the Rolls went by, the perfect picture of the happy publican, and Sir Richard returned the salute. They did a wonderful steak-and-kidney pudding at The Dun Cow and it had been too long since he had had one. Sunday perhaps.

Now the road straightened as it climbed on to the limestone ridge above the town. Meadows and farms on all sides, slashed through by the motorway that made the new town possible. Then the town itself. He knew the old village was still down there, at least part of it, but it could not be seen until you were right on top of it. The towers of the blocks of flats dominated the scene, rows and rows of them like beehives.

Beyond the flats were the low white buildings of the plant. At least these were landscaped and not unattractive. The road swung around the plant and dropped so that the large chemical tanks were outlined against the sky. Painted orange. It had seemed preposterous when he first saw them, but he had discovered since that it was far easier to live with than sooty battleship grey which became more and more depressing as time passed.

The guard at the gate saluted casually, more a wave than a military greeting, and the Rolls eased to a stop before the main entrance.

'Usual time, sir?' Andrew asked.

'Only if half six is the usual time. Perhaps it should be. I've given my solemn oath that I'll be home on time. If I am not down ring the office and remind me.'

'Yes, sir. Have a good day, sir.'

'Thank you, and the same. And Andrew, if you can, keep out of the whisky in the back. The level keeps dropping faster than my own attention should warrant.'

He turned and pushed open the glass door and went inside. A day, just like every other one, had begun.

# 9

'START THE COUNTDOWN,' Samson Kletenik said.

As he spoke the numbers on the digital clock that hung high in front of Launch Control, unmoving until now, changed from 95:00 to 94:59.

At every console the thick countdown volumes were open to the first page, volumes thicker than usual because every instruction was in duplicate, Russian in one column, English the other. Though all of the positions controlling fuelling, engines, pumps and ancillary equipment were manned by Soviet technicians, and all flight deck instrumentation and computer monitoring by Americans, there was an interface that was not simply payload or booster. Here nationals of both countries were mixed, many times two of them at the same console monitoring each other's work, ready for the instant response that can be demanded during an operation. Prometheus had been in the planning stage long enough to give Berlitz and the Soviet equivalent plenty of time to drill languages into resisting heads. Theoretically all the technicians and engineers in Launch Control spoke both languages, for better or worse. Perhaps they were not the world's greatest conversationalists, but all were adept in the limited vocabulary of rocketry and control systems. They could work together. That they could do other things together had been obvious when a female Russian technician was returned home in an advanced state of pregnancy. Seven requests for Soviet-American marriages were in the file awaiting processing, which meant that decisions would be made after Prometheus was in orbit, not before. National co-operation was not to be strained.

Samson Kletenik was Launch Control. He was a tall, long-armed slab of a man, slow speaking and fast thinking, not given to smiling. Not that he had anything to smile about. All the years of effort of construction and assembly had reached their conclusion. Every part of the complex launch function was controlled from his console. His was the ultimate responsibility. As though to make matters worse he knew that every step of his operation was being monitored by Flax and the other Mission Control people, thousands of miles away in Houston. Once clear of the ground the responsibility could be handed over to them. But that was in the future. At this moment Kletenik was in charge, carefully throwing switches, speaking in slow and measured tones, appearing relaxed and calm.

In Mission Control in Houston, Flax was neither of these. Relaxing was for afterwards, calmness was only in his voice when on the radio, a role to be played. As the launch approached closer and closer his tension grew greater. He watched the rushed order of Launch Control through the television hook-up, then looked around at his own technicians relaxed before their controls. Let them relax—he couldn't. He felt the hard knot growing in his gut, the knot he always got at this time, that never left him until splashdown and completion. While the astronauts would be enjoying ticker-tape rides and presidential handshakes, he would be slipping through a side entrance of the Naval Hospital at Bethesda and into a private room. The doctors there would shake their heads over him and attempt to drag him back from the brink before his pre-ulcerous condition turned into a nice duodenal ulcer that would punch a hole right through his gut. It wasn't just the chain-smoked cigars, the endless cups of coffee and half-eaten sandwiches or the lack of sleep, it was that knot. He usually lost about fifteen pounds during that week in the hospital. The liquid diet was without interest and the pills, so that he wouldn't miss cigars, booze and coffee, had him asleep most of the time. Then when he came out it was a good month or two before he could be back to normal, able to enjoy lobster, champagne, Havana cigars and all the other things that contributed to a good life.

But right now the knot of tension was just beginning, a tiny little twist of anticipation that would soon turn into a burning ball of flame that would have him drinking Maalox by the gallon. Nothing had gone wrong yet—but something would, something always did. In a way waiting for it was harder than experiencing it. Would it be small, or too big for Launch Control to handle? It was with a feeling of relief that he heard the words, saw Launch Control spring into action.

'I don't have pressurization in helium anti-pogo system. No pressurisation on four, until 31 down seven . . ."

'Do you want a hold?' Kletenik asked.

'Negative. At least not right now. We have ten minutes to clear it.'

'Stay with me and if I'm on something else let me know your condition in nine minutes.'

'Roger. *Oh-chin ogay*!'

An American A-OK in Russian, the new combined language of the space age, Flax thought, watching and listening, a silent spectator. And the Americans were saying *vas ponyal*, I understand, instead of Roger. Not a bad idea; a little peace went a long way in the world today. *Mir*. They could use a lot more of it, particularly in Africa where the massacres were still going on.

There was no need for a hold on the fuelling. The bypass worked and the faulty valve was replaced. But this was minor, one of the expected difficulties. There was enough time built into the countdown to correct small malfunctions. Even time for more major trouble by having a hold when the clock stopped and everyone and everything waited until the problem was licked. But there could not be too many holds and they could not be too long, because there was a limited amount of time that all the complex systems could be held in readiness. Some systems had a life that could be measured in days, even hours. After this cryogenic fuels could cause unreliability. If enough holds added up an entire mission could be scrubbed. And if Prometheus were scrubbed it might be months before it would be ready to go again. Unthinkable. Years of preparation had built towards this moment, the reputations of two nations were at stake. The leaders of both were watching and the world was watching them. And they were all watching Flax. The knot tightened.

A red light on a board, one of many thousands. Some switches thrown to test, then a phone call and an answer, then through to Kletenik.

'We have some trouble here at twenty-seven, could we see you.'

It was the toneless voice that troubled Kletenik, the forced calmness that meant someone was worried. Which had *him* worried. He unplugged his headset and walked swiftly towards console twenty-seven.

In the isolation quarters Patrick was getting into his pressure suit, with Ely's assistance. He would not need it until they were in orbit and ready to assemble the solar collector: since Prometheus was designed to be a permanent space station the entire structure was pressurized and they would wear normal lightweight coveralls. But Patrick had been having pressure suit trouble. Each astronaut had his suit made specially for him. Two suits, really, one for training that would take the wear and tear of daily use. The other for space walking. Both were made the same way, layers of fabric and rubber that had been sewn and glued together with infinite care. The suit had to be flexible enough to enable the wearer to move about, yet it had to be strong enough to contain the air pressure that kept him alive. It had to bend at the joints and be firm in between;

all in all a magnificent compromise. That wasn't always perfect. Reinforcements could dig in and irritate so adjustments had to be made. A nagging piece of metal that rubbed Patrick's shoulder had been sent back three times for corrections, returning finally just before they had entered quarantine. He hoped it was right; if it wasn't there might still be time to correct it.

First the thin cotton underwear to prevent chafing. Then the slightly humiliating, but nevertheless necessary, donning of the triangular yellow plastic urine bag; it's not possible to make a quick call to the men's room when in space. Ely held up the bag and admired it.

'What a marvellous invention, symbol of man's conquest of space,' he said.

'A lot better than woman's symbol of that conquest. I should think a catheter would be damn uncomfortable.'

'Be happy then with your little rubber ring on the corner of the bag here that fits, oh so neatly, around your thing. Another comment on the age of science becoming the age of conformity. Although men come in all sizes from three-foot pigmies to seven-foot Scandinavians, their vital organs apparently come only in three sizes. Small, medium and large. There are only three size rings on these bags, aren't there?'

'Always referred to as extra large, immense and unbelievable. The male ego must be reassured. And when you're picking the right size don't let ego overrule reality. If you pick one too big it will leak, a condition known as "wetback" that you won't enjoy.'

'I've been warned. Here, let me help you with the suit.'

Putting on a pressure suit was more like a snake getting back into its discarded skin than putting on normal clothes. Patrick struggled to get his feet through the resistance of the nylon inner lining. Once this was done he had to bend over double to work his arms far enough down the sleeves to let him put his head through the neck ring. Ely tugged strongly until Patrick's skull popped through.

'Thanks,' Patrick gasped. 'I think you took all the skin off the back of my neck.'

'You could have stayed a nice safe test pilot instead of taking this giant step for mankind.'

'Zip up the back, will you.'

He didn't bother to pull the gloves on, he was hot enough as it was. Standing, he stamped around the room, swinging his arms.

'Feels all right. Let me try some bending . . .'

Something was wrong. He was aware of it at once—and then he saw it. The countdown clock, there was one in every room, had stopped at 83 : 22.

'It's a hold,' he said. 'Find out what's causing it while I get out of this thing.'

They were all in the main room when Patrick got there and Nadya was just hanging up the phone. 'They haven't located the source of the trouble yet,' she said. 'But all fuelling has stopped.'

'That can be dangerous with the tanks only partly filled,' Patrick said.

It went on for almost five hours. Only Ely seemed untroubled by the hold, his nose buried in a chess book, replaying a master tournament. He had started a game earlier with Colonel Kuznekov, but they had to abandon it because the Colonel's concentration kept wandering to the motionless clock. The numerals were frozen still at 83 : 22. Less than twelve hours into the countdown and already a major hold.

The phone rang at the same instant as the numbers began changing again.

'Right,' Patrick said, 'we see it. Good. Let's hope it goes on this way.'

It did, for one day, then two—then the third—and it was time to enter Prometheus.

'You know,' Coretta said, kneading her hands together. 'It is one thing to say you're going to do something—and another to get around to doing it. You sure I can't have a drink, Patrick?'

'Contra-indicated. No alcohol for jet pilots twenty-four hours before a flight. Forty-eight for us. Space flight's an uncompromising business.'

'But you and Nadya will be doing all the piloting. The rest of us are sort of passengers.'

'Sorry. You're crew. I don't think any situations will arise where we'll need your help at once. But it *could* happen. Relax. Think good thoughts.'

He reached out and held her arms, sharing his strength with her. She was frightened and they both knew it, and knew as well that she must get over it. The world was watching, literally. Watching the Launch Control countdown at this moment, but all cameras would be focused on the astronauts as soon as they emerged. His hands felt good and Coretta relaxed a bit, leaning forward and placing her head against his chest. There was perfume in her hair, just a trace, and he resisted the impulse to stroke it.

'I want a rain check on this,' he said.

She turned her face up to his and smiled. 'You're very good for a girl's morale, Patrick. When we get back from this little pleasure trip I want to see more of you.'

'That's a promise,' He kissed her, and that was a promise too that they both understood.

'It's time,' Nadya said from the open doorway. 'They are expecting us all.' Her face was expressionless, her voice toneless.

'We'll be there,' Patrick said, just as emotionlessly, not releasing Coretta until Nadya had turned and left.

'You and Nadya aren't quite the partners you should be,' Coretta said, straightening her hair in the mirror. She was calm now, the moment of panic past. Doctors aren't supposed to let their feelings show. You learned early to put on an assured air like a suit of armour. She could do it now—but she knew that she had needed Patrick's help, had appreciated it.

'We work together all right,' he said, then smiled and looked at the lipstick on his handkerchief where he had wiped his lips. 'Let me tell you, this is a hell of a lot better than the all-man days at NASA.'

'I think you're oversexed and I'll give you some saltpetre pills to calm you down. You missed a spot on your lip, there. Come on, let's go.'

They were all there, dressed in silver one-piece suits. In the name of equality the Soviets had abandoned their usual red boiler suits, the Americans their blue ones. A compromise on silver, symbolic of the great silver wings that Prometheus would spread in space, had been made and that was what they wore. On each left breast was the symbol of Prometheus One. A star-shot disc of black space with the bold silver mirror of the solar generator in the centre, as it would look when opened. To one side was the red star, on the other the stars and stripes; the red star appropriately on the left. (Though a letter to the London *Times* had pointed out that left was, heraldically, the right.)

Ely was standing on a chair and adjusting the focus of the television pickup. Kuznekov sat before the screen talking to the technician imaged there.

'A little up, there, that's fine,' the man said. 'I would like the two outer books moved in a bit. Bit more, that's fine, a real winner.'

Patrick looked at the books on the floor that Nadya had been moving and his eyes widened. 'Is it permitted to ask just what the hell is going on?'

'You might very well ask,' Ely said, climbing down from the chair. 'Someone in high places has decided that our morale would be immensely improved if we had a chance to chat with B and P before the flight. They come on in a couple of minutes.'

'Not in the flesh I hope.'

'God forbid. Bandin's in Washington, Polyarni in the Kremlin, I guess. A miracle of misapplied technology will permit us all to talk together. Let's go.'

The books marked the spot on the floor where they were to stand and, more or less goodnaturedly, they took their places. They had to shuffle closer together to get on camera and then it was time.

'Stand by,' the technician said, and his harried face was replaced by a split screen with Bandin on one side, the Soviet Premier on the other.

'This is a very great moment in the history of the world,' Bandin said. Then Polyarni made almost the same remark

63

in Russian. Patrick nodded and tried to look intelligent, aware of the stiff figures standing on both sides and fighting down the sensation that they must look like a row of silver-plated teddy bears. Polyarni started to talk again but Bandin beat him to it.

'When I say a great moment in the history of the world I indeed mean just that. Yes, this is a victory for the technology, the hard work, the sheer guts of the men and women of our two great nations who created the Prometheus Project and who will see it carried through to glorious completion. But more than that it is a victory for all mankind, echoing the words of Neil Armstrong, the first man ever to walk on the Moon—this is a great step for mankind . . .'

'I agree, Mr President,' Polyarni broke in when Bandin made the mistake of pausing an instant for breath. 'A tradition for greatness in space exploration that began with the first man to fly in orbit, Yuri Gagarin.'

'Yes, of course, how true.' Score tied, one-one. 'For mankind itself is on the threshold of a great new age that will open when Prometheus blasts a fiery trail into the heavens to tap the inexhaustible energy of the sun. We will be freed for ever from dependency upon our ever decreasing store of fossil fuels, and in doing this we shall leave for ever the age of suspicion and distrust between nations and enter that of mutual peace and prosperity on Earth for all.'

There was more of this from both of them and Patrick shifted slowly from one foot to the other so his muscles wouldn't cramp or go to sleep. The countdown clock was visible behind the TV screen and he experienced a great feeling of relief when it clicked over to 02:00. He took a firm step forward and nodded at both men, and spoke in the momentary silence.

'Thank you, Mr President. *Balshoya Spaseebo tovarisch presidyent.* We are better prepared for this mission now that we have talked with you and, in the name of my crew, I offer our thanks. However the countdown has reached the moment when we must depart for the spacecraft. Thank you again, and good-bye.'

64

He walked briskly out of range of the camera and the others, trying not to hurry, came after him. The connection was broken and Kuznekov yawned and stretched widely.

'*Boshemoi!* How boring politicians can be, of whatever nation. A necessary evil I suppose, but one I've had my fill of.'

Ely nodded agreement. 'No one ever got shot for something they didn't say. Therefore politicians say nothing and get elected on their charm or charisma or PR or whatever it is.'

'Chitchat later,' Patrick said. 'The carrier should be sealed to the exit port now. Before we go I want all personal effects in the plastic bags, and this means emptying your pockets too. No ham sandwiches on this flight, or postage stamps, extra first-day covers, pictures of the Pope or Lenin. Nothing. That was the agreement and we'd better not blow it.'

'We do not have your capitalistic instincts to turn an honest buck,' Kuznekov said, smiling. 'So are happy to agree. But isn't there still a little capitalistic business to repay us for sacrificing any attempt at personal free enterprise?'

'You know perfectly well,' Ely told him. 'We have three hundred first-day covers with the special stamps from both countries. We have a handstamp and we will cancel them in space. We will have fifty each to keep or sell and do what we want with the money. Mostly pay income tax I guess.'

Patrick checked the transparent plastic bag each astronaut carried. There were only the normal personal items he expected to find. He looked at his watch.

'Right on time. Let's go.'

Patrick led the way, pausing only to shake hands with the cook and the two maids who had looked after them during their quarantine. 'I'm coming back for more of your potato pancakes, Ivan,' he said in slow Russian.

'I'll have a washtub full, a bathtub full waiting when you land, Major!'

The green light was on over the exit portal. Patrick spun the wheel that secured the door and there was a slight hissing as the pressure equalized. Their quarters for the quarantine period had been sealed away from the outside world to make sure they did not contract colds or any other infections.

All the food and water that they would need had been locked in with them. The air they breathed was pumped in through elaborate filters and the interior pressure kept higher than the ambient air outside. This was any air that leaked would leak *out* of their quarters and possible infected air could not enter. Now they were leaving—but still in quarantine.

As the door opened they could see another door just inches away, still damp from the disinfectant that had been sprayed on it. Patrick opened this door as well and they entered the hermetically sealed people carrier. There were large windows in the sides of the vehicle, which was really a large box carried on a flat bed truck. There had been no windows in their quarantine quarters, part of the psychological adjustment to condition them to sealed-in living in space. They had talked with others on the phone, usually about technical matters. Or had made long-distance calls to their families at home. In their single-minded attention to their work they had forgotten how many people were involved with the project, how much the world was interested in what was happening to them.

They found out now. People, people everywhere. Waving, shouting, pushing to get a glimpse of the astronauts, with the photographers in front clicking away and fighting to stay in position. The shouting was clearly heard, even through the insulated wall of the sealed carrier. Soldiers cleared a path for the vehicle which started slowly forward. The astronauts waved back, suddenly shocked speechless by the reality of what was happening.

This was the day.

This was the big one.

Slowly and carefully the truck moved forward and around a corner and away from the laboratory complex. At the end of the wide road Prometheus waited, white clouds coming from her venting ports, the hot sun gleaming from her metal flanks. Still looking more like a skyscraper than a structure designed to fly. The cluster of rockets was a hundred and fifty feet across at the base, rising four hundred and fifty feet above the ground. And, up there, standing above the bullet snouts, was the single projectile form of Prometheus itself, now revealed fully with the removal of the VAB. Only the Launch Tower remained, connected to the spaceship and boosters by its Service Swing Arms.

With slow precision the truck backed up to the base of the tower and locked its brakes. Clamps were loosened at the same time and the carrier was rolled backwards on to the elevator and once more locked into place. Then it shuddered and began to rise slowly into the air.

'I'm a little shaky,' Coretta said.

'So am I,' Ely told her. 'We all are, nothing else would be possible.' Endlessly, the metal flanks of the boosters flowed by outside. 'I'll bet even our steel-nerved pilots have butterflies in the stomach at this time. Is that true Nadya?'

'Of course, only a stupid person does not feel fear. But really, it is only the waiting that bothers you. Once a mission begins you're so busy there's no time for worry or fear or anything else.'

With a slight vibration the elevator eased to a stop. They had arrived. Technicians outside rolled the carrier forward. One of them was waving excitedly and pointing ahead.

'What's he trying to say?' Patrick asked, suddenly uneasy.

'Making like throwing switches and talking into something.' Ely said. 'Wait a bit, he's writing on that piece of paper.'

The carrier locked against the wall of the spacecraft, the man finished writing and held up the paper. *Use radio now* it said. Patrick nodded agreement.

'What is it about?' Nadya asked, puzzled. Patrick shrugged.

'No way of knowing yet. We'll just jump ahead in the countdown and switch on the radio first. There's the light.'

With the green light on, the door could be opened once again. The wet metal of Prometheus was just outside. Patrick flipped up the cover on the controls and actuated them, stepping back as the hatch cover swung slowly towards him. He bent and led the way in.

'Nadya, close the hatch after the last one,' he said. 'I'll get on the radio.'

He dropped on to the pilot's couch and turned the radio on.

'. . . *peat. Kletenik here calling Prometheus. Do you hear me? Please come in, Prometheus. Repeat . . .*'

'Hello, Launch Control, Prometheus here.'

'*Major Winter, we are having some difficulties. I have been discussing this with higher authorities and with Mission Control in Houston. They wish to talk with you. I am patching you through.*'

'Go ahead,' Patrick said, calmly, not showing the sudden sharp worry he felt. 'Can you read me, Mission Control?'

'*Fine, Patrick, clear as a bell. Listen . . . I haven't got the world's best news for you. I've been talking with Kletenik and I've been on to the White House.*'

'What is it, Flax?'

'*Trouble. You need a hold, a long hold, and we don't think you have enough time. It looks like we're going to have to scratch this mission and reschedule.*'


## 10

'TELL HIM to get his ass up here. Now.'

Bandin slammed the receiver back on to the phone and reached for the cup of coffee. Afternoon in Russia, crack of dawn in Foggy Bottom, and he had had maybe an hour's sleep. He pulled his bathrobe more tightly around him and sipped the coffee. Like ice.

'Lucy!' he shouted, then remembered that the room was soundproofed. He stabbed the intercom button and her voice quavered in. 'Yes?'

'Coffee. A goddamn pot of coffee.'

He switched off before she could answer. There were servants who could have brought it, but Lucy in the morning with the coffee was the habit of a lifetime. He had never asked her if she minded doing it or not, he rarely asked people this kind of question. He just took it for granted. If he was up, Lucy was up, preferably earlier to make sure the coffee was freshly brewed. She brought it in, a pale, ageing Barbie doll. He took the pot without thanks and poured a fresh cup full, then added four spoons of sugar.

'Will there be anything else you want?' she asked in a whisper of a voice. He shook his head and grunted *no* and wasn't even aware she had gone. The intercom bleeped softly and Charley Dragoni's voice announced Simon Dillwater.

'Send him in.' He sipped the hot coffee and glared at the closed door. Although the room was warm enough, he felt chilled with fatigue; he wrapped his bathrobe tighter about his legs.

There was a light tapping on the door, then Simon Dillwater let himself in. He was very tall, very thin, very distinguished looking with the wings of white hair above his ears. There was something in his movements that came only after a life of assurance; good family, best prep school, then Harvard—and behind it all far more money than he could possibly spend if he lived to be two hundred. Bandin envied him the ease with which life had treated him, had handed over all the good things on a golden platter. Would Dillwater have been the same man if he, like Bandin, had been the son of a Kansas druggist, had gone to a second-rate Bible-belt college, then dragged himself up through the ranks of the party machine? Dillwater was what he was and, though he never admitted it even to himself, Bandin was envious.

'Dillwater! Just what the hell is all this about?'

'A hold with Prometheus, Mr President. I thought . . .'

'I thought you could keep an eye on the shop while I got some sleep? While you were dreaming I was trying to get one word ahead of that s.o.b., Polyarni.'

69

'I am sorry about your sleep, Mr President. I do not imagine any of us on the project have been to bed for days. I would have handled this matter, I assure you, if it had been routine. It is not. Therefore, acting upon your instructions, I notified you at once.'

'All right—so what the hell is it?'

'A major hold. The engineering details . . .'

'Can wait. How long is it going to be?'

'At least four hours, possibly more.'

'So . . . ?'

'The technical people say that system unstabilities will develop after three hours and there is danger of mechanical failures from the cryogenic fuel.'

Bandin took a long noisy slurp of the coffee. 'Tell them to stay with it,' he said. 'They're bright boys, they can lick any problem, or so they have been telling me for years.'

'Not this one, Mr President. The danger is too great. They wish to terminate this operation and reschedule. . . .'

'*No!* Absolute goddamn no! Are they out of their minds? The entire world is watching this thing, and after what we've promised we had better damn well deliver. I have my balls on the line for this and I don't want to see them chopped off. The lobbies and the papers and now the goddamned Congress is talking about the time and cost overruns on Prometheus. We've got to get that bucket of bolts up there and working. I don't care if all they produce is enough electricity to light a hundred-watt bulb. I want it. I *need* it. We are not cancelling. That's final.'

'The danger . . .'

'None of us is going to live for ever. The astronauts knew what kind of a job they were signing up for so I know they'll agree with my decision. And I'll bet you dollars to doughnuts that Polyarni will go along.'

Right on cue the phone buzzed and Bandin picked it up, listened, grunted and slammed it back down.

'I told you. Hot line to Moscow. Stay right there,' he said as Dillwater began to ease towards the door. 'I want you to hear this historical decision so it will go on record that our two great nations are in complete agreement at this time.'

He picked up the red telephone and wiped his forehead with his handkerchief at the same time. It no longer felt cold in the room.

## I I

*Cottenham New Town*

IRENE LEWIS was worried. She peered hesitantly through the shop window at the display under the golden letters COTTENHAM NEW TOWN BUTCHERS—KEENEST PRICES. Oh no they weren't. The prices were just terrible. Steak was unbelievable, stewing meat no better, mince was cheaper but it was all fat. But she had to get something. After a long day in the plant Henry expected a good tea—and he deserved it. He turned his entire pay packet over to her every week, holding back just a little for beer and cigarettes and maybe a few pence more for the pools. It was because he was such a fair man and never questioned her that she was worried now. Not that she had lied to him, rather it was what she hadn't told him. To keep eating, even in the modest manner they were used to, was costing more and more every day. Judy and May were always growing out of their clothes and eating more all the time. Prices went higher and higher, yet everyone expected her to make do and keep things going as she always had, with a joint on Sunday and all the rest.

Well she did keep things going—and that was what worried her. Years ago they had agreed to put by a bit every week in the Post Office Savings, for the rainy day that was always coming, as well as the summer holidays. But the prices kept rising and in order to cope she had put in less and less until one day she had stopped saving altogether. And now she was beginning to withdraw. Not much, but the girls needed shoes for school, and once it started flowing out it didn't seem to stop. She was afraid to look at the balance, but she did know one thing; that Blackpool holiday that Henry was already beginning to talk about, it was out of the question. He wasn't going to like that.

'Look what they're asking for sausages!' It was Mrs Ryan from down the street.

'Shocking,' Irene agreed, happy to share her misery.

They nodded their heads and made clucking noises, searching the window once more in the vain hope that they had missed some unusual bargain.

'Did you see the interruption on the telly?' Mrs Ryan asked. 'Right in the middle of Coronation Street. Trouble with that big rocket.'

'Did it explode?'

Irene was concerned, knowing that death and destruction were always waiting in the wings of life, ready to step forward.

'Not yet, though you never know, do you?'

Once more they nodded agreement then, steeling themselves as for battle, they entered the butcher's. Whatever happened, families would still have to be fed.

## 12

'I THINK IT IS TIME we got back into the bunks and strapped in,' Patrick said. 'I know it's a drag, but in ten minutes the hold may end.'

'And how many times have you said that before?' Ely asked.

'Too many. Buckles and straps, Ely.'

The four acceleration couches were arranged two by two on the deck of the crew compartment. Each was designed and custom-built to fit one of the astronauts, to give the maximum support and protection during the acceleration. Ely sat on the edge of his, a thin book clasped in his fingers. Patrick stood over him and waited in silence. Finally the physicist sighed dramatically and swung his legs up; Patrick helped him with the hold-down straps.

Coretta's couch was next to his and faced a bank of instrumentation. She was already strapped in and studying the dials. These displayed duplicates of the biosensor information being fed continuously to Mission Control. Each of the astronauts was wired with pickups that passed on vital readings such as blood pressure, pulse, respiration, body temperature, all of the human biological measurements that had to be monitored, watched closely to ensure that these astronauts could stay alive in space.

With the four in the inner compartment secured, Patrick went through the hatch in the wall. Of course wall, ceiling and deck only had meaning when they were on Earth. Once in orbit and weightless the terms would become meaningless. The walls and ceiling of this compartment were covered with instruments and lockers for food and equipment, some of it impossible to reach now, all of it accessible soon when they could simply float in any direction.

Prometheus itself, the only part of this immense spacecraft that would go into orbit, was divided into four sections. In the nose was the payload, thirteen hundred tons of generator, reflector and transmitter, the reason for everything else. At the other end of Prometheus, over two hundred feet away, was the nuclear engine with its fuel supply of U-235, the engine that would lift them up into their final orbit. Above the engine was the biological shield, twenty-five tons of barrier to keep the radiation from the crew when the engine went into operation. Above the biological shield, also acting as a barrier to radiation, was the immense bulk of the liquid hydrogen for the engine, a tank over a hundred feet long.

Sandwiched between the payload before and the hydrogen tank behind was the crew module, the thinnest slice of the great length of the spacecraft. It was divided unevenly into two compartments. The larger, inner one, took up over two-thirds of the space. This was the Crew Compartment where the four non-piloting members of the crew had their couches, where all the food and extra equipment was stored.

73

An inner wall with a sealing hatch separated it from the Flight Deck. Here were the couches for the two pilots, all of the flight instrumentation, the windows, periscopes and TV connections that enabled them to look out and guide the ponderous vessel. But they were blind now, the TV cameras sealed into take-off position while the shroud that protected them and the pay-load from the atmospheric friction of take-off, hid any direct view. Nadya was in her co-pilot's position and talking to Mission Control.

'He's here now, Flax,' she said. 'He'll be able to talk to you as soon as he plugs in.'

'Any results?' Patrick asked her, dropping on to the couch and reaching for the headset.

'Negative. The President won't be able to talk to you.'

'What about Polyarni?'

'The same answer. Lauch Control put me through, but he's involved in a conference with your President.'

'They don't want to go on record for keeping this flight going.' He threw the radio switch. 'You there, **Flax**?'

'*Roger. About your talk with the President. I had his First Assistant, but the President is in conference by phone with Premier Polyarni and cannot talk to you now, but he will as soon as he can.*'

'Flax. Is this conversation being taped?'

'*Of course.*'

'Then I want to speak for the record.'

'*It's been a long hold, Patrick, and you must be tired. Why don't you . . .*'

'Negative. For the record.'

'*I have been talking to the doctors here, Patrick. Your pulse and heart beat show a good deal of stress. They suggest you attempt to rest, sleep if you can, your co-pilot will take over.*'

'Knock it off, will you please, Flax. I'm the Commander and what I say is of some interest. If not now—for the record later.'

'*Sure, Patrick. Just trying . . .*'

'I know what you're trying. What I'm trying to do is get some facts on record. We are almost two hours into what is called an unsafe period in the flight plan you have in front of you. . . .'

'*Just an estimate.*'

'Shut up. I'm saying something, not having a discussion. All the indications are that as this unsafe period progresses the condition of the ship deteriorates so that the mission should be aborted. Early estimates were that after a half an hour into the unsafe period the mission should be cancelled. As Commander of this mission I ask why that has not been done?'

'*Decision-making is still progressing at all levels.*'

'I didn't ask that. I want to know why the recommended procedure has been ignored and why we are still on hold despite earlier decisions to abort at this point?'

'*Observations indicate the earlier estimates possibly to be too pessimistic.*'

'Give me those results, if you please.'

There was a mutter of voices at the other end then Flax was back on, relief obvious in his voice. '*Launch Control wants to get through to you. The hold is terminated. Countdown continuing at zero minus twelve minutes.*'

Patrick opened his mouth to protest—then closed it and flicked off the mike switch instead.

He turned to Nadya. 'We can still abort the mission. I can do it as a pilot's decision, but it would carry more weight if you agreed.'

'I know.' She spoke very quietly. 'Is that what you want?'

'I don't know. What I do know is that we are heading for trouble if we take off now, possibly big trouble. But if we abort . . .'

'The entire Prometheus Project might be scratched. Is that what you are thinking?'

'Something like that. It cost a bundle and people are beginning to complain, and more and more pressure groups are jumping on the bandwagon. But that's not a problem you have in your country.'

'We have it, but not in the same way. The Politbureau is the Politbureau. One night there will be a meeting—next morning Polyarni will be Minister for State Pig Farming, and Prometheus will be dead at the same moment. So what do we do?'

'We're risking our lives if we go on now.'

'We risked our lives when we joined this project. I think —what do you say it in English?—the game is worthy of the candle.'

Patrick looked at her in silence for a long moment, nodding his head grimly. 'I've always thought the game was worth the candle. But this is different. If we take off now we risk destroying everything.'

'If we stay we have the equal risk.'

'*Come in Prometheus.*' Kletenik's voice sounded in their ears. '*At zero minus nine minutes how are the levels on your ADP?*'

Patrick was searching Nadya's eyes for an answer to his question. But she had answered it already. She wanted to go ahead. And who was he to disagree? His superiors, the heads of the government wanted to proceed. He could go against their judgment and stop the whole thing now. Ruin his career, perhaps kill the entire Prometheus Project. It was a lot of responsibility to bear. He turned on his microphone.

'APD in the green. What are your readings on fuelling?'


Flax was running with sweat, slumped in his chair like a sack of potatoes. He could not slide down any further but he felt the tension drain from his limbs when he heard Patrick's words. The mission was on. There was danger still, but nothing that the programmes and he and the computers could not handle. He was going to ride it all the way. The programme would come up with the answers and the pilots would throw the switches—but it was his mission the instant they took off. Let them space walk and get dosed with radiation and have their parades. They were welcome to it. But none of them could take his place here in Mission Control, the spider in the middle of all the webs, the interface between man and machine that kept them all working. One piece had weakened and caused

76

the hold, a bit of machinery, and he had put it right. Another piece, a human one, had acted up, but that had been put right too. Five minutes more and . . .

'Hold at zero minus five,' a voice at Launch Control said, almost shattering him like a sudden blow with an axe. 'I have a red light on sustainer propulsion. It's the lox pogo damper pressurization.'

'And it seems we have another hold, ladies and gentlemen, at exactly five minutes before blast off, and I assure you that no one is happy about this one at all. The tension is so great here at Ground Control that you can almost feel it in the air. I'm turning you over now to Bill White in the crowd in the viewing stand for a report on the reactions there. Bill.'

On millions of TV sets all around the world the scene changed suddenly, from the hectic order of Ground Control to the viewing stand five miles from the take-off site. From here, Prometheus looked like a child's toy on the horizon with nothing to give an indication of its true size. Yet there had been much discussion over siting the stands as close as this, since they would still be in danger if there were an explosion at take-off. But any farther away and there would be no point in having viewing stands at all. In the end the decision had been one more compromise; limited-size stands for what might be called the second-rate notables. Expendable notables. If a few journalists and ageing generals and politicians went up in flames they would not be missed in the general horror and destruction. Of course the reality of this decision had only been discussed at the very highest levels and a number of elderly gentlemen were pleasantly surprised to find their names on an invitation list. In the foreground between the spectators and the distant spaceship was the familiar lined face of Bill White. As he spoke the image of the distant Prometheus was covered by a superimposed telescopic version.

'The tension here in the viewing stand is exactly like that at Ground Control and Mission Control as you can well imagine. It must be the same all round the world wherever people are watching this incredible event taking place. Here in Baikonur it is already late afternoon, over two hours past the scheduled time for take-off. And now, only seconds away, we have another hold. We can only imagine how the men and women, the astronauts in their giant craft, must feel. They are professionals and trained for their work but it still must be unbearable. I don't think anyone would want to take their places. They are doing magnificently and the entire world appreciates their courage. Now, Harry Saunders at Ground Control. Any changes yet, Harry?'

'We're exactly the same here, and in Prometheus which you can see on your screens there.' The image changed, filling the screen with Prometheus, zooming to her flight cabin, then panning down the length of her great boosters, steaming vents. Harry Saunders grabbed up his notes as soon as the camera was off him. The holds had been so long that he was running out of things to say, people to interview. He wished the damn thing would take off or blow up. His voice was beginning to go. He frantically searched his scribbled notes while his voice calmly described the Leviathan of space. Detailed description, he hadn't done that one lately. He found the right figures.

'We still have difficulty in realizing how big Prometheus is. When you say as high as a forty-storey building or as heavy as a battleship, some feeling is conveyed. But not the combined complexity of its construction, for this spaceship is really seven separate machines in one. This programme is being transmitted on radio as well as television, and you lucky TV viewers must realize how impossible to visualize it must be for someone, say, in a small Asian village who has only seen a few simple machines in his lifetime. Perhaps the easiest way to understand its construction is to hold out your hand with fingers straight, then bring all the fingers together until they touch and make a circle. These fingers are the boosters, each one a completely separate rocket with its own fuel, pumps, motors, everything. Now if you take a pen with its cap on and, cap in your other hand, push it down between your fingers you will have some idea of the construction of Prometheus. The fingers and the pen, called the core body, are all the same. Complete rocket ships in their own rights. The cap is the payload, Prometheus, the part of the ship that will go into orbit high above Earth. And stay there for ever.

'At take-off all the boosters fire, as does the core body. Their fuel is the most powerful in the universe, hydrogen and oxygen, and it will be gulped and burned at the rate of fourteen thousand gallons a second. Yet this complex machine will not only burn fuel at that tremendous rate, but will *transfer* fuel from the outer boosters into the core body. This will be pumped in as fast as the core body burns its own fuel so that finally, when the boosters are empty and fall away, the core body will have a complete load of fuel. With the boosters gone the core body will burn to insert Prometheus into low orbit, then it will drop away as well, its job well done. At that point Prometheus will fire its own nuclear engine to push itself higher and higher into the correct orbit. Complex, yes, but still practical, for these Lenin-5 boosters have had a number of successful missions lifting larger and larger payloads into space. Also . . . wait a minute, yes, my countdown clock's moving again! The hold's over. Let's hope it's the final hold so I return you to Ground Control. . . .'


'Two minutes,' Patrick said, 'and this is it. The countdown now is automatic and locked in. They can't stop us.' He turned on the ship's intercom. 'Crew compartment, are you secure?'

'In position,' Coretta said. 'No changes, bio monitors functioning and all readings within predicted parameters.'

'Which means no one has died of boredom or fright yet.' Patrick said. 'Roger. You can listen in but I won't have time to talk to you until after booster shutdown. This is it crew—we're on the way!'

'One minute fifteen seconds and counting.'

The computer was running the entire operation now,

issuing instructions to men and machines, opening and closing switches—and counting down towards zero and lift-off.

'Minus eleven seconds and counting.'

'Minus ten.'

'Minus nine.'

A throb, more vibration than sound, swept through the towering metal structure as the huge engines ignited. Their flames shot down into the pit below and boiled out as smoke and steam at the sides. Second by second their thrust level rose until at zero the hold-down clamps would release.

'Three . . . two . . . one . . . zero!'

At full thrust the engines generated a fraction more lift than the immense weight of Prometheus. The clamps pulled free and flames wrapped the umbilical tower. Now the ground shook with the intensity of the rockets and the air roared and crackled with unbelievable sound.

Slowly, infinitely slowly, only ten feet in the first second, the towering cluster of rockets rose into the air.

'We have lift-off!'

Noise. Vibration. Thunder. Patrick found himself thrown back and forth against the restraint of his strap as the vectoring engines swivelled in their mounts to keep their course vertical. The first six seconds were critical, until they passed the umbilical tower and their speed built up. At lift-off the digital timer began to operate, its numbers flicking from 00:00:00 to 00:00:01, ticking off the seconds steadily to measure GET, the Ground Elapsed Time.

00:00:04 The G forces, the gravity that pushed them down into their couches was beginning to build.

00:00:06 First danger past. All instruments reading in the green.

Second by second the thrust increased until it reached 4.5G then 5G where it held firm. Five gravities pressing them down into their couches, standing on their chests and making breathing difficult. They had all learned how to breathe under high G in the centrifuge. Never breathe out all the way or it will be almost impossible to fill your lungs again. Keep your lungs full at all times, just letting out short breaths and breathing right in again.

Pressure and acceleration. Speed. The engines gulped sixty tons of fuel a second and pushed the great structure on, faster and faster.

'You are GO, Prometheus,' Launch Control said, the words tinny in Patrick's ear. The G forces pressed on his eyes, bringing about the condition of tunnel vision; he could only see directly in front of him. Turning his head was an effort, but he had to, to read all the instruments.

'All in the green.'

*'Stand by for staging at oh-one-thirty. We are turning you over now to Mission Control.'*

'Roger.'

The Gs stood on their chests as the GET digits clicked over. Although the vibration and the pressure seemed to go on for ever, the first-stage blasting took just a minute and a half. At the instant the GET read 00:01:30 the engines cut off and they were weightless. Patrick switched his microphone to intercom.

'That's the first stage shutting down. We'll be in free fall for a few minutes now so it is a good chance for your stomachs to get used to the sensation. I'll warn you before the second stage fires. Right now the boosters are pumping their reserves of fuel and oxygen into the core vehicle below us. Then they'll release . . .' A quick shudder passed through the ship. 'There they go. I'll see if I can get a picture for you. The TV is for Mission Control but I'll be able to relay it to your screens.'

There were TV cameras set into the hull, protected and obscured up until now by the bulk of the boosters. Patrick located the activating switches, three among the hundreds he had to operate, and flicked them on. At first there was just darkness—then a sudden flame. He angled the camera towards it and focused on one of the small engines that was pushing the booster away from them. As it grew smaller the surface of the Earth appeared behind it.

'It is Russia—there is Lake Baikal!' Nadya called out.

'And a second booster there,' Patrick said. 'I'm switching

to camera two and panning. We should see all five of them. Are you receiving, Mission Control?'

'*Six by six, Prometheus, a great picture.*'

One by one the boosters swam into view, dark cylinders against the hazy blue of the world below, dwindling as they dropped behind. Each of them was monitored from Ground Control in Baikonur so that the individual orbits could be controlled separately, for the success of the Prometheus Project depended upon bringing down the boosters intact. They were stable both nose up, as they had been when they left the Earth, and engines down as they returned. The plug nozzle of the rocket engine acted as an ablative shield to slow the booster and keep it pointed in the right direction. As the machine approached the Earth the engine would be fired, fuel had been left for this, to bring the booster in for a soft landing on the Russian steppe. One by one the boosters would come down to be picked up and brought back to Baikonur for the next step in the sequence. Prometheus Two. One by one the cargo to build and expand the solar generators would be lifted up until the great task was completed with Prometheus Fifty. But the project would be in operation long before that, sending electricity back to a world starved for power.

They hoped. They were still far from their final orbit 22,300 miles above the surface. At this point in the take-off, although they were far above the Earth and in free fall, they were still bound to it by the invisible ties of gravity. Prometheus was like an artillery shell fired high into the sky, to arch up and up to the summit of its climb. Then to drop back to Earth. The multiple boosters had lifted them high and fast—but not to escape velocity, the speed of a body sent off the Earth that would permit it to leave the gravitational pull never to return.

'Shroud jettisoned and ready for core burn,' Patrick said, his eyes on the GET numbers. 'It will be about a two-and-a-half-minute burn to get us into a higher orbit. Here it comes. . . .'

The core vehicle had one-sixth of the original thrust on lift-off, but it was still immensely powerful. The Gs built up more slowly, but build they did until once more 5Gs pushed hard upon them. Then, for the first time, the controlled progression of events changed. A sudden shuddering gripped the ship, building up, shaking everything hard—then stopped.

'I have pogoing,' Patrick said, sharply.

*'Under control, pogo pressurization restored.'*

As quickly as it had come the shaking ended, and did not return. All of them aboard the ship relaxed for they knew that the very worst was behind them. The three of them who were new to space were veterans now. They had survived take-off, the moment of ignition when they had thought the unthinkable, riding in a cabin on top of the greatest chemical bomb ever constructed by mankind. The energy locked there had been expended to take them into space. It could have exploded instead. With this behind them they relaxed unknowingly. Coretta and the flight surgeons on Earth noted it in their readouts of pulse and blood pressure and were aware of what had happened. Even though they were hard at work in Mission Control they had relaxed as well; there were more smiles than frowns. Flax had the victory cigar out and was chewing on it still unlit.

All was going according to plan.

'Shutdown,' Patrick said quietly as the engines cut off. 'How is our orbit now, Mission Control?'

*'Four balls, Prometheus. We have a one in the last digit, just one away from five balls.'*

A good orbit with a .00001 error from the ideal predicted orbit. Patrick stretched and unlocked his belt, talking to the crew.

'We are coasting now but please do not leave your couches. I am coming down for eyeball contact.'

He pushed away from the couch and floated towards the bulkhead. 'I'm going to cheer up the troops, Nadya, will you take the con?'

*'Nyet prahblem, vas ponyal.'*

As the opening of the hatch swam towards him, Patrick grabbed the edge to brake his motion. His feet came up slowly and brushed the wall, slowing his body to a stop. Head first he pulled himself in, floating towards the couches.

'A most dramatic entry, Commander,' Coretta said, fighting the urge to draw aside as he floated headfirst towards her. 'When do we get to try that?'

'As soon as we're in final orbit. How is everything here?'

He bent his arms as he floated to her couch, slowing and stopping. He tested her straps. She nodded and smiled.

'I'm fine now—but what was that shaking around about?'

'The pogoing?'

'If that's what you call it. Like a pogo stick?'

'That's right. As the tank empties pressure waves in the fuel line will sometimes surge backwards and forwards and cause the engines to set up a motion something like a pogo stick. There are pressurization and systems dampers to stop it.'

'It was shaking the fillings out of my teeth.'

'Everyone else all right?' Patrick asked, looking around.

There was a moment's hesitation, then Gregor spoke slowly.

'I regret the free fall, the shaking, caught me by surprise. I had . . . my stomach . . . a small accident.' He was almost blushing. 'But there is the plastic bag, it is all right now.'

'Happens to all of us,' Patrick said. 'Hazard of the profession. Are you over it?'

'Yes, finished. I am most sorry.'

'Don't be. When we are back on solid ground I'll tell you some real good Air Force whoopsie stories.'

'Spare us now, will you, Patrick.' Ely spoke above the top edge of his book, a novel with a title in French.

'Of course. Here's the situation.' They were listening closely now, even Ely. 'We're about a hundred and thirty kilometres high and still climbing. Our boosters are gone but the core vehicle still has fuel. It will fire one more time for orbit insertion before staging. After this, as soon as Mission Control is happy about the orbit, the core vehicle will be detached and we will be on our own. That will be when Ely does his thing.'

'An honest job at last,' Ely said. 'I'm tired of being a passenger and look forward to the moment when Dr Bron and his magic atomic rocket engine have a chance to perform. Though small, and without the kiloton thrust of the monsters we have dropped behind us, it is true-blue and with a heart of gold and will puff and toot and lift us up into the perfect orbit in the ideal position.'

'May it do just that. Any questions? Colonel?'

'When do we eat?'

'A good question. With all the holds we had I'm feeling hungry myself. I'd say break out the food packs now if I thought we had time. You have the tubes there so drink some lemonade if you want to keep the hunger pangs away. As soon as we get into the low orbit we'll eat. Then Ely can get to work on his engine.'

Patrick pulled himself back up into the flight cabin and buckled in once again. 'How's our time?' he asked.

'About three minutes to firing,' Nadya said looking at the GET.

'Good. I'll take it.'

Flipping up the safety lid, Patrick held his finger over the engine firing button. The computer counted down on the GET and, at the precise second, he pressed down just in case the signal from the computer did not activate it precisely.

The pumps whirred, the engine fired.

It worked at full thrust for exactly three seconds. Then it exploded.

# 13

GET 00:35

THE BLAST jammed Patrick into his couch, blurring his vision for an instant. He shook his head and when he could see again there were lights, red lights, everywhere before him on the panels. Voices hammered in his ears, from Mission Control and on the intercom; Nadya was calling out to him.

He ignored them all, scarcely aware of the intruding sounds. The instruments. Engine. Automatic shutdown, now manual shutdown. Pumps, fuel, safety interlock. And they were spinning. The Earth swam into the ports ahead then slipped out of sight. He looked at the GET and timed the rotation, lying motionless until it appeared again. Then he threw the switch that cut off the intercom, stilling the voices that cried out to him, calling over to Nadya at the same time.

'Hold the question until I contact Mission Control.' He flipped one more switch. 'Mission Control, do you read me?'

'*Yes, listen, we have . . .*'

'Condition report follows. We have had a malfunction in the core body engines. No readings at all from number three, may have been an explosion. Others shut down. Fuel flow shut off. Fuel reserves remaining at eleven per cent. We are tumbling in orbit, one rotation every twelve seconds. Give me an orbit and status report. Over.'

'*Orbit follows, perigee eighty-four point six three miles. Orbiting time eighty-eight minutes. We have an indication for lowered cabin pressure. Do you have a reading?*'

'Reading positive, seven point three pounds. You may have an instrumentation failure. Do we cancel tumbling?'

'*Negative, repeat negative.*' There was emotion in Flax's voice for the first time. '*We want to determine extent of damage first.*'

Patrick flicked on the intercom.

'Did everyone hear that?'

'I heard it, but I didn't understand it,' Coretta said.

'We've had an engine malfunction,' Patrick said. 'We don't know the extent of the trouble yet. As you know, the plug nozzle engine of the core body is really four separate quadrants that fire together. One of these is out of action, no readouts from it at all. I'd guess it's had a major malfunction. . . .'

'Do you mean it blew up?' Ely asked.

'Yes, I suppose it might be that. In any case we've three good engines. . . .'

'You *think* we've three engines.'

'Ely, shut up for a moment. We don't know yet just what we have or don't have. Find out first, panic later. We still have plenty of fuel for manœuvring and we're in orbit. The only problem facing us immediately is that we're tumbling. I'm going to correct that as soon as I've permission from Mission Control.'

'You say we're in orbit,' the Colonel said slowly. 'Might I ask what kind of orbit that is?'

Patrick hesitated. 'I don't really know. I'll get the data as soon as I can. Roughly though, we're about a hundred and forty kilometres high and orbiting the Earth once every eighty-eight minutes.'

'Eighty-five miles isn't very high,' Ely said.

'Sounds pretty high to me,' Coretta broke in.

'High enough.' Patrick fought to keep the tension from his voice. 'Up here we are above most of the atmosphere, ninety-nine per cent of it. I'm getting back to Mission Control.'

Five more minutes went by before Mission Control was certain that the computer had digested all the available information. *'All right, Prometheus,'* Flax said. *'Permission to stabilize. Suggest minimum fuel expenditure.'*

'I am aware of that necessity, Mission Control. Manœuvre begins.'

This bit of flying by the wire was uncalled for in their flight plan. The fuel he was using now would be needed to stabilize the ship in the correct final orbit. But they would never reach that orbit if he didn't stop the tumbling. He would have to use minimum fuel and hope there would be enough left when he needed it. A touch on the controls slowed the rotation. But not enough.

'You will need more,' Nadya said.

'How well I know that.' His face was grim. 'Here goes.'

With short blasts on the manœuvring jets the tumbling through space slowed bit by bit until it finally stopped. The Earth, his only reference point, moved slowly into view in the ports ahead, the horizon sensors finally settling it into fixed position bisecting the window.

'Fuel reserves in manœuvring jets at seventy-one per cent. That was wonderful, Patrick.'

'And the estimate was that we wouldn't need more than fifty to correct orbit. There's still a ball game.' He turned on the radio. 'Hello Mission Control. Tumbling has been cancelled and we are stable in orbit. Do you have a condition report on the core body engines yet?'

*Negative, Prometheus. But we have been running the programmes through the computer and need more input before we will have them finalized. Are you ready for instructions?*

'Go ahead, Flax, but make it fast. I don't like this orbit and I want us out of it soonest.'

*Confirm. Activate your P20 to C64 and let us have a reading. . . .*

While Patrick was testing the circuits and feeding the results to the computer, Nadya turned on the intercom and told the rest of the crew what was happening.

'Can we unstrap, Nadya?' Gregor asked. 'Perhaps stretch a bit, move about. It is becoming claustrophobic in here.' There was a thin edge of tension in his voice, not quite panic yet, but the edge was there. The most exhaustive tests in the world are still just tests; space flight is the ultimate test and one that cannot always be completely prepared for. Nadya was aware of the difference in Gregor's voice and thought it best to ignore it for as long as possible.

'Please don't, Gregor. We may fire again at any moment and we will have to do it at the exact instant ordered by the computer programming. We could be badly hurt if we weren't strapped in.'

'And the food, *Nadenka*?' the Colonel asked. 'You must hear my stomach grumbling up there.'

'Is that what it was, *Volodya*! I thought it was the rockets firing on their own.' Someone chuckled at her joke; no one really laughed. 'The same goes for you, I'm afraid. As soon as we're in orbit we can do what we want.'

'But we're in orbit right now,' Coretta broke in. 'Couldn't

we stay here longer, what difference does it make? I'm sorry to be such an idiot.'

'We are in a low orbit,' Nadya told her. 'Just on top of the atmosphere. And we were never intended to be in this orbit at all.'

'What would happen if we did stay here?' Coretta asked.

What indeed, Nadya thought. Is it a decaying orbit? How long will it last? They might need to know the answers very soon. But she pushed her fears aside and kept her voice calm. 'Nothing much. If we stayed in this orbit we would just whistle around the world every eighty-eight minutes. But we'll be out of it soon. Hold on, Patrick's signalling. . . .'

'Commander here. The computer has digested all the info we have for it and produced what we think is an answer. One of the engines is definitely out of order and we have bypassed it and blocked it. We'll fire on the two opposing engines, two and four. Number one engine will be cut out as well so we'll have balanced thrust. . . .'

'Will we get the proper thrust out of two?' Ely asked.

'Of course, Dr Bron. We needed the full thrust of the four engines for lift-off, along with the thrust of the boosters. Now that we are in Earth orbit we will fire at lower thrust for a longer time and still get the same result.'

'No need to be clever, Patrick.' Ely was angry, his armour of cool cynicism penetrated for the first time. 'I know as much about orbital mechanics as you do. I was talking about programming for the reduced thrust to get the correct final orbit. A programme of this kind might take hours or even days to prepare.'

'I'm sorry, Ely, I shouldn't have said that. I'm damned tired, as we all are. You're perfectly right, of course. But one of the preparations in the past year was preparing programmes for almost any eventuality. This was one of them—Mission Control is coming through now.'

Patrick killed the intercom and took the instructions from Mission Control. There was little he could do except watch because the computer was in control again. Readings and observations from Prometheus were coded by its own

89

computer and radioed back to Earth. Either a relay station on the ground or one of the comsats would pick up the signal and bounce it on. Once the information had been digested the coded message would be sent back to the shipboard computer which would follow instructions.

'*You will have ignition at 01:07:00,*' Mission Control said.

'Roger. Check your straps, everyone, and get ready. The engines will fire in about two minutes, at 01:07 on your GET clock.'

The seconds ticked away, going too fast yet seeming to take an eternity. This had to be it. Seconds to go, three more, two, one. . . .

He was ready, his body prepared for the thrust. But nothing, absolutely nothing happened.

'Come in, Mission Control. We do not have ignition.'

'*Nothing at all?*' There was unconcealed worry in Flax's voice.

'Not a fart in the engine or a light on the board. Do you know what you are doing, Mission Control?'

'*Affirmative, Prometheus. Look, Patrick, we're doing our best down here. They're running the programme through again for bugs, then we'll give you a new time and you can fire manually from there.*'

'Thank you, Flax, I appreciate your concern. I am sure your people are working hard and sweating and getting ulcers. But they have solid ground under their feet and are not whipping around orbit. Do you have the data on this orbit yet?'

'*Negative . . .*'

'Flax! Shut up and listen to me, closely. You are lying. Your computer has digested enough orbital data to belch out an answer by now.'

'*Your height is . . .*'

'I know how high and how goddamn fast we're going. What I want to know is this a decaying orbit? How long are we going to hang up here before we hit the atmosphere and start slowing and drop back?'

'*We can't be certain . . .*'

'HOW LONG, FLAX?!'

*'All right, Patrick, just take it easy. We have a figure here, but just a rough estimate so far. As we refine it we'll feed you the latest info. As of now with a possible seventy per cent reliability the best we can say is that you have about thirty-six hours.'*

'One day?'

Nadya was staring at Patrick, eyes wide, for she had heard too. He nodded slowly at her but knew better than to try to smile. He thought for long seconds before he spoke.

'Listen to this, Flax. We have to boost out of this orbit or we're going to turn into one more shooting star and burn up when we hit the atmosphere at the end of a day. Get those engines running. If they don't fire you better start your boys on the next possibility right away. We will need some figures on the chances of getting out of this orbit using the nuclear engine alone. We will drop the core body and fire on our own. Do you read me?'

*'Loud and clear, Pat. We've already considered the nuclear engines and are running a programme on it. Are you ready to try firing again?'*

'Roger.'

*'I'll read you the countdown and fire on zero. Ten . . . nine . . .'*

Nothing happened this time either and Patrick stabbed down again and again on the button until his thumb hurt. 'All right, what's next?' he shouted. 'Are you going to fix those engines or do we separate?'

*'Separation in a few minutes. We want to be sure you will have enough time for running up the nuclear engine before separation.'*

'That *would* be a good idea, wouldn't it.' Patrick disconnected Mission Control with a savage flick of the switch, then talked to the crew.

'Did you all follow that? It should have all gone on intercom.'

'It did,' Coretta said. "But—I'm going to be a fool—what was it all about?'

'Simple,' Ely said. 'If we do nothing we hit the atmosphere in a day's time and turn into one of those nice

91

shooting stars that young lovers like to look at at night. To prevent that we hope—I think hope is the right word —hope to use my engine which does not have the thrust and was not designed for this job. The only cheering note in this otherwise depressing situation is that I have been doing sums on my calculator. The computer will do a better job, but it looks like we will be able to get out of this orbit—but we had better get rid of that dead weight on our tail and start firing as soon as we can. I'm unstrapping and getting down to the engine now . . .'

'Hold it!' Patrick said. 'On the couch until I say get up. I'll query them on this. Mission Control, do you read me?'

'*Roger, Prometheus. You will have thrust for orbital manœuvres with the atomic engine. Burn should begin soonest. Prepare for staging separation.*'

Ely laughed. 'Just what I said, only a bit more pompous and long-winded. Tell them to blow the damn bolts or whatever so I can get out of bed and on with the job.'

'*Separation.*'

The explosive connections that held Prometheus to the booster behind it were felt only as slight thuds in the flight cabin. Patrick actuated the TV camera and relayed the signal back to Mission Control. They would take over control of the booster now and bring it back to Earth safely. If they could.

'Look at that!' Patrick choked out the words. 'Mission Control, look at your screens. Do you see? The core body hasn't separated. It's attached to us at an angle. Maybe one of the connectors didn't blow. I don't know. But whatever happened that thing's still on our back. And while it's there we can't fire the nuclear engine. Do you hear me, Mission Control? You have to do something about that thing and goddamned quick. Because if you don't, this mission is going to end in the biggest fireball you've ever seen.'

*GET 01:38*

'THIS IS GOING to mean replating the front page and we're forty minutes late on the streets already,' the Mechanical Superintendent said as he looked at the new layout.

'I don't give a damn if it means feeding your mother through the presses,' the City Editor told him. 'This story's breaking at the right time for us, and I'd do this on my own, but God had me on the phone and this is the way *he* wants it, too.'

When the owner of the newspaper spoke the employees simply nodded and did as they were told. The circulation of the *Gazette-Times* had been falling steadily and anything that might give it a shot in the arm would help. The Mechanical Superintendent opened the door of his walled-off glass cubicle in a corner of the composing room and went out into the hum and roar of a newspaper being put to bed. At their stones the compositors never looked up, light seared out on one side as an engraver exposed a plate.

The Mechanical Superindendent had problems of his own and almost ran into the small man who bobbed up in front of him waving a sheet of paper.

'Out of the way, Cooper, or I'll run you down.'

'Listen, you must look at this. Imperative.' The Science Editor was a shaggy man with long hair that hung in his eyes more often than not, who had a tendency to chew, unknowingly, his ink-stained fingertips.

'Later. We're changing the whole damn paper around after a message from God so I got no time for your latest breakthrough on the deodorant front.'

'No, not that, you must listen. The rocket . . .'

'Move! I got a whole front page full of rocket. In twenty-four hours it's going to burn and those six nice people with it!'

'What's the shouting about?' the City Editor asked as he squeezed by them.

'This, sir, I tried to stop him. Change the front page, I have the story here.'

The City Editor halted and turned on his heel and looked down at the excited man. He had been too long in this business to ignore anything that might be news. 'Sixty seconds, Cooper, and it had better be good.'

'It is, sir. Incredible. This rocket, sir, Prometheus, the one in the decaying orbit. There's a good chance it's going to hit the atmosphere and burn up in less than a day.'

'That's our front page story.'

'But there's more to it than that! Prometheus is the largest object ever to be put into space, it weighs two thousand tons and that's a lot of mass. When it hits the atmosphere and burns it will be a most spectacular sight. . . .'

'Our leader writer produces better copy than that, Cooper. Leave the story on my desk.' He turned on his heel and started away and Cooper's words reached out desperately after him.

'But, sir. Listen sir. Please. What if it doesn't burn up? What happens if it comes down in one lump?'

The City Editor stopped dead, rigid. Then slowly turned about and glared at Cooper. When he spoke his voice was cold as the Arctic.

'Tell me, please. What will happen if it hits in one big piece?'

'Well,' Cooper struggled frantically through the crumpled papers he carried. 'I've taken the optimum, you understand. Speed, mass, angle, ideal situation all around. I mean ideal to get the highest speed at impact. Inertia, you understand, velocity times mass, small and fast, big and slow, both hit with the same impact. But what if something very big hits very fast? That is our Prometheus. I estimate its impact explosion will be the equivalent of ten kilotons of TNT.'

'Translation, please.'

Cooper was hopping from foot to foot and chewing his fingertips so hard his words were barely audible. 'Well, simply, say it were to hit a populated area, a city, you know. It would explode with about the same force as the original atomic bomb that blasted Hiroshima. No radio-activity, of course, but it would explode. . . .'

'Yes, it certainly would. Very well done, Cooper. Clean up your copy and get it to rewrite. Right now, scoot.' He pulled out a pack of cigarettes, extracted the last one, lit it and crumpled the pack and threw it to the floor. He looked at the Mechanical Superintendent. 'You heard him. Get ready to replate the first page one more time and the hell with how long it takes. We have the story of the century here. Do you realize that flying bomb could take out a city, maybe this city right here. . . .'

He stopped suddenly and looked up. They both looked up.

# 15

*GET 02:19*

WASHINGTON D.C., on a muggy morning, at the height of the rush hour. The motorcycle escort was making heavy weather of shepherding the Cadillac at more than the snail's pace through the rest of the traffic. Once they were over the Chain Bridge from Maclean, Virginia, they picked up a larger escort of police cruisers that sirened their way down the wrong side of the parkway, frightening the hell out of the few drivers leaving the city.

General Bannerman slumped in the back seat of the Cadillac and hated the world. He had not been in bed more than an hour, and certainly was not asleep, when this shit of a captain had pounded on the door. The police escort probably had no idea of who was in the car or why they had been called out to this suburb so early in the morning. But the captain knew. He had got the address from Bannerman's adjutant—the only one who knew it— and had barrelled out with the car and woken Bannerman and even seen the blonde head in bed with the general, before he had been told to go to hell and get out and wait. The escort had picked them up at the corner and that was that.

Bannerman rubbed his massive jaw and felt the sore spot where he had cut himself shaving in a rush and wondered how much would leak out.

'You're not on my staff, are you, Captain?' he asked the driver.

'No, sir. G2 special liaison to the White House.'

Bannerman grunted, then yawned widely.

'There's some benzedrine in the bar if you're tired, sir,' the captain said.

'What makes you think I'm tired?'

'You didn't leave the party until after four, sir.'

Well, well, so someone was keeping tabs on him. He had always suspected it, but put it down to the endemic Foggy Bottom paranoia. Taking out a crystal glass he filled it with water, then washed down a benny from a little green bottle. He started to put the glass away, hesitated, then poured two fingers of scotch into it instead.

'You know a good deal about my movements, Captain. Is that wise?'

'I don't know about wise, sir, but I have my orders. It's the Secret Service that monitors your movements, for your own protection of course, and I act as liaison.' He turned his head briefly to look back at the general and had the sense neither to smile nor wink, displaying only a fixed and very serious expression. 'Your life is your own, General, but we must know where you are in order to protect you. But we are very discreet.'

'Let's hope to hell you are. Do you know what this meeting is about?'

'No, sir. I was just given your address and told to bring you to the White House as soon as possible.'

Bannerman nodded and watched the pillared buildings sweep by. He yawned again, then sipped the straight scotch. He was used to going without sleep, commanding an armoured cavalry division had given him plenty of experience. At the age of sixty-one he looked ten years younger and had the stamina of a man ten years younger than that. Beryl had told him that not more than an hour ago, and she had reason to know. He smiled at the thought. So what the hell did Bandin want him for at this hour of the morning? Arabs again, probably, it was usually the Arabs. Since he had been appointed Joint Chief of Staff nearly all the meetings were about oil and Arabs.

The car stopped before the discreet rear entrance of the White House and Bannerman emerged. As the door opened the two guards there presented arms and he returned the salute.

That little pimp Charley Dragoni was waiting inside, moving from one foot to the other like he had to pee, waving at the elevator.

'You're the last one, General Bannerman, they're all waiting.'

'Well, *good* for them, Charley. What's this meeting about?'

'The elevator, General, if you please.'

Well up yours, Bannerman thought. Bandin's errand boy was getting kind of big for his breeches. As the elevator rose he speculated happily about different ways in which he might put the kibosh on Dragoni.

A Marine guard opened the big door and the general sucked in his gut and stamped forward, hitting his heels down hard enough to make the spurs on his cavalry boots jingle. He knew a lot of them hated it, which is why he did it. Bandin was at the head of the big mahogany table, Schlochter next to him and—surprisingly—the only other person was Simon Dillwater. Interesting. The Secretary of State, Dillwater who was the top man at NASA, and himself. What did they have in common? The answer was obvious.

'Trouble with Prometheus, Mr President?' The best defence is a good attack.

'Christ sake, Bannerman, doesn't your radio work? What do you think we're doing here?'

Bannerman pulled out his chair and sat down slowly, coolly. 'I worked late with my staff, then retired and slept soundly.' Not a twitch of expression, even from Dragoni, so maybe the captain had told the truth and the Secret Service did have close mouths.

'Tell him, Dillwater, and as simply as possible if you don't mind.'

'Of course, sir. Prometheus has serious difficulties. Primary staging was fine and the boosters separated and have landed as planned. But the core body will not fire nor will it separate completely.'

'Still attached?' Bannerman was cold attention on the instant.

'Partially,' Dillwater said.

'What's their altitude?'

'Approximately eighty-five miles at perigee.'

'That's a damn crappy orbit!'

'Your description is accurate.'

'What's being done?'

'We're still attempting to separate. Then Prometheus should be able to climb to her correct orbit on her atomic engine.'

'Well work fast. That orbit must be decaying. How long before it goes bust?'

'About thirty-three hours on our last estimate.'

Bannerman tapped his fingers on the table and thought quickly. 'If that thing burns up it's going to put paid to a couple of billion dollars and maybe your whole project.'

'I was thinking more of the six people aboard,' Dillwater said, coldly.

'Were you, Simon?' He paused. 'You've got to get that thing into some kind of stable orbit as soon as you can.'

'You're damn right,' Bandin broke in. 'Listen to some sense, Dillwater. We have got national prestige to think about. We have the entire Prometheus Project to keep in mind, and the damn Russkies and the UN who are on our side just this once, and the next election and a lot of goddamn things. We'll worry about the passengers if and when we have to. Right now we don't. Schlochter will tell you what Polyarni said while Dragoni gets an update report on the thing. Top priority must be to get that thing moving up up and away before it goes bust. Nothing else matters—and I mean *nothing*!'

Dragoni, who was seated discreetly at the small table by the door, reached for the telephone before him to get the report for the President. Before he could touch it it buzzed softly. He picked it up, listened, then replaced the receiver. Then he rose quietly and stood beside Bandin until he was noticed.

'What is it? Anything new?'

'I did not call yet, Mr President. I took a priority call from your press secretary who said that a big news story has broken in New York about Prometheus . . .'

'What the hell do they know in New York we don't know in Washington?'

'He did not say, sir. But NBC is having a special news break in about three minutes and he said it might be best to watch.'

'Call him back and find out what this nonsense is about.'

'It might be wise to turn the television on at the same time,' Bannerman said calmly. 'We could learn just as much that way.'

'Yes, I suppose so. In my office then.'

They trooped through the connecting door and Bandin dropped into his chair behind the massive desk. One button slid aside the panelling, with a portrait of George Washington attached, to reveal the screen of a 72-inch projection TV. Another button turned it on and they watched fixedly while two bars of soap danced to a Chopin *étude*, then dived into a basin of water. This scene faded to be replaced by the life-sized image of Vance Cortwright. He did not have his familiar smile, known to millions, but his familiar frown, equally well known, which meant the news was very serious. He laid down a handful of papers and spoke solemnly, directly into the camera.

'Good morning, ladies and gentlemen. Many of you who stayed up last night to watch the spectacular launch of Prometheus will have retired with the comfortable knowledge that this largest of all space flights was off to a successful start. If you read the early editions of the morning

99

papers you would have known this as well. Only if you have been listening to your radio, or watching television, would you know that a most recent development has altered that situation dramatically. There has been some difficulty in firing the core body, the final booster that will lift Prometheus into its higher orbit. The orbit they are in now is . . .' he consulted his papers, '. . . approximately eighty-six miles above the Earth and the ship and booster are making a complete orbit every eighty-eight minutes.'

His image vanished and was replaced by an animated drawing of Prometheus and the attached core body orbiting the Earth.

'Our hearts go out to these six brave astronauts who are, literally, trapped in orbit. Until means are found to fire the booster, Prometheus cannot rise up to its proper place in the sky, to the fixed position in space above the Earth where it is to begin this mighty project of supplying solar energy to a power-hungry world below. Not only can they not go higher, but they cannot return to the safety of the Earth in Prometheus, which was designed to remain for ever in orbit. It does not have either the correct engines, the power or the fuel for this task. It is a prisoner in space, in orbit, and the six men and women aboard are prisoners as well. What their fate will be we cannot determine at this moment.'

Cortwright reappeared on the screen, and sitting next to him now was a small man in an ill-fitting suit, his long hair carefully combed into place by the make-up girl. This was obviously not its normal condition because, as he moved his head nervously, a long hank detached itself and hung in front of his eye.

Cortwright nodded to him.

'With me in the studio now is Dr Cooper, the Science Editor of the *Gazette-Times*. I have a copy of the morning edition of your paper here, Dr Cooper, and the lead story is a very startling one, I might even say a very frightening one. If I might just read the headline. It is in very large type and says BOMB IN THE SKY.'

He held up the newspaper so the screaming red words,

covering half the page, could be seen. 'That is strong language, Dr Cooper, as is the story that follows. Do you think it is true?'

'Of course, it must be, facts . . .'

'Could you please tell us just what *are* the facts behind this extra edition of your newspaper?'

'It's obvious, there in the sky above us!' He waved his hand over his head, then dropped it, started to worry his finger, then dropped his hand guiltily back to his lap. 'Prometheus is up there, passing over our heads about once every hour and a half. Not just the satellite itself, but the attached booster that won't fire. Prometheus at this moment weighs slightly in excess of four million pounds. We must guess at the weight of the booster, but since it must contain a great deal of fuel, in addition to its own mass, I would say that its weight must also be in the region of a million pounds. There are five million pounds up there, three thousand tons of metal and explosive fuel. If that should fall . . .'

'Hold on, please.' Cortwright raised his hand and Cooper stammered to a stop and instantly had a quick nibble on one nail. 'If I remember correctly the space scientists have been telling us for years that it takes energy to change anything in space. It took a lot of energy to get Prometheus up there into orbit, and it will take a lot of energy to get it down as well. It will stay in orbit until it is pushed out.'

'Yes, yes, of course.' Cooper vibrated in his chair with the intensity of his feelings. 'That is for an orbit well outside of the Earth's atmosphere. But Prometheus has not reached that altitude yet, there are still traces of air at that height. Air that will slow her down, more and more. It is what is called a decaying orbit.'

'I would like to kill that hairy little son-of-a-bitch,' Bandin muttered.

'As you know, altitude is speed in a satellite. The faster it goes the higher it rises, like a stone on the end of a piece of string, swung in circles. The string is the bond of gravity, the speed is what maintains the orbit. As Prometheus slows it will drop lower, as it drops lower it will hit denser and

101

denser air and will be slowed. Its speed will drop so much that it will lose its orbit and will fall back to Earth.'

'Where it will burn up by friction in the atmosphere, as have all the other satellites and boosters that have fallen back to Earth,' Cortwright said calmly.

'Why should it?' Cooper jumped to his feet so abruptly that his head vanished for an instant and the image jerked as the cameraman hurried to follow him. 'Smaller boosters, yes, burn like meteorites. But meteorites have hit this Earth before, we can see them in museums. Meteor Crater in Arizona is where one enormous object penetrated our atmosphere and dug that immense pit in the landscape. In 1908 the Tanguska meteor in Russia wiped out an entire forest, killed . . .'

'But, Dr Cooper, Prometheus is not as big as these.'

'Big enough! Big as a destroyer. Big enough to stay in one piece when falling back through the atmosphere. Do you realize what would happen if a steel destroyer, a battleship, with this mass came hurtling out of the sky and struck this city . . .'

'That seems far fetched.'

'Is it?' The camera moved again as Cooper rushed to a large globe of the Earth that stood behind him. 'Look here, at the track of that bomb in the sky. It's over our heads right now, cutting across the United States, over New York, over the ocean, hurling along, getting lower and lower over London, Paris, Berlin, Moscow. Cutting a path through the sky like *this*.' With a red marking pen he slashed a line that connected these cities. 'A bomb with all the kinetic and explosive energy of the atomic bomb that blew up Hiroshima. If it should fall and strike one of these cities—what do *you* think would happen?'

There was silence in the Presidential office at these words, silence broken by the softly spoken words of General Bannerman.

'It's in the fan now, it really is.'

# 16

THEY WERE ALL in the crew compartment, sharing the rations, eating for the first time since take-off. Nadya had opened the lockers and unstowed the meals, because the others had gone to the flight cabin as soon as they unstrapped. There were no ports in the inner compartment and it had been claustrophobic for them strapped in place and helpless. They returned to the compartment one by one, silently, the undescribable sensation of looking at their home planet from space so overwhelming that they forgot their predicament for the moment.

'The photographs, they don't do it justice,' Coretta said. 'It's unbelievable.'

Gregor was babbling enthusiastically at the Colonel who nodded his head in agreement. The sight of the Earth from space was no novelty for Colonel Kuznekov, he had logged countless hours in space, but it was a view he had always enjoyed. He had also gone along to aid the others who were inexperienced with the weightless conditions of free fall. They were all still gravity-orientated despite the conditions around them and had returned to sit on their bunks, clipping themselves into place. They found it disconcerting the way the Colonel floated with his head next to theirs, but with his feet in the air above, calmly kneading a plastic tube of creamed chicken dinner.

'I enjoy your American space rations, such variety.'

'A real boondoggle,' Ely said, removing the lid from a can of Russian salmon. 'While we spent a fortune developing space foods and special containers and all that rigmarole—you people just stuffed a lot of commercially packaged and canned food in your ships. This salmon is better than that muck.'

'Perhaps, perhaps,' the Colonel said, sucking happily on the tube.

Patrick finished his meal in the flight cabin, then drifted back in as they were cleaning away the remains.

Ely watched him intently as he floated to a bunk and secured himself.

'Any news?' Ely asked, and they all fell silent on the moment for there was really only one thought at the back of all their minds.

'Nothing they can do to change the situation. They've pinpointed the problem but can't do a thing from Earth. Here, look at this diagram.' He unrolled a large print and held it before them. 'Here, here, and these over here. The exploding bolts that secure us to the core body. That name is not quite true. They don't really blow up since gas and particular matter released during separation might damage the nuclear engine. The explosion is confined within the hollow steel of the bolt so they deform, sort of blow up like a balloon. This shortens the length of the bolt which moves the release mechanism at the end. Then these pistons, here, are actuated which push the two structures apart. Simple and theoretically foolproof.'

Ely snorted disdainfully and the others nodded. 'When we get back I want to talk to some people about the engineering on this project.'

'So do we all, Ely, but let's save that for later. We are under time pressure now. Mission Control say there's nothing more they can do to effect separation.'

'Which means they leave it up to us,' Nadya said.

'Exactly.'

'But what can we do?' Coretta asked.

'Space walk,' Patrick told her. 'EVA, Extra Vehicular Activity. Someone puts on a suit and gets out there and takes a look and sees if that damn thing can be knocked loose from us. Let's hope the umbilicals give us enough leeway to get near it.'

'Can't we unstow an Astronaut Manœuvring Unit—an AMU?' Ely asked.

'Negative. This was not planned for at this stage. We all have pressure suits with air connections in the cabin. There are two sets of umbilicals, air cables and phone line, that can be hooked up in the flight cabin. These were supposed to be used when we get to orbit to go back and open the outer hatch to get at the AMUs that will enable us to manœuvre without umbilicals. They will be used to assemble the generator, but no one thought they might be needed before that.'

'Bad planning,' Ely said.

'I don't think so. They're bulky enough to almost fill this compartment. The planning wasn't at fault—this time.'

'Can't we get to them now?' Coretta asked.

'We can, but it's a time-consuming job, two, three hours at least to unseal and power up, then maybe as much to reseal. We don't have that much time. So someone goes out on the umbilicals to see what can be done.'

'It is nice to get back to work,' Colonel Kuznekov said, pushing himself towards the upper lockers. 'I'll suit up at once.'

'Just a minute, Colonel, it hasn't been decided . . .'

'Circumstances decide, my boy.' He methodically stripped off his boiler suit and pushed it aside. 'You've had some time space walking, I know that from the records. Nadya, while an experienced pilot, has never been out of her ship, is that right, Nadya?'

She nodded agreement.

'So there you are. For the others, this is their first flight into space. Nadya mans the controls, you will handle my umbilicals, Patrick, and I shall make this mess right. Of course I am not attempting to give the Commander orders. An old army man like me, never! I simply remind you that I have had over a thousand hours in a suit in space working on my cryonic projects. The only other choice, my captain, is for you to go and for me to watch, which seems a foolish risk for the commander of a vessel when a grizzled old space dog can do the trick. *Oh-chin ogay?*'

Patrick began to protest, then laughed. 'How come you never became a general, Kuznekov?'

'It was offered, I refused. All desk work with high rank, which is not my sort of thing at all. Shall we go?'

'Right.'

With many hands helping, the suiting went faster than usual. The hanging spaghetti loops of the umbilicals were taken from their lockers and pushed through into the flight cabin.

'We'll seal the hatch between this compartment and the flight cabin since you'll still be pressurized,' Patrick said.

'Would we be of any help if we suited up?' Ely asked.

'Negative, sorry. We'll be crowded as it is. Nadya will be at the controls and will fill you in on the intercom. Here we go.'

'Good luck, Patrick,' Coretta said. 'And you too, Colonel.' On sudden impulse she pulled herself to Kuznekov, they were floating with their heads almost touching, and kissed him on the forehead.

'Wonderful!' the Colonel said. 'No warrior going into battle ever had a finer salute.'

But once in the flight cabin they were more serious. The hatch was sealed and they put on their helmets, twisting and locking them into place. Nadya was connected to the air supply next to the pilot's seat, Patrick and the Colonel's umbilicals plugged to their suits and into the air attachments near the door.

'Are we ready?' Patrick asked.

'*Oh-chin ogay.*'

He moved slowly in the clumsy suit, twisting the valve in the centre of the exit door. It opened and the atmosphere in the cabin began hissing out into space.

'Pressure dropped enough,' Nadya said.

'Roger. Unsealing the door.'

With most of the air gone the door could be opened safely without the pressure of the cabin atmosphere against it. It swung open silently. At this the atmospheric pressure dropped suddenly and the air became hazy with fog that vanished moments later as the last of the air puffed out into the vacuum of space. Framed in the opening was the sable darkness and unflickering points of light of the stars of the endless interstellar night. The Colonel floated head first through the opening.

'There should be handholds all the way along,' Patrick said.

'No problem, I feel I've been doing this all my life.'

The Colonel was indeed a skilled space walker, his solid, clumsy-appearing form moving light as a feather. Patrick paid out the coils of the umbilicals as he floated aft, just touching the handholds with his fingers so that he moved smoothly along.

'Coming to the end,' Patrick said, looking at the short length remaining.

'Just about a metre more. Let me have all the slack you have. That's it.'

The Colonel had clipped his safety line to the last rung of the handhold and was leaning far out. The umbilicals were now bar straight and taut, pressed hard against the lip of the hatch where they went out. Farther and farther the Colonel reached—until his finger seized the stern of Prometheus, beyond him was the dark angled bulk of the still-attached core body.

'What do you see?' Patrick asked.

'Very little, black as Hades in there, in the shadow. Let me get my torch out.' He unclipped his flashlight and poked it over the end. The circle of illuminations slid over the nose of the core body, the beam itself invisible in the vacuum of space, then moved out of sight.

'Aha!'

'What is it?'

'Our culprit all right. One of the connecting rods, a bit twisted but still holding. All the plungers around it are actuated and pushing to separate. The only problem being that the harder they push the stronger the connecting rod is wedged into its anchor to hold us together. But easily enough remedied, I think.'

'A little sizzling with the oxy-acetylene torch will cut that rod in two in a second. Then the rest of the mechanism will do its job and drive this great weight off of our backs and we will be free to go on our way. Except for one little problem.'

They waited, hushed, the astronauts and the three in the sealed compartment hearing every word spoken over the intercom, and even the breathing of those in the pressure suits.

'Problem? What?'

'At the present moment I don't see how we can reach the rod. It's on the other side and the umbilicals won't stretch that far.'

## I 7

*GET 03:19—Cottenham New Town*

SIR RICHARD LONSDALE did not like lunches that went on so long, but he had no choice. It was late and they were still around the table in the executives' restaurant, still wreathed in a fog of cigar smoke and the perfume of fine brandy. The Swiss seemed happy, coats open and perspiring freely.

'My congratulations to your chef, Sir Richard,' Müller said, patting his great midriff affectionately like a pet dog.

There was more light talk until eventually one of them looked at his watch. Chairs were pushed back and there was much hand-clasping and many guttural good-byes. Müller waited until he was leaving to speak the few hoped-for words. He was obviously a believer in good curtain lines.

'We shall recommend the contract on the terms discussed, Sir Richard. I hope it will be only the beginning of a long and successful relationship.'

'Thank you, thank you very much.'

Their car would be waiting, and that would be that. He ground his cigar out in the ashtray and tried not to remember the trayload of papers in his office. They would have to be tackled now, like it or not, if he were to have any chance of getting home before midnight.

The shortest way back to the executive offices was through the canteen and Sir Richard pushed his way through the swing door. He was preoccupied and would have gone straight through if the voices hadn't caught his attention. There were a number of workers here, it was already late enough for the afternoon tea break, and a group of them seemed agitated about something. Not a wildcat strike, he prayed.

Some of them were reading newspaper, two and three at a time looking over one another's shoulders.

He recognized one of the men, one of several older employees who had come over from the original works.

'Henry, what's happening?'

Henry Lewis looked up and nodded, passing over his own paper.

'Look at that, sir, enough to curl your hair it is. Just like the war all over again.'

SATELLITE BOMB SCARE. Sir Richard scanned the piece quickly.

'Like a flying bomb,' Henry said. 'Hiroshima all over again. Look at this diagram on the next page, look where the bloody bull's-eye is.'

A drawing of Great Britain with a dotted line bisecting it, the satellite's track. To emphasize the peril the artist had drawn a great bull's-eye on the centre of England and, completely by chance, the centre of the bull was over Cottenham New Town.

'I wouldn't be too concerned if I were you,' Sir Richard said, folding the paper calmly and handing it back. 'I think there is more imaginative journalism in this than rational scientific fact. Pure guesswork.'

## 18

*GET 03:25*

COLONEL KUZNEKOV'S WORDS echoed inside the helmets of the other two pressure suits, as well as from the wall-mounted speaker in the crew compartment. They answered with silence for no one could think of a thing to say. It was

Nadya who spoke first, relaying, in a professional, emotionless voice, a message from Mission Control.

'Major Winter, Mission Control wants you to come in.'

'Tell them to go to hell.'

'Hello Mission Control, this is Prometheus. Major Winter cannot speak to you at this moment. Yes, that's right, he's helping Colonel Kuznekov in a survey of the damage. Roger, he will be with you as soon as he can.'

'What did he want?' Patrick asked.

'More radio contact, and could you rig one of the TV cameras so they could observe us for general broadcast.'

'Negative. No circuses for the folks back home, not just now. Kuznekov, stay where you are, I'm coming out to see for myself.'

'Right Patrick. And bring the oxyacetylene torch with you and the tool pack. I think I know how to cut that bolt.'

'Roger. Here I come.'

Patrick clipped the tools and the torch behind him and drew himself through the open doorway, then snapped a clip on the handhold outside. After that, carefully, he pulled all of the floating loops of his umbilicals through the doorway until they hung free, writhing slowly in space. Only then did he unclip and work his way back along the length of Prometheus, stopping every few feet to check the trailing umbilicals to be sure they were not getting tangled or caught. The bulky toolpack and torch on his back were weightless in free fall.

When he had almost reached the end of the umbilicals Kuznekov reached back and seized his hand, pulling him the rest of the way.

'There,' Kuznekov said. 'You will see our problem.'

A circle of light appeared, gliding first across the smooth surface of the metal then over the nuclear motor and the angular forms of the pistons that should have pushed the two spaceships apart. The nearest ones were extended all the way, a gap showing between their ends and the base of Prometheus. But there, on the far side, was a jumble of twisted metal, half extended pistons and the intact form of a thick steel rod.

Kuznekov kept the light on it.

'Exploding bolt,' he said. 'Unexploded. An American bolt I am unhappy to report.'

'And those supports and pistons are Soviet,' Patrick said in a weary voice. 'The interface between the two techniques, the weak spot where one system meets the other. Well, we were warned. Not that it makes much difference now. But—that bolt's at least five metres away. We can't possibly reach it.'

'Perhaps we can rig a pole and attach the torch to the end?'

'We've nothing like that on board, we'd have to improvise. What would be strong enough? And we would have to light the torch here and work it over there while it was burning. Right between all that piping and the guts of the atomic engine. If that's injured there goes the entire ball game.'

'There it goes indeed,' the Colonel said, snapping open the latches on the tool pack. Inside, held in clips, were the tools specially designed to work in the cold and vacuum of space, to be operated by clumsy gloved hands. He drew out the torch. 'The very thoughts you have outlined crossed my mind. The only way to cut that bolt is for someone to go over there and cut that bolt.'

'We'll have to unship one of the AMUs.'

'No time for that, you said so yourself. So if you'll aid me I'll go over there and cut it. First the lighter, to be sure the torch is operating. Wonderful, I turn it off . . .'

'Colonel Kuznekov, what are you talking about? Your umbilical won't reach over there.'

'Obviously. So I breathe in a good deal of air, disconnect it, do the job and return. I can hold my breath three, maybe four minutes. It should be enough. If I black out I count upon you to reconnect my oxygen in time.'

'Stop him!'

'He can't, no . . .'

The intercom roared with the cries of many voices. 'Silence!' Patrick shouted. 'If you have anything to say speak up by turn. Nadya.'

111

'I . . . nothing. You are the commander, you must decide. The bolt must be cut.'

'Coretta, Ely? Anyone else?'

It took a moment for anyone to speak, then Ely's voice came over. 'There's nothing to say, I guess. Down here, we're just passengers. But isn't there any other way?'

'Negative,' Kuznekov said brusquely. 'Now we must begin. There's no time to waste.'

'Agreed,' Patrick said. 'The first problem's going to be how to disconnect your suit from the umbilicals without your losing all your oxygen. If we just unplug it goes whoosh.'

'I have concerned myself over that too and think I see an answer.'

The Colonel opened the tool pack and reached in. All of the devices bore little resemblance to their Earthly counterparts because of the unusual conditions of working in space. Small tools could not be held easily in the thick gloves, nor could fine adjustments be made on them by hand. Nor, when tools were being used, could gravity be counted upon for help. We do not think of gravity until it is not there. On earth it is a simple thing to put a wrench over the head of a bolt, to brace and push and turn it. Not so in space, in free fall. Without gravity to act as an anchor Newton's third law comes into its own. For every action there is an equal and opposite reaction. If the bit of a power drill goes in one direction, whoever is holding the drill rotates in the other. Therefore all the tools for use in space were power-operated from built-in nicad batteries. Internal flywheels spun in one direction to provide torque for tools rotating in the opposite direction. Adjustments were made by moving a sizeable lever, actuating a motor to make the adjustment.

Colonel Kuznekov took a wrench from the pack, very much unlike the crescent wrenches and open-end wrenches it replaced. The two adjustable jaws were motor driven and could be adjusted either to open or close, or to stop at an exact preset measurement on the scale.

'What are you going to do with that?' Patrick asked.

'It will be obvious in a moment. The torch now, if you please. I think the tanks would be best clipped to my back where they will not be in the way.'

The twin tanks were easily secured in place by Patrick, with the flexible hoses passed over the Colonel's shoulders to the pistol grip of the burning head he held in his hand. A large trigger turned on the gas flow and when he touched the ignition button on top the nicad batteries produced a fat spark that ignited the oxygen-acetylene mixture. A lever next to the button adjusted the mixture to a long needle of fire.

'Step one,' Kuznekov said. 'Now, Patrick, if you will just hold this burning torch for a moment, if you please, pointed well away.'

The Colonel stopped speaking and began to inhale, slowly and deeply, filling his lungs with oxygen, hyperventilating, getting the maximum amount of oxygen into his blood-stream that was possible. Through his faceplate, Patrick could see him nod and smile when he had enough. With a swift motion he raised the power wrench close to his chest and clamped it over the umbilicals, actuating the mechanism at the same time. With geared-down strength the jaws closed, tighter and tighter, clamping down on the electrical and intercom cables, squashing flat the flexible hose of his air supply, until it was clamped shut completely.

'No air flow,' Kuznekov whispered, conserving his breath. 'Torch.'

He took the burning torch from Patrick's hand. With a single pass he severed the umbilicals, leaving the stump with the attached wrench dangling from his suit.

Then he turned off the torch, waved his hand in farewell, and hauled himself over the bottom of Prometheus with a firm grip on a metal stanchion.

'What is happening?' The voice sounded in Patrick's earphones and he realized that the others could have no idea of what was going on.

'Colonel Kuznekov is going to cut the bolt. He clamped the wrench on his oxygen hose so it wouldn't leak into space, then cut the umbilicals with the torch.' He wasn't thinking clearly, Patrick realized. The severed umbilical was writhing in space like a garden hose. But instead of spouting water it was sending out a shower of frozen crystals.

'Nadya,' he called out. 'Turn off the Colonel's air at the wall valve. It's just being pumped into space.'

'It is off,' she said, and the shining spray slowed and died. 'What is happening now?'

'He's halfway there. It's slow going through that maze of hardware without a safety line—*watch out!*'

Patrick shouted the last, forgetting that the Colonel was out of communication with his umbilicals severed. Kuznekov was fighting against time, taking chances that, as an experienced space walker, he would never normally consider. He must take them now. The last yards to the bolt were across a bare patch of metal. Up until now he had been moving steadily from handhold to handhold. Now he gauged the distance—and launched himself towards his objective, floating free in space.

But he could not see what Patrick could. The bulk of the tanks on his back was in line with one of the extended jacks, aiming directly for it. Patrick could only watch, horrified, as Kuznekov drifted forward, his hand extended to grab the length of the unexploded bolt.

His tanks struck first and he cartwheeled in space, missing the bolt completely. The force of the impact swung his booted feet in the opposite direction, slamming them into the base of Prometheus. As they hit and rebounded the Colonel grasped at the bolt, but could not touch it.

He was drifting now, out from between the booster rocket and the satellite station, heading towards the depths of space, with nothing near enough to grab on to.

An inexperienced space walker would have kept on drifting, clutching vainly at the objects that passed just out of reach, but the Colonel knew better than this. He was already rotating slowly from the last impact. Bending over he drew his legs up to his chest in a single swift motion, increasing his speed of rotation. Just as a stone on string will spin faster when the string is shortened, so did he rotate faster.

Then he straightened out to his full length, reached out— grabbed the angled brace of one of the jacks. There were worried questions in his ears and Patrick realized he had been watching the drama in space in silent horror.

'It's fine now. The Colonel has had difficulty reaching the bolt but he is almost to it.'

'He will be running out of air!' It was Gregor's voice, thick with fear.

'Not yet,' Patrick told him. 'He's not only hyperventilated but he has oxygen in his suit. He'll make it.'

The Colonel was making it. With a final swing he reached the bolt and examined it for a long moment. Only then did he swing out as far as he could and attach a clip from his belt to the base of Prometheus. Then, carefully and methodically, he ignited the torch, adjusted the flame to his liking, reached out and put the flame to the length of steel.

'It's working, he's cutting it!' Patrick shouted, so loudly that his voice echoed inside the confines of the helmet and rang in his ears. 'It's tough steel but it's glowing, I can see it, drops of metal coming off—almost through—THERE!'

The end was dramatic indeed. The pressure of all the jacks and hydraulic plungers was so great that, before the metal was cut through completely, the bolt snapped. Released at last the metal arms extended. In complete silence the two great metal shapes were pushed apart. Once started the motion continued, the core body drifting slowly away from Prometheus.

'It did it, it worked!' Patrick called out. 'We have separation. And Kuznekov is all right, he's unclipping and starting back.'

He did not add that the Colonel was obviously in trouble. The minutes had ticked by, one by one, and his oxygen was finally exhausted. His movements were slow, clumsy.

Kuznekov pushed himself forward, grabbed the stub of the bolt and used this to accelerate himself towards Patrick. But his hand slipped as he fumbled his hold, drifting slowly. He shook his head, trying to drive away the blackness that pressed in on him. Then, with his last strength and consciousness he planted both feet on the bolt, waited until he was lined up—then pressed down firmly.

Floating across the bottom of Prometheus, beside the bell-shaped mouth of the atomic engine, straight towards Patrick. Limp now and barely conscious.

But not straight enough. His hand was out, hanging slackly, his arm kept in position by the pressurized fabric of the suit. Patrick seized the lip of metal with his left hand, pushed hard, straightened against the pull of the taut umbilicals, reaching out towards Kuznekov's hand drifting close.

Close, moving, but not close enough. He gasped with effort as he fought the tug of the umbilical cables, stretching, fingers extended as far as they could go.

Silently drifting, Kuznekov's hand went by scant inches from Patrick's groping fingertips. In the full light of the sun Patrick could see the Colonel's closed eyes, his lined face calm and at ease.

The suited figure drifted by him, arm still extended as if in a last salute, into space and oblivion.

# 19

*GET 05:32*

FLAX was washing down his Maalox with black coffee and it was not doing him any good at all. His gut rumbled continually and sent out sudden gusts of flame like a volcano about to blow up. Not only that but the coffee was going right to his bladder and he forgot the last time he had been to the john so he felt as if he had a full basket ball down there.

But he couldn't leave the console now.

'Listen, Patrick, we need this.' He was pleading and he knew it. 'You were out of contact for almost forty minutes there, it was only the readouts from the bio-sensors that let us even know you were there at all. And when Kuznekov cut his umbilicals I'll tell you things were hairy down here. And you haven't had the TV cameras broadcasting more than a total of fifteen minutes the entire flight.'

'*We have had some problems, Mission Control.*'

'I know that—and I'm not making light of them in any way. But the situation here, without going into many details, demands your aid. We *need* that broadcast, Patrick— desperately.'

'*I read you, Flax, and I'm getting agreement here. Before we repressurize the flight deck I'll give you a shot out of the hatch. Stand by, Mission Control.*'

Flax sighed and leaned back, hooking his thumbs inside the front of his belt and pulling outward, relieving some of the pressure on his bladder. He took a sip of coffee. He could see the display below him on the TV monitor console, a breaking-up signal and picture that quickly was put under control. He switched the picture to his own TV screen and switched his phone through to the network liaison console.

'We have a picture, Bob, what's your status?'

'All networks vamping and ready to take our broadcast.'

'Tell them to stand by. Sixty seconds.'

A light blinked on his board and he flipped the switch beside it; the voice sounded in his earphone. 'Mr Flax, I have Mr Dillwater on the line for you . . .'

'He'll have to hold.'

'But . . .'

'You heard me. I'll get back to him as soon as this broadcast from Prometheus is over. I'm sure he will understand that.' He switched off the voice before there could be any response, and nodded approval as the picture on his screen steadied and the hatch loomed large, then vanished and the Earth, as seen from space, appeared on the screen.

'We're receiving a perfect picture, Patrick. Just hold it there please. The networks are standing by, are you ready to go?'

'*Roger.*'

'Give them the signal,' he ordered, and saw himself,

small on the screen, from the network camera to the rear of Mission Control.

'Switching over now to the camera on Prometheus. There, you can see it now, the Earth from the open hatch. Major Winter is holding the camera and is moving it now. Over to you, Prometheus.'

*That's Earth as we see it, plenty of cloud. We are now ending our third orbit and, I don't know if you can make it out through the cloud, but we are going over the Pacific with Peru just coming up, the air is clear there. I'm going to move the camera . . . just a moment . . . there, you can see the detached core body. It's in orbit behind us at a bearing of about fifteen degrees.'*

Flax pressed one of the buttons on his console. 'Kill the sound to the networks, but keep the picture. Tell them it's a technical difficulty.' He switched back to Prometheus. 'Hello, Prometheus. A good picture, great commentary, Patrick. What I'm saying now is not going out to the networks. Do you see that spot of light just to the left of the booster?'

*'Affirmative.'*

'Is it . . .?'

*'Yes, it's Colonel Kuznekov. He's also following us in orbit. And before you ask—the answer is no. I'm not going to zoom in on his corpse or anything like that.'*

'Just a report, that's all I ask.'

*'You've had that already. I'm going to give you about one minute more of this then close the hatch and pressurize. We have work to do.'*

'Going live again,' he sighed and gave the signal.

*'The core body will gradually drop behind us in this orbit until it is brought back to Earth for a soft landing. In the cabin now, I'll hand the camera to Major Kalinina while I close this hatch. Once we're pressurized we can begin preparations for orbital firing.'*

The picture jumped around as the camera was passed over. Flax groaned to himself and wondered if his bladder really would burst. A light flickered on and he threw the switch.

'Mr Dillwater insists on talking with you, Mr Flax.'

'A few moments more.'

'He's not waiting. He's gone into Mission Control.'

'Damn!' Flax disconnected and turned his chair about. There he was all right, the dark figure just entering the upper tier. It had to be him, the only man in Texas in the summer who wore a dark suit—with a vest. Striding steadily, right up to the console.

'Mr Flax, your presence is required in the press conference chamber.'

'Mr Dillwater, I wish I could, but as I told you on the phone I can't leave this position now. The atomic engine . . .'

'Your assistant controller will take over. I have flown to Houston from Washington for this conference which I could have done just as well from there. The venue is here for your benefit. I realize your worth, Mr Flax, and commend your attention to duty. But if you do not come with me now your assistant will take over and you will be relieved of your duties and will no longer be an employee of NASA. Do I make myself clear?'

Flax, for the first time in his life, could think of nothing to say. The seconds ticked by dumbly and he realized that there was nothing he could really argue about. Realistically, he could take a break now as the flight cabin was repressurized and they removed their suits, he had the time. 'Spendlove, take over,' he said, then took off his headset and threw it on to the console before him. 'I'll come with you, Mr Dillwater. Only I have to go to the bathroom first.'

He heaved himself erect and thought his bladder would explode now with the pressure on it. He tried not to waddle when he walked. The men's room sign looked before him like the gates of heaven and he fell against it and pushed it open.

Dillwater was waiting when he came out—were his eyebrows elevated ever so slightly? Maybe they were, he must have set the world's peeing record, but did not feel he could explain this to Dillwater.

They went to the elevator.

'Can you brief me?' Flax asked.

'It is simple enough. A New York paper broke a story a few hours ago, this morning New York time. Since then all of the media have picked it up, all over the world, and it's snowballing. Have you heard about it?'

'Just a couple of words, someone told me who was watching TV. A crackpot idea about Prometheus turning into an atom bomb. Insane!'

'I am glad you feel that way, Mr Flax, but please save your arguments and indignation for the press. As soon as he heard the first reports President Bandin sent me here to arrange a conference to destroy these rumours before they spread. I have just spent a very uncomfortable time in a supersonic Air Force plane, so you must excuse me if my temper is short.'

'Who's here? What kind of coverage?'

'Everything and everyone. All the media. We must be on our toes and I look upon you for aid in every way.'

Flax was scared. He did not like big crowds nor did he enjoy being cross-examined by suspicious journalists. When backed into a corner he tended to squeak like a rat, which everyone enjoyed but which sapped his morale. He wished he could have a drink before he went on. There was the bar in the office behind the conference hall. But what would Dillwater think? The hell with what he thought.

'I'm going into Jack's office for a moment,' he said, turning the knob.

Dillwater's eyebrows arched up.

'Whatever on earth for?'

'For a drink, if you must know.'

The eyebrows slowly dropped and a suspicion of a smile touched the corners of the rigid mouth.

'I will join you.'

Dillwater had a small dry sherry while Flax poured a half glass of whisky, diluted it with water, then drank it straight down. 'My God,' he said, striking himself lightly on the protruding stomach with the thumb of his closed fist. 'That is going to cure or kill me.' He belched cavernously and shuddered. Dillwater finished his last sip of sherry, tapped his lips with his handkerchief, and waved to the door. 'Into the lion's den, if you please, Mr Flax. I'm afraid we have no choice.'

They came in by the side entrance and were unnoticed for a few seconds. Minford, the PR man, was behind the podium and fielding the questions. If his sweat-drenched face was any indication, he had not been having an easy time. Heads turned, one by one, as they crossed the front of the hall and the cameras began to click. Minford had the expression of a man just saved from the lion pit as they came forward.

'Now if you would please hold those questions for a moment or two you will be able to ask the people who are completely in the picture. Mr Simon Dillwater you all know. He has just jetted down here from Washington to give you a full report. With him is Dr Flax who has been in the hot spot at Mission Control ever since take-off, and has been in contact with the astronauts all of that time. Will you please address your questions to them. . . .'

Hands, pencils and pads were being waved; there were hoarse shouts for attention. Minford looked them over quickly, and pointed to the Science Editor of the *LA Times*. They had worked together for years and he might just be a little more sympathetic.

'Dr Flax, just what is the situation in space at this moment?'

Flax relaxed, ever so slightly, no trouble here. 'Separation has been achieved as you know. At the present time the crew is repressurizing the flight cabin so they can work in shirtsleeve environment again. The programme now calls for the check-out of the nuclear engine in the lower compartment, the engine which will now be fired to lift Prometheus to its final orbit. . . .' Hands were waving again and Minford stabbed his finger at the nearest.

'What about the core body, the last booster still there in orbit? If it fell couldn't it cause immense destruction? As much as an atomic bomb?' They were silent now, waiting for his answer. Flax spoke slowly, counting off the major points on his fingers.

'Firstly, nothing can "fall" from orbit despite what you might have heard. This last booster, like the previous five, will be inserted into a proper descent orbit and soft-landed just as the others were. Secondly, if anything were to go wrong, though this is unimaginable, the worst that would happen would be the destruction of the booster by combustion in the atmosphere. . . .'

'If a malfunction is unimaginable,' a voice called out loudly, 'what do you call the failure of the core body engines and the failure to separate?'

Flax was beginning to sweat heavily. 'Perhaps I chose the wrong term. We can imagine an uncontrolled landing, in which case the booster would burn up.'

'It couldn't hit a city, explode?'

'Impossible. Thousands of rockets have been launched, all of them with disposable stages. All of these have burnt up on re-entry and none have ever caused the slightest damage.'

One man had been calling for attention since the interview had begun and Minford could ignore him no longer. 'Mr Redditch,' he said.

The *Newsweek* correspondent was one of the senior men present, well known to all the reporters. They quieted, waiting for his questions, knowing he could speak for most of them.

'I appreciate your arguments, Dr Flax,' Redditch said. 'But aren't you referring to far smaller boosters than this one?'

'Possibly. But the scale isn't that great.'

'Isn't it?' There was frank unbelief in Redditch's voice. 'This type of booster is bigger than any other, and Prometheus is many times bigger than the booster. Is that not correct?'

'Yes, but . . .'

'So forget the booster for the moment. What would happen if Prometheus itself slammed back to the Earth? Wouldn't it make one hell of a hole in the ground?'

'But Prometheus is *not* going to return to Earth,' Flax could feel the sweat trickling down inside his shirt. 'It's already in orbit and will soon be firing its engine and going into higher orbit.'

'Isn't it in now what is called a decaying orbit? Is it not true that if the engine does not fire soon that the entire satellite itself could plummet back to Earth after contact with the atmosphere? Is it not true that this decaying orbit will not last more than eighteen hours more?'

Flax did not know what to say. Where had he obtained those figures? Someone had talked—they were NASA's own figures. What the hell could be done?

Dillwater saved his bacon. Cool and calm as always he coughed into the microphone and nodded in Redditch's direction.

'There has been too much loose talk today,' he said. 'Unfounded speculation by a certain irresponsible minority. You gentlemen of the press are absolutely correct in your attitude, in your questions. You have heard these speculations and you wish to know about them. To determine the truth, if there is any truth, to lay to rest rootless and absurd speculations, dangerous speculation I might say, if that be the case. You are not gossip mongers, but representatives of a free press dedicated to telling the truth. . . .'

'Well, could we have some?' Redditch said, unimpressed. 'My question still stands. If, at the end of the sixteen-hour period, Prometheus hits the atmosphere—what is going to happen?'

'Nothing. Because Prometheus is not going to do that. As we are talking here the fusion engine is being tested and will soon be building up thrust. There have been difficulties and they have been surmounted. We are on our way.'

Oh, baby, you had better be right, Flax thought. You had better be very, very right. His fingers crept out, unseen by the newsmen, to the back of the podium, where he knocked, ever so lightly, on wood.

## 20

*GET 05:39*

'IT LOOKS LIKE it belongs in a submarine,' Coretta said, looking down at the round hatch with a handwheel in its centre which was set into the floor of the crew compartment.

'It serves the same function,' Patrick said, turning hard on the wheel. Ely had anchored himself and was holding Patrick's legs, giving him something he could thrust against. 'Right now there's just space on the other side of this hatch. The crew compartment and flight deck of Prometheus are a single unit designed to be ejected in an emergency. We sort of shoot out sideways propelled by rockets. Since we didn't eject we can now hook up with NTECS, the Nuclear Tug Engine Control Station which is behind us. The engine room. I'm pulling up a retracted tube now that will seal against the other side here. There! Your turn, Ely. Use the wrench to take all the sealing nuts off.'

It was not easy work. In a few minutes Ely was muttering with exasperation. 'Why the devil does it have to be dogged down so hard?' he said, wrestling the wrench to the next stud.

'You know why,' Patrick said, carefully putting the removed nut with the others in the plastic bag hanging from his belt. 'There's hard vacuum out there. Any leak would evacuate the engine room and we'd have to operate in suits. But if the pressure readouts are fine we can do it in shirtsleeves—which is much easier.'

Ely fitted the jaws over the last nut and tripped the switch. The flywheel spun and the nut came free. But he did not kill the motor quickly enough as he lifted the wrench off, so the nut was propelled violently across the compartment to clang loudly into a locker door. The thin metal dented and rebounded, slinging the steel nut back with a good deal of its energy still remaining. It struck Nadya in the leg and she shouted with pain.

'Ely, you stupid . . .' Patrick broke off the shout and

called to Coretta who was in the flight cabin above. 'Coretta, down here at once!'

He shoved Ely aside rudely, in fact using the other man's shoulder to launch himself across the compartment. Nadya was floating in a small circle, holding her wounded calf in both hands as the blood seeped through the fabric. Patrick reached her, pulled her down towards the couch.

'It's not much,' she said. 'I was just surprised at the suddenness . . .'

'Let's see it.'

He clipped her to the couch and took the clasp knife from the pocket on his leg, then carefully slit the fabric of her suit. The wound was bleeding freely but did not look bad. Coretta floated next to him, the first-aid box ready in her hands.

'Let me see that,' she said, pressing a sterile pad over the cut. 'It's not big at all, won't even need stitches. I think a butterfly here will do. Will you hold the box please, Patrick.'

She worked swiftly, professionally. Patrick turned and looked at the other two men, Ely shame-faced and hangdog, Gregor shocked at the suddenness of the accident.

'Listen to me carefully, all of you,' Patrick said. 'You have just seen an accident. It didn't amount to much—but it might have been fatal. We have already had one death on this mission. Colonel Kuznekov died to correct someone's error, someone back on Earth. Malfunctions do not happen by chance in space. They are caused by human mistakes, things people have done wrong or do wrong. I want an end to it. We cannot afford *any* more trouble, do you understand? We have only one thing to do now, nothing else matters. We have to get that engine fired up. So you will all stay here, clipped to your bunks. It may be uncomfortable for a while—but you'll be out of the way. And that includes you, Ely.'

'But I . . .'

'Shut up. We have no time for explanations or recriminations or even any goddamn conversation. Shut up and stay that way. Every one of you. I'm going to take off that hatch and stow it. I'm going to go through the tube to the bottom end and remove the hatch there. When I've done that I'll plug in my intercom and call you. You'll join me, Ely, and we'll start the engine. The rest of you will stand by here in case you're needed.'

He was irritable and abrupt and knew he should be more politic. But he was too tired to make the effort, too singleminded about what he knew had to be done. Nadya was an experienced cosmonaut. Even while he had been speaking she had clipped Coretta to the couch beside her and was sitting quietly waiting for further instructions. Coretta was finishing bandaging the wound—but she had heard. Ely was livid with rage, yet he kept his mouth shut. Fine. Only Gregor was out of it, turning away sullenly. He was cargo, useless, in the way and with nothing to do. Well he would just have to stay that way until they were in orbit and he could get on with his job.

Patrick lifted the hatch cover and stowed it in its clips against the bulkhead. Then, with the wrench clipped in his belt, he floated headfirst into the tunnel. It was little wider than his shoulders and claustrophobic. If he let himself give in he could feel the walls pressing against him, his breath growing shorter and shorter. He kicked away the sensation, knowing he felt this tension, this incipient claustrophobia, only when he was very tired. Like now. How long had it been since he had slept? He had lost track with the seemingly endless holds. A day or more at least. Best not to think about it. The hatch cover that he was drifting towards, that was what was important. He bent his arm as his outstretched fingers touched it, slowing his movement to a stop. He clipped to the nearest ring and swung up the wrench. He was working in his own shadow from the single bulb behind him. Another wonderful bit of applied technology, but he could see well enough to remove the nuts one by one. Slowly. Stop wrench. Nut into the bag. The next one. The hatch floated free and he turned its oval shape sideways so he could push it ahead of him into the engine compartment. When it was safely stowed in the clips he plugged in his intercom.

'Ely, down here with me.'

The nuclear physicist floated out of the tube and neatly checked himself on a handhold, swinging about. They were all getting more facile in free fall, after a few hours in space. Ely smiled, despite himself.

'What a lovely machine. Look at that thing, seven million bucks worth of fission reactor powered by a small fortune in uranium dust.'

The engine itself was invisible, outside in space, beyond the hydrogen tank and the 25-ton biological shield that would protect them from its radiation when it was operating. All that was seen inside NTECS was the complex control station with its many readouts. Ely pushed over to it, smiling happily, and strapped into the chair facing the console.

'Now let's fire this thing up and get it operational as soon as possible.'

When he touched the proximity switch the controls came to life. He ordered the computer to display the starting sequence on one screen while the main screen lit up with the many-coloured schematic diagram that showed the status of all the valves and control circuits. Ely ran through them all very quickly, then turned off the safety inhibit. One by one he went down the list. Propellant status showed the hydrogen tank full. Start-up system motors and valves ready, nozzle throttles closed, heat exchanger operational, pipes purged . . .

Patrick watched in silence until Ely went through the last display of the neon-closed loop, then settled back, satisfied. He made a thumbs-up sign to Patrick.

'And that takes care of the check-list. All in the green, A-OK, *oh-chio gay*. Plug into Mission Control and tell them we are ready to fire when they are.' He looked at the GET readout on the wall. '09:16 and they gave us about twenty-four hours in this orbit before things warmed up. Fourteen hours and forty-four minutes to go, which is not very much time. Tell them we're in a hurry and have an orbit to catch.'

127

## 21

*GET 05:45*

ACADEMICIAN A. A. TSANDER was an old man and well aware of it. He looked the picture of the frail octogenarian, with his wispy white beard and crown of floating hair. Never a large man, he had been bent by age so that he walked now with a perpetual stoop that forced him to bend his head back to look up at people. Yet he was neither as weak nor as frail as he appeared, as many had discovered through the years. Reaching his now exalted rank in the Academy of Sciences had taken a good deal of scientific skill—as well as a wicked talent for political infighting. He was liberally endowed with both, but he was eighty-three and knew it, so he husbanded his energy for the times it would be needed.

He was asleep now, lying on his back on the leather couch in his office, his long white fingers laced together on his chest. His breathing was so unnoticeable that he could have been a corpse. Yet, deeply asleep as he was, his eyes opened instantly when the doorknob turned silently and a beam of light came into the room.

'What time is it?' he asked.

'Almost midnight, Academician. The American colonel is here, you asked that you . . .'

'Of course. I will be down.' Three hours' sleep, more than enough preparation for what was sure to be a long night ahead. He poured some water into the basin from the jug, bathed his face and hands then dried them. Then he lighted a *papirossi*, one of the thin cigarettes he favoured, more paper than tobacco, shoved the rest of the package in his pocket and went out. The halls in the office floors were dark and quiet and he walked through them slowly, gathering strength. He had a feeling he would need it.

Inside the Ground Command Control Centre there was light and sound in direct contrast to the dark halls and tiny bulbs in the rest of the building. Here was the beating heart of Kapustin Yar, the central command to which all inputs fed, from which radiated all commands. Standing at the rear of the great room, Colonel O'Brian was very happy to be there. This entire area had been Top Secret for generations, mentioned only in CIA reports, and then in only general terms. GCCC in KY—the Soviets were as fond of alphabet names as the Americans were—the centre of ICBM and satellite launches. Well the ICBM controls were gone now, where he didn't care, though the CIA probably knew. What was left were the satellite controls which were now being used to land the Prometheus boosters. And, since this was a joint Soviet-American project, it was necessary to have liaison and at least one observer here.

How the Soviets had wriggled and twisted over that one! How responsibility had been passed higher and higher, until the Communist Party Central Committee had finally inherited the buck, since it had nowhere else to go. Back, after a long time, had come a reluctant yes. Arriving, the very next day, was Colonel O'Brian who had been waiting for years for just this opportunity.

It had been a bit of a letdown, most of the Soviet secrecy being just bad habit as always. There wasn't anything done here that wasn't done in Houston. Only better. Yet it was interesting to see how they did it because it told him a lot about the operation of their ICBMs. O'Brian was not a cold warrior, but he was still in the Army and the more he learned the better it was for his side. He was the new kind of officer, with degrees in mathematics and physics. But he was still an officer. He held the briefcase under his arm and looked around at the now familiar consoles and general bustle. Not the world's most modern set-up, but it worked, it worked very well indeed.

'Are those the promised figures?' a deep chesty voice asked in Russian.

'They are indeed, sir,' O'Brian answered in the same language, completely fluent. He turned and saluted the massive form of Lieutenant-General V. F. Bykovsky, the man in charge of it all. Bykovsky returned the salute with an airy wave of his hand, looking relaxed and a little dull. O'Brian was not fooled in the slightest. The general was chairman of CEUS, an outgrowth of ICIC—Commission for Exploration and Utilization of Space of the Permanent Interdepartmental Commission on Interplanetary Communications. This made him top man of all Soviet space activities, responsible only to the Central Committee. A very big man indeed. O'Brian opened his case and took out a thick ream of paper. 'All of the latest orbital data, observed up to an hour ago, calculated for the next three orbits,' he said.

'Very good,' General Bykovsky said, holding out his hand.

'Not very good, but excellent,' Academician Tsander said, coming up behind them. 'We will need them to refine our own orbit.'

He came only as high as the shoulders of the two big military officers—but height was not what counted here. Responsibility was. The booster landings were his responsibility. The papers were his.

He glanced through them as he shuffled away, muttering to himself.

'What do you plan to do with the core body booster?' O'Brian asked, casually. Bykovsky's lips smiled slightly at the question; his narrow Tartar eyes did not.

'Why, land it of course, Colonel. Isn't that what we are here to do?'

'Absolutely, General. But you are surely aware that there have been some troubles with ignition. The more excitable sections of the world press are beginning to kick up a stink about possible impact landings.'

Tsander reappeared, cigarette dangling from his lips, white hair floating behind him. The file of papers under his arm far thicker now. 'Gentlemen, we must talk,' he said. 'Could we use your office, Valery Fyodorovich?'

'Of course,' Bykovsky said, pointing the way, knowing full well what the Academician had in mind. His office was wired and bugged and every word would be recorded for later study. There could be no secret arrangements, or later accusations of secret arrangements of anything discussed there. It was no accident that Tsander had reached his advanced age and high degree without coming to harm.

'Be seated, gentlemen, vodka of course.'

Tsander waved it away with his hand but O'Brian accepted with pleasure. He knew just how much of this white lightning he could drink to keep sharp, and never had a drop more. It was Polish vodka, flavoured with the buffalo grass, the kind he enjoyed.

'*Zdarorvya!*' Bykovsky said and they downed the small glasses which he instantly refilled. 'What is the matter under discussion, Academician?'

'You know perfectly well what it is. Landing that last booster. What I want to know from you, now, is do we do it unilaterally or is Colonel O'Brian to be represented in the discussions?'

Bykovsky sighed inwardly as he downed another vodka, thinking of all the microphones in this room and all of the ears that would be listening to this conversation soon. It was a good thing that he had considered this possible contingency ever since the trouble had begun, and a number of phone calls had resulted finally in a decision from above. He was covered.

'The answer is obvious,' he said. (Hours of continuous phoning—obvious!) 'Of course this is a joint project in every way. The orbital figures the Colonel has brought will be invaluable. But naturally he has no responsibility in the actual landing of the booster. Is that satisfactory?'

That way they can have their cake and eat it too, O'Brian thought, sipping the next vodka and showing no expression at all. If the landing is faultless—then they did it alone. If there's trouble the responsibility is shared and they can blame the US figures for the trouble if need be. The Soviet mind. It made Pentagon politics look like cat's cradle. Finally, he nodded his head.

'Then it is decided,' Tsander said with finality. 'Here is our problem. Earlier attempts to obtain ignition on the core body were not successful. It appears that engine three is in difficulty and it has been isolated. Engine one has, we hope, also been isolated to obtain balanced thrust with the two remaining, opposed engines. Yet these would not fire at all.'

'What about the attitude engines?' O'Brian asked.

'They have not been tested yet, nor will they be until decision has been reached as to how we are to proceed. A big concern is also the remaining fuel in the booster. It is approximately twenty-four per cent of total capacity.'

'That would be—how much?' Bykovsky asked.

O'Brian had been tapping quickly on his calculator. 'About six hundred thousand kilos,' he said. 'Hydrogen and oxygen. The most explosive chemical combination that can be used for fuel.'

'I'm aware of that,' Bykovsky said, tonelessly. 'Please go on, Tsander.'

'I said the fuel was a big concern, but not one that should worry us unduly. A good percentage will be used in the landing and my people assure me that the balance represents no threat. It will boil off harmlessly after landing. If we can fire the engines and bring the booster in under control. Please take note of that *if*. We must be prepared for the fact that we may not be able to fire the engines under precise control.'

O'Brian nodded. 'Yes, you may be asking a lot of a control system that has failed twice and now appears to be inoperative?' O'Brian said.

'Perhaps. But we have programmed around the earlier difficulty and should have direct digital control of the firing now. You must realize that our only other choice is to do nothing so that in a few hours the orbit will terminate and the booster will be destroyed.'

'Will it?' O'Brian asked, quietly.

'Ah, yes, Colonel,' Tsander said, blinking at him through deceptively mild eyes. 'You are of course referring to the press reports. Rubbish written by people with no knowledge of physics or orbits or science at all. This booster would be incapable of supporting its own weight if it were not pressurized. It is a tin can with the thinnest of walls—that now contains a good deal of high explosive as you pointed out. It would burn nicely in the atmosphere, quite spectacularly I assure you. But it is also a very expensive machine and the heart of the Prometheus Programme is our ability to re-use the boosters. Without this capacity we would never succeed. We would also like to examine the engines and circuitry to discover what the difficulties were, so they will not be repeated.'

'All good reasons,' O'Brian said, nodding. 'But I also bet you would not like to be responsible for blowing a great big hole in the landscape somewhere and maybe taking some citizens out at the same time.'

Tsander finished lighting a fresh cigarette and nodded benevolently. 'Spoken in your straightforward American way. Yes, that is the crux of the matter. Wouldn't you agree, General?'

'Of course,' Bykovsky said. He paced the floor like a caged bear, hands behind his back, thinking hard. 'It comes down then to two possible courses of action. We do nothing and watch the booster burn up, with the very remote possibility that there might be an impact afterwards. Or we attempt ignition and bring it down under control. Isn't there a third possibility—that if we do have ignition we just send the thing into a higher orbit for future consideration?'

'Possible, but self-defeating. If we do that we admit some possibility of danger, admit as well that we cannot control our own machines and shoot them out into space when they give us trouble.'

'Things that we do not want to admit, Academician. Therefore we really have only two choices. Do nothing and watch it burn. Do something and perhaps bring it back intact. Or, if we fail, watch it burn in any case.'

'My thoughts exactly, General,' Tsander said. 'Inaction destroys the booster. Action may also destroy it—or it may be brought back for a soft landing which would be invaluable.'

'Then the answer seems obvious, wouldn't you say so, Colonel?' the General turned to face O'Brian, his head tilted slightly as though waiting expectantly for an answer.

'I would be tempted to agree,' O'Brian said, slowly. 'Either way the booster burns up, though one way may get it back. I cannot advise you, since obviously I am just an observer here, but you seem to have a decision on your hands.'

Tsander's eyes opened wide as he considered O'Brian's comments. 'I love the unqualified qualification of your un-qualified remarks,' he said dryly. 'If you leave the military you have endless possibilities in politics, Colonel.'

O'Brian made a slight bow and smiled. Then it was all seriousness again.

'Time is running out, General,' Tsander said. 'Do we have a decision I can act on?'

'It seems to me that the decision has been forced upon us. We must do what we can do to bring the booster down intact. Begin retrieval programme.'

There was little to be added. Tsander looked on while the others downed a last vodka, then they returned to the Ground Command Control Centre. O'Brian had an office here, specially constructed for his liaison work. It was in one corner, glassed in, with readouts from most of the consoles that were grouped outside. He had a staff of six, all sergeants, and one of them was on duty here at all times. Discipline was very loose and Sergeant Silverstein just gave him a thumbs-up when he entered—and instantly typed the fact of his presence into the teletype at which he sat. It chattered back in return.

'They have been eagerly awaiting your presence, Colonel,' Silverstein said. 'Washington and Houston want to know soonest status Soviet opinion re orbital soft landing capacity core body booster.'

'You mean they want to know what's going to happen to the damn thing?'

'That's about the size of it.'

'Report that attempt is now being made for complete soft landing retrieval through orbital accelerating and braking. Details follow.'

'Roger.'

The teletype hammered again while O'Brian plugged into the communication circuits. The computer outside was in direct contact with the smaller computer aboard the booster, asking questions and getting answers. The attitude of the booster was most important; which way the nose was pointing, up or down, at the stars or at the Earth was the first consideration. Since the faulted staging from Prometheus the core body had turned and was no longer in the correct attitude for acceleration into a new orbit. The manœuvring rockets would have to be fired to adjust the attitude. This would be the first test of their ability to control the great rocket, hurtling along in orbit eighty-five miles above their heads.

'Begin programme,' Academician Tsander said calmly, when everything possible had been done.

'Rolling.'

It took some minutes for all of the data to be correlated and when it had been there was jubilation in the high chamber.

'The Russkies seem happy, Colonel,' Silverstein said.

'They're halfway home, Sergeant, you can report that orbital manœuvre appears to be successful. Booster in correct attitude for firing of main rockets. *If* they fire—and don't send that last.'

'Gotcha, sir.'

This was the big burn and almost two hours passed before the programme and responses appeared to be satisfactory. The faulty engine and its opposed engine should be shut down now. The original failure should have been bypassed. The fault that had prevented firing from Prometheus should have been corrected. It should fire correctly.

There are an awful lot of *shoulds* here, O'Brian thought and was very glad indeed that this was not his decision. He poured coffee from the thermos and watched the countdown clock as it was set in motion. Here it goes, he thought, here it goes.

The count reached zero and the radio signal flashed out to the waiting receiver in the booster above.

Unseen switches were thrown, the report of the monitors sent back instantly.

'We have ignition!'

There was controlled jubilation. A big success, for they had started the engines when the Prometheus team could not. So much for American engineering. These were Soviet boosters and they took well to Soviet control.

Then a needle snapped over, then another. The computer readout chattered and columns of figures appeared on the blank pages.

'There is trouble.'

'Firing has become erratic.'

'Shut down!'

'Firing continues. Firing cannot be terminated.'

O'Brian spun about and shouted to Silverstein.

'Top priority. Ignition trouble on booster. Erratic firing. It appears to be out of control. More follows.'

'Is this bad, sir?' Silverstein asked, his fingers busy on the keys while he spoke.

'It's not very good, that's for certain. Just how bad it is we're going to find out very soon.'

## 22

*GET 07:20—Cottenham New Town*

WHAT COULD SHE DO, oh-h, what could she do, Irene wondered despairingly. Yesterday evening Henry had settled himself at the kitchen table and written to the boarding house in Blackpool where they had stayed the last two summers. His holiday dates for the coming year had just been fixed and he was writing well in advance to reserve the same rooms again. He had given her the letter to post but it still sat on the mantelpiece resting against the china Blackpool Tower, fond memory of the city it was addressed to.

But dare she post it? Just this morning, running short of money for the Sunday joint, she had taken the last penny out of the Post Office account. The last—she couldn't believe it. But it was all gone, every bit of it. Instead of the pounds and pounds that should have been there for the

Christmas presents and next summer holiday there was nothing at all. Henry would find out, he had to find out sooner or later, and what would she do then?

Seizing her apron she pressed it to her face and sobbed, rocking back and forth in quiet agony. What could she do, what could she do?

Judy and May did not know of their mother's worries. If they had they might have cared, but not for long. Their lives contained far simpler problems: getting good enough marks in school without working too hard, getting new clothes, new shoes, things that were directly related to their new, sudden overwhelming interest in boys—creatures considered as filthy pigs best avoided until a few short months ago.

Henry Lewis's body was tense, taut, his toes against the hockey, his right arm raised, his left eye half-closed. With grim intensity, backed by years of practice and experience, he sighted along the steel point, drew his arm back—and let the dart fly.

Bloody hell! A fraction outside the double seven that would have won the game.

'Well played, Henry!'

'At least you missed t'lav door.'

He took a long swig from his pint of mild and said nothing, outwardly unmoved by the comments. He wasn't shaken, just annoyed. Should have been in. But he would have another chance, Alf wouldn't be able to go out yet. The glass ran dry and he took it to the bar for a refill. George was polishing a glass and keeping an eye on the telly at the same time. Henry pushed the empty pint over to him.

'Rooshins got trouble with that rocket, announcer said.' George pumped in a bubbling stream, then topped it with the whitest of collars.

'Waste of money if you ask me.'

Alf had missed so he would have his chance after all. Do it this time. Henry turned back to the game, determination in his step.

'Could be dangerous, that's what paper said.'

137

'Nawt to do with us, nawt at all,' Henry said, putting the glass on the table and turning to do battle.

For Giles Tanner the warm evening held no attractions. He had been up since four that morning and he was bone weary. Running the farm was tiring enough at any time, but this summer it was exhausting. The days were too long, there was too much to do. Once the rains had stopped and the corn had dried he had to get it in. And his son down with the flu as well, he couldn't blame him for that, though it couldn't have come at a worse time. A whack of the stick brought the erring cow back to the path, behind the others towards the barn. Here he was doing the milking that Will should have done long since. He had to break off the reaping and do two men's work, and even with the milking machines it was a labour. Then afterwards back to the field and the waiting tractor and the reaping. It was a bastard, it really was a bastard. The stick lashed out again, with no reason this time, and the cow jumped forward with a mournful moo.

Giles looked up before he followed them into the barn. A quiet evening, the sky was clear, there didn't seem to be any rain in it. Thank God for that, at least he could get the corn in. The first star twinkled low on the western horizon. That late already. He grunted and went into the barn, closing the door behind him.

Andrew saw the star and looked at his watch. Time to go. He didn't want to get to the plant early and wait outside the entrance, nor did he want to keep Sir Richard waiting. He drained the last drops of whisky and sighed happily. Straight malt, the very best. Then he wiped the decanter and put it away. The metal cup went into the glove compartment and, with a single turnover, the engine caught instantly. A wonderful beast the Rolls. He engaged gear and rolled down the hill towards the plant. It was a dull life but a happy one.

Sir Richard turned off the recorder and threw the un-answered letters back into the basket. They could wait until tomorrow. He yawned and stretched, then pulled up his tie and buttoned his collar. Only after he had slipped his jacket on and had started towards the door did a little needle of doubt pierce him. Did he really have to take his briefcase home every night? Reason tonight anyway. He hadn't looked at the new estimates on their bulk chemical and they came up at the eleven o'clock meeting tomorrow morning.

He grabbed the bag, turned off the light and went to the front entrance. The night watchman, bent over his desk at the night book, stood up when he came by.

'I'll just unlock the door, Sir Richard. Lovely evening, sir.'

'The weather's been good lately, hasn't it? Good-night.'

The car was waiting and Andrew was holding the door open. It was indeed a lovely evening and he stopped a moment to savour it, looking up at the last sunset colours in the sky.


The last booster was alone. Earth was far below, the men who had built it were distant—but the men who wished to control it still had contact. They had been talking to it for hours, their invisible messages picked up by the loops and lattices of the aerials. Fed into the solid state circuits of the computer, the unliving brain of this creature in space. This brain had communicated with the greater computer brain on earth and had answered questions in exhaustive detail. And finally had received orders. The orders were simple and easy to obey. Small jets of compressed gas had puffed out from their nozzles on the metal flank, had rotated the great mass while it sped along in orbit. Moved and stopped it when the computers and their masters were satisfied.

Now it waited the final order. The signal that would begin the final operation.

It came. A coded burst of radio waves. Picked up by the

aerials, relayed through the communication circuits to the computer that issued its commands. Electric currents moved through wires and relays were thrown, switches clicked over, valves opened. Pumps whirled up to speed and hurled the hydrogen fuel through the orifices into the motors, where it met the oxygen that it needed to burn. Ignition. A spark —and the flame burst out in a tongue of fire hundreds of yards long.

One engine stuttered, of the two that were firing. The flame went off, came on again, stopped a second time, clouds of unburnt particles gushing forth. The other motor roared on for some seconds before the first one started again, firing now with its full-throated flame to match its companion. Pushing evenly together to raise the acceleration, the speed, higher and higher.

But they were not supposed to be firing now. A short burn had been programmed to start the core body in orbit downwards towards the empty Russian steppes where the engines could be fired one last time to slow it and bring it down for a soft landing.

This was not going to happen. The continuous firing brought the rocket into the atmosphere sooner, faster, the acceleration climbing until the engines stuttered and were silent, out of fuel.

Within seconds the force of the atmosphere struck it and heated it, the molecules of air impacted by the metal rushing downwards at five miles a second. The fittings on its end, the jacks and arms, glowed red, then white, then were torn away in droplets of molten metal. The pressure was uneven and the great rocket wobbled, was buffeted by the thin atmosphere, began to turn.

It had been designed that way, to be stable nose up upon take-off, stern down for landing. With ponderous ease it turned end for end so that the great plug nozzle of the engines came first. This was made of ablative material and intended to resist the heat of re-entry. But not this speed, not this heat. It glowed hotter and hotter, then began to break away in burning fragments. Short moments later the entire structure of the rocket began to disintegrate.

Too late. It was going too fast. The incandescent mass of fire and metal punched a hole through the atmosphere, through the clouds.

Towards the Earth, towards the growing, expanding landscape below.

A last look at the evening sky for Sir Richard, a last breath of the evening air. The first stars on the horizon, a star above, almost directly above, a shooting star perhaps.

Not a star, a light, a flame, one moment a point, then a disc, then an unbelievable flame-shedding spear pointed directly at him, dropping to impale him.

For an instant his horrified face was bathed by the red glow, the grounds, the building, all illuminated as by the light of a terrible red dawn.

Then it struck.

Six hundred tons of rocket struck the earth at five miles a second and turned this frightful speed into energy, heat energy that exploded outward with the force of an atomic bomb. One moment the plant, the towering flats of Cottenham New Town, the Library Gardens, the shops, the pubs, were standing there. The next instant they were not.

Buildings, bricks, bodies, trees, furniture, cars, everything was destroyed in a fraction of a second, vaporized in the heat, torn apart and wiped from existence. Half the town and all the factory went in the first explosion. The rest followed so closely behind that there was no time, no warning. Perhaps some were momentarily aware of the incredible sound of impact and the light that followed; perhaps a few knew that something impossible had happened and had the beginning of a burst of fear that was destroyed before it could be formed.

After the explosion came the shock wave. The air, compressed far beyond its capacity to absorb more energy passed on its tremendous charge an instant later, an expanding canopy of death that radiated in all directions. It passed through a flight of birds a mile away and, unmarked, they all fell dead from the sky.

On the ground it was a rolling barrage of invisible guns that lifted up the ground, the trees and hedges, the plants and animals and buildings and obliterated them, pulverized them as it passed. It ran over the Tanner farm and mixed man, cow, milk, machine into a hideous jumble, exploded the house of Giles's wife and son the same instant.

The dart was never thrown, the game never finished, the holiday plans left unfulfilled. Irene would have to worry no more about her Post Office account. There would certainly be no Blackpool this year.

There would be no life, no future, no existence for twenty thousand nine hundred and thirty-one men, women and children. Where this town and all its bustling life had been there was now only a seared wasteland, a desert of death in England's green countryside, decently concealed for the moment beneath the shroud of dust and smoke that hid the horror below.

# 23

## GET 07:52

PRESIDENT BANDIN was in the toilet, in his own private toilet when someone pounded on the door. He burst out seconds later, holding the towel, his hands still wet, fire in his eye. Bannerman was standing there, white faced, almost trembling. This in itself was enough to stop Bandin, who never in his life had expected to see that leathery skin drained of blood, the man suddenly as old as his years, older. The words came quickly.

'My God,' was all that Bandin could say, in a hoarse whisper, not even knowing that he spoke, slumped against the open bathroom door with the forgotten towel clutched in his hand.

'My God, oh my God. . . .'

\*　　　\*　　　\*

It took seconds, then minutes, then almost an hour to find out what had happened in any detail. Colonel O'Brian, the silent witness at Ground Command Control, in Kapustin Yar, knew that something had gone completely wrong at the precise moment the controllers did. He had the same read-out before him, the same information. His fist tensed, tighter and tighter, as he saw the first erratic firing, then the continuous firing—then the change in orbit. The new orbit could not be measured quickly or easily and he was aware of the growing panic, hysteria in the voices calling to each other and he was to verify this in many secret interrogations in the coming months. But right now all he could do was watch.

As the figures flowed in, the computer worked out an orbit. An unbelievable one. Slowly the voices died away and all sound ceased as the orbit was plotted on the screen. Changing, turning, downward, accelerating. With their mind's eye they could see the danger growing unbelievably before them, watch enacted out minutes after the tragedy the last flight of the core booster of Prometheus One. Watch until the utterly incomprehensible moment when the orbit, the path of the booster in space, ended.

The computer, which had been printing out the rows of figures, came to the end of its information and fell silent. The chattering of the printer stopped at the same moment. The silence was absolute.

'Send this!' O'Brian ordered, and was surprised at the roughness in his voice. Silverstein looked up at him, taken unaware, for he did not know one word of Russian and even less of space technology, and had not the slightest idea of what had gone wrong. 'Top priority, and I mean top. For the President. Core booster malfunction. Appears to have impacted the earth. Site unknown.' He scrabbled in the papers before him and made some quick calculations. 'First estimate would be area fifty-two degrees north latitude, zero degrees longitude.'

'Where is that, Colonel? Where is it?'

The sergeant was beginning to have some realization of what was happening.

'Zero longitude? Greenwich, England . . .'

They looked at each other in mutually shared horror. They both knew England well. Knew how crowded with people that island was. Silverstein slowly tapped out the information that O'Brian gave him, but knew this was only the outline of the tragedy. When there was nothing more to report he typed a query for return information soonest on point of impact.

The orbit analysis from Kapustin Yar was sent directly to the White House, followed by Houston's own orbit from their tracking stations. Then Houston ran their own figures and the Russian ones through the computer once more and came up with an estimated point of impact, theoretically correct to within a quarter of a mile. Instead of bringing the raw data to the President the Information Officer in the White House made a xerox of the southern half of England and drew a red circle with a felt tip pen on the site. He then put the map and the final figures in a leather attaché case and ran for the elevator. Because he was well known, plus the fact that rumours of what had happened were already circulating, the guards at the conference room door opened it as he approached. Almost the entire cabinet was there, hastily summoned, and every eye was on him when he entered. The President held out his hand and the officer gave him the papers. Bandin looked at them in silence until the door had closed, then raised his head slowly. There was a faint tremor in his hands.

'It looks from here, I can't really tell, as though the rocket came down in the countryside. There's a lot of countryside in England.' His voice was hollow, his words unconvincing even to himself. General Bannerman reached for the map and he passed it over in silence. Forgetting that he had never worn them at a public meeting before, Bannerman took the gold-rimmed pince-nez reading glasses from his breast pocket and put them on.

'Countryside, yes,' he said. 'But the motorway cuts right through here. It's heavily travelled, I know. And there is one name here, not easy to read in the xerox. Looks like Gottenham New Town.'

'Cottenham New Town,' Dr Schlochter said in his best scholastic voice. Unlike the others the Secretary of State seemed outwardly unmoved by the developing events. 'One of the more successful British attempts to move light industry out of the cities into areas in need of development. You will remember that I was there at the dedication ceremonies with the Minister of Labour.'

No one remembered or cared. The President turned to Charley Dragoni who sat at the secretarial table, a telephone pressed to his ear. 'Well?' he called out.

'I have your office holding on calls to Whitehall and the Embassy in London, Mr President. They know nothing more than we do, but will report as soon as they do. I'm holding myself here on the scrambler line which has been patched through to 10 Downing Street. The Prime Minister is in conference, taking reports, but he knows you're waiting for his call. I . . . excuse me. Yes?' He listened to the phone for a moment while they all waited in silence. 'Yes, thank you, I'll pass on the information.' He looked up. 'The Prime Minister will be with you in a few moments, sir, as soon as he has finished a call to the Kremlin.'

'Has anyone found out what sort of impact this thing would have?' Dr Schlochter asked. 'Perhaps we are making mountains out of molehills. There are airplane accidents every day and they are forgotten the next.'

Bannerman had the figures scrawled on a piece of paper and his words filled the silence.

'The estimate sent through from GCCC at KY is that approximately twenty per cent of the fuel was unused at the last engine shutdown. That, with the total weight of the vehicle, gives us a total impact mass weight of over a million pounds. Speed is important here. Going at sixty miles an hour that would make a big hole in the ground and nothing more. Houston reckons that, even allowing for reduced speed from atmosphere friction, that must have hit a velocity of over twenty thousand feet per second. Or if you want it on a speedometer, that is just about eighteen thousand miles an hour. About half the explosive power of a tactical atomic bomb.'

'The Prime Minister, Mr President,' Dragoni said. Bandin picked up the phone by his elbow.

'Yes, I'm holding. Yes. Mr Prime Minister, President Bandin here. I am shocked, as I am sure you are, at this terrible accident. All of us here are hoping, praying, that there has been no loss of life, minimal loss of life. Yes, I'm sorry. There has been *what*? . . . Yes, I understand. Good God, this is terrible. I have no words, no, none. . . . Whatever aid, anything we can do. . . . Of course I do understand. Though of course we are not responsible for this terrible tragedy we do feel responsible in that it is a joint project, although this rocket was Soviet, and we wish to do everything in our power in this hour of need. Yes, thank you, good-bye.'

Bandin put the receiver gently down and looked around at the silent men.

'That does it,' he finally said. 'The goddamned rocket did hit that town, that Cottenham place you were talking about. Took it out just like it had been aimed at. No exact figures yet of course but the PM says the first estimates are at least twenty-one thousand dead. . . .'

'Those are just the people who were in the place,' Bandin continued. 'There are roads hit, the motorway, accident reports still coming in. Fires too. He's called a national alert, mobilized troops, ambulances, fire departments, everything he can get.'

'We could offer the assistance of our armed forces stationed there to aid in the relief work,' Schlochter said.

'No,' Dillwater said with great firmness. 'I would advise issuing orders for all American personnel to be restricted to their bases. The British have enough manpower to handle this themselves. Soviet rocket or no we're in this up to our necks. I don't think our people are going to be very popular over there for a while.'

'I second that,' Bannerman said. 'If you agree, Mr President, I will issue an order to that effect right now.'

'Yes, you're probably right considering the circumstances.' Bannerman picked up his phone. 'But what else can we do? There must be something.' Bandin looked around at the men in his cabinet but no answers were forthcoming. 'What effect is this going to have upon the Prometheus Project?' he asked.

'It should not affect it in any way,' Dillwater answered. 'We have back-up boosters to replace the one destroyed. The project can go ahead. But there can be no question about not having a second disaster like this.'

'I should hope not. Maybe we can ride out this one, but two strikes and we're out. And I don't have to tell you how much is riding on this project. National prestige, one in the eye for the Arabs—and the next election. If Prometheus goes down the drain, and the public doesn't see any return for the money spent so far, you are going to see one of them from *that* party sitting in this chair next year. I want to talk to Polyarni as soon as it can be arranged. And what *is* happening with Prometheus? Have we forgotten all about them in this brouhaha?'

'No, Mr President,' Dillwater said. 'The engine is now being prepared for ignition and will soon be firing. You will be informed as soon as this happens. Final orbit will not be reached for at least forty-eight hours after that. Then the generator assembly will begin.'

'It better. Set up a call to Polyarni. I want to find out what the Kremlin thinks about this. This is one time when we have got to stick together.'

# 24

*GET 12:06*

THE NUCLEAR ENGINE countdown was almost finished when word of the disaster reached Prometheus, relayed from Mission Control. Flax had not mentioned the fate of the core booster until all the facts were in, until the complete extent of the catastrophe was known. Then he had talked to Nadya, telling her what had happened in exact detail.

She had called Patrick and Ely back from the nuclear engine control compartment so she could speak to them in person at the same time. When Major Gagarin, the first man ever to fly in space, had been in a plane crash his voice had been like hers. His engine had failed but he had stayed with his plane and flown it into the ground in order to miss the school and the houses below. His voice was calm and emotionless up until the instant of the crash. Nadya had been trained the same way.

They did not want to believe it, they had to believe it, but it still seemed so impossible.

'It couldn't have happened,' Ely said. 'It just couldn't.'

'It did,' Patrick said, his quiet words cutting through the shocked silence. 'It happened. But there's nothing we can do about it. It is just a fact we are going to have to live with. I don't know who's to blame—if anyone *is* to blame. It won't be easy but we are just going to have to put it out of our minds while we get on with the work here. Nadya, stay with the radio and give us reports of any developments. Ely and I are going to start the engine.' His eyes went to the GET readout and the others looked as well. '12:42. We're running out of time. We've less than twelve hours to build up speed and get out of this rotten orbit. If we don't the same thing could happen to us. And we would make a far bigger hole when we hit.'

In silence he pushed into the tube and back to the engine compartment, with Ely right behind him.

'I'll contact Mission Control,' Nadya said, shoving off from the couch towards the opening to the flight cabin. Her eyes were red, from fatigue not from tears, and her motions were slow.

'You should take a rest,' Coretta said. 'Speaking as your doctor.'

'I know, thank you, but not right now. There is too much to do right now. It is checklist time for the air scrubbers to be examined. The fuel cells as well.'

'Can I help?'

'No. This is a particular job that either I or Patrick must do.' Then she was gone.

'It is always that way,' Gregor said. 'Nothing for us to do—just wait. You are a physician, you have your work, but I am only a fifth wheel. I do nothing.' His face had sunk back into Slavic melancholy.

'You get gloomy too quickly,' Coretta said, moving over to him. 'This trip has not been one of joy unrelieved, admittedly, but it's not that bad. Enjoy being a passenger while it lasts. When we get into orbit you're the only person who counts, the one this whole trip is about. The pilots are just cab drivers, and I'm here to make sure you don't get sniffles. As I remember this thing is called the Prometheus Project and it's supposed to put some kind of solar generator in orbit. And, with the Colonel gone, it looks to me like you're the only one who can do that.'

He wrung his large hands. 'It will be difficult without Vladimir,' he said.

'Gregor, you are just going to have to snap out of this.' She was totally professional now. Opening the medical cabinet she took out a small tube of pills. On her way back to the couch she grabbed up a squeeze bottle of water as well.

'Take these,' she said, holding out two white capsules. 'Wash them down with water, and I'll give you two more in six hours.'

'What are they?' he asked, suspiciously.

'The pharmaceutical industry's answer to the rigours of the age of technology. Tranks. Tranquillizers. They file the thin edge of hysteria off life.'

'I do not take medicines, thank you. They are not necessary.'

'Don't be afraid of these pills, Gregor. They are to help, not hurt.' She saw the signs of strain around his eyes and lips. 'I feel in the need of a little tension-relieving myself.' She put the pills in her mouth, showed them to him on her tongue, then swallowed them with a mouthful of water. And took two more from the vial.

'Your turn now. No arguments.'

This time he took them without protest and she sighed with relief.

Ely, in the nuclear engine control station below, felt no relief at all. In fact, even in the controlled environment of the ship he was sweating. From tension, not from physical effort. The checkout was almost done, the preparations for starting up the nuclear engines almost finished.

'Ready to go,' he said.

'Begin,' Patrick said. 'Is there anything I can do to help?'

'Negative. We're in the green so far. This engine is complex—but theoretically simple. The uranium dust is trapped in a vortex of neon inside the light bulbs. The quartz tubes with this mix are surrounded by hydrogen, mixed with some tungsten so it won't be too transparent to the heat. Hydrogen moderates the U-235 plasma which heats up to twenty-three thousand degrees Kelvin which really warms up the rest of the hydrogen and sends it blasting out of the reaction chamber. So we move to the last step in the start-up, power to the turbo-pumps in the secondary hydrogen closed loop. . . .'

His voice cut off suddenly as a buzzer sounded and red lights appeared on the board before him. He threw switches quickly.

'Is that normal?' Patrick asked.

'No, that is not normal,' he answered, lips peeled back from his teeth in a most unhumorous grin. 'We have had shutdown. Something is wrong.'

Their eyes moved to the GET clock at the same time.

13.03.

Now it was less than eleven hours before they were due to run out of room in space and have first contact with the sea of atmosphere waiting below.

'How wrong? What you you mean?' Patrick asked.

'I don't know yet.' Ely had programmed the computer to display an eight-colour diagram of the relevant circuits and controls and was tracking through it. 'There are five engines out there, but they function as a single unit and are far more interconnected than the chemical engines. We're having a malfunction in one of them. That's what I am trying to track down now. Let me alone, will you Patrick, I have to do this alone.'

'Right. I'll be in the flight cabin. Plug into the intercom when you need me.'

Patrick kicked off up into the lower compartment. He saw that Gregor was lying face down on his couch, really floating a few inches to it and held in place by the clips. Patrick started to speak but Coretta raised her finger to her lips and shushed him, then waved him to the far side of the compartment, went to join him.

'Gregor is sleeping,' she said in a whisper. 'I don't want him disturbed. Emotionally he's not in very good condition. The fatigue and strain have been almost too much for him to handle. I gave him some sleeping pills, told him they were tranks. Had to take two myself to con him into it, but I managed to spit them out without swallowing them.'

'How bad is he?' Patrick asked, looking at the sleeping figure.

'I can't say. Back home I would give you a guess, but this is different. He must have been stable enough or the Soviets wouldn't have him on this project.'

'Don't bet on that. The report I saw said that he was the only microwave transmission authority fit enough to go on this flight. I have a feeling he was drafted.'

'If that's true it would explain a lot. He doesn't seem to have the right temperament or the right constitution for this kind of work. But he's going to be needed when we're in orbit. With the Colonel dead, Gregor is now our only authority on getting the generator working. So if I can get him to sleep, to relax now, he should be functional when we need him. Once he's doing that I don't think there'll be any problems.'

'Thanks, Coretta. You're right. Let me know if you need any help. . . .'

'He doesn't like to take pills.'

'He can be ordered to. I'll take care of that.'

Patrick started for the flight cabin but Coretta caught his sleeve and pulled him back.

'Just a minute. You're under doctor's orders too.'

'Pills?' he asked, looking grim.

'Food—and drink. And bring some up for Nadya.'

'Of course, thanks. Hunger and thirst strike like lightning as soon as I think of it.'

He took the plastic meal bags and squeeze bottles from the locker before he went to join Nadya. He strapped down next to her and passed over her ration.

'Doctor's orders. Chow time,' he said.

'Thank you, I am thirsty.'

'Eat too.'

Patrick forced himself to finish most of the pulverized beef stew before calling Mission Control.

'A little engine trouble,' he told Nadya as he sent out the call.

'No! Not more, it cannot be.' She was horrified, her hands clasped against her breasts.

'I'm sorry,' he said, reaching out to take her hands in his. Her skin was cold. 'I hope it's something small. Ely is checking it out now. . . .'

*'Prometheus, Mission Control here.'*

'Hello, Flax, Patrick here. I am reporting an apparent malfunction with the fission engines. Checklist fine, but barrage of red lights when we tried to fire it up.'

There was the slightest delay before Flax spoke again. Fatigue and tension were just as bad on the ground. *'Do you know the extent of the malfunction, Prometheus?'*

'Negative. Dr Bron is on that now. Are the fission engine team standing by in case we need them?'

*'Absolutely, all here. They want to know if you will transfer engine housekeeping data dump?'*

'Roger. I'll set it up.'

All the steps Ely had followed in starting up the nuclear engine had been recorded by the ship's computer. Patrick used his commander's controls to retrieve the information. When he was satisfied he pressed the transmit button and all the details were radioed at high speed back to Mission Control on earth. While he was doing this he was aware of the intercom bleeping and Nadya taking a call. She tapped his arm.

'Yes,' he said, turning towards her.

'It was Ely. He thinks he knows what has happened. I

152

told him you were on to Mission Control so he's on his way up here.' Patrick nodded and turned on his microphone again.

'Mission Control, I have more information on the malfunction. Dr Bron will report shortly. He appears to have located the source of the malfunction.'

'You better believe I have,' Ely said, coming in. He saw the squeeze bottle of water in Nadya's hand and realized suddenly how dry his mouth was, how thirsty he had become without knowing it. 'Can I have a swig of that? Thanks.' He drained half the bottle before sighing and passing it back.

'It's not good, Patrick, not good at all. I'll check with the team in Mission Control and they can run it through their mockup, but I'm pretty sure about what has happened. You know that the heart of these nuclear engines are heavy quartz tubes—which is why they are called light bulb reactors. That quartz is good stuff and the way the engine is set up the tubes are immune to thermal shock. But the pogoing and the abortive separation of the core booster must have done something. . . .'

'Physical shock?'

'Exactly. Quartz is just a fancy kind of glass. Something must have bashed around back there during separation because I think one of the tubes is broken.'

'But—can you replace it?'

Ely laughed, very bitterly. 'Replace it? Even if I had a spare it would be impossible in space. That tube is broken and it is going to stay broken. Those engines will just not run.'

'Something can be done. Something *must* be done,' Patrick insisted.

'Like what?'

'Like we take a look at the motors and see just what happened, send a complete report back to Mission Control and have them see what can be worked out.'

'You're an optimistic bastard, you know that, Patrick.' After the intensity of his work something seemed to have gone out of Ely. He was hunched, seemed smaller.

'No, I'm not. Just doing the job I was trained for. There are programmes that cover a lot of *what ifs*. Now we've got a problem here, but we need more data on it. You're going to space walk and assess the damage. That's what we need to know next. There's only one undamaged umbilical left. Use it. Let's suit up.'

'Whoa, not so fast. I've never space walked before, and I certainly hadn't planned to do it alone for the first time. You have the experience and could save a lot of time. . . .'

'I'm not an atomic physicist. You are. You helped design the motor, as you've often told us, so you should know what's wrong just by looking at it.'

He started towards the suit locker, then turned back as a sudden thought struck him. 'You're not afraid of going out there, are you?'

Ely smiled. 'Yes, if you want to know, I'm frightened shit-less of being out there on the end of a rubber tube and a couple of wires. I'm frightened of this whole trip and every-thing about it. But I'm here anyway because I wouldn't miss it for the world. So let's get suited up before I change my mind.'

Patrick wasn't sure what to say. 'I'm sorry I said that. Please understand, it wasn't personal. . . .'

'It was personal as hell, my boy, but all is forgiven. This hasn't been much of a pleasure cruise, has it? And you've been awake and working for what? Two days now?' He glanced up at the GET clock. '13:57 and still counting. And the estimate was that we would run out of space at twenty-four hundred. Ten hours left. Why doesn't someone ask Mission Control if they've any revisions on that original estimate? It would be nice to know.'

'Nadya, as soon as we're all suited up, talk to them about that. Tell them Dr Bron is going to look at the motors and they want to listen and record everything he says, then get to work on the information as soon as it comes in. Our time is running out.'

There was not a second to be wasted now. As soon as the suits were sealed and the flight cabin evacuated, Patrick opened the hatch. His cabin walk-about umbilical stretched

154

far enough to enable him to help Ely through and feed his umbilicals after him.

'Slowly,' he said. 'The one thing you can't do is rush now.'

'Rush!' Ely laughed. 'It's all I can do to move.'

'There are rings all the way along. Clip on to one before you release a handhold.'

'Right. Moving now. Faster than I thought, guess the experience inside the ship in free fall helps. Here's the base of the first motor, trumpet bell looks fine, I'm moving to the next—Christ, there it is!'

'*What?*' Flax's voice sounded loud in Ely's ears. '*We read you well, Dr. Bron, What did you find?*'

'The source of our trouble. I can see what happened now. The pogoing and that aborted separation we had with the core body booster. There was plenty of misaligned thrust then, knocking about. The shroud must have been shifted because it bashed into one of the motors. There are quartz fragments floating out of it and the thrust chamber is all askew and dented. I'm close to it now. Motor four. The others look okay. Going up it now to look into the trumpet. I can see now ... my God ... it's a mess. A real mess. Broken tubes, quartz everywhere ... must have a massive gas leakage.'

Ely looked down at the ravaged interior of the engine, then pulled back slowly and stared at the great globe of the Earth that half filled the sky. It was infinitely more impressive when viewed from space rather than through the port. Big and close, far too close. Mission Control was saying something but he was not listening to their words. Flax's voice broke off when Ely began talking.

'That engine is not going to fire, ever again. Do you read that, Mission Control? Unless you can come up with some way to by-pass it so we can fire the other four engines we've had it. End of mission. End of Prometheus. So get cracking. We need some advice.'

## 25

*GET 13:12*

IT WAS AFTER TWO in the morning and Red Square in
Moscow was deserted; even the line of visitors waiting to
enter Lenin's tomb had vanished for a few hours. The two
armed guards stationed there looked on with little interest
as a large black Moskva limousine turned into the square
and accelerated towards the Kremlin. Cars of this kind
arrived at all hours of the day and night for that destina-
tion. Perhaps a few more tonight than was usual, but of
course there was no indication why. No public announcement of the destruction of Cottenham New Town had
been made on the radio yet nor, for once, had The Voice of
America been in a hurry to carry glum news to the Russian
people.

Engineer Glushko led the way and easily penetrated the
outer circle of functionaries and guards. Both he and
Academician Moshkin who trailed after him had been here
on a number of occasions. Their identification helped because anyone connected with the Prometheus Project certainly had business here tonight. Within these walls everyone knew what had happened. They also knew that Glushko
was senior project engineer and the little professor with
him was also involved, somehow, with the project.

Despite the fact that the two men had no reason to be in
the Kremlin this morning, they progressed quite far before
being brought up short. The inner circle of senior civil
servants owed their seniority to intelligence, ability and
suspicion, in almost equal parts. The greying man behind
the desk, with ash on his lapels and the cigarette in his
mouth trickling smoke into his half-shut eye, resembled all
the other officials the two men had recently seen and bypassed. But this one would not be as easy.

He turned their identification over and over in his hands
as though looking for some fact he had missed the first time
through.

'Of course, *tovarichi*. I appreciate your positions on the

Prometheus Project, it is all detailed here in your papers I assure you. But nowhere can I find the message or the reason that has brought you here today.'

'As I told you,' Glushko said, 'the Academician and I must see Comrade Polyarni at once. It is of the utmost importance.'

'I am sure it is or you would not be here. Such a rush, a few hours ago in Baikonur, a military plane, a car waiting for you at the airport. A rush indeed—but nowhere do I see a reason for this rush. What business brings you here?'

'You know about the . . . affair with the booster rocket?'

The official nodded gravely. 'I do. A tragic accident. All of the country will mourn. Then you come in regard to this?'

'In a way, though not exactly. Look, comrade, I do not like to be misunderstood. Do you think that either I or Academician Moshkin, one of the leading astronomers in the nation, do you think that either of us came here to play silly games?'

'No! Of course not. But without stating your business it would be impossible for me to do anything to aid you. You realize my position, don't you?'

Glushko sighed and straightened up. 'I certainly do. But, as I told you earlier, what I have to say is for the ears of the Premier alone and for no others. Therefore I wish to see your immediate superior and explain the same thing to him.'

'He is in conference, if you wait . . .'

'Eventually, we will see the Premier. He will want to hear what we have to say as soon as possible. Anyone who is responsible for delaying us will not be viewed with favour. Do you understand?'

The civil servant understood, only too well. He had heard this sort of talk, this kind of veiled threat in the past. If they meant what they said why then, yes, he would be in trouble. But if they were bluffing and he aided them he would only be in for a reprimand.

It was a simple decision. He pushed his chair back and stood.

'But I do understand. And I am sure you understand that I want to help you in any way I can. If you will stay here I will see how soon he can see you.'

'Good,' Glushko said, voice firm and carriage erect. He remained that way until the door had closed, then dropped into the nearest chair.

'This is exhausting, Academician, I hope you realize that. If you are not correct we are both going to be in very big trouble.'

'That is not the kind of trouble to worry about at this time. *This* is the trouble,' he said, tapping his worn leather briefcase. 'The facts are correct, they can be checked. It is all here.'

Glushko looked at his watch, then drummed his fingers on his leg.

'In that case,' he said, 'they had better hurry.'

Halfway around the world, in Philadelphia, Pennsylvania, it was still early evening. Not quite dinner time, but late enough. All the offices in the East were closed, the labs shut, the college professors gone home. Professor Weisman sat in his scruffy office watching the shadows grow longer, listening to the ring-ring of an unanswered phone in his ear. Not for the first time either. He carefully put the receiver back, steepled his fingers on the desk before him, and wondered what to do next.

The few people he knew who might have been able to help him had not answered their phones. Or some moronic answering device had beeped at him and told him to record his message. He did not think there was time for that. He was still not sure how to go about passing on the vital information he had, nor was he exactly sure whom he should pass it on to. Of course the people involved with the Prometheus Project would want to know, but he had had only busy signals from both numbers given him by the information operator. He rarely listened to the radio and had no television set, so he did not know of the news story that was just breaking about the disaster in England. He would have been interested to hear it, but it would not affect what he had to do.

Washington, that was it, he would just have to go to Washington. Normally he hated to travel, but always said that getting out of the Fraunhoffer Institute and out of Germany and staying one step ahead of the Nazis all the way across Europe had been enough travelling for a lifetime. Life at the University of Pennsylvania was very easy, very calm, and he preferred it that way. But now his peace would have to be broken for a bit. He would have to go to Washington. Even as he decided this he began carefully placing a thick sheaf of notes into a briefcase as old and disreputable as the one Academician Moshkin was clutching on his knees in the Kremlin at this very moment.

There were footsteps in the corridor outside and the rap of knuckles on the frosted glass of his office door. Weisman did not respond because he was concentrating so he did not hear the sounds. Only when the door swung open did he look up.

A bearded face poked in.

'Say, Sam, isn't that something? Did you hear the broadcast about the town in England?'

'Ahh, Danny, come in, I want to ask you something.'

'You didn't hear, then. One of the boosters from Prometheus took out an entire city, they don't know how many dead, worse than an atom bomb attack. . . .'

'Danny, do you know how to get to Washington, D.C.?'

Danny started to gape, then changed his mind. He had taught in the university long enough to realize that his associates on the staff weren't really fruitcakes, just individualists with different powers of concentration and different interests. Sam Weisman had a world-wide reputation and a Nobel Prize. And he didn't care about blown-up cities nor did he know how to get to Washington, which was maybe all of a hundred miles away.

Danny shrugged and forgot Cottenham New Town for the moment.

'You can drive, you can take the bus, you can take the train.'

'I cannot stand motor vehicles.' Weisman frowned in thought, then took out an old-fashioned clasp purse and looked inside. 'Four dollars, I don't think that will be enough.'

'Not really. What do you want to do in Washington?'

Weisman ignored the question, his mind involved in the logistics of the journey. 'The banks are closed. But you can cash a cheque for me, can't you Danny. Do you think five hundred dollars will be enough?'

'Five bills is more than enough but I don't always carry quite that much on me.' He looked in his wallet. 'You're in luck, I just cashed my pay cheque. I'll give you two hundred bucks, pay me when you get back. Your credit is good.'

Weisman pulled on his jacket. 'Is there more than one train station in Philadelphia?'

'Don't worry, I'll drop you off. You buy a ticket for D.C. and try to get on a Metroliner because the old rolling stock will give your haemorrhoids haemorrhoids inside five miles.'

'Very kind.' He put on his hat. 'Would you know if the Smithsonian Institute is hard to find? I have a friend there.'

'I am going to control myself and not ask you why you are going there in the middle of the night when it is closed. I'm afraid you'd tell me. Grab a hack at Union Station when you get in and tell him Smithsonian. Maybe the night-watchman will know where your friend is. All I can do is wish you good luck.'

Professor Weisman sat calmly, his old briefcase on his lap, as they drove to the station. In Moscow Academician Moshkin was sitting in the same position holding a very similar briefcase. Yet this wasn't the only thing they had in common.

Each was an astronomer with a world-wide reputation.
Each specialized in the study of the sun.

# 26

'HAVE A CIGAR, Cooper,' the Editor said. 'You won't have smoked anything like this in years. A real Havana, claro, the first batch in after the trade treaty with Cuba.'

'Excuse me, sir, I'm sorry, I don't smoke.'

Cooper was too nervous to twitch or even think of nibbling his fingers. He rarely met the Editor of the paper, and certainly had never been in his office before. Here even the City Editor, that tower of strength and vituperation, was subdued and in the background. The Editor opened the liquor cabinet; his fingernails were shining and pink, his hands plump and white, his tailoring immaculate. None of the ink or dirt of the newspaper had rubbed off on him. He held up a cut-glass decanter and smiled showing two rows of perfect white teeth.

'But you'll have a drink of course,' he said. 'Twenty-year-old bonded Canadian, I think you might like it. Water?'

Cooper just nodded at every question, still unsure of himself, not knowing why he was here. To be fired? No, the underlings would take care of tasks like that. Then why?

He took a large sip of the drink and tried not to cough. His throat was on fire; a cherry coke was the strongest thing he normally indulged in.

'Good, isn't it? I knew you would like it.' He glanced at the City Editor. 'Time yet?' he asked.

'A few more minutes, sir.'

'Well, warm it up.' The City Editor waded through the carpet to the TV on its carved mahogany case and turned it on. 'A special broadcast from Great Britain, Cooper. I though you ought to see it.'

'Yes, fine idea, thank you, sir.' He got more of the drink down and blinked through his tears at the familiar face of Vance Cortwright on the screen. Cortwright wore his most sombre expression and when he spoke it was in deep, funereal tones.

'There is neither Moon nor stars in the clouded skies of Britain tonight, as though the very heavens themselves have gone into mourning for the dead. This country has known many disasters in the past with plagues, the Great Fire in London, the trench deaths in the First World War and the bombings in the Second. These people know how to fight and how to survive—and how to die with dignity if they must. But never before have they experienced a disaster to match the one that happened here short hours ago. Reports are still coming in about isolated tragedies, but the central, unbelievable core of the holocaust that struck without warning from the sky is behind me here. The site where Cottenham New Town used to stand. I say used to because there is no other way to describe this.'

The scene changed as he continued to talk and little could be made of it at first, just moving lights and rolling clouds of some kind. It was only when the camera zoomed back from the close-up that a demolished structure of some kind could be distinguished. Spotlights were on it and firemen, wearing breathing apparatus, were working on it, tearing at it, in the midst of clouds of smoke and dust.

'This was a prosperous farm on the outskirts of the town, a solid structure going back hundreds of years. It was destroyed in an instant by the blast, turned into this jumble of broken timber you see. There can be little hope that anyone could have survived this destruction but a search must still be made. No need to search the town itself.''

As the camera moved, the site of Cottenham New Town came into view. Spotlights and Army searchlights illuminated the area. Nothing could be made of it, nothing comprehensible could be seen. There was no connection at all between this vista of blackened, smoking rubble and the city of buildings, homes and people that had existed there. There were still fires; the smoke clouds were lit from below as from an opening to hell. Even Cortwright's modulated voice broke at the sight.

'Perhaps all that might be said good about this . . . this inconceivable disaster is that they had no warning, no premonition, no pain. It was over in an instant. Full details are not in on the rocket booster that struck here, but it was obviously moving at many times the speed of sound. The V2 rockets of the Second World War, of which this booster was a descendant, moved faster than sound and the residents of London only knew of their arrival when the explosion occurred. The same is true here. One second this was a living city, the next a burning hell. Fire brigades and hundreds of policemen have converged on this site from all directions. Troops are on their way. The roads are sealed off so that rescue workers can get through. Yet, tragically, there is very little to rescue. Except on the periphery, the outer edges of the shock wave that radiated out from the explosion. Here there are car accidents, one multiple pile-up involving over seventy vehicles on the motorway. Buildings have collapsed, mostly isolated farmhouses and homes, and people in the street have been struck down. We'll have a report from the hospitals in a moment, but first this message . . ."

The Editor switched the set off before the commercial came on. He was smiling, satisfied, like a cat after a large dish of cream. He raised his glass.

'Here's to you, Cooper,' he said. 'You made this story, saw what was coming before anyone else did, and we broke it first and we're now breaking circulation records. I have three reporters and five cameramen on the way there now in a chartered jet, and we're going to give this the kind of coverage that has never been seen before. And we're not forgetting you, Cooper. There will be twenty dollars more in your pay envelope and a bonus as well. . . .'

'Oh, thank you, sir! Thank you so much.'

'Not at all. Only fair. But you want to earn this raise, don't you, Cooper? Yes, I see you do. No, don't bother about that, a little spill. The City Editor will wipe it up. I want you to think about bigger things. I want you to go out of here and write the follow-up story that will kick our circulation into a world-busting figure!'

'What follow-up, sir?' Cooper gaped.

'You're kidding, of course. The goddamn rest of the rocket, that's what! What will happen when it comes down, how much worse the disaster will be then. Put in everything, I want it all.'

'B-but, there doesn't seem to be any indication yet that Prometheus will crash. Just a minor difficulty with the engines . . .'

'Don't believe a word of it. They didn't tell us their damn booster was going to blow up half of England so they're not going to tell us what's happening to the rest. I want figures and I want facts. I want the bulldog in the morning not just to have the entire story of the disaster that has happened but all about the one, the bigger one, that's in the making. How many people on that rocket?'

'Six, five I mean, one is dead.'

'The first victim.' He stabbed his finger at the City Editor. 'Biographies on them all, personal stuff. The next in line to die—and who will die with them. You know what to do.'

'I certainly do, sir.'

'Then get on with it. I'll be here all night. Let me have a proof of the front page as soon as it's locked up. I'm writing an editorial, boxed on the front page, thirty column inches. Allow for it.' He finished his whisky and slammed the glass down with a triumphal gesture. 'TV and radio is the big thing, and they said the day of the newspaper was over. They'll find out—and we'll be showing them!'

## 27

*GET 14:21*

IT WAS ALMOST seven-thirty in the evening in Washington. The government offices were empty as well as the streets, and all the workers were home with the air conditioning turned up full. Electricity consumption was at its usual evening high as all the stoves came on, and the television sets. They were all on this night, every TV, almost all tuned to the continuous coverage of the disaster in England. Only one channel, in the middle of an important series game, did not join in the coverage for fear the baseball fans would burn down the station as they had once before when a technical failure had blacked out the last, scoring, inning of a drawn game. But only the real diehards were watching the game. There was more action in England.

In the White House the cabinet meeting still continued. Two and a half hours now and no sign of it ending. Bandin had talked briefly with the Soviet Premier but it had resolved nothing. Polyarni was holding his cards very close to his chest and saying little. He and his advisers were still formulating policy, or rearranging the facts for presentation in the proper order, or looking for ways to make sure their American partners shared in the present Prometheus failure. Until they decided just how to go about it they were being a little hard to talk to.

The American cabinet was considering the same thing, only from the opposite direction.

'We can't leave the Soviets with complete responsibility for this,' Simon Dillwater insisted.

'Why not?' Dr Schlochter asked. 'This is a political matter now, not a technical one, so the State Department has ultimate responsibility. They are our partners, yes, but this disaster is their responsibility and we must be sure that we are not hung with them for the crime. Statecraft, as the great Metternich said, is the art . . .'

'Balls to Metternich,' General Bannerman said, savagely biting at the end of his cigar and spitting the piece on to the floor. 'You drag out your Kraut and I'll drag out mine, and I'll give you a quote every time from Clausewitz that tops your guy. We are just going to forget the diplomacy and cold war bit this once and stay in the barrel with the Russkies. It's our joint project. If we kick them in the ass now they take their marbles and go home. Prometheus is not going to get up there without their Lenin-5 boosters. Do you agree, Mr President?'

General Bannerman was an old hand at this kind of gamesmanship, which is why he was Chairman of Joint

Chiefs of Staff instead of still riding herd on a combat division. Schlochter had had his mouth open ready to speak when he had passed the buck to Bandin, so now all Schlochter could do was shut his trap and turn even redder. Bannerman liked the Secretary of State; he was so easy to needle. Wouldn't have lasted a day in the Army.

'I have to agree,' Bandin said. 'No official releases from any department about this being a Soviet booster. This is a tragedy of the space age, it's not the first sacrifice for the betterment of mankind, nothing but an unavoidable accident like being hit by a truck crossing the road. And we offer the British plenty of aid. And that includes plenty of money. They're dead broke and they'll appreciate it.'

'Call from Mission Control in Houston, Mr President,' Charley Dragoni said.

'Put it on the speaker phone.'

'You may go ahead, the President is on the line.'

*'This is Mission Control, Mr President. There have been developments on Prometheus which I would like to report to you and Mr Dillwater.'* The voice rattled from the loudspeaker on the table, clearly audible to everyone in the room.

'He's here with me, Flax. What is it?'

*'It is the fission engine on Prometheus. The trouble has been localized. There has been shroud damage to the thrust chamber and engine four is unoperable. Possibility of restoring function is zero.'*

'What, what?' Bandin said. 'Dillwater—what's that gobbledegook? What the hell is he saying?'

'The shroud, that's the metal covering over the nuclear engines that protects them during take-off. It shifted, probably when the core body failed to separate, and damaged one of the engines. It is broken beyond repair and cannot be fixed.'

'Are you telling me that Prometheus is stuck up there too, and in trouble—like that piece of junk that took out the British town?'

'I don't think the situation is that bad yet, sir. The four other engines appear to be undamaged. May I talk to Flax?'

166

Bandin nodded. 'Hello, Mission Control. What is being done about by-passing the damaged engine in order to use the other four?'

'*The computer is working on a programme for that right now. We will inform you as soon as a solution has been found.*'

'Will it be possible? In the time remaining?'

'*It is the only chance. One moment please . . .*' There was a mutter of voices at the other end then Flax came back on the line.

'*We have a request from Prometheus. They wish to talk to you.*'

'I'll have this call transferred to another phone.'

'Put it through here,' Bandin said.

'I didn't want to bother you, Mr President. . . .'

'Bother! This is the only business on our agenda until that thing is up where it should be. Put them through, Flax.'

'*Yes, sir.*'

There were electronic splutterings and clicks while the patch was made from radio to telephone. This took a few moments, then Flax gave his okay.

'*Prometheus, you are through to Director Dillwater who is with the President at this moment. Over.*'

'*Mr Dillwater, Mr President. Major Winter on Prometheus here.*'

'Go ahead, Patrick,' Dillwater said.

'*You know about our difficulties with the nuclear engines?*'

'We do.'

'*Well, we have been looking at the figures and we appear to have a problem. It seems that we are running out of time.*'

'What do you mean?'

'*With the core body gone, the changed mass gives us approximately twenty-eight hours before this orbit decays and we contact the atmosphere. There have been no changes in that estimate. Taking into consideration the amount of time to get the nuclear engine operational we*

167

*may have a time overrun. We just may not be able to get thrust in time to lift out of this orbit. Do you understand?'*

'Yes, of course.'

*'Then I would like to respectfully ask what plans you have to take the crew off Prometheus before atmospheric impact?'*

'Crew—why, none. We had not considered the possibility.'

*'Well I hope you are considering it now.'*

There was an edge to Patrick's voice that had not been there earlier.

'Of course, yes. But you know that your relief space-shuttle is not due to take off until a month from now. It takes at least six days to get it on the pad.'

*'I know that. But I am thinking of the Soviets. Do they have a shuttle operational that might make orbital rendezvous? Or maybe the Air Force? They have been doing shuttle work with the fast turn around time. Do they have one operational right now?'*

'I do not know. But General Bannerman is present and I will ask him.' He glanced over at Bannerman and raised his eyebrows.

'Negative,' Bannerman said, his face expressionless. "There'll be a shuttle coming on line in a few days. It cannot be launched in the ten hours left.'

'Did you hear that, Prometheus?'

*'Yes. But we still want to know the situation with the Soviets. Please report soonest.'*

'We will do that, Prometheus. Just a moment, the President would like to speak with you.'

'This is your President, Major Winter. I just wanted to say that our hearts are with you and your crew at all times. The utmost priority is being given to the safety and success of Prometheus, and of course your personal safety. Be assured that no task will be left undone, no stone unturned in our efforts to assure your safety and success.'

*'Thank you, Mr President. Out.'*

'That kid is kind of snappy,' Grodzinski said. 'He oughta watch his mouth.'

'They are under a certain amount of tension up there,' Bannerman said.

'Still. . . .'

'Shut up, Grodzinski,' Bandin said. 'We have a problem on our hands. We've got to think of those people up there. We've also got to think of the million tons or whatever of US hardware they are riding around in. Dillwater, if they can't be helped, what happens in twenty-eight hours?'

'Prometheus will impact the atmosphere.' He took off his glasses and pinched the sore bridge of his nose while he spoke. 'What happens after that, well we cannot be sure. Something the size of Prometheus has never been in this situation before. She might break up and burn, or she might hold together and impact the Earth's surface.'

'Are you telling me there could be a second crash? Like the first one?'

'I am very unhappy to tell you, Mr President, that it might be much worse than the first one. Not only does Prometheus weigh much more, but it still has its fuel for the fission engines. About five hundred pounds of radioactive uranium pellets. It is doubtful if these would explode on impact. . . .'

'They wouldn't have to explode,' Bannerman said. 'They would burn, melt, be diffused as radioactive gas. Wouldn't that be a nice thing to land in our back yard.'

'Our back yard, anyone's back yard. Depending where it was in orbit at the time it could strike almost anywhere in a large section of the globe.'

'I don't understand that,' the President said.

'It has to do with the rotation of the Earth, sir. Prometheus goes around the Earth once every eighty-eight minutes in a roughly oval orbit. But while it's doing that the Earth is rotating, moving under the orbit. So with every circle of the Earth the satellite passes over different places on the surface below. At one point, unhappily, the orbit passed over Britain as we now know and regret.'

Bandin had a sudden thought.

'Has anyone bothered to work out where the orbit will be

at the end of the twenty-eight hours when that thing is supposed to come down?'

'Yes, sir. It has been done.' Dillwater put a slip of paper on the table before him. 'The orbit will be swinging down from the north Pacific at that time, cutting across the Gulf of Alaska at that time.'

'That's good,' Bandin said. 'We're not going to worry about icebergs and some polar bears.'

'No, sir. But this orbit, the twenty-eighth orbit, continues south in a track along the entire west coast of this country. Going over in turn Seattle, Portland, San Francisco, Los Angeles and San Diego.'

In a stunned silence the enormity of what he had said slowly sank in.


# 28

## GET 15:08

'THIS IS A CREW MEETING,' Patrick said. 'I want you all to know what's been happening with the engines, with everything. . . .'

He was surprised to find himself stumbling over his words. In his years of test piloting he had become used to long hours, even long days of work. Fatigue was something he had learned to control. But he had never been as tired as this before; if he had not been floating in free fall he would have been collapsed on the couch. Not that the others looked any better. If his eyes were as red as Nadya's, he did not want to look into the mirror. Ely's skin was pale with strain and fatigue, the dark marks under his eyes looked as though they had been brushed with soot. Only the other two looked remotely human. Gregor, still looking dim after his drugged sleep, fought to keep his head erect. Coretta was calm and relaxed. If she was feeling any strain she was not showing it.

And she was looking at him with deep concern.

'You look like hell, Patrick,' she said. 'And you know you're having difficulty talking?'

'I sure do, doctor. Because I'm plenty tired.'

'I suppose you wouldn't try to get some sleep.'

'You suppose correctly.'

She kicked off to the wall and opened her medicine locker. 'In any other circumstances I would not be doing this. But I've plenty of uppers here, benzedrine, dexadrine. Do you want something? You know you'll only feel worse afterwards?'

'There may be no afterwards. Let me have a handful of them.'

'What do you mean?' Coretta was shocked at the sudden brutality of his words.

He swallowed the pills and washed them down with water before he spoke. They were all listening now, rigid with attention; even Gregor snapped out of his drugged haze.

'Let us lay all the facts out, get them absolutely straight,' Patrick said. 'We cannot afford to kill ourselves by making any mistakes. The chances are slim as it is. Right now——' he looked up at the GET—'it is 15 : 11. We're still in a low orbit that it is estimated will terminate at forty-three hundred hours, about halfway through our twenty-eighth orbit.'

'How can they be so sure?' Coretta asked. 'I mean we'll be slowed by the air, won't we? That will be sort of a gradual thing.'

'Not really,' Patrick told her. 'We're already being slowed now by the traces of the atmosphere at this altitude, slowed just enough to drop us lower and lower all the time. But you must remember that our orbit is not really circular, but more like a big ellipse in space. At apogee—that is our highest point in the orbit, when we are farthest from Earth —we are about a hundred kilometres higher than at perigee, the closest. On our twenty-eighth orbit when we hit perigee we will hit the atmosphere and that will be that. End of the voyage.'

'The engines,' Gregor said abruptly. 'You must start the engines.' The tension was back in his face again, his fists closed so tightly the knuckles were white.

'We'd like to, Gregor, believe me we would. But the four good ones can't be fired until we find some way to disconnect the broken one. Ely, you have any ideas about that?'

'I do.' He shook out a complex diagram he had been studying. 'Mission Control is doing this in more detail, but I've been trying for myself. The trouble is that the five engines are interconnected. They share a common supply of hydrogen, for both moderator and the fuel supply as well. Theoretically it's possible to seal off engine four. It would mean a space walk and closing a lot of valves, cutting pipes and wires and isolating them, sealing them. But it's dangerous. Cut the wrong pipe and that is the whole ball-game. Plus the fact that when you're through with the spatial plumbing job and the engines get fired up, if they do, what kind of thrust do you get? Can the off-centre thrust be allowed for? I don't know, but I hope the boys in Houston do. Plus one final and vital factor.' Ely stared around at the circle of watching faces and could not look them in the eyes. He turned away abruptly. 'You tell them, Patrick. You're captain of this sinking ship.'

'Not quite sunk yet,' Patrick said. 'But the final difficulty is that even if we fire up the engines—will we have time enough to break out of this orbit before the twenty-eighth orbit? The upper atmosphere is a strange area about which nothing can be predicted precisely at any given time. We might have time enough, we might not. But all we can do is try.'

'Is that really all?' Gregor asked, his voice too loud.

'No. I've already contacted Dillwater, and the President, about getting us off Prometheus before the twenty-eighth orbit if the worst comes to the worst.'

'It can be done?' Gregor asked, eagerly.

'It's a long shot, but a possibility. The space shuttle that was supposed to change crews in a month's time is not ready. However there are US military shuttles and Soviet ones. All the possibilities are being looked into. So that's

172

the situation. As soon as Mission Control tell us it can be done we try to isolate the knocked-out engine. Then fire up. Then, with luck, get up into our correct orbit. In case it can't be done, alternative plans are now being made to get us off.'

'And if we don't get off . . . ?' Coretta asked, her voice very low.

'I just don't know,' Patrick said. 'If you mean do we get out of this alive, why then the answer is no, we don't. This thing may burn up, or it may ride in in one lump. In either case we won't be walking away from it.'

'But—couldn't it be landed, somehow?'

'Negative. No chance at all.'

'But, if Prometheus hits, could something horrible happen like with that English city?'

'The chances are against it,' Patrick said, as calmly as he could. 'The odds are well against it. Two-thirds of the Earth is water, so Prometheus will probably impact the ocean. And about three-quarters of the land areas are mountain, jungle, desert, things like that. I doubt if there's another disaster in the making. . . .'

'You doubt it!' Gregor shouted hoarsely, turning in the air as he tried to push himself erect. 'The disaster is for us, is that not bad enough? We are going to die and that is the end of it!'

'You're going to have to keep your cool, Gregor. For your sake as well as for ours. . . .' The radio contact signal beeped and he turned towards the hatch.

'I will take that,' Nadya said, and pushed by him and was at the hatch before he could respond. She was right, his place was here.

'It is tough on all of us, Gregor,' Patrick said. 'I know how you feel, shut in here with nothing to do. But we may get through yet and if we do you're the indispensable man. Don't forget that. All this effort is to get you up there, not us, into orbit with the generator. You are the guy who has to do the job.'

Nadya came floating back into the group and they turned to her.

'Mission Control says there is a good possibility that the faulty engine can be isolated and the other fired. It will have to be done from outside the ship.'

'I knew it,' Ely said, and sighed. 'Back to the salt mine.'

'They think it will all work out well,' Nadya told them. 'They're sure that the eccentric thrust can be compensated for. And that there will be enough thrust to lift us out of this orbit. But firing *must* begin as soon as possible.'

'You can bet your sweet bippy on that,' Ely said, warmly.

'Mission Control has worked out a programme of step-by-step procedures that are to be done, and they'll relay it one item at a time. They ask if two people can space walk at the same time. They know we have only one operational umbilical.'

'The answer is yes,' Patrick said. 'I'm going to break out one of the Astronaut Manœuvring Units from the cargo hold. Ely, suit up and stay on the flight cabin umbilical until I get back. Then you can use the long umbilicals and I'll fly the AMU. It's going to work.'

'It better.' Ely said. 'Let's get suited up. Coretta darling, let me have some of those pills before we tackle this last one.'

'Of course. How about you, Nadya?'

She started to shake her head no, then stopped. 'Normally I do not like stimulants, but I feel this situation is very different.'

'About as different as they come, *dooshenka*,' Ely said. 'Join the junky brigade.'

'You will seal the hatch again?' Gregor asked. 'Seal us in once more?'

'I'm sorry,' Patrick said, hearing the fear in the man's voice, but unable to help him any more. 'This should be our last space walk. So let's get it over with.'

'I could wear my suit as well,' Gregor said. 'I could help.'

'He could do something, couldn't he?' Coretta asked, trying with her tones to tell Patrick how she felt. As a doctor she was well aware of Gregor's borderline state. Patrick shook his head *no*.

'Sorry. I don't want to have to evacuate the entire ship—

and there is just no room for anyone else in the flight cabin. And really no need for anyone. Nadya will relay instructions to Ely and me—and we'll do the work. We'll be as quick as we can.'

Then they were suited up and out of the hatch. Coretta and Gregor looked up as the hatch closed and the wheel spun and locked it. Soon after the red light came on beside it showing that the air was gone on the other side.

Coretta turned around to find that Gregor was sitting, hunched over, his arms clasped before him and his head bent. Of course he couldn't sit, but was floating a few feet above his couch.

'Would you like something to eat, Gregor?' she asked, but received no answer. 'There are some nice things here. I must say you Russians do things with your food that we would never consider. Look at this—caviar! This little jar is easily twenty-five dollars on earth, and here we are with a dozen or more. It's worth going into space for this.'

'Nothing is worth it. It is too terrible.' You did not need to be a doctor to hear the terror in his voice.

'Well, it hasn't really been exactly a pleasure trip so far. But do have some of this, I've opened it.'

No, nothing. I shall never eat again, for life is at an end.'

He was raising his voice to shout above the sound from the wall speaker, hooked into the radio circuit and repeating the instructions from Mission Control about the spacewalk. She turned it off, it was too distracting and too much of a reminder of their plight. On impulse Coretta turned to the music bands, flipping through them until she found a pleasant piano concerto, Rachmaninov it sounded like. In one of the cabinets a microminiaturized tape player ran continuously, producing six channels of music that could be tapped at will. The clear piano notes and the warm sound of the strings filled the compartment.

'It should not have ended like this,' Gregor said. 'Too many mistakes have been made, too much was rushed. We were pushed into space too quickly, more care should have been taken.'

'Can't cry over spilt milk, Gregor,' Coretta said. 'This caviar is delicious. Too bad there's no champagne to go with it. Hey, wait a minute. I have some two-hundred proof surgical alcohol in there. Cut that in half with water and you have one-hundred proof vodka. How about that, *tovarich*, does a shot of vodka sound interesting?'

'There were mistakes, and they rushed too fast and we are going to die.'

Gregor was pounding his fists together. He had not heard her. He needed something a lot stronger than the vodka. Coretta looked into the medicine cabinet, then back at the distraught Russian. There seemed to be no effect left of the sleeping pills she had given him, which should have been strong enough to put him under for hours. Could she get him to take any more? Unlikely, he seemed unaware of her, uncaring. He had deteriorated very rapidly.

She opened a metal box and removed the pressure hypodermic, then rooted out a plastic bottle of noctex. Enough of this would put an elephant to sleep. And the advantage of the pressure hypo was that you didn't have to have a needle to break the skin. Just press the device against the body anywhere and a blast of high pressure air sent the droplets of chemical right through the skin. She would have to put the Russian under whether he liked it or not. A good shot to keep him down until the danger was past. Or all over—but she wasn't going to think about that. He was a patient and she had to do her best for him. Very quietly she closed the locker and held the silver bulk of the hypodermic behind her leg. Then pushed off towards Gregor. He had his back turned, his head lowered, was unaware of her. The back of his neck with the curly blond hairs, was the right spot. Just place and press. She floated close, raising the hypodermic.

'It is a crime what they are doing to us!' Gregor shouted, straightening, his legs banging against the couch—just as Coretta pushed the hypodermic at him.

The nozzle slammed into his shoulder, jarring it, sending a gust of droplets past his face.

'What is this?' he roared, seeing the apparatus extended

like a gun towards his head. 'You are trying to kill me! You cannot do that!'

He lashed out with his hand, slapping the hypodermic from her grasp, sending it hurtling across the compartment to crash into the wall, the force of his blow sending them both tumbling and turning. They collided and he struck again—this time at Coretta.

'You want to kill me!'

The slap was clumsy, the reaction of his movement spinning him about even as he struck. A fist fight would be impossible in free fall. But the flat of his palm struck her forehead and his wedding ring gashed her skin; small droplets of blood formed in the wound. The sight of the blood angered him even more and he lashed out again, but with little effect.

His eyes were blank, his temper overwhelming. He clutched madly at the fabric of Coretta's jumpsuit to pull her closer, punching with his free hand, clumsy blows that she twisted away from.

'Gregor, stop it,' she shouted. 'Stop it, please!'

They drifted and spun, bouncing from the couches, drifting towards the wall, their insane ballet in space accompanied by the soaring music of the concerto. Gregor was panting now with the effort, still wild with fear and anger. To avoid his blows Coretta pulled him close to her, put her arms around his body and buried her head in his chest so he could not strike her face.

His anger spluttered out. He sobbed deeply and placed his hands over his eyes.

'My God, what am I doing. . . . I did not know. . . . There is blood on your face. I did that.'

'It's not important, it's all over now.'

'No, I'm so sorry. Very sorry. I ask you to forgive me. I have hurt you, I have broken bones.'

'No, nothing, really.'

Gregor was distraught now, his anger forgotten, running his hands down her arms, holding them, as though expecting to find the bones broken there. Pulling her to him, wrapping her in his arms.

His breath loud in her ears, coming faster now. She reached to disentangle his arms.

'I'm sorry,' he said softly, '. . . sorry.'

'Don't be,' she said, equally as quiet, aware that his hands were on her back, moving lower, pressing his body tight to hers. The passion of his anger turning suddenly to another kind of passion.

Coretta knew it had gone far enough and knew how to stop it. Yet, even as she thought of that she wondered why she should stop it. She was a woman, and had been married. She found that this big, gloomy, passionate Russian attracted her. And—she fought hard not to laugh at the thought —turning the laughter into a smile instead—by God, this was a first in space; one for the books. Gregor saw the smile on her lips and touched it with his fingertips, whispering soft Russian terms of endearment as he did. A single, long zipper closed the jumpsuit she wore and he slid it open slowly, revealing the brown warmth of her bare skin inside.

She wore no bra—what need without gravity?— and her breasts were full and round. He bent his face, burying it in their warmth, kissing her over and over. She held his head tightly against her. Helped him to open the long zipper, all the way. She slipped out of her suit and helped him from his.

It was good, strangely good, floating weightless in space as though deep in the ocean. The waves of the music broke over them . . . and broke again. . .

## 29

*GET 16:41*

'POLONY, SALAMI or rat cheese, Mr Flax, that's the lot. And you can have them on white or white.'

Flax glared at the tray of unappetizing-looking sand-wiches.

'Why is it, Charley,' he asked, 'that the second a mission starts the commissary runs out of everything edible and starts sending us up this kind of *drek*? I suppose the bread's stale too?'

'You got it right, Mr Flax. But, after all it's after seven at night, you can't expect. . . .'

'I can't *what*? I can't expect decent food because it is after union hours or something? I got men here been working twenty-four hours without a break and the best you can come up with is horse-cock sandwiches?'

'Not me, I just bring 'em. You want one?'

'Can beggars be choosers.' Flax grumbled, anger dissipated as fast as it had come, and he shifted his weight in the chair to ease his numb legs. He ought to walk around. After he ate something.

'Give me one of each. Thanks.'

He threw away one slice of bread from each sandwich, and mashed the remainder together into a triple decker. It was almost edible. He chewed slowly on a big mouthful and listened to the instructions from the fission engine team in his earphones.

'. . . that's the one, painted yellow, to the right of the mounting. You're going to have to cut out a section of the pipe and crimpseal the lower end. Right. . . .'

All of the time he was talking, eating, he was aware of that voice and of the two men in the vacuum of space trying to repair the atomic engines. Working always against the clock. At the thought his eyes went up to the GET readout. 16:43. It flipped over to 44 as he watched. Time was running out.

A light blinked and he threw a switch.

'*Russian desk here, Flax. I've been on to KY and Baikonur and they swear they have nothing operational that could rendezvous with Prometheus before the deadline. They have a Soyuz coming on line in about two days but they have no way of cutting this time by more than a few hours. This matches the info in our records and, if you will pardon my saying so, the CIA intelligence. I got through to them without asking you, I know I should. . . .*'

179

'No, not this time. You were right, thanks. Then we're sure there's no chance of getting a Soviet rocket to rendezvous in time?'

'*Absolutely. Sorry. A real zero.*'

'Thanks anyway.' He threw the switch.

No help coming from the Soviets. And the NASA shuttle could not be rushed on line for a week at least, at utmost speed. They were doing that in any case, readying it as fast as they could. If Prometheus could get out of this orbit they still might need help. It was coming as fast as it could.

If only the Air Force had their shuttle on the line now. By hindsight he could have arranged it, as a backup measure. Spilt milk again; no point in kicking himself. It was all hush-hush and secret projects, but there was no way that secrets could be kept from other people in the same business. The shuttle payload, yes that was hush-hush enough, though everyone was guessing what they needed a twenty-ton capacity for. The military never stopped playing their expensive games. Bannerman had said that a shuttle wasn't on line now, and he was the one who should know. But he hadn't said just how long it would take to ready one. That was a thought. If it was only a day or two away it could be of help if Prometheus did get into a slightly better orbit. Ask Bannerman? No, no point in bothering the White House again; they were still in the cabinet meeting.

Should he call the Cape itself? As he thought this he groaned and reached for the black coffee, washing the last of the tasteless sandwich down with the cold coffee. A gourmet feast. No, he couldn't think of calling directly to a classified project. Maybe two years from now they would let him know what they were doing. Then what could he do? In through the side door. Who was working on this project that he knew well enough to phone, who might cut through some of the red tape? Among the military, no one, the engineers—of course! Ask the right question, get the right answer. Wolfgang Ernsting. They had worked together countless hours before Wolfgang had opted for bigger money and secret research. One of the original Peenemunde team that Von Braun had brought. He grabbed up the phone.

'I want to make a person-to-person call to Florida.'


A sudden summer storm lashed rain against the windows of the tiny cubicle, rivulets of water cutting streaks through the New York soot. Cooper, Science Editor of the *Gazette-Times*, looked at the rain but did not see it, was not aware of it. His mind was centred on turning hard fact and soft speculation into purple prose. He gave a last chomp on his ink-stained nails to drive the ideas into place, then began to peck feverishly with two fingers on the ancient Underwood standard.

'A greater disaster is in the making,' he wrote, 'one that will make the tragedy of Cottenham New Town insignificant by comparison. The *screaming death* that hurtled out of the clear sky on that helpless city was just a *single* booster of the complex array of boosters, six in all, that lifted Prometheus into orbit where it now rests unstably, hurtling over our heads once every eighty-eight minutes. The boosters are *toys* compared to Prometheus for with its payload this vehicle weighs in excess of two thousand tons. A figure so large as to be meaningless—until we compare it to something we know. A *US Navy destroyer*. An entire *destroyer* is up there over our heads. The weight of all those guns, armour, engines, bombs, shells, munitions, all of that weight ready to fall. And fall it will—and bring down with it something far worse than sheer mass. *Radioactive poisoning!* For as fuel for Prometheus's motor there is carried five hundred pounds of *uranium*. When Prometheus hits the ground and explodes with the forces of a small nuclear bomb it *will* have a nuclear fallout, for that poisonous radioactive metal will be turned to *poisonous radioactive* gas in an instant. Enough to kill *two million* people if it were dispersed finely enough. And where will this *atomic bomb* from outer space hit? It will strike. . . .'

Where would the damn thing come down? Cooper thought. He turned to a Mercator map of the world that he had spread on the desk. On top of it was a transparent overlay sheet with the sine-wave shaped orbit drawn upon it. With each orbit the track changed as the Earth below revolved out from under the satellite. So . . . there . . . on the twenty-eighth orbit, when they had announced it would impact the atmosphere, it would be going . . . Christ! . . . right over the middle of the US!

Cooper shivered and looked out at the dark sky. The black birds of his predictions were coming home to roost. Far closer to his own head than he liked.


'We must face all the possibilities, Mr President,' Dr Schlochter said, nodding as he spoke. 'There is a good chance that Prometheus may be destroyed. . . .'

'I don't want to think about it. I get an ulcer when I do. Dragoni, another bourbon and step on it.'

'We *must* consider, I am afraid. Must consider the international aspects of another disaster. What effect this would have on our relations with the Soviet Union and with other nations.'

'Hey, do we consider the five people in that thing and what we can do to help them?' Grodzinski asked. Dillwater nodded in the direction of the Secretary of Labour, a nod that was almost a slight bow of recognition. Grodzinski, for all of his gross and obvious faults, was at least thinking like a human being, about human beings.

'They are not our consideration,' Schlochter said, his nostrils flared slightly.

'I beg to differ with the Secretary of State,' Dillwater said. 'I speak for NASA when I say the lives of those people are most valuable to us. It could not be different.'

'They're valuable, they're valuable,' Bandin said, ice rattling in his glass. 'But that is not what we are talking about right this moment now. This is another consideration completely. What if they don't get that thing patched up? What if it does come down in twenty-six hours? Can we let it take out some American town like it did that Limey one? How are we going to stop that?'

'There is a way,' Bannerman said.

'A way to save this whole thing?' Bandin asked.

'I did not say that, Mr President. I said that there was a way to prevent Prometheus from falling and causing another disaster on Earth.'

'What's that?'

'If it could be destroyed in space——'

'Are you saying what I'm thinking, Bannerman?'

'I am, sir. We have defence rockets in silos and on the alert at all times to prevent a sudden nuclear surprise attack. These rockets are designed to intercept other rockets aimed at the United States and to destroy them. This would be a good test of the ability of the system.'

Simon Dillwater had to fight to keep the revulsion from his voice when he spoke. 'Are you talking about deliberately destroying five human beings, General? Three of whom are American citizens?'

'I am,' Bannerman was calm, unmoved. 'We take far greater losses in combat during a war and no one complains. By tomorrow morning ten times that number will be dead in auto accidents on our highways. It's not the number of lives that should be considered, nor the citizenship of the persons involved. Our only thought must be preventing a larger disaster that could be caused by the rocket striking the Earth.'

'Have you thought what would happen to the Prometheus programme if this were done?' Dillwater asked.

'That is not a consideration at this moment,' Bannerman answered in his coldest drillfield voice. 'If you'd done a better design job of building Prometheus we wouldn't be in this trouble right now.'

'You cannot say that. . . .'

'That's enough!' Bandin shouted. 'You people can fight later. Now we have a problem on our hands. General, get me an up-to-date report on the defence rockets. You know, are they ready to go and so on—and when is the latest moment they would have to have the command to fire to knock this thing down before it hits the US.'

'Yes, Mr President. I'll have that in a few minutes.'

'How would it be done, I mean what kind of war-head . . . ?'

'Atomic. You'll excuse me if I use the phone.'

There was silence in the room. Grodzinski fumbled with his pencil on the table before him, looking shrunk. Dillwater was silent and erect but he could not keep the horror he felt from his face.

Only Schlochter seemed unmoved.

'We must plan for the worst,' he said. 'The complete loss of this mission in every way. If this occurs—what will the effect be on the Prometheus Project as a whole, Mr Dillwater?'

'The project . . . yes, of course. It will set us back a year at least, to replace the space station. You must realize that, after initiating construction of the generator, the vehicle with its atomic engines was to be used in high orbit as the last stage in the shuttle to ferry up the additional building materials. Without it we can't get the construction operating.'

'A year. You don't mean a year?' Bandin said, his face grey.

'I am afraid that's the minimum, sir.'

'Then that's the election,' Bandin said. 'There'll be some corn-fed yokel sitting in this chair and you will all be out of a job as well. If you don't want that you are going to have to think of something pretty quick.'

'Unless they repair the atomic engine,' Bannerman said. 'That's the only chance we have now. They must stick with that until it's done.'

'You bet your butt on that,' Bandin said. 'How are they doing, Dillwater? What's the status, the latest?'

'No change, Mr President. The pilot and Dr Bron are outside the vehicle making the repairs as instructed by Mission Control. Things are going as planned.'

'How much longer?'

'I hesitate to say . . .'

'Force yourself.'

'At a guess, and I really am guessing now, I would say that they could be finished inside another hour.'

'Let's hope they are.'

'We all pray that they are, Mr President.'

## 30

'IT LOOKS LIKE a chicken wrapped up for the oven,' Ely said, looking at the great mass of crumpled aluminium foil that was wrapped round the stern of Prometheus, around the nuclear engine. There seemed to be acres of it, a mound fifty feet wide with only the mouths of the engines projecting from it. He was clipped to the hull with Patrick floating nearby in the AMU.

'Well, it's a chicken we are going to have to unwrap before we can get at the engine's guts. Which one is it?'

'On the far side, that one, there.'

Patrick worked the AMU's controls and drifted across the base of the ship while Ely worked his way around from clip to clip. By the time he reached the site Patrick had already peeled free a great sheet of foil and was digging deeper. They laboured in silence, tearing at the aluminium foil, hurling it aside so that lengths of it were soon floating away in all directions. They were panting before they were done.

'*Are you ready to proceed with instructions?*' The voice sounded in their ears.

'No we're not and we'll tell you when we are.'

Ely snarled the words, then gasped to get his breath back. Mission Control had enough sense not to answer. His back ached, every muscle in his body was sore, and he panted heavily, close to exhaustion. He couldn't wipe away the sweat because of the pressure suit and drops of it ran down his nose, itching and annoying. He shook his head to clear them away but it didn't work.

'Are you all right?' Patrick asked, touching the control

185

on his AMU so that a jet of gas puffed out and floated him along the base of the engine; he grabbed a support to stop his motion.

'No I'm goddamned well not all right.' Ely choked out the words. 'I don't know how much longer I can go on.'

'I'm bushed too—but we have to stick with it. Right now it takes two of us. Let's finish it then you take a rest while I go on to the hydrogen-helium heat exchanger.'

'If I could only get out of this suit for a few minutes. . . .'

'Negative. We don't have the time to repressurize and start the whole thing all over again.' Patrick tried to keep his voice cool, keep composed, but he was just as tired as Ely. Or more so, his nerves stretched taut. 'No time, do you understand that? We've got to stick to this, there's nothing else we can do.'

'*Are you ready to proceed, Prometheus?*'

'No fucking lectures, Patrick, I can live without that. And shut up, Mission Control, we'll tell you when we're ready. I don't know if I can do it, my eyes won't focus. . . .'

'I'm sorry about the lecture. This is getting to us all.'

Patrick floated close to the other man, until their face-plates almost touched, reaching out a hand to Ely's shoulder. Through the layers of fabric and plastic he could just feel the human being inside when he closed his fingers hard. They were alone there in space, in the vacuum of eternity that reached away on all sides, the sharp points of the stars just markers along the way. The steel shell of Prometheus was next to them, a capsule of life in the terrible emptiness, while filling half the sky was Earth.

'We've no choice, Ely,' Patrick said. 'It took billions of dollars to get us up here and millions of hours of labour. And it's all a waste if we don't finish this job. There's really nothing else we can do.'

'Right,' Ely said. 'Sorry about that. Let's get on with it. What's next, Mission Control?'

They had been waiting in Houston, listening in silence, powerless to help. All they could do was describe what had to be done and hope that the two exhausted men in space would do it correctly.

'*The plate before you, it should have a stencilled number Peter Alfred seven six on it. There are four duz fasteners.*'

'Roger. Can I have the screwdriver, Pat?'

Patrick unclipped the safety line and passed the bulky form of the machine to Ely. 'I have the big blade in it. Set for extract, minimum speed. Ready to trigger.'

'Right.'

Ely swung about, braced against the clip he had fastened to the hull and put the blade into the slot of the first fastener. When he pressed the trigger it whined rapidly, the flywheel inside spinning against the torque of the head, turning swiftly.

'What is the . . .' Ely started to say just as the blade dug into the aluminium and was torn from his hand. 'Too fast!'

The power screwdriver floated away from them, a mote of light in darkness.

'I'll get it—hold on,' Patrick shouted, kicking the AMU about and levering the gas for forward flight. He soared out after the power screwdriver, grabbing it to him as he passed, then braked to a stop. His return flight was much slower.

'You had it on high,' Ely called angrily. 'It pulled right out of my hand when it dug in.'

'I'm sorry, a mistake, but you should have attached the safety line. If you did this wouldn't have happened . . .'

'Ely, Patrick, the time on the GET is 17 : 34,' Nadya said, her quiet words cutting through their angry ones. 'How is the work proceeding?'

Patrick took a deep, shuddering breath. 'Proceeding as planned. Thanks, Nadya.'

'Would you like me to relieve one of you?'

'A very good idea. As soon as we get this plate off I'm sending Ely in. If he transfers to the flight cabin umbilical you can take his place out here.'

'I'm all right,' Ely said.

'No, you're not. Neither am I. As soon as you feel better you can take my place. If we work in turns like this it should help us all. Now get on with the plate.'

187

'Right.'

The plate was finally free, disclosing a maze of pipes and cables below.

*'Can you see a black cable with a green tracer?'*

'It looks like a lot of spaghetti,' Ely said, moving his head closer. 'This looks like it, yes, green markings.'

*'You are going to have to cut it. You'll find if you pull up there is some give and you can work a loop of it up high enough.'*

'It's . . . not easy. . . .'

'Let me see if I can get a hand on it,' Patrick said, drawing himself close.

Each pulling, they managed to get a black arch of the cable up from the others below, two, three inches high.

'It'll be a bitch to cut,' Patrick said. 'Too thick for any of the tack we have. We'll have to burn it through.'

'Isn't that dangerous, with the other wires just behind?'

'Our only choice. Fire up the torch and pass it down to me.'

Ely pulled himself back to the engine support to which they had clipped the tools. He detached the oxyacetylene torch and fastened it to a loop of his own umbilicals. Then he turned on the automatic gas regulator and thumbed the spark switch. The shining exhaust of frozen gas particles turned to a lance of flame.

'Here it is——'

'WATCH OUT!'

Patrick shouted the words—too late.

As he turned with the flaming torch Ely did not see the top of his own umbilicals floating up before him. The umbilicals seemed to have a life of their own as the slightest motion started them moving, the motion passed along their length like some half-sentient serpent.

The loop reared up and the flame burned into it.

Patrick grabbed the torch, turned it off—and they both looked in frozen horror at the blackened oxygen hose. It had been half burnt through, the wire-wound outer casing penetrated, the flexible inner rubber lining swelling out in a great blister.

Only for an instant did it stay like that, for even as they reached to contain it, it burst.

Ely screamed as his air bubbled out in a torrent of crystals, the sound of his voice getting weaker and weaker as the air that carried the sound ebbed away.

'Hold your breath!' Patrick shouted. 'Hold your breath, I'll get you inside.' He grabbed the burst hose in his glove but could not contain the gas which bubbled out between his fingers. 'Inside! Nadya, start pressurizing now, we need every second.'

He seized Ely with his free hand and worked the jets on the AMU, a short hard blast, then a course correction, full on. It was a crawling pace, a drift towards the distant safety of the open hatch, floating forward with the loops of the umbilical trailing out behind. Patrick had his faceplate close to Ely's and could see his mouth shut, then his eyes, slowly, with ice crystals already beginning to form on them.

The open hatch. Brake, grab the edge. Then shove the unconscious man through it, pushing the loops of trailing umbilicals after him.

'Get him near the air inlet,' he called out, fumbling with the belt that held him to the AMU, disentangling himself from it and forcing himself to take the time to clip it to a ring in the hull before diving through the hatch. The very last thing he did was to close the valves and disconnect himself from the air supply of the AMU. Holding his breath, not taking the time to reattach inside, closing the hatch.

The white snow of the air turned to invisible gas as the atmosphere was pumped into the flight cabin. Nadya was bending over the still form on the floor. Patrick jumped to the pressure gauge. Quarter atmospheric, good enough. Then he was rotating the wheel of the hatch to the crew compartment—was blown back as the air rushed into the only partially pressurized cabin.

Nadya was turning Ely's helmet, removing it. Patrick realized that he was still holding his breath so took off his own helmet as well, gasping in welcome lungfuls of air.

'Corretta, in here at once,' Patrick shouted.

'The air, what happened to the pressure?' she said, coming out through the hatch.

'It's Ely, his hose was cut.'

'Let me see him. Someone bring the big green metal case from my locker.'

*'Prometheus, you have an emergency with Dr Bron,'* Mission Control's voice rattled from the wall speaker. *'Medical monitoring reports no pulmonary activity, heart functions weakening.'*

'Give me running reports on respiration, pulse and heart,' Coretta called out as she put the oxygen mask over Ely's face and triggered the valve. 'Get this suit off him so we can use artificial respiration.'

She let the oxygen tank drift away and bent her lips to his, sealing his nose with her hand, giving him the kiss of life. Aware of the crystals of frozen perspiration on his icy skin.

*'We have treatment suggestions from the medical team, Prometheus, are you ready to copy?'*

'Copying,' Nadya said, taking the notepad from the pocket on her leg. Patrick slumped, he would have fallen if there had been gravity, totally exhausted by the last spurt of effort.

Coretta bent over the unconscious man while Gregor looked on in shocked silence.

'What . . . will happen to him?' Gregor asked. No one dared to answer.


# 31


*GET 17:45*

'MISTER, IT'S GONE a quarter to eleven at night. The old Smithsonian been closed maybe five hours now. Ain't no one there.'

The cab driver was fiftyish, amiable, black, and didn't

want to strand this nice little old man in the middle of the Washington night. Not with the muggers and such around.

'I have a friend that works there,' Professor Weisman explained patiently, holding tight to his briefcase.

' 'Fraid she's gone home now.'

'I'm sure she has, but someone there must know her address or her phone number.'

'Tried the phone book?'

'Unlisted.'

'Better get in. We'll drive around and maybe find the night watchman. But I don't want to just leave you there, not this hour of the night.'

At this hour of the night it was a short drive from Union Station to the Smithsonian Institute. It loomed up ahead, redbrick and Victorian, a castellated fortress appearing very much out of place among its ultramodern, Greek-templed neighbours. The cab driver stopped before the entrance and looked carefully into the shadows before he opened the back door.

'There's a night bell under that light there, street looks okay now,' he said.

'Thank you, I wouldn't worry too much,' Weisman said, climbing out of the cab.

'I got reason. A girl mugged and killed last night just a block from the White House. This ain't Funsville.'

'Oh dear! Thank you.' Weisman moved faster than he usually did and arrived, panting, at the door. He leaned on the bell which he could hear ringing dimly deep inside the building.

It took a minute before the watchman appeared. His large belly pushed out the blue of his uniform shirt; he kept his hand on the butt of his revolver as he came slowly towards the door.

'Whaddya want?' he shouted through the glass, making no attempt to open it. 'We're closed.'

'It is Dr Tribe I want to see.'

'She's gone home, come back in the morning.'

'I need to contact her now. Do you have her address or her home phone number?'

'Listen mister, we're closed. And we can't give out that kind of information anyhow.' He started away, then reluctantly turned back when the bell started ringing again.

'You don't understand, this is an emergency, a matter of life and death really. Could you phone Dr Tribe and tell her that Professor Weisman is here and must see her at once. She will know my name.'

With the utmost reluctance at this break from routine, the watchman agreed but he did not open the door before he slumped off towards the phone. Weisman stood on the steps, looking worriedly at the shadows as the minutes ticked by. The cab driver watched him and shook his head unhappily. And kept his window rolled up most of the way despite the heat of the night. It was less than five minutes before the watchman returned, but it seemed an age to Weisman.

'The doctor said to come to her place because I said you had a cab waiting. The address is 4501 out on Connecticut.'

'Yes, thank you, very much indeed.'

Weisman dropped happily into the security of the cab and dabbed at his forehead as they drove. By the time they had crossed the bridge in Rock Creek Park he was feeling better. Dr Tribe would know what to do.

She made him sit down and have a cup of coffee while she listened to him. As he explained, she forgot her own coffee which cooled before her. In the end she just clutched the papers he had given her and looked at them unseeingly.

'You're sure of this, Sam, absolutely sure?'

'How can there be any other answer? There are the figures, the photographs, all laid out before you. There can be no other conclusion.'

'No, of course not. Have you told anyone else about this?'

'No one. I had no idea who to tell and the few people I called for advice weren't there. It was most confusing. I thought you, being in Washington, would know what to do.'

'I certainly do.' She stood and went to the phone. 'I know an under-secretary at State. He'll come around in his car and take us there.'

'There? Where?' Weisman was tired and more than a little confused.

'To the White House, of course. The President is the only one who can act on information like this.'

## 32

GET 23:24

'HE'S BREATHING,' Coretta said. 'More than that—I'd hate to say.'

She looked down at the unconscious form of Ely Bron. He had been strapped down to his couch and the extra sleeping bags tied to him for warmth. His face was waxy and pale and he did not move at all. The others grouped around him, Patrick floating free, the others clipped down.

'Will he stay unconscious like that?' Patrick asked. Coretta nodded.

'Yes. He's had a severe shock, superficial freezing of his skin and eyelids, suspended respiration, oxygen deprivation —and the last is the one to worry about. Mission Control took the time from the tapes they made of our communication with them, also from Ely's biological scanners. It was almost four and a half minutes from the moment of the accident until the time I started mouth-to-mouth resuscitation.'

'I went as fast as I could. . . .'

'Patrick! No one's blaming you. Quite the opposite, I doubt if anyone else could have got him back that quickly. That's not what I mean. It is just the time he went without breathing. No breath, no oxygen. Most human organs can last a long time without oxygen.'

'The brain can't,' Gregor said.

'That's right. He may have irreparable brain damage. We won't know until he regains consciousness.' Coretta hesitated before she spoke again. 'If he ever does.'

'It is that bad?' Nadya asked.

'I'm afraid so.'

'All right then,' Patrick said, taking a deep breath. 'He's your patient, Coretta, and I know you'll take the best care of him possible. Do you need any help?'

'No, I can handle it myself.'

'Good. Nadya, get on to Mission Control and tell them what's happened. Tell them you and I will be going out again to finish the repairs. There can't be much left to do. Ask them for an estimated time on that, how much more we have to do. They know by now how fast we can work —or rather how slowly.'

'*Vas ponyal*, Patrick. *Nyet prahblem.*'

She pushed herself towards the flight cabin and Patrick turned to follow her. Gregor took him by the arm.

'I would like to help,' he said. Patrick looked at him closely.

'Are you sure that you're up to it?' he asked.

'Do you mean am I still chattering with fear? Yes I am. But now I can control it. Coretta helped.'

'Pills?'

'Well . . . sort of. She is a fine doctor.' He was smiling, and so was Coretta. Patrick blinked at them through a haze of fatigue.

'I hope you're right, Gregor. I'm really bushed. If you could get out there and help Nadya I could monitor from the flight cabin. It would really help—and might make the difference between doing and not doing the job. I am so tired that I don't trust myself any more.'

'I have rested and I am fit. And you can trust me.'

'I always have.' On impulse he reached out and took the big Russian's hand. 'This has been no joy-ride until now so maybe it will have to get better. Whatever happens working with you, Nadya and the Colonel, it's been worthwhile. Hands across the sea, hey? A little co-operation in this mixed up world.' He shook his head. 'Sorry, I'm going on too much, just tired.'

'No, I understand, *tovarich*. It has been the same for me as well.'

'Right, then. Your pressure suit's in that locker there. Coretta, can you help him into it? Or should I?'

'No, it's all right,' she looked at Ely. 'There's nothing to be done for him at the moment, I'll help him.'

'Okay. Suit up and join us, Gregor. I'm afraid we're going to have to lock you in again, Coretta. You'll be on your own.'

'That's fine. I'm the only one who can take care of Ely in any case. Now fix those damned engines and get us out of here.'

She smiled as she said it, softening her words.

'Will do.'

He kicked off into the flight cabin and pulled himself down into his couch. 'Mission Control,' he said into his microphone.

'*Come in, Prometheus.*'

'Flax. You know what's happened to Ely. It doesn't look good.'

'*I know, Patrick.*'

'Listen, even if we do manage to kick into the higher orbit, it's not going to help him. He has to get back to Earth, to a hospital. When's the soonest a shuttle can rendezvous?'

'*Two weeks on the resupply.*'

'What about the Air Force?'

'*I'm looking into that now. I'll let you know as soon as I have a report.*'

'Can you impress upon them how urgent it is.'

'*I think they know, Patrick. I think everyone knows. . . .*'

'Out.'

Patrick disconnected and looked over at Nadya on the next couch. She looked exhausted. 'Can anyone possibly know?' he asked.

'I think they do. I'm sure everyone is doing everything possible. There's just so little they can do. We will just have to do it ourselves, won't we?'

'How right you are.' He smiled, crookedly and tiredly, but still smiled. 'We do it ourselves. As consolation we have the fact that it certainly can't get any worse.'

Searing light, incredibly bright, a quick stab of burning light outside where only the blackness of space had been a millisecond before.

Light that was pain.

Nadya screamed, again and again, pressing her hands to her tortured eyes, screamed without stopping at the endless agony.

In the crew compartment the light came from behind, through the half-closed hatch, like the beam of an intensely bright searchlight swept suddenly across the opening. Coretta was bent over, closing a fastening on Gregor's boot and she straightened up, blinking, shocked.

'What was that . . .' she said and the screaming cut off her words.

They moved together towards the hatch, but he was clumsy in the massive pressure suit and she reached the opening first, pushed through. Darkness and night outside, the stars as always, and Nadya still screaming and clutching her eyes. Patrick was pulling himself blindly towards her couch, his eyes closed and streaming with tears, his face drawn with pain. His breath came in great gasps and Coretta knew that he should be screaming too. She pushed off towards them and as she did something white and obscene swam into view outside.

It was a disc of ghostly pale light below them, changing and moving, slipping away behind them even as she watched. There was no way to judge its size or distance against the emptiness of space. But it was large. And streamers of fire arched overhead. She could make no sense of it all.

'Boshemoi . . .'

Gregor was beside her, breathing the words in a prayer, transfixed just as she was.

'What is it . . . what is happening?' she asked.

'It's the atmosphere, stimulated air glow emission, the streams of light, like the Northern Lights. It could only be caused by, but it cannot be, an atomic explosion in space. We are moving away from it now.'

'But how . . . I mean here . . . what?'

'*What?*' Patrick roared the words, roaring with pain and anger, holding the sobbing Nadya. 'A bomb, that's what it was. A missile with an atomic warhead!

'Someone has just tried to blow us out of space!'

## 33

*GET 23:27*

SIMON DILLWATER clutched the sheaf of papers tightly and stared at the large photograph of the sun. Then he riffled the sheets of computations before looking up.

'I assume that you have checked all of your figures most thoroughly, Professor Weisman?' he said.

Weisman nodded. 'A thing like this, you don't like to make mistakes. I ran them through the computer many times. Backwards and forwards, up and down. There's no mistake.'

'Might I ask if you have any idea why our people did not come up with this?'

'Why should they? It's a small field, a new one. There aren't that many solar astronomers in any case. And those interested in the interaction with the upper atmosphere, who really knew their business, a handful. Not even a handful. In fact just two. Me and Moish.'

'Moish?'

'I just call him that, to myself, we have never met. But we correspond all the time. Academician Moshkin.'

'A Russian?'

'Of course.'

'Yes, of course.' Dillwater stood up, his tall lean form overshadowing that of the little professor. 'I must thank you for what you have done, for making the effort to contact us quickly. My thanks to your associates as well.' He nodded, bowed slightly, in the direction of Margaret Tribe and the under-secretary. 'I'll bring these facts to the attention of the President at once. He will want to know. Where can I contact you, Professor Weisman?'

'Philadelphia . . .'

'Not at this time of night,' Dr Tribe said, firmly. 'The professor will be staying at my house. I'll leave the address at the desk.'

'Thank you, thank you very much. . . .'

His words trailed off, interrupted by the distant slam of a door. A *slam*? Doors weren't slammed in the White House! And running feet. The corridor outside hammered to their sound and a moment later an Army officer with a briefcase, flanked by two MPs, ran by.

'Please excuse me,' Simon Dillwater said, composedly, and turned and left. Inwardly he was not composed at all. Something important was happening. He must return to the cabinet meeting at once. He fought back the desire to run and instead walked at a firm and regular pace. There seemed to be a buzz of activity on all sides, something unexpected here after eleven at night. There were extra guards outside the entrance to the executive offices; the captain in command stepped forward and raised his hand.

'Could I see your identification, sir.'

'What—but you just let me out of this door some minutes ago.'

'I'm sorry, sir. Identification if you please.'

Good gracious—his hand was actually resting on his gun butt. Dillwater dug out his identification card, which should have been on his jacket pocket, and handed it over. The officer consulted a list and nodded.

'That's fine, Mr Dillwater.' He raised his hand as Dillwater started to step forward. 'Just one more formality, if you please. Would you tell me your wife's mother's first name.'

'What, why on earth should I?'

'You won't get in unless you do. ASCM. Accelerated Security Check Measures. I've just taken this book from the safe.'

'But . . . why?'

'I'm afraid I don't know, sir. Just following orders. The name . . . ?'

'Maria.'

'That's correct. Please go in.'

More guards at each door and in the corridors in between until Dillwater finally entered the conference room. He stood, dazed, unbelieving. When he had left short minutes ago the atmosphere had been subdued, everyone too tired to talk, going over the latest reports from Mission Control.

Now it was near to bedlam. Bandin was standing and shouting—and Bannerman was shouting back.

'. . . I want them up there and the frigging button pressed and everyone scrambled on the alert. . . .'

'Mr President, you have just got no goddamn business to do that. It might be the very wrong thing. The Hot Line, get on the Hot Line to Polyarni and find out what he knows. Tell him that all we know is that it's not one of ours. Tell him that loud and clear or the missiles could start flying soon.'

'The alert . . .'

'The Interception Alert has gone. That's all internal and no one on the outside will get their balls into an uproar. But that is *all* we must do until you talk to Polyarni.'

The President was still upset, too tired to make his mind up. In the brief silence the Secretary of State spoke.

'The General is correct, Mr President. Everything that should be done at this moment has been done. You must talk with Polyarni, tell him what we know. That our satellites and tracking stations have recorded an atomic explosion in space over the Soviet Union. And it was not one of ours. Period.'

Dillwater sat down heavily, trying to get the facts into perspective. What could this mean, an atomic explosion? The answer came quickly. His through line to Mission Control rang and he answered it automatically. Flax was on the other end and, as he spoke, Dillwater felt his body grow numb, cold. What he heard was impossible—yet he knew it had to be true. He made notes on his pad and, finally, spoke.

'Thank you, Flax. I will tell them, yes, that's right.'

He hung up the phone and rose slowly to his feet. 'Mr President,' he said, but his voice was ignored, unheard. He spoke again, slightly louder, but still no one gave heed. Anger gripped him, he shook uncontrollably and his face grew red.

'SHUT UP, ALL OF YOU!' he shouted at the top of his lungs.

They shut. Shocked, by this cry of rage from a man who never raised his voice above a polite conversational level. The whole room was silent for a moment and Bandin was the first to recover. But, even as he opened his mouth to speak, Dillwater spoke first.

'Mission Control reports that the atomic explosion was directed at Prometheus. Someone tried to blow it up.'

'Who . . . why . . . ?' The President spoke for them all.

'That is not known yet. Mission Control reports that apparently the missile, bomb, whatever it was, did not hit. But there have been injuries. As soon as there are more details they will call back. . . .' The phone at his elbow buzzed and he answered it, nodded. 'Mr Dragoni, will you please patch this call through to the speaker. It is a report from Prometheus.'

'*Mission Control calling Prometheus. Go ahead.*'

'*This is Prometheus, Gregor Salnikov here, it is unbelievable, that this could have happened. . . .*' His voice died away to a mumble.

'*Please come in, Prometheus, the President and his cabinet are listening. What was it that happened?*'

'*An explosion. An atomic explosion in space. I have no way of estimating how close it was. Dr Samuel and I were in the crew compartment, we were only aware of the blast. But the pilots, they were facing out, they saw it. There is pain, they are blinded. . . . I must go, the doctor is calling me.*' The voice switched off.

'Mission Control,' Dillwater said. 'How close was the explosion to Prometheus?'

'*Unknown as yet. We have attempted to activate TV cameras at stations two and three and they do not respond.*'

*If they are burned out the blast was below and behind the spacecraft. Cabin radiation count confirms this.'*

'What do you mean?'

*'There was only slight elevation of background radiation count in the cabin at the moment of explosion. This could only have occurred if the base of the ship was pointed at the explosion. The bulk of the engine, the biological shield and the hydrogen tank would have stopped the radiation.'*

'Thank God for that. But what about the pilots' eyes. Is there blindness . . . ?'

*'We cannot tell yet. Reports will follow. Out.'*

There was a buzz of comment after the call. And confusion. The facts were there—but what did they mean?

'Who would lob a bomb at Prometheus?' Bandin asked, as confused as all the rest. Except for Dillwater. He was staring at the speckled photograph of the sun.

When he spoke it was so softly that they had to strain to hear.

'I know who did it. And I know why.' He glanced up from the photograph. 'Mr President, is this room security shielded?'

'Of course.'

'Then I must tell you that it was undoubtedly a Soviet missile that was fired at Prometheus.'

'Can you verify that?' Bannerman asked, icy cold.

'No, General, you will have to do that. I can only tell you my reasons. Prometheus is now entering its sixteenth orbit. In approximately eighty minutes it will be over Stalingrad. A few minutes ago, at the time of the explosion, it was passing over the wasteland of Siberia. There are Soviet atomic missile sites there. This was the last opportunity to take out Prometheus before it completed its final orbit and fell on Moscow.'

'What are you saying, Dillwater?' The President was livid. 'There are twenty hours yet before that thing is due to fall. And on the US, not on Russia.'

'No, Mr President. I have just received new information that alters this. Information that I am sure the Soviet authorities have as well.' He held up the photo of the sun.

'There is a very good chance that this is the last orbit and that they will crash and burn in about an hour.'

'But—what changed?'

'The sun, Mr President. If there should be a solar flare now, a sunspot, the sudden burst of radiation will strike the upper atmosphere and cause it to expand. Prometheus is just brushing the fringes of atmosphere as it is. If this were to rise it would cause the satellite to impact the atmosphere and crash.'

'That picture of the sun has something to do with it?' Bannerman asked.

'It does, General. It was taken a little over two weeks ago. You see this series of black spots? These are solar flares about to be carried around to the back of the sun by its rotation. They will be reappearing on the other limb of the sun at any time now. They are the beginning of a solar storm. If they progress as normal they will have developed into giant flares while out of sight on the far side of the sun. When rotation brings them to this side of the sun again their immense radiation will be flowing out. Eight and a half minutes later it will impact the top of the atmosphere . . .'

'And Prometheus will run into a solid wall of air,' Bannerman said.

'That is correct. The Soviets must have learned this and made an attempt to destroy the ship before it could impact in Russia.'

'The dirty bastards!'

'You were discussing doing the same thing yourself, General, if I remember correctly.' Dillwater did not need to speak sharply for the impact of his words to strike home. Bannerman's neck reddened but he did not speak.

'You're sure the Russians knew about this?' the President asked.

'Almost certain, sir. Why else would they have fired the missile?'

'Charley, get the Hot Line working. I want to talk to Polyarni. His story had better be good.'

# 34

THE CAB TURNED into Rockefeller Plaza and stopped before the canopied entrance.

Cooper emerged, nodding his thanks to the doorman, unsure if he should tip the man or not.

'May I help you, sir?'

'The Mike Moore show. I was told . . .'

'The receptionist will take care of you.' The doorman was turning away as he spoke, giving all his attention to the white Rolls-Royce that had slid into the space just vacated by the cab, obviously considering journalists not worth his notice. Cooper tried not to slink as he entered the lobby—and forced his knuckles away from his mouth. The receptionist was good-looking, in a very lacquered way, and she actually smiled at him.

'Good evening, sir, welcome to the home of the world's finest television.'

'What? Oh, yes, thank you. My name is Cooper, I was told to come here for the Mike Moore show.'

'Why yes, Mr Cooper.' She kept smiling while she ran her finger down a list of names. 'They're expecting you. Would you please use the third elevator in the bank and press the button for the forty-third floor. Good-bye.'

It was all very efficient, very smooth. As the elevator bent his knees and shot him into the air he looked in the mirror beside him, made an attempt to brush the hair from his eyes and to straighten his tie. Though he had scrubbed his fingers there were still the black marks of ink on them. Perhaps no one would notice.

'Come in, come in, you're the last one and we were waiting for you.'

Mike Moore ushered Cooper in himself, with a propelling hand in the small of his back. He was shorter and looked a lot smaller than he did on the TV screen, Cooper thought, but had a really nice coppery tan. Cooper was too myopic to see that it was television make-up.

'Dr Cooper, this is Sharon Neil whom I'm sure you know by reputation. She's just won her second Emmy, isn't that really great, and we are going to talk to her about that. And Bert Shakey of course.'

Very much in awe he took Sharon Neil's hand, she was just as beautiful up close, then shook hands with the fat comedian.

'What's up, Doc?' Shakey said loudly, the only tone of voice he knew. 'The end of the world in sight yet?'

'Not really, but——'

'Thass good, because I wouldn't wanta miss it!' Shakey laughed loudly at his own joke; Cooper managed a polite smile.

'Well you good people are my show tonight, and I really am looking forward to talking to you.' Mike smiled whitely and waved towards a coffee trolley. 'Help yourself if you like, the cheese danish are really great. After the show the bar is open but I hope you don't mind just coffee, now, fine. All of us here, and I know all of America, if not the world, is interested in what you have to say about the rocket, Dr Cooper.'

'It really gonna drop on our heads? I gotta hard head but not *that* hard!'

'Unless the engines are started up in time, and each minute's delay makes the risk greater, I'm afraid that Prometheus will fall back to Earth.'

'And hit *here*?' Sharon widened her eyes dramatically and laid her hand delicately on her imposing bosom as she spoke.

'I wouldn't want anything awful to hit *there*, darling!' Shakey looked deep into her cleavage and sighed.

'I meant this country, New York, you horny borschtbelt fart.'

'Tempers, tempers,' Mike said brightly. 'Will it hit New York, Dr Cooper?'

It was too late for Cooper to correct the honorary doctorate he had been given, and he was rattled by the touch of profanity on those hallowed lips. He struggled to get his thoughts together.

'It could, yes, it is possible. And of course if it did impact it would be a far bigger explosion than the one that destroyed the English city. Not to mention the danger of radioactive contamination from the uranium, U-235 fuel it carries. But the explosion would be the greatest danger.'

'A new way to dig reservoirs.' Shakey excavated in his teeth with a long fingernail.

'Shakey, old *landsman*, save the gags for later. What are the odds, Dr Cooper, of that thing wiping out the Apple?'

'I'm not sure, it would depend where in its orbit Prometheus is at the time of contact. But the danger is not only to New York City but to the entire country when it sweeps across it. And not only to the United States, you must remember that it circles the entire world. On its sixteenth orbit it will be going over Moscow, will be easily visible as a moving light in the sky. . . .'

'Or it could go ploughing in instead of going over?'

'That is correct. . . .'

'It couldn't happen to a better place!'

'. . . perfectly correct, Mike. Prometheus is a deadly bomb in the sky now, but where it will fall after hitting the atmosphere is anyone's guess. But remember, it wouldn't have to hit a city. It could destroy the countryside, contaminate growing crops, burn down whole forests. Or land in the ocean close to shore and cause tidal waves. This could be the largest man-made disaster in the history of the human race.'

'Even worse than mothers-in-law!'

Mike Moore flashed his famous TV smile. 'Well,' he said, rubbing his hands together, 'I think we're going to have a real nice little show here tonight. Here's an authority on a danger facing this nation. And we have beauty and the beast. . . .'

'Watch da lip, Mike! God will get you for dat!'

'So have some more coffee if you like, then we get you down to make-up, with the exception of the lovely Sharon, and I'll see you all in auditorium three. A live and lively audience that includes the entire Rotary Club of Potlach, Michigan and their wives. . . .'

'Oy!' Shakey groaned. 'Double equity rate for that!'

'So don't get lost and I'll see you there in about a half an hour.'

The door opened and a man stuck his head in and waved a piece of paper. 'Mike, a newsbreak just in on the wire. You can use it with your guest.'

'My mother-in-law died?' Shakey said brightly.

'Even worse than that,' Mike said reading quickly. He looked up at Cooper. 'What can this mean, Dr Cooper? NASA has just released the news that there was, and I quote, '. . . . an atomic explosion in the vicinity of Prometheus. The satellite appears to be undamaged although there have been crew injuries. The cause of the explosion is unknown, although the origin of the explosion is known not to be American.' What do they mean *origin*? Are there spaceships up there taking potshots at the thing?'

'No, of course not. It would be technically feasible I suppose for the atomic fuel to explode—but that could not be done, certainly, without damaging the vehicle. Origin, of course. They must mean an atomic missile. They are saying that we did not fire an atomic missile at Prometheus. . . .'

'But if we didn't—someone else did! Who?'

'I don't know, really. France, England, China, the Soviets, they are all armed with this type of ground-to-satellite defence missile. A lot would depend where Prometheus was at the time of the explosion, since these rockets are for national defence and have a limited range. Of course, they can be fired from submarines.'

'How awful,' Sharon said.

'Awful is the least of it, baby.' Mike was pacing back and forth excitedly. 'Someone is so worried about being blown up by the rocket that they tried to blow it up first. The whole world trembles in fear. Death from the skies. Atomic poisoning. We've got a programme coming up, folks, that'll send our Neilsen rating higher than that satellite!'

# 35

'I CAN'T TELL them this. You can't expect me to tell them this!' Flax shook his head so emphatically that his heavy cheeks flapped. He was almost shouting into the phone and he realized that the men at the other consoles were turning to look at him. That didn't matter. Nothing mattered any more; tragedy was closing in from all sides. He could not cope with it all. Simon Dillwater was still speaking when Flax hung up the phone. This was no way to treat your boss, but nothing did really matter very much any more. He turned slowly, blinking through fatigue-sore eyes.

'Mike,' he called to the man at the nearest console, and waved him over.

'What's up, Flax? Not more trouble?'

'You'll hear about it. Look, take these keys, they unlock the big desk in my office. Bottom drawer. There's a bottle of slivovitz there. Get it and bring it to me.'

'Shliv-o-what?'

'Plum brandy. It's the only bottle there. Get cracking.'

'Flax, you know the rules, about drinking, you wouldn't want to . . .'

'I would. Screw the rules. My people are dying up there.'

He was surprised, shocked, to find tears in his eyes. They ran slowly down his cheeks and he really did not mind. He was mourning the dead. This last thing about the solar flares was almost too much to handle. How could he tell them? Nothing had gone right with this mission from the beginning and it wasn't over yet.

He sighed tremulously, not even realizing he had made the sound, a tired fat man at the end of his tether. He mopped away sweat and tears with his sopping handkerchief. And stared at nothing until the slivovitz arrived. It was transparent and moved like oil in the bottle and appeared harmless. So was nitroglycerine and it looked the same way. He uncorked the bottle and inhaled deeply of the rich odour of decay. It smelled even worse than tequila, which he also adored. There was a half-empty container of coffee at his elbow and, scarcely aware he was doing it, he poured the cold remains on to the floor, then filled it halfway with the slivovitz.

Marvellous! It cut a track down his throat and exploded like a bomb in his stomach, sending waves of warmth out to his extremities. Marvellous, and while the effect still lasted he threw the microphone switch.

'Come in, Prometheus, Mission Control here.' He had to repeat the call twice before there was a response.

*'Hello, Flax.'*

It was Patrick, his voice thick and slurred. 'Yes, Flax here, is that you, Patrick?'

*'Yes. Coretta's given me a shot, for the pain. Can't talk too well. Pain is A-OK. I told her to give Nadya a bigger one and she did and Nadya is sleeping. No change with Ely. Our eyes are bandaged. The doctor does not know if the blindness is temporary or permanent.'* There was no alteration in his voice as he said this. *'Did you find out yet who threw that thing at us?'*

'Negative. You'll have the news as soon as I hear.'

*'I hope so. Gregor is suited up and ready to go out. I'll relay from the engine team. Coretta will handle his umbilicals from inside the hatch.'*

'That is contraindicated.'

*'What the hell do you mean, Flax? If that engine isn't fixed there goes everything.'*

'Look, Patrick, it looks like there isn't enough time to get the engine firing before atmospheric contact.'

*'According to my clock we have about eighteen hours yet before we are due to hit.'*

'The clock's been changed . . .'

*'What!'*

'Listen to me. I've been talking to a Professor Weisman who is a solar physicist, a high atmosphere specialist. Solar storms are due soon that will raise the top of the atmosphere, change everything.'

*'When are they due?'*

'Almost any time now.'

'*This is straight, Flax? No chance of error?*'

'No chance of error on the sun's rotation. The storms were just small ones when he observed them about two weeks ago. If they follow the normal solar activity pattern they should be full-blown by now.'

'*Give me the odds, Flax. The sun is no goddamn oven that goes on and off with a timer. What are the odds of a major eruption?*'

Flax hesitated, but in the end he had to speak. 'Eighty to ninety per cent that there will be a major solar flare.'

'*Well that's nice.*' There was more than a little bitterness in Patrick's voice now. '*I'm going to tell the others. Out.*'

Flax switched off the radio connection and hooked through to the communication desk. 'Get Professor Weisman back. Ask him who the people in Europe are who are doing continuous solar studies. I want names and phone numbers. Then contact them. I want a continuous report here on these solar flares, levels of radiation. Hook them through to astronomy who can record the data. Do it now.'

'*I have an incoming call for you.*'

'No calls.'

'*This is one you asked for. A Mr Wolfgang Ernsting.*'

'Yes, right, put him on.'

Flax sipped at the slivovitz but it didn't seem to help any more; he threw the container into his wastebasket. 'Hello, Wolfgang, is that you? Flax here.'

'*I've heard about your trouble. Terrible . . .*'

'That's the least of it.' He pressed his forefingers hard into his forehead. 'I'm sorry to bother you. It's too late now for what I wanted to know.'

'*I'll be glad to help, in any way.*'

'I know, thanks. But I don't think we will be able to kick Prometheus into a higher orbit now. So it doesn't matter. I was going to ask you how long it will be before your Air Force shuttle can be readied for launching. I know you have a week countdown and I was wondering how far into it you were. Originally I hoped we could maybe get a few more days in a better orbit and there might have been a chance of a rescue launch. Get those people off of there.'

'Yes, well as you say, there is no chance now. If it is any consolation remember the old German expression. "Rufen Sie mich zu Hause in dreizig Minuten an." Good-bye.'

'Good-bye, Wolfgang.'

Flax slowly broke the connection and wondered just what was going on. That was really some old German folk saying. *Phone me at home in thirty minutes.* He looked at the clock and scratched a note on his pad. Why couldn't Wolfgang talk now? Someone listening, security? It could be anything. The only way he could find out would be by making the call, but why should he bother? But maybe it was important. Some hush-hush business with the Air Force shuttle. Not that it made any difference now. Still, he hated to leave ends untied. The thoughts whirled around and around in Flax's head, whirling like snowflakes around the hard black central core of realization that Prometheus was doomed. He crumpled the note and aimed it towards the waste-basket.

Then smoothed it out and clipped it up before him where he could see it. At least he owed Wolfgang the courtesy of returning the call. The Communications Console light blinked and he made the connection.

'Mr Dillwater for you, Flax.'

'Right. Flax here.'

'Ahh, yes, Mr Flax. President Bandin has a personal message for the astronauts . . .'

'They've shut down.'

'It is a matter of some urgency.'

'It always is. Hold on and I'll see if I can raise them.'


The makeshift oxygen tent was made of plastic bags that Gregor had patiently glued together at the edges. It billowed out like a crumpled balloon, holding its shape from its own internal oxygen pressure, slightly more than the ambient air pressure of the compartment. Ely's face was sallow, his respiration so slight it was scarcely noticeable. Coretta had

to look at the bio readouts next to his head to reassure
herself that he was still alive. Heartbeat steady but weak,
the same for his breathing. He was alive—but barely. She
adjusted the pressurized glucose drip in his arm vein and
realized that there was little else she could do. What use was
it all in the short time remaining? Whenever she remembered they had but short hours, perhaps just minutes, to
live the same jolt of fear passed through her. She did not
want to die and it was becoming harder and harder to
keep up a front.

'How is he?' Gregor asked, coming close.

'The same, no change.'

'Perhaps he's the lucky one. He will never know when
it happens.'

'Oh, God, it's just too terrible to believe.' She clutched
to him, buried her face in his chest—but could not cry.
You can weep at others' death, not at your own to come.

'*This is Mission Control, come in, Prometheus.*'

The call was repeated over and over—but it was not
answered. On the other couch Nadya stirred in her sleep.

'Why doesn't Patrick answer it?' Coretta asked.

'We should look, find out.'

Patrick had fallen asleep. The total exhaustion of the
past days, the pain, the drug to kill the pain, all had taken
their toll. Topped by the news that all their efforts were in
vain, that there was no time left, it all had just been too
much for him. There was simply no reason to stay awake
now, he could die just as easily awake as asleep, so he had
simply let go.

'*Come in, Prometheus, come in please. The President is
on the line.*' The call sounded over and over from the wall
speakers.

'Shouldn't we awaken him?' Gregor asked, looking down
at the sleeping commander. Coretta was next to him. Their
hands were clasped together, both to keep from floating
apart and for the pleasure of the human warmth. She shook
her head.

'I'm not sure. Patrick needs the rest—and what could
they possibly tell us of interest after the last good news that

the trip was about over?' She said the words lightly, or at least tried to, but within she was overwhelmingly afraid.

'But it is your President who wishes to talk to you.'

She smiled at his worried look.

'You respect the mere idea of authority too much, Gregor darling. Bandin is a political hack, always was, always will be. When he was still a congressman he was on the committee for school bussing—and his district was split, half white half black. That was when they first started calling him Rubber Bandin. He could stretch to reach anything, any side, and never lost a vote. Or accomplished anything. Anyone that adroit had to be elected President.'

'Coretta, please, you should not talk about your leader in that manner. . . .'

'For a revolutionary you make a damn good bourgeois, my leetle Russian bear. Isn't your Polyarni the last of the old Stalin gang? Wasn't he involved with all those camps?'

'You should not talk like that,' he said worried, looking over his shoulder. Coretta saw the gesture and burst out laughing, uncontrollably, over and over, tears rolling down her face. She was still laughing when she spoke.

'You should have seen your face! Looking about to see if you could be overheard—in a rocket in space about to blow up. I'm sorry, I'm not really laughing at you. But at us, all of us. With all our little nationalisms and fears. At least we few, here, can forget about them in the little time we have left.' She pulled herself close and kissed him warmly. 'I'm glad I met you, really I am. It doesn't make all this worthwhile—but it sure makes it feel better.'

'And I, you . . .'

'The call, take the call . . .' Patrick said, thickly, twisting against the restraining strap. His hands went to his bandaged eyes; he had forgotten what had happened, wondered why it was dark. Then unwelcome memory returned and he let the air out of his lungs and dropped his hand to the con switch.

'Prometheus here, come in Mission Control.'

'*The President would like to talk to you all. Are you ready for this call?*'

'Put him through,' Patrick said, uncaring. After a few moments Bandin spoke.

'*This is the President of the United States speaking* . . .'

'He can even make a phone call sound like the Gettysburg Address,' Coretta said, turning her back in a gesture of defiance.

'. . . *it is with a heavy heart that I address what might be a final message to you brave astronauts, citizens of two countries, united in the bond of brotherhood in this great mission that seems to be terminating disastrously. It is my sad duty to tell you the details of the atomic explosion that so recently occurred near your vehicle.* . . .'

'They found out!'

'Be quiet!'

'*I have talked with Premier Polyarni at length and he wishes me to extend his heartfelt regrets that such a terrible accident could have occurred. For that is what it was. A single man, deranged, in the Soviet Defence Command, launched the missile* . . .'

'One of ours, no,' Gregor said, shocked.

'*He has been apprehended, but the deed was done. His breakdown was understandable since the world is filled with fear at this time. After the unbelievable catastrophe in Britain the rest of the world beneath the track of Prometheus has lived with the terrible knowledge that their turn might be next. We should understand this officer, though of course we cannot condone the dastardly action he has taken. I join Premier Polyarni in his pleas for understanding, his depth of sorrow at your plight, his unhappiness at what appears to be a disastrous end to this beginning of a new era, his hope that others will carry on the gallant battle you brave few have begun. Good-bye.*'

In the silence that followed the end of the President's message Nadya could be heard calling out from the crew compartment.

'Where are you? I can't get free of this couch.'

'I'll help you,' Coretta said, pushing towards the hatch.

'Is that you, Coretta? That voice, it woke me up. I heard what he said. Please, take me to the others.'

They emerged together, Nadya with her hand protectively before her blind eyes.

'Did you hear it, Gregor?' she asked. 'Do you believe it?'

'What are you asking, Nadya?'

'You know perfectly well. This story of the mad officer with his finger on the button. Is it true?'

Gregor took a deep breath—then shook his head despairingly. 'No, it cannot be true. This sort of thing does not happen in our country. This now is, what do you call it? A cover-up. That missile was ordered to be launched. If there was panic it was closer to the top. Now they attempt to hide the truth. I am ashamed for my people, I apologize. . . .'

'Forget it,' Patrick said. 'It's not going to make any difference in the long run—or the short run—in any case.'

'He's right,' Coretta said. 'It'll all come out the same way. And I'll bet we have a couple of generals who're jealous of your boys and wish they could throw some of their bombs around too. . . .'

'That's enough, Coretta,' Patrick said, sharply. 'I'm a military officer. I won't hear that kind of talk.'

'I'm sorry, Patrick. Nerves I guess.' True or not, she knew she shouldn't have spoken that way. At least they could have peace in their last moments. 'You're right. It just won't make any difference, will it?'

'I'm afraid not. What is the time?'

'The GET says 24:59.'

'We should be into the sunspot time now. Does it look any different, Coretta?'

'I'm no astronomer. . . .'

'Doesn't matter. Could I have a drink, that stuff you gave me makes me thirsty.'


Flax glanced at the GET. 24:59, and no rise in solar radiation yet. The piece of paper caught his eye and he noted the time. Wolfgang would be home by now. So that was the official excuse, the old madman and the button routine. Would anyone in the world believe it? Probably not. But it would save face, very important to big nations and small. Maybe they were still thinking of keeping Prometheus going. Why not. The energy need was still there, growing larger every day. Another launch, another attempt. What could Wolfgang possibly want? Flax put the call through. The phone rang and rang, but there was no answer. The hell with it. Flax crumpled the scrap of paper for the final time and threw it away.

# 36

GET 25:03

'WHERE IS Prometheus now?' Bandin asked.

Dillwater flipped through the pages of computation and made a check mark against the GET of 25:03. Then he rose and went to the Mercator map of the world that hung on the wall of the conference room, the eyes of the tired men following him as he moved. With precise motions he checked the latitude and longitude and moved the magnetized red circle that showed Prometheus's position from moment to moment. It was now in mid-ocean.

'That's better,' Grodzinski said. 'Hit the water there and it would be all right.'

'But it will be over land again in a few minutes,' Bannerman pointed out. 'What then? That thing is still a threat to the whole world. I wish to hell the Soviet aim had been better and they'd taken it out.'

'General, there are still five human beings aboard,' Dillwater said stiffly.

'And they'll be aboard whenever it hits and they'll buy it then. I'm a humanitarian, Simon, just like you. But I'm also a realist. A soldier who isn't doesn't win battles. Like it or not we have a big explosion coming up in the near future. If those solar flares do the job they can impact at any moment, like right now, even while we're talking here.

And if the sunspots don't do their job the thing will still go bang in a couple more hours. Or have there been any changes in the first estimate?'

Dillwater shook his head. 'None that matter. Closer measurements have brought the time forward a few minutes if anything.'

'Then there we are. The people aboard are dead, any way we look at it. Now what about the bomb that they're riding? I suggest we take it out with one of our missiles while it's over the ocean and that is that.'

'Are you insane?' Bandin shouted. 'Do you want me to go down in history as the President who atom-bombed his own people?'

'A lesser instead of a greater tragedy,' the General insisted.

'I think you will find that the President is right,' Dr Schlochter broke in. 'Public opinion is a force that we cannot discount. There are already reports coming in of fallout from the Soviet missile, which was none too clean as none of their bombs are, and the world press and politicians are up in arms. By morning they will be in full cry —and the American press will be running in front of the pack. Atomic fallout is not popular. We have banned atmosphere testing for years. If we reverse our policy now and authorize this destruction I doubt if our party will get four votes in the next election.'

'Less,' Bandin said. 'We'd be insane to vote for ourselves. So the bomb is out, forget it, Bannerman. As much as we would like to do it or need to do it we are *not* going to do it.'

'What about TNT or nitro?' Grodzinski asked. 'I handled them in the coal mines when I was a kid. They ought to break that thing up into little pieces.'

'They would,' Dillwater told him. 'But there is the little matter of their delivery to the satellite. Admittedly they already have a full tank of hydrogen and possibly enough oxygen to cause a chemical explosion if the two could be combined. But it would be difficult, and also out of the question. Any chemical explosion at that altitude would liberate most of the U-235 to fall back to earth. If spread out this could be a bigger disaster than it might be localized in one area. A chemical explosion is out.'

'Then what the hell do we do?' President Bandin asked, looking around the table. 'Just sit here and beat our meat until it comes down and hope it doesn't hit anything important? Is that the best we can come up with?'

Apparently it was because only silence followed his question. Simon Dillwater watched and waited, seeing if anyone could come up with a suggestion. No one did. Eventually he knew that what he had to do, had to be done. He rose to his feet and held out a thin, orange-bound folder. The dark letters SECRET were stamped on its cover. All eyes were on him now.

'Since there seems to be no other solution to this trying problem I feel I should inform you gentlemen of the existence of this contingency programme. I do not advise that it be adopted, nor do I say that it should not be. I just bring it to your attention. This is a programme titled HOOPSNAKE. As you know, many different programmes are worked out before all missions that cover many possible contingencies, accidents in space, mishaps that might occur. Most are realistic, some very far-fetched. HOOPSNAKE is in the latter category, worked out by some engineers whom I feel were a bit on the morbid side. I learned of its existence by accident, read it—and classified it and had it filed——'

'Come on, Dillwater, what the hell is it?' Bandin's patience had worn thin.

'I beg your indulgence, Mr President, but I wanted to make all of the details clear. What HOOPSNAKE is, is an outline of a technique by which a self-induced nuclear explosion could vaporize Prometheus. It would destroy the ship and, of course, the radioactive fuel.'

'I don't get it,' Grodzinski said.

'It sounds quite simple,' General Bannerman answered. 'You mean they can jury-rig the atomic motor to blow the whole thing up?'

'Not quite like that, but that is basically the idea. I have been assured if the procedures are done correctly that a nuclear explosion will follow. I must bring to your atten-

217

tion the fact that these procedures must be done by someone aboard the craft. In other words the people who arrange the explosion must be blown up by it. No means of remote control, even if that were possible, could be set up easily and simply for the desired effect.'

'You're asking them to commit suicide to save the world?' Bandin said.

'I am asking them nothing, sir. I am just outlining a programme which I have here. The implementation of it, thank God, is not my decision.'

'They're dead anyway,' Bannerman said, calmly. 'I say we send them the details now so they can get to work. It's the only chance we have.'

'Perhaps they might be asked first if they want to,' Dillwater said.

'We've no time for that kind of luxury,' Bannerman answered. 'Major Winter is an officer, as is Major Kalinina. They can take orders. They should be told at once what must be done. I am sure that they'll be proud to seize this opportunity to avert a catastrophe here on Earth. We have no time for argument if this plan is to be implemented. Mr President, I ask for your decision now.'

'I should talk to Polyarni, have them talk to Kalinina. . . .'

'He didn't talk to us when he threw that bird at the ship —and we backed him on his half-ass story. He'll back us on this one. We are waiting, Mr President.'

'Anyone else have anything to say?' Bandin asked, an edge of desperation in his voice; he had risen to his high station by avoiding decisions—not making them. 'All right. We can't order them, not yet, but we can explain to them about HOOPSNAKE. Give them the details. If they jump the right way, make the right decisions, we won't have to order them. That's a last resort, Bannerman. Find out how they feel before we make them do it. Honey and vinegar, you know. They're good people, I have faith in them. They will die anyway and this way they can make their deaths meaningful by saving the lives of possibly thousands of their countrymen. That's a great thing to do. Contact them about HOOPSNAKE now.'

'Hoopsnake,' Grodzinski said, brightly. 'I just got that. The snake that swallows its tail and eats itself up and vanishes.'

'Shut up,' Bannerman said, tiredly.

## 37

*GET 25:28*

WOLFGANG ERNSTING put on the car's brake and threw open the door. Damp Florida air rolled over him and he gasped; he had never become acclimatized to the abrupt change from the chill air conditioning to the tropical breathlessness. At his front door he fumbled for the key—and stopped. Was the phone ringing? Yes, he could hear it dimly, the drive had taken longer than he thought. He rushed, unlocking the door and throwing it wide, running to the phone.

The ringing stopped abruptly just as his fingers touched it. When he picked up the receiver all he could hear was the dialling tone. He replaced it quickly, watched it, hoping it would ring again.

It did not. He looked at his watch. Yes, it had to be Flax. No one else would be calling him, not at this exact moment. Flax was an immensely punctual man. Then what was to be done? Wait, Flax would surely ring back, yes, that's what would happen.

Wolfgang went into the kitchen, neat and spotless, just as he had left it that morning when he had washed up after his breakfast. He had never married, had never found the time or the opportunity, and as a perennial bachelor he was far more fussy than any old maid. There was a stein he favoured on the shelf, an antique from some long-vanished Bavarian brewery, pressed glass with a metal lid to be lifted with the thumb, the top of the lid proudly proclaiming the brewery's coat of arms.

There was only one bottle of beer left and he poured it carefully into the stein. He would have to buy more. In the back of the fridge the stone crock of Schinkenhäger was cooling—but it contained only a meagre glass. He poured the last of the schnapps out and realized this was serious. None of the local liquor stores carried imported schnapps; he had never learned to like whisky of any kind.

He knew he would want something else to drink when this ration was gone. He drained the Schinkenhäger and washed it down with a draught of cool beer. What would he do?

What would he do if Flax did not call back? That was the thought foremost in his mind no matter how much he tried to avoid it. This was really not his responsibility and he did not need to go out of his way to cause himself trouble. If Flax didn't call back, why that was the end of it. He pushed his chair back with an angry gesture and paced the kitchen, trying to walk away from his thoughts; the room wasn't big enough. It took a good minute to undo the many bolts on the kitchen door, crime was very bad in the neighbourhood, and let himself out into the garden and the steam-bath night. After all these years in the United States he could never get used to the climate. The crisp winters and gentle summers of Bavaria were still in his bones. He would have to make a visit there soon. It was not his responsibility to talk to Flax—the thought slipped in despite his strongest defences.

Responsibility. There had been much talk of that in Germany after the war, that and collective guilt. He had tried not to think of it at the time and he would not think of it now. He had been a scientist, that was all, following instructions. What else could he have done? Right out of university and assigned to Peenemunde, one of the youngest on the team then. Was it his responsibility that the rockets he helped design had fallen on London, killing helpless civilians? It was not, he had never been accused, in fact the Americans were glad to whisk him away to work for them before the Russians could get a grip on him. He had been happy to come, had never regretted it. In this rich country the magazine articles about post-war conditions in Germany had seemed very unreal. As had the War Crimes trials. People had followed orders—yet they appeared to have committed crimes. This troubled his orderly mind and, in the end, he had stopped reading about it or even thinking about it. There was nothing he could do other than the work he had been trained for. He was a good worker and good at following orders.

Though the day was humid and hot it was cloudless, the sky a watery blue. Wolfgang stood and looked up at the sky, wondering if the satellite was above him now. Prometheus might well be hurtling along up there scant miles above his head. With its crew, its people there in space, living now and soon to die.

Uncontrollably he bent, heaved, threw up over and over again until there was nothing left inside him. When the spasm was done he looked around guiltily, dabbing his lips with his handkerchief. No, he had not been seen.

It was the people up there, not the fate of the tons of metal that had reached through to him. He could feel guilty about them because, he realized suddenly, he had been guilty for years. The collective guilt the German papers were always on about. He had been guilty once and had not acted. Could he do that again?

Wolfgang went into the house, washed and dried his face, then reached for the phone. And stopped. No, he could not call Flax directly, that is why he had asked him to call here instead. If he should call Houston there would be records, his name, the time. His involvement would come out. There could be reprisals, it would be a security violation. He backed away from the phone, turned to the door.

The car started easily, still warmed up, and a blast of cool air washed over him. He drove slowly, unthinkingly, until the neon sign BAR appeared ahead. He parked and went inside, his ears assailed by the too-loud jukebox. One regular sat at the bar, a young couple huddled in a dark booth, the bartender was reading a newspaper but looked up when the door opened.

'A beer please.'

'Draught?'

'Draught, yes, thank you.'

Wolfgang took out his wallet, his fingers touching the bills. There was a phone booth in the back corner. Duty and guilt, guilt and duty. He was sweating although the bar was cool. A one-dollar bill, break it for the beer.

With a volition of their own his fingers pulled out a ten and laid it on the scarred, damp wood.

'Might I have some change too, if you please. Quarters, a lot of quarters?'

The bartender, grey and unhappy, looked with faint disgust at the bill.

'You know this ain't no bank.'

'Of course, I'm sorry. I would also like a six pack of beer, no, two six packs.'

'Sure, you understand. For customers it's one thing, but anyone can walk in off the street.'

Wolfgang drained the glass of beer and seized up his change, the bills and the silver, and hurried to the phone booth before he could change his mind. The feeble light came on when he closed the door; the booth smelled of stale tobacco and rank sweat. The operator answered almost at once.

'I would like to make a person-to-person call to Houston, Texas. Houston, that's right. . . .'


'This is Flax calling, do you read me, Patrick. Please come in.'

Flax was tired, so tired it didn't feel like fatigue any more but a wholly different state. A new kind of terminal disease maybe. Did people who were dying feel like this? Dying would be easy now, far easier than what he was doing, what had been done this day. A series of disasters, one after another.

And now. He stared at the scribbled note before him, and it did not register. Logically, yes, but emotionally it had no impact.

'Prometheus here.'

'I've just received a report from the medics, from the bio monitors . . .'

'Yes, I forgot about them. I was going to call, but you know already, don't you.'

'This just says bio monitor cessation Dr Bron. It could be a communication failure.'

'It is. Ely is no longer communicating with the world. He's dead.'

'I'm sorry, Patrick, we all are. . . .'

'Why bother. All of us up here are dead anyway. Ely was just in a little more of a rush.'

A runner shoved a note under Flax's nose. DILLWATER WANTS TALK PROM. it read.

'I'm sorry, Patrick. This thing isn't easy for any of us. Look, I've been informed that Dillwater wants to talk to you. . . .'

'Tell him to take a running jump. There's nothing to talk about now.'

'Patrick, Major Winter, the director of NASA is coming through.'

There was a long pause. Flax had the feeling that Patrick was about to tell him what he could do with the director of NASA. If he had, he wouldn't have blamed him. Instead Patrick answered calmly; if his voice held any emotion at all it was simply that of resignation.

'Prometheus to Mission Control, ready to accept your message.'

Flax jabbed his finger at the Communications Console and the connection was made.

'Simon Dillwater here.'

'Prometheus. What do you want, Mr Dillwater?'

'Major Winter, have you heard of an emergency engine programme entitled HOOPSNAKE?'

'No. The person you would have to ask about that is our engine expert, Dr Ely Bron. I would let you talk to him only he is being very discourteous. He's just died.'

'What? Did you . . . I'm very sorry, I had not heard. This is terrible. . . .'

'*Everything is terrible, Mr Dillwater. Now what is this HOOPSNAKE you were talking about?*"

Flax wondered as well, he had never heard of it either.

'*It is an emergency programme. I classified it myself because at the time I thought it both a dangerous and foolish suggestion. But, in the light of changing circumstances . . . and under the orders of the President . . .*'

'*You're hesitating Mr Dillwater, which is not like you.*' It was hard to make out from the even tone of his voice if Patrick was being serious or sarcastic. Either was possible now.

'*I am sorry, Major Winter. Believe me I am. I do not relish this duty. But I must tell you that a programme exists, HOOPSNAKE, that details how the atomic engine of Prometheus may be detonated. That is how the fuel and the engine may be used to cause an atomic explosion.*'

'*That's interesting as hell, Dillwater, but why are you telling me now?*'

'*You are making me spell it out, Major Winter, and I do not blame you. Simply said, if and when Prometheus crashes it will cause widespread destruction and death. You can appreciate what this will mean.*'

Patrick interrupted. '*I do, Mr Dillwater, and I'm sorry I spoke the way I did. Understandable but not justifiable. When this thing hits we die in any case. If Prometheus could be exploded in space it would not crash and many lives would be saved. Is that what you were going to say, Mr Dillwater?*'

'*Thank you, Major Winter. You put me to shame for I know I could never do what you are doing. But that, in essence, is what I was going to say.*'

PHONE CALL FOR YOU the note read.

'Tell them to hold,' Flax said.

'Person-to-person,' the messenger said. 'Can only hold a couple of minutes.'

'For Christ's sake, not now. Who is it?'

'A Wolfgang Ernsting.'

'Get the number. I'll call him back.' Patrick was talking again. He had missed part of what they had said.

'. . . not my decision. I'll explain to the rest of the crew and we will contact you. I don't know what they will say but, since time is a consideration, I suggest you put the programme on the teleprinter to us so we will have a copy here.'

'I don't know, is that possible?'

'Mission Control here,' Flax said. 'There is a classified military telex in the White House which hooks into our printer here. Begin sending soonest and I'll have it relayed to the printer in Prometheus.'

'Yes, I'll take care of that.'

'Prometheus out.'

Flax threw the switch and collapsed back into his chair. Just too much. Then he stirred and called Communications Console. 'See that a copy of that HOOPSNAKE thing reaches me as soon as it's printed. I want to know just what they have in mind.'

'Yes, sir. Do you want me to place that call now?'

'What call?'

'Wolfgang Ernsting.'

'No, hold that. Get me through to that French observatory, the solar one that's been looking at the sun spots.'

They must have been holding a line open because the call went through in seconds. The conversation was less satisfactory. The astronomer had little English, and Flax, tired as he was, could hardly think of a word of French. But the meaning, or lack of meaning soon became clear. Yes there was solar activity as predicted. No, not yet was it as strong as predicted, but that could change at any moment. Any guess when? Any time. Great. Thank you and goodbye.

Flax groaned as he broke the connection. No contact yet from Prometheus. They must still be talking about HOOPSNAKE—what a wonderful conversation that must be! Or perhaps, like him, they were too stunned for any of this to have much effect any more.

There was something he must do. What? Take a leak. That could wait, but barely. Something else. Right, Wolfgang. What the hell had he called him about in the first place? It was only hours ago that he had placed the call yet it seemed like weeks. Prometheus was still silent. Call him and get it over with.

'Put that Ernsting call through,' Flax said.

Fatigue and the pressure of events pressed Flax deep into the chair, his mouth hanging slightly open, his skin grey and damp. No one noticed—for they were all in approximately the same condition. The connection was made and his phone buzzed; he switched it to his mike and headphone.

'Hello, Wolfgang. I tried you earlier but ... *what?*'

The words whispered quickly into his ear were like some new form of energy because, as he listened his body grew tense, drew taut, sat up and leaned forward, his hand pressing the headset hard against his ear so that he would not miss a word. The fatigue was gone and replaced by a savagely burning anger.

'Yes,' he said. 'Yes. You are absolutely sure? I know. I'll try not to involve you if I can, I know what it means. I'll do my best. Yes. You were right to have told me. Whatever comes of this, *whatever* happens you remember that. It is something to remember for the rest of your life, *Mein lieber Freund.* Good-bye.'

'*Prometheus calling Mission Control. Can you patch us through to Mr. Dillwater ...*'

'No,' Flax shouted, then louder, jumped to his feet. '*NO!* I am connecting you to the President of the United States, Dillwater as well, and the entire cabinet who are meeting at this time. Before they hear what you have to say I want them to hear what *I* have to say.'

At every console heads were turned, the strained faces staring in awe at Flax's massive form as he stood, quaking with anger, shouting into the radio.

## 38

'GREGOR, I need your help in here,' Patrick called out.

'One moment, I will be there.'

Nadya was on the far couch, the one that had been Colonel Kuznekov's, possibly asleep; with her eyes bandaged it was not easy to tell. Gregor was helping Coretta to put Ely's body into a sleeping bag. She went about it so calmly that he was ashamed of his emotions as he felt the cold skin, the limp arms. He had never touched a corpse before and it was doubly horrible here in space. It was too soon for *rigor mortis* to have set in, he had always thought it happened almost instantly after death, but the corpse was still difficult to handle, to force into the tight confines of the bag.

'This is not working,' Coretta said. 'Pull it off. Hold him while I fix the bag.' She rolled it back on itself then, like putting on a stocking, rolled it neatly down over the body.

'What should we do with him . . .?' Gregor asked.

'Nothing, I imagine,' Coretta said, slowly. 'No burial, no service either I guess. Let's just strap him to the bunk.'

'Here on this one,' Nadya said, sitting up. 'Someone guide me, if you please.'

Gregor was glad to leave the compartment, to answer Patrick's call.

'Turn on the teleprinter, will you,' Patrick said, his blind eyes looking into darkness, pointing where he knew the machine was. 'Just throw the switch to on, then the other switch to transmit. Type "ready to receive" and turn the switch back to receive.'

'Easy enough.' Gregor did this and, as soon as he had switched to receive the machine began to chatter rapidly. The first thing it typed was HOOPSNAKE OPERATION DESCRIPTION. 'What is this?' Gregor asked.

'Get the others in here, I want to tell them too.'

In a calm, unemotional voice, Patrick explained what Dillwater had told him, what the programme was that was coming out line by line from the teleprinter. Gregor accepted the news stoically, with Slavic resignation. Coretta was not quite sure what it meant.

'Engine self-destruction programme?'

Patrick nodded. 'It would be simpler to say make-the-engine-a-bomb programme. They want us to rig the thing to blow ourselves up to prevent greater loss of lives on Earth.'

'That's nice,' Coretta said, not hiding the bitterness in her voice. 'They get us up here, strand us up here, shoot a bomb at us, then expect us, out of gratitude, to commit atomic suicide. Why don't they just shoot off another bomb? Maybe the American aim will be better than the Soviet.'

'They must have their reasons,' Patrick said. 'Probably because there could be no guarantee of the complete destruction needed to eliminate us and our atomic fuel. What do you think, Gregor?'

'I? Nothing. If we die a few minutes earlier or later we are just as dead. You are the Commander, the decision is yours.'

'No, we all have to vote on this. Nadya?'

'Follow the instructions, blow us all up, get it over with.'

There was more pain than resignation in her voice; Patrick knew how she felt, shared the same emotions. The ache in his eyes was only dulled by the drugs, the pain of their failure was even stronger. 'Your vote, Coretta?' he asked.

'Me? Does it matter what I think? You are going to be real Gung Ho and logical about it in the end and put the safety of the world ahead of a few minutes more of our happy lives. So go on and do it and don't bother me.' Her voice was rising, she was beginning to shout, and she realized suddenly that she was losing control. The trained physician, cool and abstract, getting hysterical while the two blind pilots remained calm and stoical in the face of this final adversity. She took a shuddering breath and tried to imitate their control. 'Sorry to blow my cool.'

'You have every reason,' Patrick told her.

'I guess I do, but so do the rest of you, with even more

228

reason, and I don't see you enjoying any self-pity. I'll try to be logical. If we are going to die in any case in minutes, hours, whatever the latest estimate is. . . .'

'The solar output hasn't varied, the beginning of the storm is not the size anticipated.'

'With our luck it's going to get bigger, sooner, and if it doesn't we still have only seventeen hours left, so the hell with it. Rig the bomb and have someone press the button.'

'Do you really believe what you're saying?' Patrick asked.

'Hell yes, but why the cross-examination?'

'Simply because neither Nadya nor I can help. The physical preparations will have to be done by you and Gregor.'

'That is logical,' Gregor said.

Coretta was shocked at first, then she smiled wryly. 'Well, well, it comes to that. The good Dr Coretta Samuel, saver of lives, ends her days building an atomic bomb. Why not, Commander. They'll be singing folk songs about me in the ghettos before you know it.'

'Then we are in agreement,' said Gregor. 'It will be done.'

'Agreed,' Nadya said.

'I'll tell them.' Patrick switched on the radio. 'Prometheus calling Mission Control. Can you patch us through to Mr Dillwater . . .'

'*NO!*' Flax's answering shout was so loud that the wall speaker rattled with it. '*I am connecting you to the President of the United States, to Dillwater as well, and the entire cabinet who are meeting at this time.*'

'Flax, what is it?' Patrick asked, but the crackle of static was his only answer.

'He sounded angry,' Coretta said. 'What can it possibly be?'

'Mr President, Mission Control insists on speaking to you as well as the entire cabinet.'

'Why? What is it?'

'I'm not sure, sir. He sounded very disturbed. He informed me that the Prometheus crew had reached a decision on HOOPSNAKE but he wanted to speak first, Mr Flax that is.'

'What the devil is the matter with the man? He can't order me around like that. . . .' Bandin was getting angry and Dillwater made some attempt to soothe him.

'I don't think it's like that, sir. The man is tired, we all are, I am sure it's a matter of some import . . .'

'Put him on, get it over with.' Dillwater nodded and spoke into his phone. Flax's voice blasted from the loudspeaker.

*'This is Mission Control. I have Prometheus on this open circuit, am I through to the White House?'* Dillwater spoke quickly, before the angry President could.

'Yes, you are, we are all listening.'

*'Good. You as well, Prometheus?'*

*'Roger.'*

*'Then I want you all to listen to General Bannerman's answer to a question I have for him. General, is it true that you informed us some hours ago that the resupply shuttle for USAF Research Satellite would not be ready to fly for some time?'*

'That is correct.'

*'No, it is not correct. It is a lie. The truth is that the shuttle is now on the pad at the Cape, on the line and ready to take off as soon as it is fuelled. Isn't that true?'*

'It is not.' Bannerman's face was expressionless, conveying nothing. In contrast to Dillwater and the other cabinet members who were stunned, shocked by the question. Flax continued to speak.

*'You are lying. The two pilots, Cooke and Decosta, are in the ready room there right now, at the Cape. Why don't I pick up the phone and call them?'*

There was dead silence in the Cabinet room. General Bannerman did not move or answer. They sat like that for seconds until Patrick's voice, from Prometheus, sounded through the room.

*'We heard that question here—but we have not heard the answer.'*

'I'm sorry,' Bannerman finally said. 'The USAF shuttle is classified, top secret, and we cannot discuss it. . . .'

'But we must!' Dillwater was shaking with anger as he jumped to his feet. 'I cannot believe this. If the shuttle is on the line it could have been launched already, could have taken the crew from Prometheus. . . .'

'Break the connection,' Bandin said.

'But, Mr President, we must know, they must know in Prometheus, it is an unforgivable crime if it is true. . . .'

'Break off, that's an *order*,' Bandin snarled.

Dillwater hesitated, staring at the President, his eyes widening with sudden knowledge. 'I'll call you back in a few minutes,' he said into the phone.

'*You can't* . . .' Flax's voice was cut off and Dillwater spoke to the President.

'You knew, didn't you? All the time those crewmen have been fighting to save that ship, have died, been blinded, all that time you knew that they could have been taken off by the shuttle. And you agreed to have them commit suicide with HOOPSNAKE. You did this knowing that the shuttle . . .'

'Shut up and sit down, Dillwater. You don't talk to the President of the United States that way.'

'Oh yes I can when the President has done as repugnant an act as you have. . . .'

'Dillwater, you're out of your depth and getting into deep trouble,' Bannerman said. He stood and faced Dillwater, eye to eye. 'We'll hear no more of this.'

'We will hear all about it, General,' Dillwater said firmly, not wavering an inch. 'This is, I hope, still a free country. You cannot have me shot for speaking. You tell me the entire truth now or I am walking out of here and straight to the press and air every bit of your squalid lying to the world.'

'You are talking treason, Dillwater,' Bannerman's hand slapped at his belt where his pearl-handled automatic pistol usually hung.

'Am I? Then you shall have to arrest me and kill me because I shall go on speaking it until this filthy mess is exposed. And you will have to shoot everyone in Mission Control as well since they heard everything we heard.'

'He's right, Mr President,' Dr Schlochter said calmly. 'The cat appears to be out of the bag and it will not get back inside. We must take some concerted action here, very quickly, before rumours spread from Mission Control. If the shuttle is on the line it should be manned and a rescue mission should be launched. It may still not be too late.'

'Negative!' Bannerman snapped, whirling on his new adversary. 'The shuttle is loaded, its payload is classified and cannot be touched. If word of it leaks out there will be a lot bigger trouble than Prometheus to answer for.'

'What is the payload?' Schlochter asked.

'You've seen the memo. The CIA package, PEEKABOO.' Schlochter went white, slumped back in his chair.

'Yes,' he said. 'That cannot come out, something must be done. . . .'

'I want an outside line,' Dillwater said into his telephone. 'Operator, I want to place a conference call to the Washington news desks of the television networks. That is correct, CBS, NBC and ABC. Please call me back when the call goes through.' He hung up and faced Bannerman, still speaking softly. 'You have about one minute to tell me what this PEEKABOO business is.'

'You're through, Dillwater,' Bandin shouted. 'Out on your ass.'

'I have resigned, Mr President, from this position in NASA and from any other in your administration. As soon as this present affair is concluded.'

'You are jeopardizing this entire nation, goddamn it, and I could have you shot. PEEKABOO is a very sophisticated twenty-ton package that this country will be mighty glad it has in the case of any emergency.'

'Exactly what does it do?' Dillwater asked.

'In time of emergency, for defence only, this bird carries just about the biggest laser ever made, completely computer controlled to defend itself, take out any missile homing in on it.'

'And why should missiles be homing in on it?' Dillwater said.

'Because PEEKABOO will be hung in orbit zeroed in on Moscow. That laser is powered by a nuclear generator and is probably the closest thing to a death ray that we will ever have. When it is fired it punches straight down through the atmosphere and burns whatever target it is aimed at. Very precisely. It has a map of Moscow and it is very accurate. It can take out the Kremlin without touching a cobblestone in Red Square right next to it, zap the Army barracks without touching the Gum department store adjoining it.'

'I see,' Dillwater said, very quietly.

'Well I don't,' Grodzinski broke in.

Dillwater answered him. 'It is a secret violation of our agreement with the Soviets not to militarize space. A weapon that will be placed in synchronous orbit covering Moscow. Once again what we have agreed publicly we evade in secret. The CIA keep their stock of poisons despite orders to destroy them, the FBI keeps lists of radicals and says they have been shredded. And General Bannerman and his military associates build a bomb that threatens the peace of the world.' He turned his head. 'And you knew about it all the time, did you not, Mr President?'

'Of course I did—because I put the safety of my nation first. If you liberals had your way there would be a red flag over this building right now.'

'Mr President, gentlemen, the present contents of the shuttle do not matter,' Schlochter said, using his skills as an international peacemaker closer to home for a change. 'The payload can be removed, stored away, forgotten. The shuttle must be prepared at once for a rescue attempt. Nothing else is possible. Too many people now know of its state of readiness. You have no choice, sir, but to issue orders to that effect.'

'You don't have to, Mr President,' Bannerman said, wheeling about to face Bandin. 'This thing can be kept quiet, the leaks can be plugged. PEEKABOO cannot be jeopardized. The project has gone too far. Once it is in orbit we're safe, the Soviets won't dare to try anything.'

Bandin was wringing his hands together, looking for an easy way out of this dilemma that did not exist.

'Mission Control and Prometheus are on the line,' Dillwater said, his hand over the mouthpiece. 'And I have the networks waiting on another line. What should I tell them?'

Bandin hammered his fist on the table in a mixture of frustration and rage. 'Tell the TV people to hold for a new break. Tell the Cape to get the goddamned bomb out of the bird and under wraps at once. Tell Prometheus that we didn't want to tell them for sure until we knew we could have the shuttle ready, that people have been working night and day on it and it looks like now there is a chance. And not one word of what has been said in this room ever gets out of this room.'

He dropped back, exhausted. Rubber Bandin had snapped through one last time.

## 39

*GET 26:19*

'WE ARE SORRY to interrupt this programme, ladies and gentlemen, but dramatic new developments have just been reported about the fate of Prometheus.' The reporter clutched the single sheet of paper, fresh from the teletype, and looked briefly into the eye of the TV camera. He knew he was breaking into every one of the network programmes across the country, being picked up by radio and sent overseas by short wave. He looked appropriately serious as he spoke.

'It appears that a rescue attempt is now being launched from the Kennedy Space Flight Centre. This is the home of the Space Shuttle, the workaday rocket that ferries men and experiments up to Spacelab. No announcement was made earlier, President Bandin reports, because of the possibility that the Shuttle would not be ready in time. But now, with scant hours left in the life of the brave astronauts trapped in that decaying orbit round the Earth, a rescue mission is being launched. There may still be time to reach them before the end. We will bring you up-to-the-minute reports as they develop, and hope to hear from the astronauts themselves if this is possible.'

'No, not now, of course not, Minford,' Flax said, shouting into the phone. 'Sure I know how important your PR is and how we have to keep the public image and improve it, particularly after you-know-what in England. But you still can't put Prometheus on to a public broadcast. Those people up there are bushed and they're sick, and they have their own goddamned problems that make yours look like a missed period. And I've got a call for them, out.' He flipped switches quickly before he spoke. 'Mission Control here, come in, Prometheus.'

'*Flax, the Space Shuttle rescue attempt, is it going ahead?*'

'That is a large and positive A-OK, Patrick. I've just been trying to get through to verify the time they need to get on line, but if they say they can do it we have a window for them.'

'*When?*'

'In just about four hours' time. Your track will bring you across to US then and an East Coast launch will be favourable for your orbit. Match-up will be forty minutes later. I'll give you a more exact ETA as soon as our programme people have been through to theirs.'

'*And the only reason this announcement was not made earlier was because they were not sure that the Space Shuttle could be readied in time?*'

'That's what the official announcement said, Patrick.'

'*That's just pure crap, Flax, and you know it.*'

'I do. And I agree.'

'*The Space Shuttle has a turn-around time of about a week. I'm sure they can shave hours here and there, but they know exactly how long it takes almost to the minute. If they knew this thing was coming on line now why weren't we informed?*'

'I don't know the whole story—and it's possible we may never know.'

'*Let's try. Ask around, Flax, you have the connections. I would like a few answers, if and when we get back.*'

'So would I . . .'

'*Out.*'

Patrick broke the connection with an angry slap at the switch.

'What is all that about?' Coretta asked.

'I don't know, and I'm afraid to guess,' Patrick said, his hands touching the bandages over his eyes, lightly. He hated the blindness, the handicap it put upon him now. 'Something very strange is happening or Flax wouldn't have patched us through to the White House that way. He was forcing someone's hand over something. But we can worry about that some other time. We have more pressing problems.' He touched the bandages again. 'Doctor, don't you think we can loosen these, maybe take them off for a quick look? You don't know until you try.'

'We know, Patrick,' Coretta said, working to keep her voice calm and professional. 'Whatever the final result is, that shock you and Nadya had to your eyes will render you sightless for a day at least. You gain nothing by removing the bandages—and may even cause more damage. I'm sorry I can't be more specific. But that's the straight of it.'

'It could be permanent then?' Nadya asked, quietly.

'Perhaps, though I doubt it strongly. There is a very good chance that the blindness is only a temporary thing.' She spoke flatly and emphatically because she was lying; she had no idea of the extent of the damage. But morale building was more important than truth at this moment.

'All right,' Patrick said. 'We'll put that aside for the moment. Gregor, did the entire HOOPSNAKE programme come through on the printer?'

'It did. I have cut it into sheets and put them into a binder as you directed,' Gregor said.

'Get it, will you?'

'Why?' Coretta asked, surprised. 'If a rescue ship is on the way we surely can forget about blowing Prometheus up.'

'The basic situation has not changed,' Nadya said. She lay, strapped in her couch next to Patrick on his. Just as blind, just as calm.

'That's the truth of it,' Patrick agreed. 'There are still too many bugger factors in the equation. Our orbit *may* hold out the hours needed for rescue. Or end any minute now. The observatory is sending a running report on solar activity. Minor flares, no excess radiation. But the sun is still rotating and we've no idea of what's coming next. One big flare and that's the end.'

'It's terrible!' Coretta cried out.

'It is only the truth,' Gregor said, going to her and holding her.

The two pilots could not see them, and even if they could —it would not matter. There were only a few vital things that mattered any more.

'Gregor's right,' Patrick nodded into his private darkness. 'We have to proceed as though the Shuttle will never arrive. If it does get here in time, well then well and good. But if it doesn't then all our reasons for going ahead with HOOP-SNAKE still hold. It will take some time, so I suggest you start at once.'

'How long?' Coretta asked.

'Considering the fact that neither of you has had EVA experience it could be three or four hours.'

'What do we have to do? I still have no real idea of the whole thing.'

'The programme is explained here in great detail,' Gregor said, holding up the sheaf of printout.

'For you maybe, baby, but that stuff is worse than Greek to me.'

'I better take the time to explain,' Patrick said. 'You should grasp the principles before you proceed. Are you acquainted with the operating principle of the nuclear engine?'

'Just the theory,' Coretta said. 'Hydrogen is used as a nuclear moderator as well as fuel. Those quartz tubes, some of them were broken, are what they call the light bulb. The uranium isotope in granular form is mixed with neon gas in the tubes, that's where the reaction takes place. This heats the tubes up, how hot . . . ?'

'Three thousand degrees.'

'A little on the warm side. Outside the light bulbs is a hydrogen atmosphere which gets hotter, meaning it gets bigger, meaning it gets pressurized in the chamber and goes squirting out the hole in the back and we get pushed along and that is that. Right?'

'Perfectly right, nice and simple. The whole process is much more complex and detailed but that doesn't matter a damn right now, since all you and Gregor have to do is bugger it up and turn it into a bomb.'

'How do we do that?'

'In four stages. First you will have to space walk and make an access to the pressure chamber. This will mean cutting into one of the cones. It will be hard, but it can be done. One of you will have to use the Astronaut Manœuvring Unit, the AMU, in order to reach the area. Then, Gregor, what comes next? My memory is shot.'

It wasn't memory, it was pain. The drugs were wearing off and his eyes ached so much it was difficult to think. Gregor had read the programme to him once, he remembered it clearly. Patrick just had difficulty talking. He would need another shot soon, but had to put it off as long as possible. He was too groggy afterwards. Gregor flipped the pages and touched a line with one long finger.

'Entrance must be made and the quartz tubing broken away to enlarge the chamber. Although very resistant to heat the material of the light bulbs is most frangible. When this has been done a four-metre section of U-235 storage tubing is removed and rolled upon itself until its diameter is approximately forty centimetres in diameter . . .'

'You lost me with that one, Gregor.'

'It's plastic tubing,' Patrick explained. 'It is the container for the uranium fuel. You can't store the stuff in a tank or it goes critical and goes bang. So it's in this plastic tubing that's wrapped around the base of the ship. A section of the tubing, with the fuel, has to be cut off and rolled up into a compact mass.'

'Just a minute,' Coretta said. 'If I recall my atomic medicine crash course that can be dangerous. Won't it blow up?'

'Not yet. There will be greater activity, but it won't go critical.'

'Whoever is doing the rolling is going to be mighty sick.'

'Whoever is doing that is going to be dead,' Patrick said grimly. 'A lethal dose in minutes. But it won't really matter.'

'I guess it won't,' Coretta said, trying to match his calm. 'It will take hours for even that kind of dose to kill someone. But the whole ship will blow up well before that.'

'That is correct,' Gregor said, turning to the last page. 'When the fuel is ready the flow of hydrogen must be turned on from the controls here. Then the mass of fuel is thrown forcefully into the pressure chamber. That is all.'

'All?' She was puzzled. 'What happens next?'

'The hydrogen in the chamber acts as a moderator, slowing down the radiation that has been escaping up to this point. The mass of U-235 goes critical . . .'

'And goes bang. An atomic explosion. I get the picture. So when do we get started?'

'Now,' Patrick said. 'Someone please tell me the GET time.'


The Payload Changeout Room was just being locked into place against the Orbiter when the Launch Controller, Gordon Vaught, climbed on to the spidery steel framework. He was a big, solid man, with muscles and tendons furrowing and cording his bare arms. Born and raised in Dothan, Alabama, just a few hundred miles from Cape Canaveral, he was used to the damp tropical climate, was scarcely aware of it. He pushed through the airlock into the cooled and sterilized atmosphere of the Room. The clamps were being thrown that sealed the entire structure tight against the body of the orbiter. Colonel Kober was supervising the operation. Kober was a short, nasty type who was always in uniform, always fresh-pressed and spotlessly clean. Vaught knew that he had a good mind, had an engineering degree as well as his military rank, yet he still disliked him immensely. The feeling was mutual. They worked together because they had to, but that didn't mean they had to enjoy it.

'You preparing to remove your payload, Colonel?' Vaught asked.

'We are, Mr Vaught.'

'How long before you get it out and we can seal the doors?'

'We will do it as fast as possible, if that is what you were asking.'

'I wasn't. I was sort of interested in a figure. Minutes, hours, days, you know the sort of thing.'

Kober flashed the big civilian a cold look of loathing, brushing back his toothbrush moustache with his knuckle as he spoke. 'An estimate, of course, Taking into mind past performance. Disconnect the utility bridges, attach supplementary power, unbolt, unship; move to the pallets, close up—it will be a good two-hour job.'

'We don't have two hours to wait. I'm starting fuelling now.' Vaught turned away but Kober's harsh words stopped him in his tracks.

'You cannot do that and I absolutely forbid you to. Civilian control on this project is lax enough as it is, but I will not permit criminally dangerous procedures that might endanger this project or my personnel. Do you understand, Vaught?'

'Do *you* understand, Colonel, that my first name is Mister as far as you are concerned. I want to hear you use it. As to your forbidding me to do anything, why you got as much chance as a hound dog winning an elephant farting contest. The fuelling starts now.'

'You cannot. It is forbidden. I'll contact . . .'

His voice shut off sharply as Vaught closed the airlock door. My oh my, the man did rile easy. It really was a pleasure to get the toe of the boot into him. Vaught pulled the CB radio from the holster on his belt and thumbed it on.

'Station two. Are the feed lines connected yet?'

*'Last one going on now, Gordon.'*

'Good. Make sure your men on top are watching the bleed valves and start pumping. I want that fuel in there just as fast as you can get it.'

*'Right.'*

Vaught put away the radio, then leaned on the hot metal of the railing and looked at the bird. The square bulk of the Payload Changeout Room was locked against it, covering most of it, with just the nose cones of the three big boosters rising above it. The orbiter was well hidden. The tiered form of the servicing tower stood beside it, now a scene of organized bustle. Underground fuel lines would bring the liquid oxygen and hydrogen, liquid only when kept at hundreds of degrees below zero. Fuelling must have begun because a white plume of vaporized gas puffed out of a relief valve high above. Begun. Now it would be at least three hours before the tanks were filled. Three hours until the tanks *had* to be filled because that was the time of the only window they could use, the few minutes when the Space Shuttle had to be launched to hurl itself into space on an accurate course, to rise up and arrive at the same moment in space and time as Prometheus which would be hurtling up from behind. One chance at a meet, and only one. Well he would do his part, get the bird fuelled and counted down and ready to fly when they needed. If the military payload was removed in time. Observation satellite they said, big hush deal with MPs with sidearms around all the time. Something more than a usual observation satellite the rumours said.

He didn't know or care. All he wanted was it out of the way in time.

Fuelling was going well so he had time to go in and bug Kober and make sure the thing was plucked out and taken away.

He liked riling Kober, even though it was very easy to do. He had been in the Army himself when he was young, been made a corporal before getting out. Anyone above the rank of Sergeant Major was instantly suspect. Chicken-shit chicken colonels were the best bait of all. He smiled and turned back towards the door.

The solar observatory was on Capri, the isle in the Bay of Naples, Italy. Monte Solaro rose up behind it where the terraced slopes, silver with olive trees, ran down through the village of Anacapri to terminate in high limestone cliffs above the blue sea. Three-quarters of the way down was the solid-walled building that housed the Solar Observatory of the University of Freiburg. It was not the best site for an observatory of this kind, the sea haze meant that seeing could not begin until late in the morning and ended well before sunset in the afternoon. But Capri is every German's idea of heaven, so heart had led head for just once and the observatory had been built here. The short day left more time for wine and peaches. A tour of duty on Capri was not considered by the astronomers, or their wives, to be much of a sacrifice.

A mirror on top of the building rotated and tilted automatically to follow the sun, reflecting its image down a chimney-like tube to the telescope room below. Here the magnified image passed through a specially designed filter that screened out all except the wavelength of hydrogen. Thus purified, modified and enlarged, the sun was captured on film by a Leica camera. Every two minutes during the day it took a picture, then advanced the film automatically to be ready for the next shot. When the camera was not operating the image could be projected on to a white screen. A burning, angry disc a yard in diameter, pocked with solar activity, rimmed with tendrils of flame.

Dr Bruzik was studying the image now, puffing complacently on a well-stained Meerschaum pipe. Astronomy is a very placid occupation, demanding more patience than energy, and he had practised this science for a number of years. His wife, Jutta, came into the room.

'It is that man in Texas again, on the phone. He is very angry because the Naples operator cut us off for almost fifteen minutes.'

'If one were always to be angry at the Italian telephone system, one would die of apoplexy before reaching puberty. Was there any message?'

'Just as always. What is the state of the sun?'

'You can reassure him that there was no change while we were out of contact. Activity normal . . . *Gott in Himmel!*'

Bruzik gasped, forgetting that he held the stem of the pipe between his teeth, a very favourite pipe indeed. It fell and broke on the tile floor—and he was not aware of it at all.

Because, hypnotized, he was watching a solar flare growing on the sun's disc. A tongue of fire that leapt up higher and higher, arched out into space. He was watching millions of tons of burning gas being ejected from the sun's surface, the explosive power of a gigantic solar storm.

What he knew also existed, what was not visible here, was the gigantic activity beneath the sun's surface, the incredibly powerful magnetic fields that twisted and churned. And sent out radiation. Radiation that, when it struck the atmosphere of Earth minutes later, could cause the Northern Lights, ruin radio reception, jam telegraph cables.

And so excite the upper atmosphere that it would rise up and strike Prometheus from its orbit. Change the relatively empty space at this altitude with its few molecules of air, to a thin atmosphere that would be like a rock wall to the satellite travelling at five miles a second.

'Keep the telephone connection,' Bruzik called out. 'I want to speak with them in a few moments. Try and make that cretin of an operator understand that the line must be kept open at all costs.

'It looks as though a period of intense solar activity is beginning. Just as Professor Weisman said it would.'

## 40

'JUST DO AS I tell you, step by step, slowly and carefully, and nothing will go wrong,' Patrick said. 'Are you ready, Gregor?'

'*Da.*'

'Coretta?'

'*Da* as well, Patrick.'

The hatch was open and they were facing it; Patrick could see it clearly in his mind's eye. The only way he could see it. Coretta had taken off the thick top bandage and secured the pads on his eyes with a tape, had done this for Nadya as well. So they could be able to fit their helmets over their heads.

Getting into their pressure suits had been a fumbling, time-consuming job, with Coretta and Gregor doing all the work for the four of them. The two pilots in their unyielding space armour had to be guided, carried really, to their couches. Moving them in this manner was the easiest and most logical thing to do; Patrick had hated it, the total dependency, but had said nothing. Now the atmosphere was gone, the hatch open, and each of them was sealed away from the others in a thin capsule of life. And they would stay this way until the end. Until help came—or didn't come.

'The AMU is tethered just outside the hatch. Do you see it?' Patrick asked.

'Still there,' Coretta said.

'All right. Gregor, cut through the hatch, taking it very easy. If you just float through easy Coretta will handle your umbilicals.'

'I don't think they will reach as far as the AMU,' Gregor said.

'We know they won't, they're designed for manoeuvre inside the cabin. But you'll be able to get at least a metre outside which is enough leeway for you to strap into the AMU. Pull it as close to the hull as you can—but don't take off its safety hold-down yet. There's a wide lap strap to hold you into position. Take both ends at once, pull up on them which will seat you, then latch. Do you have that?'

'Roger.'

'Then exit through the hatch. Coretta, try and give me a running commentary so I'll know how it's going.'

'Sure. Going out now. A tight squeeze, but going through nicely. I'm paying out the umbilicals . . .'

Gregor was sweating heavily, panting with exertion. By now he was used to the lack of gravity and the way inanimate objects seemed to have life and motions of their own. This moving around would not have been too bad if he had not been restricted by the suit. Every action had to be a forceful one and, if he dared relax his arms, they tended to stick straight out from his body. The simple act of getting into the bulky, chair-like form of the AMU, the Astronaut Manœuvring Unit, proved almost impossible. Either he was moving or the AMU was, usually in opposite directions.

'Take a rest,' Coretta ordered. 'You're panting like a bull-dog in heat. Let things quiet a bit or you are going to over-load your cooling unit.'

'She's right,' Patrick said.

'Must . . . finish this . . . a moment more . . .'

Angry at himself for being so clumsy, Gregor seized both ends of the straps and pulled them tight, damping the movement of the AMU. They were spinning together now —but at least it was together. He closed his eyes against the vertigo and hauled on the straps until the ends came together—and he clipped shut the belt.

'A great job,' Coretta said, smiling at his victorious thumbs-up signal, using the umbilicals to damp his motion. 'In the AMU and ready for the next step,' she said.

'Be very careful about sequence now,' Patrick said. 'Coretta, have you the safety line rigged? With one end attached inside?'

'Done as directed,' she answered, giving the nylon line one last tug to make sure it was secure.

'Good. Clip the other end to Gregor's belt—not to the chair. After this is done plug the short leads of the AMU umbilicals into the receiver on Gregor's suit.'

'In place.'

'All right, Gregor, you can turn the selector valve from the U position to the AM.'

Gregor took the lever clumsily in his gloved fingers and pushed, hard.

It did not move.

'It won't go,' he said.

'It happens.' Patrick's voice was calm, emotionless. 'Traces of water in the oxygen, there can be ice. Try working it back and forth, a little at a time.'

'There . . . it is moving a bit . . . a bit more . . . *done!*'

'Very good. Coretta, first close the valve on his umbilicals, there at the bulkhead, then disconnect them.'

It was done quickly, the disconnected umbilicals floating inside the cabin; Gregor was in space outside totally dependent upon the life systems of the AMU.

'Can you read me, Gregor?' Patrick asked.

'Very clearly.'

'You are on the AMU radio connection now which is channelled through the intercom circuits. On the outside of the hull is an aerial to pick up your signal. You may get far enough around the ship for it to thin the signal or even lose it. Keep thinking about this so we don't get out of touch. You're on your own now, but you will keep the safety line connected. That way Coretta can pull you back in at any time. You can start working your way back down the hull now. Moving safety clips as you go.'

'Shouldn't I use the gas jets . . .'

'Negative! They are tricky to use and take a lot of practice. Forget about them now. Just think of the AMU as a big pack on your back and drag it along with you.'

'*Vas ponyal,* here I go.'

'Do you have all the tools you need?' Nadya said, speaking for the first time.

What a fool I am, Patrick thought. I can't see what is going on out there, can't keep track of everything. 'Thank you, Nadya,' he said. 'I should have remembered. The cutting torch is still back by the engines, along with most of the tools. But for this you will need the hydraulic jack as well.

Coretta, will you get it and clamp it to the AMU where Gregor can reach it.'

It was not easy going. Coretta leaned far out of the hatch to watch Gregor's progress; they could all hear the rasp of his breath in their ears. The AMU was like the old man of the sea on his back. Instead of giving him freedom, moving him about, it got in the way of all his motions. Of course it had no weight in free fall—but it still had mass. It took effort to get it moving, and once in motion the same amount of effort to stop it. Whenever he moved the off-centre mass had a tendency to start him spinning. All he could do then was reel in the short line that clamped him to the hull, hold himself tight against it until the motion had been damped. Then attach to a new anchor and crawl slowly on.

'At the engine,' he finally gasped, a breathless cry of victory.

'Well done,' Patrick said, and the others called out agreement. 'Anchor yourself well and listen to Coretta. She has the programme that outlines the best way to get into the engine cavity. Are you tired?'

'Yes . . . a little.'

'Then take a breather first. Drink some water. . . .'

'*Prometheus, this is Mission Control. Come in.*'

'We're here, Flax.'

'*Patrick, I'm going to patch you through in a moment to Major Cooke in Florida. He is Commander of the Shuttle that is coming up after you. Captain Decosta is his Pilot.*'

'Cookey and Des, this is going to be old home week. We all trained together.'

'*A-OK, make things easier. That's what Cooke wants to talk to you about. There is one other thing. The solar activity is hotting up. The report has just come in.*'

Patrick felt the tension grip him, the sharp cold realization that there might be no rescue at all. A hope of safety offered—then whipped away. There was no hint of this in his voice.

'When will it hit us? What will the effect be?'

'*The first jump in particle count is here now. Very slight, but it's sure to grow.*'

'Can you give me any figures? Any times, Flax?'

*'The astronomy boys say it's difficult to predict with any accuracy. It is only after events that correlations can be made.'*

'In other words we'll know it first up here. All right, Flax, give me any time estimates at all if you get them. You can patch through to the Cape now, whenever you're ready.'

The line was already open, the connection was made at once.


'Major Cooke here, come in Prometheus.'

*'I thought you would never call, Cookey.'*

'My pleasure, Pat. Dee is here with me, just adding weight sitting around the ready room, waiting for the bird to be counted down.'

*'Been waiting there long, Cookey?'*

Cooke looked up at Decosta who was sitting across the table from him, listening in. Decosta, a dark, small man who always wore an expression of gloom, looked even sadder now as he heard the question. He put his finger to his temple, his hand shaped like a gun, and pulled the invisible trigger. Cooke, a solid, meaty blond, looking more like a lineman than a pilot, nodded his head in silent agreement.

'Just long enough,' he said. 'We're going out to the shuttle in a few minutes, run through the countdown early then hold while the fuelling is finished. We want to hit that window.'

*'So do we up here. Believe you me.'*

'Roger. I want to settle the transferral details now before link-up. Are we going to have any problems?'

Patrick's laugh was very cold. *'That is all that you're going to have. Two of us can't see so we'll have to be towed. And we'll need walk-around bottles of air.'*

'No problem. When we rendezvous Dee will get them to you. The configuration of this Orbiter has the air-lock opening into the cargo bay. So we'll have to crack the doors to the bay so he can get out that way. They'll have to be open in any case, since two of your people are going to have to ride back there. We are set up to carry only four in shirtsleeve environment.'

'*I know. What do you plan to do?*'

'Right now they are fixing two acceleration couches on pallets to go into the bay. The walk-arounds hold enough oxygen for two hours. We'll be on the ground before they run out.'

There was a continued silence after that, filled only with the gently hissing static. Then Patrick spoke again.

'*Cookey, tell them to put in four couches. Just in case. Your cargo bay is as big as a barn, so there's plenty of room.*'

'Positive—but we do have the room for two inside.'

'*Do as I ask, Major. We may be in a hurry when we arrive. It could very well be a matter of getting the hell out of there fast without worrying about cycling time through the air-lock.*'

'I read you, Prometheus.'

'*Great. Now just get cracking and get your ass up here in that brick rocketship.*'

'Will do. We'll get four couches in. Dee and I are suiting up now. Next time we talk to you will be from the bird.' He broke the connection.

'They know, don't they?' Decosta asked.

'He knows something.'

'But how much? Does he know we been sitting here in ready since before his launch? Because we had so many aborted holds on the schedule flight that we had to hold again until after they took off.'

'Drop it, Dee, will you.' Cooke turned to look out of the sealed window at the pad. The bulk of the Space Shuttle stood out clearly, white plumes leaking from the relief valves. The winged form of the Orbiter itself appeared small clamped to the three torpedo-like rockets of the main fuel tank and the twin boosters. 'We're doing a classified job and we got into it with our eyes open. They asked for volunteers for this one and we opened our mouths. They even gave us a chance to get out after we knew what the mission was. A lot of people maybe don't agree with us, but I think getting that package into orbit over Moscow will help peace in this world.'

'We agreed to that. We didn't agree to sit on our duffs and play pinochle instead of going up to help those people on Prometheus.'

'We're going, aren't we?'

'A little late, that's all. Maybe too late. They'll burn before we get there.'

'You shut up before I spread your Mex nose all over your face.'

'Not before I cut out your gringo heart and make *tacos de corazón*.'

The racial insults meant nothing; they were too good friends for that. They were just words used to cover up their real emotions, their real knowledge that they had permitted themselves to sit by without doing anything all this time. Until it was possibly too late to help.

# 41

*GET 28:54*

AS SOON as the President had left the Cabinet room, the Secretary of State leaned over to speak to Dillwater.

'Come on, Simon, I'll buy you a cup of coffee,' he said.

'I've had a good deal already, Dr Schlochter, thank you.'

'Well a drink then, I don't think I have seen you have anything other than coffee all the time we have been in here.'

'I rarely drink spirits, but, yes, a small sherry perhaps.'

They walked past the table laden with sandwiches and coffee to the small portable bar which had been rolled in a few hours earlier. Bandin had felt in need of a few more large bourbons and had, he thought, covered this up by encouraging the other to drink as well. Schlochter poured out a Tio Pepe with a steady hand, then a vodka on the rocks with a twist of lemon peel for himself.

He handed the sherry to Dillwater and raised his own glass.

'To a successful rescue mission,' he said.

'Yes, I will drink to that. But to very little else.'

'The President is a very occupied man, Simon, with more problems than you can perhaps understand.'

'Ever the peacemaker, Dr Schlochter, are you not? But I am afraid there is little you can accomplish this time. I tendered my resignation to go into effect the instant those people are back on the ground. Or dead. Both the President and General Bannerman knew that the shuttle was available for a rescue mission—yet they did nothing until their hand was forced.' He looked pointedly at Schlochter. 'Did you know about it as well?'

'No, I did not, I am relieved to say. If I had I might have been as divided in mind and as concerned as the President was.'

'You will make me cry in a moment, Dr Schlochter.'

'I appreciate the reasons for your irony, Simon, and I won't argue with them. But you should remember that the President has the larger job of being leader of this great nation, of guiding its destiny in war and peace. As long as there was even a slim chance that the engines could be started to lift Prometheus out of orbit he did not dare jeopardize our national security by cancelling the PEEKA-BOO operation. The fate of a few sacrificed for the greater need of the many. The cleft stick that many statesmen are forced into.'

Dillwater looked into his empty sherry glass, then put it back on to the bar. The only signs of fatigue he had, after all these hours, were the tightened lines around his eyes. He drew himself up and spoke quietly and quickly so only Schlochter could hear him.

'I come from a class and background in America, Dr Schlochter, that has almost vanished. I was taught early not to use profanity and low language and I have followed that course through life because I found it the most agreeable

251

way. However there are exceptions. What you say about President Bandin is the pure quill well-refined and first grade absolute bullshit. The man is a political opportunist who will sacrifice anything, anyone, to guarantee his re-election. Morally he makes Mr Nixon look like a choir boy.'

Schlochter nodded seriously, listening to the words as though they were some highly refined argument.

'Yet you took a position in his administration? Knowing what you did about— shall we say—his moral drawbacks?'

'I did. He needed me as a member of what is called the Liberal East Coast Establishment to get him some votes. I felt that NASA was important enough on its own to justify my aid.'

'Then what has changed?' Schlochter drove home the points of his arguments with slow shakes of his forefinger. 'The President is the same person you always knew he was. And NASA and the Prometheus Project are even more badly in need of your expertise and aid than they were when you first joined.'

'My mind is made up. I have resigned. I cannot be any part of a government that that man is the head of.'

'Think again, if you please. I have been talking to Moscow and we are agreed that Prometheus must go on, whatever happens now. Too much has been invested, the need for energy is too great——'

'And Bandin needs re-election too badly.'

'Precisely. You are probably the only person who can see the project through to completion.' He raised his hand before Dillwater could speak. 'Do not answer now, please. Think about it. I will talk to you again, later. Now, I believe, yes—isn't that your phone that is ringing?'

Dillwater moved swiftly to it and picked it up.

'Simon Dillwater speaking.'

'*Flax here. A progress report to date. About an hour to go to take-off of the Space Shuttle. The countdown going well there. The solar storm—it's . . . getting worse.*'

'What does that mean in time?'

'*No one seems to know exactly. Solar activity will lift up the top of the atmosphere. How much and how fast is still a guess. But soon. It could be before rendezvous, or just after it.'*

'Not very heartening news.' Dillwater realized he was holding the phone so hard that his finger hurt; he forced himself to relax. 'You have kept the crew of Prometheus informed, I take it?'

*'Yes sir. They know everything we do as soon as we get the information. They are proceeding with the HOOPSNAKE project.'*

"What? But I thought . . .'

*'That it had been abandoned? No, sir. They feel that the threat of impact is a real one. And the chances of their being taken off before atmosphere contact only a fair possibility. Therefore they are initiating the HOOPSNAKE programme just in case."*

'We should never have asked them,' Dillwater whispered, pounding his fist on the table as he spoke.

*'I didn't hear that last. . . .'*

'Nothing. Please keep me informed of everything.'


Eighty-five miles high, Prometheus hurtled in its steady course. The great globe of the Earth below moved slowly by. They were over the Panama Canal now, but clouds and storms obscured any clear view. Beyond the blue of Earth the stars shone clearly in great profusion, the moon a clear disc, the sun a burning presence that could not be faced directly. Gregor kept his back to it, looking outward at the incredible vision of space as seen from space. He was the pendant spectator, the godlike eye, the vision apart from the world of his birth. Separated by space, was the warmth, the water, the air of the planet, a bit of which he carried with him, just a few centimetres thick, the only barrier between himself and the deadly vacuum of space. Looking at the Earth like this he felt distant, yet so much a part of it, could see it more clearly than he ever could from the ground.

'Feeling rested, Gregor?' Patrick's voice echoed inside his helmet, drawing him back.

'Yes, much better really, just tired and hot there for a moment.'

'You've done a lot.'

'Not everything.' He turned and looked at the jagged metal at the base of the ship. 'The supports have been cut away so I can get close to the orifice. I've cut into the trumpet mounting and managed to fit in the jack so I levered it aside to get access to the thrust chamber. All that's left is to get inside the chamber and knock the light bulb out of the way.'

'How do you plan to do that?'

'I have a steel rod I cut loose. That should do the job.'

'Good luck.'

Coretta and Nadya spoke as well and he nodded, half listening, but did not answer. This was the last challenge. He held the bar in his left hand, he had no way to tie it down securely, which made moving about difficult. The line he had clipped to the ship prevented much movement, and he saw no way to unclip it, move, then reclip it with one hand. He opened the fastening and let it float free. On the base of Prometheus here Coretta could not see him so she would not know what he had done. And she did hold the other end of the nylon safety line. She could reel him in to safety if he did move free of the ship. He did not intend to. There were handholds enough here among the braces and pipes.

Handgrip by handgrip he worked up to the thrust chamber he wanted. The two-metre-high trumpet mouths of the other chambers were on all sides of him, the other pipes and gear beneath his clutching hand. When his head was over the open mouth of the chamber he stopped, held on firmly until all movement had been damped, then clipped back on to the ship. The opening was like a black O-shaped mouth before him. The extension light was on the left side of the AMU. With precise motions he transferred the steel rod and groped for the light. It flicked on and cast a disc of light on to the dark metal, lit only by Earthlight. He found the mouth of the chamber, aimed the light inside and gasped.

He had not expected this. Instead of the soot-lined cavity or the burned mouth of a rocket, here was a three-metre-long chamber like Aladdin's cave. It was smooth lined, shining with reflected light, filled up the centre with a delicate crystal structure. This was the tube everyone had referred to so disparagingly as the light bulb. It was more like a crystal chest of diamonds, glinting and glowing with gemlike sparkle as the bright light played across its surface. As he moved, the light shadows and illumination changed and the colours flowed and merged.

'Will you be able to break it up in there?' Patrick asked, his voice coming from a great distance.

Gregor sighed and forced himself to return to the reality of the situation. This was no cathedral to the glories of the gods of science. It was a demolition site.

'Yes, I should be able to,' he said.

With the light in his left hand he pushed the steel rod slowly through the opening, down its full length until it hit against the quartz and rebounded. Now the shadow of his arm and the rod changed the illumination even more and the colours and lights sparkled and spun.

For one moment more he looked at it—then struck out.

It was a slow motion ballet of destruction, independent of gravity and air pressure. When the steel struck, the quartz fractured, particles and fragments moving out in all directions.

The opening was about half a metre wide and Gregor had his arm in as far as it would go now, his body writhing slowly in reaction as his arm and the bar moved back and forth. When he finally looked in again the destruction was complete; only glittering fragments filled the chamber. He pulled out the rod and hurtled it from him, out into space, getting smaller and smaller until it vanished, still in orbit trailing behind Prometheus, though invisible now.

'It is done,' Gregor said, really speaking to himself though the others heard.

'Come on in, then,' Patrick said. 'Right now if you're done.'

There was a strain, a touch of tension in his voice and

Gregor heard it. He shrugged. Why not? There was tension enough for all of them. But had something new happened? His mind was on this, not what he was doing. He unclipped his short safety line, pushed off towards the side of the ship, reached for a stanchion.

And missed.

Horrified, he watched the base slide by next to him, just out of reach, then the burnished side of Prometheus moved into view, the projecting hatch a good fifty metres away with the shining globe of Coretta's helmet protruding from it.

'You shouldn't be that far from the ship,' she said.

'Not on purpose. I'm afraid I lost my hold.'

'I'll pull you in . . .'

'STOP!' Patrick shouted. 'Don't do anything yet. There is no danger as long as the safety line is still attached. Is it, Coretta?'

'Secure both ends.'

'All right—describe to me exactly what you see, where Gregor is.'

'Well, he's just come into view now. Floating straight out away from the ship it looks.'

'How fast?'

'I don't know. It took maybe one, two seconds for all of him to come into view.'

'Good, very good.' Patrick guessed at Gregor's speed, the distance he had to go, then made a quick calculation. 'Pull in the line slowly, until it's straight, just the slightest tension. When it's taut then pull in a yard more *very* slowly, take about three seconds to do it. Remember, it's not a matter of hauling him in, just starting him in the right direction. He can't get lost as long as the line is attached. The worst thing you can do is to get him moving too fast, slam him to the ship at the end of his arc.'

'There—it's done,' Coretta said.

'That's great. Now keep the rope as short as you can without exerting any more pull on him, just reel it in as he moves closer.'

It was frightening, though safe, Gregor had to keep telling himself that. But he was still moving *away* from the

256

ship, though up along its length at the same time. Very logical, he must remember that, a simple problem in mechanics. He had originally imparted a motion away from the ship, Coretta had added a motion along its length. His direction now was a vector of those two forces, moving still away from the hatch, but along the ship towards it all the time. An interesting problem—abstractedly. Not so interesting when he was the weight at the end of the string.

Patrick strained to imagine what was happening, having only Coretta's description to guide him.

'Closer,' she said.

'Wait until he is even with the hatch—then stop taking in any more line. That will start him in an arc towards the ship. But do it gently or he'll speed up and slam into the hull. That is what we must watch out for.'

'Right—here goes.'

There was a gentle tug on the line on his belt—then Gregor found himself moving towards the hull again. He put out his arms, bent his elbows when he struck in slow motion, and absorbed the shock. Before he rebounded he grabbed an anchor ring nearby.

'Done it!' he gasped, victoriously.

'Come on in,' Patrick ordered, as tired as the others with the strain. He waited until Gregor was back at the hatch, securing the AMU, climbing inside, before he spoke again.

'Put some extra lashing on the AMU, then close the hatch,' he said.

'Why, what reason?' he asked. It was Nadya who answered him, speaking in quiet Russian.

'We talked to Mission Control while you were outside. There is a prediction now, about the atmosphere. They have an eighty per cent estimate that we may impact at next perigee, in about ten minutes.'

'But that is one orbit too soon! On the next orbit the Space Shuttle will be here, we'll be taken off!' He looked around at the others, their faces dimly seen through the filters on their helmets.

'We know,' Nadya said, simply. 'Perhaps our luck has run out. A few more minutes will tell.'

Gregor started for the hatch. 'I must go back, finish the HOOPSNAKE programme.'

'No time,' Patrick said. 'It will take too long. Let's see if we ride this out, then we can decide. What is the GET?'

'33 : 23,' Coretta said.

'Six minutes more. Then sixty-five after that if the Shuttle is launched on schedule.'

They could only wait then. For Patrick and Nadya it was harder to wait in the darkness.

## 42

*GET 33:14*

'WHAT DO THEY SAY about the fuel?' Decosta asked.

'Almost done,' Cooke told him.

'And about time too. This is a very uncomfortable position to lie around in.'

Both pilots were strapped into their seats in the Orbiter flight deck, in normal flying position. But the Orbiter had the dual role of being both space vehicle during take-off and operation in orbit, then airplane when the time came to land. The two pilots sat in their stations, their seats more like those of an ordinary cockpit than a space vehicle. Perfect for manœuvring and landing, but uncomfortable now since the vehicle was standing on its tail, pointing straight up into the air. Like sitting in a chair that was lying back down on the floor.

'What about the couches?' Decosta said, speaking into the microphone.

'*Locking into place now,*' the cargo engineer's voice said.

'And the walk-arounds?'

'*Stowing them in the airlock. . . .*'

'No! Not good enough.' Decosta began pulling at his belt fastening.

'And what do you think you are doing?' Cooke asked.

'Getting the hell down there and putting things right.'

'You're out of your gourd! We've less than twenty minutes to zero, we're into the countdown now. We can't ready for take-off with you rattling around there.'

'You just might have to. This is not the usual operation.' He was moving as he spoke, climbing about his chair until he hung from the back of it—then dropped the five feet to the rear wall of the aft flight deck, now a floor. 'We're not going to have much time up there. I want that gear set up so I can use it instantly without extra farting around.'

He dropped through the interdeck opening into mid deck below.

'If you're not back on time I'm leaving without you,' Cooke called out to his vanishing back.

The bulk of the airlock was like a closet lying on its back next to him. Decosta undogged it and heaved it open. He looked straight down through the airlock and the open outer door beyond at the vast open area of the cargo bay below, its far end a sheer drop of sixty feet. A cherry-picker cage was just beyond the airlock hatch and he stared into the shocked face of the technician there.

'You're not supposed to be here, Captain,' he said.

'Blame my mother, I was premature. Move over.'

Decosta climbed down into the airlock, swung from the edge of the outer hatch—then dropped neatly down in the cage. Trying to ignore the sheer fall beyond. The cage bounced with his sudden weight and they both clutched the rail.

'You're gonna give me a heart attack,' the technician groaned.

'Are these the walk-arounds?' Decosta asked, pointing to the oxygen bottles on the floor of the cage.

'Yes, sir. I was gonna lash them——'

'Forget it, I have a better idea. Drop us down.'

They moved slowly down the length of the bay, between the wide-gaping jaws of the open doors. This great tubular cargo space, sixty feet long and fifteen wide, was usually filled either with cargo or the palletized experiments bolted into place. Or a satellite like the one so recently removed.

The only cargo now was a single pallet that was sealed into place just behind the cabin. Four acceleration couches had been roughly welded to it. They were askew, not lined up in a neat row, and the welds were bumpy and uneven. But they were secure and they were in place in time—nothing else counted now.

'Down to the bottom,' Decosta said, pointing. 'To the end effector on the end of the manipulator arm.'

The remote manipulator arm ran almost the length of the cargo bay, a jointed tube fifty feet long. It was absurdly thin for its length and the motors in its joints were scarcely able to move its own weight now. Because it was designed for operation in space only, in free fall, beyond the reach of gravity. At its far end was a jaw-like mechanism designed to seize the cargo and lift it free. Decosta looked at it, thinking fast, thinking of what the situation would be like in space.

'Hey, Captain,' the technician on the nearby tower wearing earphones and microphone called out. 'Major Cooke says you have only fifteen minutes left.'

'I know, I know,' Decosta called back, beginning to sweat now. 'Take this thing down to the bottom end of the cargo bay and let's unload the walk-arounds.'

Decosta jumped out on to the circular platform and took the heavy oxygen tanks the technician handed him, placing them in a row at his feet. 'Do you have any nylon rope?' he asked.

'Yeah. White and red . . .'

'Pass me the white.'

As quickly as he could he lashed the walk-arounds side by side to the ring bolts set into the metal. He used a single length of line, weaving it back and forth over the tanks, then securing. A single cut anywhere in the line would free them.

'Knife.'

The technician handed him a heavy pocket knife. He opened the large blade, cut the line—then reached for the end of the red line and passed it quickly through the clasps on each walk-around, tying them together. He climbed back into the cage.

'To the end of the manipulator.'

The cage rose and he let the line reel out behind it.

'You got about eight minutes left!' the communications man called out. 'It takes us that long for the final check and to close and dog those doors.'

'Almost done.' He slashed the line off and tied the free end to the end of the manipulator. Then he cut off another short length and used it to tie the knife close beside it, dangling free on a foot of line.

'Hey, that's my knife!' the technician called out.

'It's about to take a trip. Put in a statement of charges. Now get us *out* of here.'

The cage rose up, higher and higher, until it hovered just under the door to the airlock above. The outer doors of the cargo bay were slowly closing at the same time, Decosta put one foot on the rail of the basket and, with the technician steadying him, managed to reach up and grab the opening. Pulling, and pushing against the groaning man's shoulder with one foot, he worked his way up into the airlock, the door slammed shut and sealed right behind him.

'Get up here!' he heard Cooke shouting. 'Christ, we're in the countdown. Two minutes to take-off. I can't wait.'

'Coming . . .' the pilot gasped, closing and sealing the door, climbing hurriedly up the handholds on the wall, grabbing out for the lip of the opening in the floor above. He looked up, gasping, into Cooke's strained face.

'Thirty seconds!' Cooke shouted. 'Pumps going, ignition coming up, strap in, damn it—*strap in*!'

Decosta pulled himself into his chair with the last of his strength, grabbed for the ends of his belt—as the engines fired.

Roaring out streams of flame the Space Shuttle lifted, moved faster and faster, rising up towards its rendezvous in space.

'*The Shuttle is go*,' Flax said, his words sounding in the ears of all four aboard Prometheus. '*One minute into the burn*.'

Patrick had flown the Shuttle more than once so he knew what was happening, knew the sensations of the two men piloting her. The first burn, the big kick by the solid fuel boosters. Three minutes of their firing along with the Orbiter engines as well. Then, one hundred and sixty miles down-range . . .

*'Burn out, separation.'*

The two big tubes, empty now, arching away, falling back towards the Atlantic Ocean. Then the snap of their parachutes and the slow drop down towards the retrieval ships waiting below. But the Orbiter was still climbing, still sucking the last drops of fuel from the external tank, still not in orbit. Any trouble now and the Orbiter would have to fall back to Earth. They wouldn't make it. *What was happening?*

*'I can't hear you, Orbiter, right, okay now. Roger. External tank jettison.'*

Engines still firing as the tank fell away to burn in the thin atmosphere. Still climbing, still aiming for orbit insertion. On the way.

'What's that?' Coretta shouted. 'Something burning, outside the ports.'

But even as she spoke the shuddering began, hammering and vibrating.

'Atmosphere impact!' Patrick cried out. 'Atmosphere. . . .'


The television programme director sat looking at his monitor screens and muttered to himself unhappily. What a choice, what a miserable choice. The Vance Cortwright picture was going out now, as well as his doomladen voice. That was on monitor two. On one he had a picture of Mission Control, everyone busy as hell at the consoles as they had been for the last god-only-knows how many hours. Without voice, Flax had cut them out again. Forget them, the viewers had seen enough of that picture to use again right now. On three a studio with a science-fiction author-space expert, ready to go again with explanations and little models and everything. The director had got a lot of mileage out of him, and there would be more to go, but not right now with things maybe breaking. Four was blank now, ready to roll any of the special films they had made. They had just used the Space Shuttle take-off animation, but with the Shuttle Orbiter up there now that was finished. The director cut in on Cortwright's voice while he thought.

'. . . dramatic events of the past hours drawing now to a conclusion. A conclusion still clouded with doubt as Orbiter reaches up into space, hurtling after Prometheus, rushing to catch up. Their engines are shut down now as the final calculations are made, calculations that cannot be off by as much as one-thousandth of one per cent. For, at this moment, the two spacecraft are in different orbits, at different heights, moving at different speeds. When Orbiter fires her engines again they should lift her up for the final and dramatic meeting that everyone, all over the world, is waiting for. The gallant crew of Prometheus have worked hard, and some have died, to reach this moment in time and space. How unspeakably cruel it would be if victory, life itself, should be torn away from them at this last minute, for they *are* reaching the end of their painful journey at last. Approaching their last orbit . . .'

'Start rolling the Prometheus burning film,' the director said into his mike. As soon as the animated drawing of the ship came on he switched to it with Cortwright's voice over.

'. . . unbreathable at this altitude, as thin and rarefied as the inside of a light bulb. But at the tremendous speed of five miles a second, eighteen thousand miles an hour, that trace of air will be like a solid wall to Prometheus.' The model's nose began to glow and send off sparks. 'Heat it up, burn it, eventually to . . .'

Cortwright stopped talking, his eyes widened, and he pressed the miniature earphone harder against his head. When he spoke again he was excited, fatigue vanished.

'It's happened, my God it's happening at this very instant. Prometheus reported atmosphere impact and then their signal faded. We know that the heated, ionized atmosphere prevents communication, that is all it may be. Or the worst may be upon them at last, the fated moment we have all been dreading may be here. This may be the end. And if it is, we can only say that though these people may die, these brave astronauts, they have not died in vain. Because their efforts have kept this giant in the sky up there until now, until this moment when it is hurtling over the empty wastes of the Pacific Ocean. If it falls now no one below will be hurt, the tragedy of Cottenham New Town will not be repeated. . . .'

'Great, really great,' the director chuckled to himself and rubbed his hands together. 'They hit while we had the burning animation on. What really great timing!'


'*I don't know,*' Flax said. '*Honest to God I just do not know anything yet.*'

'I understand, Mr Flax, and I do appreciate your position.' Dillwater could hear the exhaustion, the pain, in the man's voice and knew he could ask no more, push him no farther. 'This line will be open and I will be standing by, we will all be standing by, waiting for whatever news you may have. We are all praying it will be good.'

Dillwater slowly hung up the receiver and looked at the circle of watching faces. 'Nothing additional is known,' he said.

'They have to know!' President Bandin shouted. 'Eight billion dollars worth of equipment and they don't have a clue? Can't they just look up, point a telescope?'

'They are doing everything technically possible. We will know what happens in a matter of minutes.'

Bannerman walked over to stare at the big plotting board, at the red circle that was Prometheus's location on last contact.

'They had better find out something pretty soon. If that thing burns now, it will just knock a hole in the ocean. But if it stays in orbit just a few minutes more it's going to come down right on top of Los Angeles.'

They could not speak. There were no words to convey their feelings as they realized this unthinkable—yet possible—greater tragedy.

\*       \*       \*

'Nothing,' Cooke said. 'Nothing yet.' He looked out at space, at the stars, unseeingly.

'They can't burn, not when we're this close,' Decosta said. He opened his belt and kicked up, floating away from his chair. 'I'm getting into the pressure suit.'

'We don't know for certain or not if you are going to get a chance to use it.'

'Don't you think I know that?' His voice was bitter, angry. He opened the locker in the rear and hauled the suit out. 'It's like knocking on wood. You do it even if you aren't superstitious. I am putting this thing on and I am going to use it, hear?'

'You tell them, tiger.' Cooke tried to be funny, to smile as he spoke, though he had never felt more depressed in his entire life. He pressed the microphone switch, 'Orbiter to Mission Control. Have you heard . . .'


'Nothing,' Flax said. 'Sorry Cooke, nothing at all yet. The programme is still running and you're due for a burn in about twenty minutes.'

*'Roger, Mission Control. Out.'*

Flax was beyond all fatigue, beyond all caring. That it should end like this, now, so suddenly with salvation just beyond their grasp. He looked at the GET. Less than an hour from hook-up . . .

*'Something on the wavelength.'*

The voice from communication jerked them all about like puppets on a string, to stare at the wall speaker that hissed and roared with interference, to strain to hear if that was a voice behind the electronic waterfall. There were words, barely comprehensible words.

*'. . . in . . . Control . . . come . . . this . . . is Prometheus . . .'*

# 43

'THERE'S NO MORE OF IT,' Coretta said. 'The fire, the burning pieces, they're all gone.'

'Five minutes now, at least,' Patrick said. 'We're through and into our last orbit.'

'What do you mean?' Coretta asked.

'We were at perigee, the closest part of our orbit to Earth, going past it and moving higher. That's when we hit, grazed the atmosphere. Any more than that and we'd have slowed and burned. Just touched lightly like a skipping stone on water, then away. Now we know almost to the minute how much time we have. At next perigee we go down. A little over an hour.' He fumbled in his darkness to find the mike switch, turned it on. 'Mission Control this is Prometheus. I want to talk to Orbiter.'

'*Roger, Patrick, Orbiter is listening.*'

'How's your bird, Cookey?'

'*A-OK and in the green all the way.*'

'What's your ETA for hook-up?'

'*Just about forty minutes.*'

'That'll be fine as long as you get here on time. It will give you about twenty minutes for the approach and exit. Might I suggest you make the approach a good one and get us on the first pass.'

'*Suggestion accepted, Pat. I will do my goddamnest.*'

'I know you will, Cookey. Out.'

Nadya waited until the radio connection was broken before she spoke. 'Do we have time to repressurize and evacuate this cabin again before hook-up?' she asked.

'Yes, more than enough time,' Patrick said.

'Could we please, my eyes . . . there is discomfort, a little pain perhaps.'

'You should have said something—Gregor, pressurize, you know where the controls are.' Patrick groped out through their darkness until his fingers found the other couch, felt along it until he reached her arm, her hand. He held it tightly, realizing that they had forgotten about her and she had not bothered them while they got on with the job. Blind, locked in her pressure suit, uncomplaining.

'I'm sorry,' Patrick said.

'Don't be silly. You have done everything possible for all of us.'

'Pressure,' Gregor said, loosening his helmet and removing it. After the stink of his own body inside the suit even the canned, recycled air of the cabin smelled good.

Coretta had her helmet off now and was helping Nadya with hers.

'I'm going to put a fresh dressing on and give you a shot,' she said.

'I don't want to sleep.' There was a sharpness in Nadya's voice that had not been there before.

'Don't worry, honey. Just a little one for the pain. And for Patrick too.'

She bent efficiently to her task and Gregor watched her. Her hair was rich and dark, a contrast to his blond curls. And her skin; brown, warm, soft. She was different from anyone he had ever met before. He wanted to bend and kiss her throat, there above the hard neckring of her suit. He did not, did not want to interrupt. Instead he looked up at the numbers clicking over on the GET, then out of the port at the darkness.

'When Coretta is finished we must depressurize. I must go out and finish HOOPSNAKE.'

'No!' Coretta gasped out the words, turning about. 'We don't have to now, they're coming to get us.'

'That does not alter the fact that this spacecraft must be destroyed completely. For the benefit of the people below.'

'But you heard Mission Control, they think it will hit the ocean. . . .'

'*Think* is not good enough. There is just as good a chance it will strike California. I must not allow that chance to be taken.'

'I'm afraid we have no choice,' Patrick said. 'We did our best but I don't think you'll be able to finish the job. There's a very good chance that the AMU was carried away, if the debris was as heavy as you say. Without it you won't be able to get back to the engines again.'

'I hadn't thought!' Gregor said. He pushed off, floundered, slammed into the wall by the port, then righted and pressed his face closely against the cold glass. He could see the outside of the hatch. Nothing else.

'It is gone,' he said, wearily. 'That is the end of it.'

Coretta broke the disposable hypodermic needles in two and pushed them into the waste holder, then went over to him. She had moved too fast, forgetting, and had to grab him as she floated up so she would not hit too hard. She held on to his arms and did not let go.

'Why so sad? We did our best. No one's to blame.'

He gazed at the pilots, at their bandaged faces, a look of pain cut deep into his face. When he spoke it was a soft whisper that only she could hear. 'I wanted to do it, it was important. Look at them, there, blinded, perhaps for ever. It was my country that did that and I am ashamed. I thought we could, I could, make up for it somehow by putting things right. Destroying Prometheus. Destroying the threat to the world.'

'But you heard the radio. It wasn't the Soviet Union that sent up the bomb. Just one man . . .'

Gregor smiled crookedly and raised his gloved fingers to her lips.

'You are a child, *darogaya*, a lovely woman yet a child when you say that. Accidents like that don't happen in my country. It was planned, a scrapegoat was found. . . .'

'It's a scapegoat, not a scrapegoat, and I believe anything you say. But there's nothing you can do about it now—except put it from your mind. If that bus gets here in time we'll be alive and out of it and back in the State of Florida in time for dinner.'

Her dark eyes were wide open, staring into his blue ones, as she leaned forward and kissed him full on the mouth. The metal collar rings of their suits clattered together and she had to lean far out so their lips could meet. It could have been funny, two thick figures swaddled in fabric and plastic, holding to each other like shapeless bundles. It could have been funny, but it was not. He kissed her as she did him, eyes open, saying more than words ever could.

'What is the GET?' Patrick asked suddenly.

'34:23,' Coretta answered, drawing back from Gregor and looking up at the numbers.

'Time to depressurize. Helmets on. Take care of that, Gregor, when we're all secured. The Orbiter will be making the final approach now.'

'Prometheus, I have you on electronic ranging and we are closing,' Cooke said.

*'We are waiting for you, Orbiter. Our hatch is open and we are standing by.'*

'Burn is complete and we're closing at one two oh feet per second.'

'There they are!' Decosta called out as Prometheus swam into view. Cooke nodded, hands busy at the controls.

'We have you in sight now, looks like we're making a high side pass. Your crew module is in the shadow of the payload so I don't know if hatch alignment is in the green.'

*'My people here are on the lookout—they see you now. Coming in just fine. Our hatch is about thirty degrees away from earthside your approach.'*

'Okay, Pat. I'll lift a bit and roll as we come in. A piece of cake.'

Of course it wasn't. Cooke knew he had to get it right the first time because there could be no second attempt. Right so far. 2,727 feet out, closing at 19.7 feet per second. He hit the forward gas jets. 1,370 feet, 9.8 feet per second. The spacecraft grew steadily larger, closer.

'Good thing they are carrying their payload on their nose,' Decosta said. 'All burned to hell. Better it than them.' He turned his oxygen on, then put on his helmet. 'Radio connection okay?' he asked.

'Fine.'

'I'm getting the doors open, the tanks ready.'

He dived headfirst through the floor hatch, kicked off the wall and grabbed the dogging handle of the airlock, twisting it, pulling up on the door. Once inside he sealed it behind him and punched the bleed valve. The pressure reading wound down and down until the red evacuation light blinked on. The outer door of the airlock opened easily and just outside it were the door controls. Decosta trained his light on them, switched the selector to open and pressed the activate button. A crack of light appeared, widened, as the curved, sixty-foot long doors began to swing back. Light poured in and he could see the base of the remote manipulator no more than a yard away. He moved off towards it, seized it, and using it as a guide pushed himself the length of the cavernous hold, to the far end. As he went he permitted himself only one quick glimpse of Prometheus.

It was no more than a hundred yards away and closing smoothly. An immense scarred cylinder in space, two hundred and fifty feet long. The crew module was still in the shadow of the payload but he knew they were there, waiting for him.

'On the way,' he said, grabbing the working end of the manipulator as he came to it. The knife was just where he had left it, floating free at the end of the length of line. He reached out carefully and grabbed the handle, then used the blade to sever the line where he had tied it. An easy steady push sent him floating the last ten feet to the end where the walk-arounds were lashed, to grab the ropes and saw through a length of white nylon, to pull it free loop after loop.

When the tie-down line had been removed and was floating away into space he tied the knife to the red line that held the four tanks together, then retraced his way back to the manipulator controls. Only then did he take the time to look out.

Prometheus was there. No more than fifty, sixty feet away, filling the sky with its bulk. Light glowed in the ports and from the open hatch where he could clearly see the helmets of the crew.

'Ready to go,' Decosta said.

'You're through to Prometheus,' Cooke answered.

'I have you in sight,' Decosta said, pushing an actuator handle forward.

'What do you want us to do?' Patrick asked.

'Here come the walk-abouts, on the end of the arm.'

The long tube of the manipulator rose up and up, pulling along the tanks at the end of their length of line. 'I'll try not to bang them into you, but they are swinging around a lot. Grab them when they get close. There is a knife tied out there with them, watch out for it, so you can cut them free.'

In Prometheus they could only wait, grouped by the hatch, two of them watching the welcome sight of the Orbiter as it drew close. It was like a great airplane flying towards them, an illusion destroyed when it rolled slowly until it was drifting topside in their direction. Then it split down almost its entire length, long doors gaping wide, and the thin shaft of the manipulator was reaching out in their direction, the tanks floating free at the end.

'What's happening?' Patrick said, angry that he had to ask.

'I'm sorry,' Coretta said. 'I forgot. There's a long arm coming over with the tanks, they are whipping back and forth, swinging around. They've stopped now. . . .'

*'Can you reach them, Prometheus?'*

'No.' Gregor reached out as far as he could. 'They are still at least two metres away.'

*'I'm out all the way,'* Decosta said.

'Coming closer,' Cooke answered.

There was a brief spurt of gas on the directional jets and the Orbiter drifted sideways, looming up.

'Enough!' Gregor shouted as the long arm seemed about to impale the ship. White gas spurted into the vacuum and the motion stopped. 'I can reach them now. Coretta, hold my feet.'

Gregor leaned far out, floated out farther and farther from the open hatch. Coretta held his ankles in one hand, the edge of the hatch opening in the other, watching, holding her breath, as his fingers reached out towards the bulk of the swinging tanks.

'I have them!'

A swift slice of the blade cut the walk-arounds free and Coretta pulled him and the tanks through the hatch.

'Put yours on first,' Patrick said. 'Then disconnect from the cabin oxygen. Then you can attach ours.'

Gregor clipped the tank to his belt, made the hose connection, then severed the link with Prometheus. His hands were steady as he fastened Patrick's tank to him, making the connections with sure movement. Coretta was slower, first her tank, then Nadya's. When she turned around she found there were just three pressure-suited figures in sight.

'Gregor?'

'I am outside, going to the engines. I should have stayed to help but there are only about ten minutes left. I have turned on the hydrogen flow. There will be enough time for you, but I have little to spare.'

'What are you doing?' she shouted, knowing even as she said it what was happening.

'HOOPSNAKE of course. You should be leaving now.'

'*Affirmative to that,*' Decosta said. '*Get your people on the end of the manipulator so I can bring you in.*'

'You don't have to do it, Gregor,' Patrick said.

'I know that, thank you, but I must.'

Coretta lifted Nadya, guided her, pushed her to the hatch.

'Open your hand,' Coretta said. 'I have the rope in your palm, close quickly, do you feel it?'

'Yes, fine, please help me through the hatch, then get Patrick.'

Coretta was doing the same for Patrick, helping him through the opening towards the end of the metal arm where Nadya waited, floating head down with her feet stretching out above. Then Patrick had seized the end effector and she grabbed the metal next to him.

'We're all here,' she said.

'*Keep your grip secure, I'm bringing you in.*'

As they swung out and away from the hatch Coretta could see Gregor for the first time. He was close to the engines, pulling at the loose plate of shielding he had partially detached before.

'Gregor . . .' she said, but there were no other words.

'It has been . . . very good to serve with you all,' Gregor said, breathing heavily as he struggled with the shielding. 'Thank you very much for the opportunity. . . .'

*'We have less than five minutes left,'* Cooke said, the calmness of his voice more emphatic than any strain.

*'We need the light to see by. I'm closing the doors as soon as these people are strapped down,'* Decosta said.

*'I can move out with the doors open. Let me know as soon as you are all secure.'*

The long arm moved slowly, ponderously, bending in the middle now like the great limb of some giant insect. Turning, carrying its human cargo towards the waiting acceleration couches, slowing, slower, stopped. The instant Decosta locked the mechanism he kicked off towards the others.

'One of you can see, I can't tell which, sorry, lash yourself in. I'll secure the other two,' he said.

Coretta groped for the couch and as soon as she moved, Decosta grabbed one of the others, prising at the gloved fingers. 'I have someone's hand, let go, I'll take care of you.' He could see the blind, bandaged eyes through the faceplate. The hand opened and he pushed the spacesuited figure against the couch, held it there, locked the belt into place. Then the other one. There was still one empty couch.

'I'm getting the arm stowed now so the doors can close,' he said.

'Can you take any acceleration? We've reached zero. Any time now . . .' Cooke's voice was strained, tight.

'Negative. A few more seconds. Manipulator stored. Doors closing, controls locked in that position, I'm in the lock, door closed . . . *now!*'

Gregor heard their words clearly, broadcast to Prometheus's radio and repeated on the intercom-radio circuit. He had the plate aside at last and he turned his head for a brief instant to look. Flames sprang from the Orbiter's engines, long tongues of it in space. The winged spacecraft began to move.

'Good-bye,' he said, pushing himself inside the shielding, the light before him. If they answered he did not know, because his suit radio did not work in this area. The light moved over the rows of plastic tubing.

'Just as described,' he said aloud. He had read the HOOP-SNAKE programme many times, had memorized it. 'Sever the tubing. With this fine knife supplied by the Shuttle.' He took the knife and sawed through the resistant plastic, cut into it and saw the poisonous granules of uranium isotope inside. 'U-235, very deadly.' He smiled when he realized that he was no longer afraid at all. 'A remarkable discovery,' he said. 'I wish I could tell Colonel Kuznekov about it. Well perhaps I shall, if the Church is right and the Communist Party is wrong. I would like to tell the Colonel that courage is not a unique property of his generation.'

The plastic tubing pulled free easily now. He pulled off the required length as instructed by the programme, making sure that the loose end was going through the gap in the shielding. Then he went out after it, pushing it ahead of him, towing it behind as he worked his way around the base of the engine towards the torn-away thrust cone. Droplets of gas, freezing as they emerged, shot out in a steady stream, making a comet's tail behind the ship.

'This could be dangerous now,' he said, working his way around the stream. 'It has to be done right, absolutely right the first time.'

As he reached the right spot he looked up, startled, as burning fragments of the ship tore by.

They were into the atmosphere.

Just moments left.

Gregor took one second to snap his safety line to the ship. He must be steady now, and would need both hands. The plastic tubing was stiff but bent as he applied pressure, rolling it upon itself, compacting it into a ball he could clasp between his hands, heavy, twenty-five kilos or more. He was aware that he was dead now in more ways than one, that the radiation of the U-235 increased as the mass of metal was brought closer and closer. But not to critical mass, there wasn't enough of it for that. The hydrogen would have to moderate the reaction for that, slow down and trap the particles so that it went critical, became an atomic bomb.

'Yes,' he **said**, 'now is the time.'

Holding the heavy sphere of uranium before him he moved to the engine, looked in. The sun was behind him now, shining into the chamber.

It was breathtaking. The hydrogen had been pumped in steadily for some minutes now. At first it had turned to gas, but in doing so it had chilled down the quartz chamber walls. As more and more hydrogen had poured in it had stopped vaporizing. The chamber was now filled and brimming over with the pale, transparent fluid, two hundred and fifty degrees below zero. As still more was pumped in globules formed at the open end and drifted away, touching Gregor's faceplate and puffing away as gas.

For a long instant he stared into that cold pool—then plunged in the uranium ball. It was heavy and he had to push to accelerate it and it moved firmly from his hand, down the length of the engine. Surrounded by a constantly renewed cloud of gas as the hydrogen boiled when it came near the warm metal. A gas cloud that prevented the liquid hydrogen from coming close enough to moderate the fast particles emerging from the uranium, prevented the chain reaction from starting.

This did not last very long.

The metal cooled and the liquid collapsed on to it and touched it.


Strapped down, her body pressing out against the restraint, Coretta saw the shining form of Prometheus grow smaller, shrinking, framed between the gap of the closing doors, visible for one last instant. Then vanished as the doors slammed shut.

'*We are at least forty miles from Prometheus,*' Cooke said, his voice sounding in all their helmets. '*Lifting up and— God . . .*' He was silent for a moment. Then spoke. '*We're facing away. Thank God. You all right back there? A light, an explosion, I have never seen a light like that. It went up. It did. It's not going to impact after all. They're safe back on Earth.*'

It was black inside the unlit cargo bay, as dark for Coretta as it was for the blinded pilots.

'Good-bye, Gregor,' she said, softly, into the darkness.

# 44

'AIR SPEED three hundred knots,' Decosta said.

'Looks good,' Cooke said. 'I'm making the last turn into the glide path now. Drop the landing gear.'

Decosta threw the switch and watched silently until the green light flicked on. 'Gear down and locked.'

There had been clouds over the entire East coast, with Florida socked in solid. They had watched it from space, seen the clouds grow closer and closer as they dropped back into the atmosphere, until they were in them and flying blind. It made no difference to their flight plan since that was controlled by the computer. There was an invisible highway in the sky they had to follow, a trace on the screen that told them just what to do, just where to be. When the Orbiter broke through the low-hanging clouds the rain-washed length of the runway stretched out before them. Cooke handled the wheel with a light touch, squinting through the tendrils of steam above the nose as the rain vaporized when it struck the silica tiles that covered the hull. Tiles still radiant hot after the 2,400 degrees temperatures they had withstood during re-entry.

'Down,' Cooke said as the heavy tyres impacted the wet concrete. Decosta took off his belt and stood up.

'I'm going to look after our passengers,' he said.

'Give me a report, soonest.'

Decosta climbed down through the access hatch to the mid deck below and opened the inner hatch of the airlock, leaving it open as he opened the other hatch into the blackness of the cargo bay. One of the pressure-suited figures was sitting up, looking in his direction, hands on helmet.

Coretta twisted, pulled at the helmet, tore it off and took in breath after breath of the damp air.

'I can smell the sea,' she said, then raised her hand. 'And you can take that damn light out of my eyes.'

'Sorry. Everything all right?'

'It will be when we get their helmets off. Give me a hand.'

The Orbiter slowed, rocked as its brakes were applied, then eased to a stop. As soon as his helmet was off Patrick pressed his hands to the bandages over his eyes, then sat up and turned in Nadya's direction. But he was silent; there seemed to be nothing for any of them to say.

'Be right back,' Decosta said, turning away.

'Hey, leave the light,' Coretta called out. 'Or can you turn on the lights in here?'

'There aren't any. Why don't we all go into mid-deck compartment.' The floor moved as the tractor hooked on and began to tow them slowly from the runway.

They were clumsy after their stay in free fall and willing to be helped by the pilot. The pressure suits were hot and cumbersome and they took them off before going into the compartment. The numbness persisted; they said nothing, just sat there and waited until they had finally stopped and the outer door was opened.

Only when they heard the wild cheering did they realize that the voyage was over at last.

'There, in the middle of your screen, ladies and gentlemen, you can see them coming out, three figures, small at this distance though giants in the history of mankind. The ambulance is drawn up and they are entering it, no wait, they're stopping. Turning. Dr Coretta Samuel is saying something, we can't hear it, there's no microphone up there. Now she's turning and following the others inside the ambulance and the door is closing. So this epic adventure is over at last. In a moment we will be talking to Major Cooke and Captain Decosta, the pilots of the rescue mission. . . .'

\* \* \*

One by one the consoles in Mission Control were shut down, the lights flickered off, the needles on the meters dropped to zero. The big screen showed a commercial TV channel now, with a picture of the crew of Prometheus entering an ambulance, the announcer's voice echoing hollowly in the silence of the hall. Flax looked up at the screen, then down at the big cigar clutched in his hand. The victory cigar. Light up and smoke when the mission was successful. He closed his fingers slowly and the cigar broke, flaked, rained down in crumbled pieces to the floor.

Three of them were back, that was something. Grabbed from the fire at the last moment. But two of them pilots, good pilots, with bandages on their eyes and maybe they would never see again. But the greater disaster of a crash had been averted. Prometheus would not be ploughing into San Francisco. The Russian had been good, really good.

Flax's thoughts rambled in exhausted circles, fatigue washed through his limbs, the ball of fire that had been growing steadily in his stomach spread out as though to fill his entire chest, his body.

He slumped forward, very slowly, his head dropping to the cold plastic of the console, his arms slipping off and flopping at his sides. Gravity asserted itself more and more as he slid to the floor and lay there. Motionless.

'Oh my God!' one of the technicians shouted. 'It's Flax. Get the doctor!'

They straightened his great form out on the tiled floor, opened his collar wide, loosened his yards-long belt. There were running footsteps and they parted to let the doctor through.

'Is he dead, Doc?' someone asked. 'A heart attack?' The doctor ignored him, feeling for a pulse in the thick wrist, pushing down hard with his stethoscope on Flax's chest, trying to make out a heartbeat through the layers of fat. The doctor finally lifted one heavy eyelid, then closed it again, before climbing slowly to his feet.

'Dead . . . ?' a voice asked, weakly. The doctor shook his head.

'Asleep,' he said. 'This man's exhausted, totally exhausted.

Call down for a stretcher. I want him in bed as soon as possible.'

It took six men to lift Flax on to the stretcher—and four to carry it. They went out in solemn procession. If not in a victory procession at least not in total defeat.

The engineer at the communications console was the only one left. He shut down his circuits one by one until he came to the last. He switched this to his headphones and rang it one final time.

'Mr Dillwater,' he said.


'Yes, thank you very much. Good-bye,' Simon Dillwater dropped the phone and rose. He felt dizzy; it had been a long, long time.

'If you're going I can drop you off,' Grodzinski said, standing as well and stretching broadly, yawning. 'I gotta car waiting.'

'That's very kind.'

'Please don't go yet, Simon,' Dr Schlochter said. 'The President would like to see you. You and General Bannerman.'

'I am not so sure that I want to see him.'

'You do, Simon. Believe me. I have had a long and heart-to-heart talk with him and I think he understands your position.'

Bannerman looked at them, then turned away and went to the bar. He still stamped hard when he walked and his spurs clinked metallically. It had been one bitch of a time and he was tired. One more large drink was in order. He poured a half glass of whisky, dropped two ice cubes into it and swished it around. He looked up as the door opened and Bandin entered. He had shaved and changed and the TV make-up hid the blackness under his eyes. He looked fresh as a daisy compared to the others, though he felt the same inside.

'I have a few minutes before I address the nation,' he said, in his most dignified manner, the speaking-to-the-nation tones already in his voice. 'Therefore I will take this opportunity to inform you both about certain decisions that I have made. First, General, I wish to tell you that Operation PEEKABOO is being shut down. . . .'

'We can't do that, not after what's gone into it,' Bannerman said, angrily.

'I am afraid that we can. That we must. The operation has been compromised and too many people know about it. If we shut it down now it will be as though it never existed. If there are rumours later we can deny everything.'

'Cancelling PEEKABOO will jeopardize the fate, the very future of this great nation, Mr President.'

'One bomb less?' Dillwater said. He knew he should not speak out, but his fatigue hampered his control. 'This country and the Soviets have the capacity between them to destroy the world eight times over with atomic bombs. I should think that that would be enough.'

'And we *will* be destroyed if people like you have their way,' Bannerman roared out. 'We can only stop communist aggression by being prepared, by being stronger, by being one jump ahead of them at all times.'

'I am sorry for you,' Dillwater said, his quiet voice in striking contrast to the General's angry one. 'With your archaic boots and spurs and even more ancient jingoistic mind. You are not aware that your kind is as dead as the dodo, extinct but without the brains to lie down and die. Mankind now has the chance to wipe itself out, your course, General, or co-operate and try for a future. We must co-operate to husband the limited resources of our plundered planet and see that they are shared out equally. We must co-operate or die. Perhaps that is something that you will never understand.' He turned his back on Bannerman, abruptly, rudely. 'I welcome your decision, Mr President.'

'I thought you would,' Bandin said. 'I've been talking with Polyarni and we're going full steam with the Prometheus Project. We need that energy from space. And we both want you to go on heading the project. Okay?'

'I have been thinking of nothing else, Mr President. My resignation still stands—unless I have the final authority on the project.'

'You always have . . .'

'No. I beg your pardon, but I have not. There have been too many political decisions overruling the technical ones. I believe the catastrophe of Prometheus One was caused by the rush to launch, the pressure, the lack of time from political not engineering reasons. If I have the final authority on all matters I will go ahead with the work.'

'You're asking a goddamned lot, Dillwater.'

'I'm promising a goddamned lot, Mr President. We will get the first of the power flowing, if all goes well, within the year.' He smiled slightly. 'So I might be promising you the next election.'

Bandin hesitated, looked at the Secretary of State. Dr Schlochter nodded.

'All right then,' Bandin said. 'You have the job. . . .'

'And your promise in writing of course, Mr President.'

Bandin took a deep breath, glared at Dillwater, turned and slammed out.

Simon Dillwater left as well and General Bannerman was alone.

He raised his drink, glared at it, then downed it.

'Well maybe PEEKABOO is dead,' he said, as he tightened his belt and pulled down his jacket. 'But NANCY JANE is almost out of the planning stage and at least that bastard Dillwater doesn't know about *that* one yet.'

His nostrils flared like a war horse going into battle as he stamped, jingling, from the room.

Cooper tapped the figures into his hand calculator and watched the little red numbers flicker and change. And come up with the same solution each time. If the *Gazette-Times* had upped their circulation because of his stories on Prometheus, then at the end of the year they would have added to their profits $850,000, more if the additional advertising revenue were taken into consideration, but that was good for a rough picture. Or an additional profit of $16,346.15 a week. While he had a twenty-dollar raise, or about one eighth of one per cent of the profits his brilliant writing had earned them. Not **only** **t**hat but, after taxes, the raise would be about seven bucks a week and if you considered the growing inflation his annual income would be down about thirteen per cent by the end of the year. He clicked off the calculator and threw it into the drawer in his desk. A copy boy dropped an envelope on to his typewriter.

From the editor! Things weren't going to be as black as he thought. He tore it open and took out the boldly typed sheet inside.

NOT REALLY SATISFIED THIS LAST STORY OF YOURS. WEAK PUNCH. GET SOMETHING NEW. WHAT ABOUT CHROMIUM POISONING IN JAPAN? COULD IT HAPPEN HERE? COPY SOONEST.

There was fine beading of sweat on Cooper's receding forehead as he groped down his copy of *Annual Abstracts, Chemical Contents of Industrial Waste.*

'You can't go in there, nurse,' the MP said. 'There's a debriefing going on.'

Coretta stopped and looked at him scornfully, lifting one eyebrow high. 'Look again, soldier,' she said. 'I'm a doctor not a nurse. And if you look a little closer you might even recognize me.'

The man started to smile until he saw the look in her eyes.

He snapped to attention. 'I'm sorry, Dr Samuel. But I have my orders.'

'Not in a hospital, sonny. Don't try to get between a doctor and her patient. Now move.'

He moved and she threw the door wide.

The four officers grouped around Patrick's bed looked up, startled.

'What is the meaning of your presence here?' she asked.

'Just talking to the Major, Dr Samuel,' the colonel holding the tape recorder said. 'A de-briefing. Dr Jurgens said it would be perfectly all right.'

'Thas is my patient, Colonel, not Major Jurgens's. I insist you leave at once.'

'This will not take much longer. . . .'

'You're dead right. Just about as long as it takes you all to walk out the door.'

Senior officers in the Army are not used to being addressed in this manner and the situation was rapidly approaching an impasse when Patrick spoke.

'I called for the doctor, just before you arrived,' he said. 'It's an injection, the pain. I thought we might be able to finish, but . . .'

'We understand, Major, of course. Dr Jurgens will advise us when we can return.'

They exited in order of seniority, honour saved, and Coretta closed the door behind them, and turned to Patrick.

'Is there really pain?' she asked, worried. He shook his head and smiled in her direction.

'No, none at all now, I just wanted to get rid of them.' The smile vanished as he touched the bandages. 'What do the eye people say?'

'Just what they told you earlier, too early for a prognosis. But I have been talking with them and they're guarded, but seem to feel that if the retina damage is not too widespread then a measure of function will return.'

'Meaning?'

'You'll be able to see, but not too well. Glasses like the bottoms of bottles, you know the drill.'

'Well at least they won't be black glasses with a tin cup. Where is Nadya?'

'Just down the hall.'

Patrick threw off the blankets and swung his feet over the side of the bed. 'Help me, will you,' he said. 'My robe, somewhere in here. And take me to her room.'

'Be happy to. Here, put it on.'

The MP was still there when they came out, looking frightened, not knowing what to do. Coretta felt sorry for him.

'Don't you worry,' she said. 'We're not going far. Right there. You come with us and stand outside the door and you'll still be on the job.'

Nadya was sitting up in bed when they came in, wearing a white hospital nightgown.

'Who is it?' she asked.

'Coretta. I have Patrick with me.'

'Come in if you like.' Her voice was tired, empty of any emotion.

'I'll leave you two now,' Coretta said.

'Whatever you wish,' Nadya said.

'No you won't,' Patrick told her. 'Close the door. We were all in that thing together. We're still together.'

He felt his way to the edge of the bed and sat on it. When he did Nadya shifted away from him so he would not touch her; only Coretta could see this.

She looked at the blind faces and stiff bodies and wanted to weep.

'Listen,' she said. 'I have something for you, for both of you.' She reached into her pocket and took out the two bundles and handed them over.

'What is it?' Patrick asked, feeling the paper edges.

'The first-day covers. You people forgot all about them. That comes from having military minds. You're too used to having people take care of you. But Coretta can't get out of the habit of looking after number one. And her friends. When we suited up, the first time when there was a chance of getting out of this in one chunk, I took a hundred of them and put them in my suit pocket. That should be enough. Scarcity is value in the stamp business, or so I am told. Twenty-five for each of us.' Her smile vanished then, but they couldn't see that, so she tried to keep her feelings out of her voice.

'Well Gregor won't be needing his now. I've divided the rest. Thirty-three for each of you, thirty-four for me, the extra one being my commission. I'm sure these things will be very valuable. Saved from the burning spaceship at the risk of life and limb, the ends of the envelopes still brown from the flame. . . .'

'*What* flame?' Patrick asked.

'The one where I used a match to singe them just a little bit. I'll bet that adds a hundred bucks to the price of each one!'

Nadya looked puzzled, but Patrick burst out laughing.

'Coretta, I'd make you my business manager if you weren't my doctor already. I doubt if there'll be much piloting in my future so maybe I better think about going into business. How about that, Nadya, you want to go into the stamp business with us?'

'I know nothing about that. In Russia . . .'

'Don't go back to Russia. Stay here with me.'

He moved his hand over the covers until he found hers, capturing it before she could move it away. He held it in both of his and spoke, hoarsely. This was what he had wanted to say since he came into the room, had been looking for some way to say. He was not experienced at this sort of thing.

'I'll leave you alone now,' Coretta said, standing.

'No, please don't leave,' Patrick said. 'There's no secret here, we've all been too close for that. Nadya, don't go back. I mean stay here with me. Or let me go back with you. About all I can offer is a military pension—and Coretta's stamps.'

'Patrick . . .' She looked up towards him, blind eyes straining to see.

'Look, I love you. I've loved you a long time. Now you can throw me out. But I just wanted to get it on record.'

Seconds ticked by before Nadya spoke. 'That is a very kind offer. You may leave now.'

'Well what the hell!' He was shocked, unbelieving. 'Is that all you can say?'

'Just what do you expect me to say? Oh, thank you sir for your kind offer. When a man speaks as you do any woman should be swept off her feet happy to rush and say *yes* and look forward to a lifetime of darning socks and raising children. You are asking a lot.'

'Not of a woman. Not much at all. But maybe too much for a flying officer and test pilot. . . .'

'Shut up!' Coretta shouted. 'Before you say too much and go too far and can't get back. Listen to the doctor. Patrick, just because you love her—and neither of us doubts it—that doesn't mean that Nadya stops being what she is and forgets everything and is ready for the rose-covered cottage.'

'I know that——'

'Maybe you know it—but you don't feel it. She is still the person she always was and you mustn't ever forget that. And you, Nadya, it's no crime to think like a woman, feel like a woman. Sensuality can be very, very good. Do you understand?'

Nadya nodded. Her voice was very quiet now, strained. 'I really do not find it easy to talk about these things. It is perhaps my training. Romantic love has always been something in the cinema, not in the life of a test pilot or a cosmonaut. Perhaps I learned to play a role—but it is a role that works and whenever I step out of it I find that I can be hurt. . . .'

'Are you talking about that time—you and I, in Texas?'

'Yes . . . I think I am.'

'Try to understand me. I suppose I was acting like an over-sexed male chauvinist, and I'm sorry. But I did mean it too, what I felt towards you, and I mean it now. Will you marry me, Nadya?'

'No.'

'Will you at least think about it?'

'Yes, of course, and more than that. When you are like this and trying to understand how I feel, then I want very much to be with you. Then I want to stay with you. Stay together, get married perhaps, perhaps not. But at least find out. Be patient with me, Patrick. It's not easy.'

'I will. If you'll be patient with me.' This time when he sought her hand in blindness he found it immediately. It was a beginning.

Coretta took one last look at them, lifted her hand in a little wave that they could not see, then slipped quietly out of the door and closed it behind her.

'The Major, is he . . .' the MP said.

'Don't worry, Corporal. The Major is doing fine, just fine. He's safe and sound in there so you just let him be.'

Then she turned and walked briskly down the corridor and around the corner and was gone.


Above the hospital, above Cape Canaveral and the shrouding clouds, high above the atmosphere the sun shone as it always did. The solar storms raged across its surface and radiated their energy into space. Light streamed from the solar disc, light and radiation spread profligate in all directions. A small portion fell on the Earth, warmed it, made it habitable to man.

Ceaselessly, timelessly, the sun shone. One day, soon, another gleaming speck would soar through the thin atmosphere of Earth and into space, where it would spread its silvery net to capture more of that abundant energy before it disappeared in the eternal interstellar night.

Then yet another spark . . . And another . . .